Indulekha

Aristocratic, accomplished, educated in English and incomparably beautiful, Indulekha loves her cousin Madhavan who returns her devotion and holds revolutionary views. She fights a composed and witty battle to fob off the lecherous and elderly Surinambuthiripad who seeks a *sambandham* with her. When Indulekha uses the first person singular as she rejects his advances, her action reverberates across Nair society.

Oyyarathu Chandumenon (1847–99), a pioneering Malayalam novelist, made important contributions as a social reformer. Beginning his career as a clerk in the government service, he became Sub-Judge of the Madras Presidency, a post which he occupied until his death.
A member of the committee constituted to inquire and report on the Malabar Marriages Bill, his observations on the Nair matrilineal society during his time are of historical importance. Following *Indulekha*, he began a second novel *Saradha*, the first part of which appeared in 1892.

Anitha Devasia is Lecturer, Department of English, St Teresa's College, Ernakulam, Kochi.

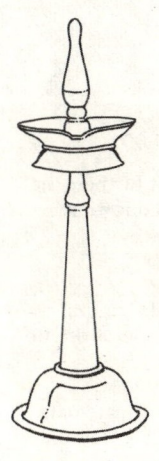

Indulekha

O. CHANDUMENON

Translated from Malayalam by
ANITHA DEVASIA

With a Foreword by
SUSIE THARU

UNIVERSITY PRESS

OXFORD
UNIVERSITY PRESS

YMCA Library Building, Jai Singh Road, New Delhi 110 001

Oxford University Press is a department of the University of Oxford. It furthers the
University's objective of excellence in research, scholarship, and education
by publishing worldwide in

Oxford   New York

Auckland   Cape Town   Dar es Salaam   Hong Kong   Karachi   Kuala Lumpur
Madrid   Melbourne   Mexico City   Nairobi   New Delhi   Shanghai   Taipei   Toronto

With offices in

Argentina   Austria   Brazil   Chile   Czech Republic   France   Greece   Guatemala
Hungary   Italy   Japan   Poland   Portugal   Singapore   South Korea   Switzerland
Thailand   Turkey   Ukraine   Vietnam

Oxford is a registered trademark of Oxford University Press
in the UK and in certain other countries

Published in India by Oxford University Press, New Delhi

© Oxford University Press 2005

The moral rights of the author have been asserted
Database right Oxford University Press (maker)

First published 2005
Second impression 2005
Oxford India Paperbacks 2005
Fifth impression 2008

All rights reserved. No part of this publication may be reproduced,
or transmitted in any form or by any means, electronic or mechanical,
including photocopying, recording or by any information storage and
retrieval system, without permission in writing from Oxford University Press.
Enquiries concerning reproduction outside the scope of the above should be
sent to the Rights Department, Oxford University Press, at the address above

You must not circulate this book in any other binding or cover
and you must impose this same condition on any acquirer

ISBN-13: 978-0-19-567877-2
ISBN-10: 0-19-567877-X

Typeset in Aldine401 BT
by Eleven Arts, Keshav Puram, Delhi 110 035
Printed in India by Pauls Press, New Delhi 110 020
Published by Oxford University Press
YMCA Library Building, Jai Singh Road, New Delhi 110 001

To
My appachan and ammachi—

DEVASIA AND CATHERINE KOIKKARA

Contents

Foreword by Susie Tharu	ix
Preface	xiii
Acknowledgements	xix
Beginningss	1
Indulekha	5
An Angry Man's Oath	30
A Separation	34
Panchumenon's Anger	41
Panchumenon's Anxiety	50
Kannazhi Moorkillatha Manakkal Surinambuthiripad	59
An Arrival from Madras	73
The Coming of the Nambuthiripad and Other Things	76
A Letter from Madras	85
What People Said about the Nambuthiripad	92
Conversation between Indulekha and the Nambuthiripad	100
Second Conversation between Indulekha and the Nambuthiripad	129

The Nambuthiripad's Wedding	144
A Calamity	153
Madhavan's Tour of the Country	164
How Madhavan was Found	170
A Conversation	184
Things Which Actually Happened at Home during the Period of Madhavan's Journey	215
The End of the Story	224
Afterword	226
Appendices	237
I: *Preface to the first edition of* Indulekha	237
II: *Preface to the second edition of* Indulekha	241
III: *Dumergue's Preface*	245
IV: *Chandumenon's Memorandum to the Malabar Marriage Commission*	248
V: *The President's Supplementary Memorandum to the Malabar Marriage Commission*	263
Bibliography	275
Glossary	284

Foreword

Even today, *Indulekha* would be considered a runaway success. Much to the author's surprise, the first edition sold out in three months; an English translation of the complete novel was ready and out the very next year; and by its 1989 publication centenary it had gone into an estimated 72 reprints. The novel fell on bad times in the middle years of the twentieth century, dominated as they were by canonical modes of reading and disciplinarian aesthetic that trivialized its scope. But *Indulekha* has found fresh life over the last two decades as questions of region, gender and minority engage us anew and we search out a history that will illuminate our discussions. Today—and critics of all persuasions would agree—this foundational work holds pride of place in the canon of Malayalam literature. And what you are now holding in your hands, dear reader, is a new translation, one that is alert to the history as well as the current vitality of this extraordinary work. Like Chandumenon's contemporary, Krupabai Satthianadhan's *Saguna* (1887–8), it is also, in all seriousness and in more senses than one, a book that makes a bid for the heart.

The focus on feeling and taste is all the more compelling since the novel took shape in a vortex of social and jurisprudential upheavals. I will annotate these briefly—just to put the reader on the scent of the momentous issues that are at stake in the labour of this text. In 1792 the British captured Malabar, the centre of the legendary trade in spices, ousting the Portuguese (who had in turn ousted the Arab traders) and bringing the region into their map of India. Meanwhile, changes taking place in agriculture (increasingly tuned to export and the money economy) and land ownership/tenure had increased the wealth and standing of the Nairs (a martial group, Sudra by caste) in relation to that of the Nambuthiris (Brahmins and principal owners of temple and private lands). Open to the new rulers and to learning English, the Nair men also found employment in the government, often rising to hold important positions—Chandumenon himself being an example of this. More immediately relevant to our discussion here is the common cause found by two groups—British administrators and some of the new Nairs. They put forward a principled and vociferous critique of Nair marriage and inheritance practices and, in 1879, set afoot initiatives for changes in marriage laws that would polarize this society for the next half a century.

The Nairs in the forefront of the movement were disturbed by two things: the joint nature of family (*taravad*) life and property which made it impossible for individuals to claim or alienate property, and the fact that Nambuthiri men could claim access to Nair women. British administrators were also invested in the issue of individual ownership which for them connected up with the promotion of enterprise and undermining the power of the taravad. But administrative discussion tended to foreground 'abnormal' matrilineal inheritance practices and the 'sanctioned polyandry' of Nair culture—since Nair women were as free as the men to dissolve an alliance and enter another.

The discussion centred on three points. One, the suffering of the junior men in the family (*anandravan*) who had no right to separate property and were victims of taravads that would not even pay for their education. Two, the informal and temporary nature of Nair alliances as reflected in the contractual, non-sacramental *sambandam* ceremony. This made it possible, they claimed, for Nambuthiri men to enter into a sambandam with a Nair woman and treat it neither as a marriage nor as binding under Nambuthiri custom. The idea that Nair alliances were actually 'concubinage' also gave rise to the perception that Nair women were unchaste and 'polyandrous'. Three, the strange (to the British) practice of inheritance through the female line and the relative unimportance of the father in everyday family life. Of the major players in the discussion were those arguing from universalist principles, traditionalists who wanted no change, and those, like the author of *Indulekha*, who fought to create a third space.

It is evident from the long note of dissent that he had appended to the 1891 report of the Malabar Marriage Commission that Chandumenon opposed the new legislation. He wrote that it was always difficult to 'defend or justify the social and religious customs of Oriental nations according to the European notions of morality and theology. Many customs, sanctioned by our law and usage and observed by us daily, appear to Europeans extremely immoral and quite unjust'. However, he pointed out, laws relating to marriage have their root in 'the very deepest feelings and the whole history of a nation'. They cannot simply be forced into 'harmony' with those of other nations 'whose institutions and characters had been cast in a totally different mould'. Nair marriage, he argued, may not contain Vedic elements (since as Sudras, Nairs were not allowed to read the Vedas), but it was a solemn rite and in normal practice the bond was respected as lifelong. He feared that 10–15 years after the bill became law, the taravad system and Nair culture would be destroyed altogether. One cannot but note that a substantive part of Chandumenon's anxiety related to that aspect of the bill that sought to make legal the bonds between Nairs and other (lower) castes. By no means, however, is he a no-changer.

His arguments are compelling. All the same, Chandumenon's most significant contribution to this debate and to the shaping of Indian modernity, is the fictional world that he was able to establish in *Indulekha*. It is a world in which the Nair household—its history, its everyday life, its current crisis, and its spoken tongue, its strong women—is the setting for the seduction of the reader. And if readers fall in love with its unusual and charming protagonist—equipped with a classical education as well as English, independent, witty, open-minded, and just, in addition to being beautiful in a Nair (as against Sanskritic) way—it is also because *she is a rebel*. When Indulekha uses the first-person singular as she rejects the advances of Surinambuthiri, the attitude reverberates across Nair society, much as the door Nora would slam a few years later when she leaves her 'doll's house', echoes through Europe. This is not modernity by fiat; it is a modernity muscled and shaped in combat with its immediate antagonists (among them those who depict Nair society as perverse and Nair women as victim to their strange customs).

This book should interest all serious students, not just of literature or culture, but also of political theory, history, legal theory, and gender studies. With the wider readership that this translation makes possible, I believe *Indulekha* will find life and place in many new terrains.

SUSIE THARU

Preface

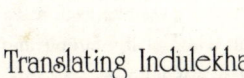

Translating Indulekha

'All good translation,' writes Talal Asad, 'seeks to reproduce the structure of an alien discourse within the translator's own language. How that structure (or 'coherence') is reproduced will of course depend on the genre concerned ("poetry", "scientific analysis", "narrative", etc.), on the resources of the translator's language, as well as on the interests of the translator and/or his readership.'[1] Asad's influential formulation of what is involved in the activity of translation reflects a break in translation studies generally. This break involves a shift from a framework where the issues are those of faithfulness to the meaning of the original and readability in the target language to a framework that takes into consideration politics of representation, and what Tejaswini Niranjana has called the 'force' of translation.[2]

The question of translation is at the heart of the very writing of *Indulekha* and, by extension, also at the heart of the Malayalam novel. In the preface to the first edition, the author provides us with an account of why he wrote the novel. Around the end of 1886, after he was transferred from the busy port city of Kozhikode to the village of Parappanangadi, Chandumenon found himself spending a great deal of time reading English novels. Resentful because he was not paying enough attention to them, the circle of his intimate friends/his wife (there is some ambiguity here) demanded that he share his reading with them. He first tried by providing a plot summary or gist of a few of the novels that he had read; that failed to arouse any interest. He then experimented with an extempore translation of *Henrietta Temple*. He found himself adding explanations and examples, using tone of voice and expression in such a way that he became more like an interpreter than a translator in the conventional sense of the word. His wife enjoyed this so much that she wanted him to translate more. Encouraged by the success, he began work on a written translation of the novel. His observations regarding the difference between his oral rendering and the formal translation are worth citing in some detail:

I do not think that it is particularly difficult to read a novel and then translate it orally in such a way that close friends of mine who do not know English can understand it reasonably well. On the other hand, I believe it is practically impossible to do a written translation in such a way that they will really grasp the import of the story. When one reads a written translation, one only understands what has actually been written. That is not enough. The actual force of an English work can be put across quite well in an extempore rendering because it is possible, even as each incident is being recounted, to supplement the translation with detail, example and commentary, and to draw out the meaning implicit in the words with gesture and tone of voice. If you incorporate such description and commentary into a faithful written translation, there is no doubt that the work will get completely out of hand. Furthermore if one were to simply translate the romantic episodes/love scenes in an English novel into Malayalam, they would not be particularly enticing.[3]

Chandumenon decided that the only way he could solve the problem was to actually write a novel in Malayalam. What he did might be thought of as creating—in Malayalam and in relation to the Malayali world at the time—the experience of the novel.

John Willoughby Francis Dumergue, the then collector in Malabar and Malayalam translator to the Madras government, was enthusiastic about Chandumenon's achievement. 'Mr Chandumenon,' he writes, 'has quit the well-worn track, paved with plagiarism; modern Malabar is depicted in his pages and the language of *Indulekha* is the living Malayalam of the present day.'[4] This depiction of contemporary reality as well as the colloquial language, Dumergue argued, was of immense 'value to Europeans'. The novel was, therefore, of 'far more importance to the ends of administration than all the monuments of archaic ingenuity which we read and mark and leave undigested....'[5] He undertakes the English translation—he terms it a translation into the 'lingua franca of the East'—in order to ensure that the new departure made by Chandumenon is not 'limited to the narrow sphere' of Malayalam, but will also be available to others working in the 'East'. In this he considers himself as assisting in the author's objective.

It is significant that Dumergue finds he has to 'add a few notes in which

I have endeavoured to explain certain passages relating to the social and family system peculiar to Malabar'.[6] In fact, just as Chandumenon felt it necessary to add to the discourse of *Henrietta Temple* when he translated that book for his Malayali audience, Dumergue must add something to make Chandumenon's novel appropriate for the audience he is addressing. What he is forced to add—the notes explaining the *peculiarities* of Malabar—are in fact an indication that his project and Chandumenon's are not identical. In fact, in this case they are quite radically different. And one might go so far as to say that the project of the original and that of a translation are rarely the same.

Dumergue regards the representational and linguistic realism of *Indulekha* as a resource for colonial administration. The novel, he writes, 'supplies a distinct want felt by colonial administrators'.[7] Unlike the classical texts, this work makes the land and its people accessible to him in a way that he finds useful. In other words, they are presented in a way that already readies them as it were for administrative intervention. This overall orientation is clearly evident in the notes, and in subtle but sure ways also affects the nature of Dumergue's translation. We have no evidence that Chandumenon wrote the novel in order to meet such a need. On the contrary, the novel would appear to have been part of a public disagreement that he had with British administrators and the initiatives that they were proposing.

No doubt also because of the fluency and the idiomatic elegance of the English Dumergue uses, and his general 'faithfulness' to the original, his translation has generally been considered a 'good' translation. It has been reprinted several times. Going by the controversy that it raised in the press, it would appear to have also been the basis for the widely circulated textbook that was prescribed at the Class X level. There are two ways of thinking about this, and both of them are relevant here. First, the aesthetic success of the translation, its smoothness and readability, has deflected our attention away from the colonial/orientalist leanings and the administrative inspiration of the Dumergue translation. The aesthetic success is related to the ease with which the original seems to have travelled into English and made itself at home there. In fact, an approach that is concerned primarily with the transfer of meaning, and the readability of the text in the target language is likely to miss these issues that concern the politics of representation. Second, the authority of Dumergue's translation is such that its reading of *Indulekha* became definitive. Tejaswini Niranjana points to this tendency as a general one in a colonial situation. She writes: 'Influential translations...interpellated colonial subjects, legitimizing or authorizing certain versions of the Oriental, versions that then came to acquire the status of "truths" even in the countries in which the "original" works were produced.'[8]

Thus, in his 1965 foreword to a new edition of Dumergue's translation, T.C. Sankaramenon, who is also the author of the Sahitya Akademi monograph on Chandumenon, tells us that Dumergue saw in the novel a 'faithful, fascinating picture of life in Malabar, and such a picture, he believed, would not only be interesting but also useful to administrators and historians'. This is a paraphrase that touches up Dumergue's 'original' in a very significant way. There are two key additions: Chandumenon's original novel is now read through the lens that Dumergue held up to it, as a 'faithful and fascinating' picture of life in Malabar. There is no mention here of the controversies over Marumakkathayam, or the debate over modernity that culminates in the detailed discussions of Chapter 18. Likewise, neither has the problems of transforming the taste of Malayali readers nor of capturing his wife, Laxmikuttyamma's interest been mentioned here. Furthermore, Chandumenon's realist depiction, we are told by this urbane nationalist critic writing in independent India, was not only valuable to administrators—and here he appears to be in agreement with Dumergue—but also to historians. While it may not be justified to read too much into this phrase, one can, I think, point out that the needs of administration and scholarship are depicted as identical. It is ironical that Chandumenon's enthusiasm for English education comes in for criticism by this nationalist critic as does Chapter 18, which he considers a 'structural blemish' and a 'vexatious hurdle' in the reader's 'eager pursuit of the plot'. For Sankaramenon, the novel is a 'well-told, pleasing love story which would have a wide appeal'.[9] By and large, this is the frame in Leela Devi's 1979 translation of *Indulekha* entitled *Crescent Moon*, which indicates her reading of the novel as a romance (a crescent—not 'new'—moon) rather than as a political or cultural initiative (there is no echo even of the other meaning of the word Indulekha—a new/fresh line/inscription). Not surprisingly, Leela Devi also chooses to improve the original by omitting Chapter 18.

What is also obscured, or rather undercut, in both these translations is Chandumenon's effort and achievement of creating a modernity that not only takes issue with colonial representations of Nair family life, but is also Nair and Indian at the same time. Partha Chatterjee writes of this task as that of creating 'our Modernity'. Interestingly, he also points to the hazards of translation in this enterprise.[10] Many of the tensions, the paradoxes, the finer, more ambiguous and multi-accented details of the transformations that Chandumenon attempts as he wrestles with modernity at various levels, are not only invisible, but also of no value to Dumergue's translation.[11]

In many instances, the genius of Chandumenon's novel would appear to have been completely lost. For example, the sculpting of the Indulekha figure is one of the most creative and politically radical aspects of the novel. Through her, the author is taking issue with the colonial characterization of Nair society and especially of Nair women. In the novel, Indulekha's charm and attraction is that of a Nair woman who brings a certain distinctive sheen to Western education. In fact, it might be more accurate to say that the value of Western education is in that it gives a sheen to this spirited and intelligent Nair woman. Further (and no less important in terms of regional politics), she is able to use the new education to help consolidate the strength of her own community in relation to the Nambuthiris. In Dumergue's translation, Indulekha is presented as a vivacious and attractive young woman who owes her charm to her natural beauty, her English education, and a certain universalized youthful femininity. Dumergue's reading, and consequently his translation, glosses over the difficult initiatives that Chandumenon is making in the context of late nineteenth-century Kerala and substitutes them with a world that is familiar and comforting to a Western reader.

In a sense, my own ideas about translation have developed through my critical reading of the earlier colonial—and postcolonial/national—translations. I read the novel both as a historical intervention in the debates about Nair marriage and inheritance practices and as an initial scripting of the detailed micrologies of what Chatterjee has called 'our Modernity'. I have therefore tried, as best as I could, to avoid slipping into a pan-Indian or universalist mode. I have tried to remain alert to the cut and thrust of the many historical issues at stake in the text. I am, in a sense, inviting contemporary readers into a dialogue with those times and this text, taking my inspiration from Walter Benjamin, who wrote about the task of the translator, 'Our translations, even the best ones, proceed from a wrong premise. They want to turn Hindi, Greek, English into German instead of turning German into Hindi, Greek, English.'[12] This is of course a very difficult task, especially when, as in this novel, the text is creating a revolution in the source language. I have, on occasion, especially when it is significant, tried to recreate the thrust of Malayalam etymology, diction and syntax, rather than subjugate it to the smoothness of well-bred English. Thus, when the Malayalam original presents dialogue in a dramatic form, I have retained that echo of Kathakali and of performative modes and have avoided reworking it, as Dumergue and Leela Devi both do, into the conventions of dialogue in realist narrative. This is also why I have in the translation, retained the names as they appeared in the nineteenth-century original: Shankaramenon, Chatharamenon and so on, rather than the fragmented manner in which such names were presented in English in the twentieth century.

ANITHA DEVASIA

Notes

1. Talal Asad, 'The Concept of Cultural Translation in British Social Anthropology', in *Writing Culture: The Poetics and Politics of Ethnography*, James Clifford and George E. Marcus (eds), Berkeley: University of California Press, 1986, 156.
2. Tejaswini Niranjana, *Siting Translation: History, Post-structuralism and the Colonial Context*, Berkeley: University of California Press, 1992, 58; Talal Asad, 'The Concept of Cultural Translation', 141–64; Anitha Devasia and Susie Tharu, 'Englishing *Indulekha*: Translation, the Novel and History', in *Critical Theory: Western and Indian*, Prafulla C. Kar (ed.), Delhi: Pencraft International, 1997, 56–78. Nearly all of them draw inspiration from Walter Benjamin 'The Task of the Translator', Walter Benjamin, *Illuminations*, tr. Harry Zohn, Hannah Arendt (ed.), London: Collins/Fontana Books, 1973, 69–82.
3. Preface to the first edition of *Indulekha*—my translation, 8–9.
4. W. Dumergue, Translator's Preface. *Indulekha: A Novel from Malabar*, by O. Chandumenon, tr. W. Dumergue, 1890; Ernakulam: Mathrubhumi, 1965, vii.
5. Ibid., viii.
6. Ibid.
7. Ibid.
8. Tejaswini Niranjana, *Siting Translation*, 33. She is of course basing her argument on Edward Said's analysis of the politics of representation in the imperial venture.
9. Sankaramenon (tr. by W. Dumergue), Foreword, *Indulekha: A Novel from Malabar*, by O. Chandumenon, Ernakulam: Mathrubhumi, 1965, vi.
10. Partha Chatterjee, 'Talking about our Modernity in Two Languages,' in *A Possible India: Essays in Political Criticism*, Delhi: Oxford University Press, 1998, 263–85.
11. Talal Asad and John Dixon point out, '...in representations of Europe's others, what your style cannot accommodate, you leave out.' What happens in the Dumergue translation is not simply a 'leaving out'.
12. Walter Benjamin (tr. by Harry Zohn, Walter Benjamin), 'The Task of the Translator', *Illuminations*, Hannah Arendt (ed.), London: Collins, 1973, 80. For a masterly and impressive practice of translation in this mode, *see* Gayatri Spivak's translations of Mahasweta Devi's stories (tr. by Gayatri Chakravorty Spivak), Mahasweta Devi, *Imaginary Maps*, Calcutta: Thema, 1993.

Acknowledgements

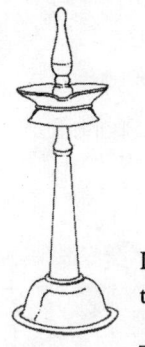

It is a pleasure to acknowledge my debt and express my gratitude to:

—Prof. Susie Tharu, Centre for English Literature, Central Institute of English and Foreign Languages, Hyderabad, for her invaluable friendship, support and encouragement;

—Prof. D. Venkat Rao, Centre for English Literature, Central Institute of English and Foreign Languages, for his warmth and friendship;

—My school teachers, Mrs Lily Anne Abraham and Mrs Ratnamala Sinha, who introduced me to the English language and to the wealth of its literature.

—All my friends for their generosity, patience and affection.

—My friend Mini Krishnan of Oxford University Press, India, for sensitive editing, working with whom has been an enriching experience.

—Gratitude and thoughts that go beyond thanks to Appachan, Ammachi, Antony, Tessy, Joe, Preston, Thomas, Ansu, Poly, Anju, Shanthi, Tina, Diya, Kirti, Anu and Sanya for their love and support.

The years this work took to finish were often dark and troubled but happy memories linked with the joy of creativity helped greatly to erase them.

ANITHA DEVASIA

chapter one

Beginnings

CHATHARAMENON: How on earth did you dare to speak so, Madhavan? No, you shouldn't have. You should have let him have his way. We don't have to yield to our elders and their authority. You spoke too rashly.

MADHAVAN: I don't think I was rash. Such mulishness should not be tolerated in anyone. He needn't educate Shinnan, if he doesn't want to. I am going to take Shinnan with me. I will give him an education.

KUMMINIAMMA: No, my dear. Shinnan is not old enough to live away from me. Take Chathara or Gopalan and educate them if you must. Anyway, the *karanavan* is no longer pleased with you. He may never have liked us much, but he used to think a great deal of you.

MADHAVAN: True. But how strange it would be to take Chathara*jeshtan* and Gopalan at this point in their lives and suddenly give them an English education!

As they stood talking, a servant arrived with the message that Madhavan had been summoned by his uncle, Shankaramenon. Madhavan left immediately for his uncle's room.

Before we proceed further with this story, it seems necessary to describe Madhavan and his situation in life.

About Madhavan's age, his relationship with Panchumenon, and the examinations he has passed, we have already spoken in the preface.[1] What remains to be said about him, can be done briefly.

Madhavan was a brilliant and extraordinarily good-looking young man. His performance and credits that he acquired in due course, from the time he began to learn English till his BL degree, fully revealed his extreme intelligence. Not one examination had he failed to clear in the very first attempt. He had passed both FA and BA in the first class, with Sanskrit as his second language. During his BA course, Madhavan developed into a first-rate Sanskrit scholar. In the BL, he stood first among those who passed with a first class. In addition, he won prizes in various examinations at school and had received several awards and scholarships for higher studies. As for Madhavan's school-teachers, every one of them was convinced that there had never been a student more accomplished than he.

Anyone who made Madhavan's acquaintance would be convinced that his physique had been specially cast to house his extraordinary intelligence. Convention decrees it unnecessary that the delineation of a man's qualities encompass a discussion of the beauty of his physique. It is enough to speak about his wit, intelligence, learning, courage, and courtesy. Yet, I fear that if I were not to say even a couple of words here about Madhavan's physical magnetism, some day or other my readers would regard it a defect in the narrative. Therefore, I gather together the essentials.

His body was the colour of pure gold. It had the beauty of a youth nurtured in the rites of daily exercise; it was irresistible. What could be seen of Madhavan's limbs and chest was neither too stocky nor too lean and seemed cast in coppery gold. As for his height, it was more than average. His cascading, ankle-length *kuduma* was measure enough for his body. Madhavan's glowing face, the beauty of the different parts of his body, their individual and mutual proportion and harmony, the manly charm of his figure and face can only be termed as amazing. No European who made Madhavan's acquaintance could help but be charmed by his appearance and all of them quickly became his friends.

Madhavan realized what an advantage it was at the very bloom of youth for people to consider his person and name to be of great worth. Between the age of around eighteen and the time they marry and set up a household, young men are unfortunately prone to unethical behaviour. Either as a result of careful reflection, or due to his natural intelligence, Madhavan, let me assure you, did not indulge in anything of the kind. As a result, at maturity, his natural glow, his intelligence, and virility were a joy to behold.

Surely, I do not need to reiterate that Madhavan used the English language with remarkable dexterity. He also excelled at English games like lawn tennis and cricket. At a very young age, Madhavan had tried his hand at hunting, a taste he had acquired from his father. Govindapanikkar was crazy about hunting and Madhavan's interest in this sport was deep. Two or three excellent rifles, a couple of pistols, a revolver and other sundry equipment always found a place in his kit. Hunting was Madhavan's chief entertainment till his interest finally found another direction.

When his uncle sent a servant summoning him, Madhavan went in and stood before him.

SHANKARAMENON: What is all this high drama about, Madhavan! The karanavan is such a senior person, how could you have spoken so disrespectfully to him? Is this the fruit of the English education he equipped you with? And to think of the vast sums of money he has spent on you!

MADHAVAN: It is truly our misfortune that you too hold the same opinion. When I discuss serious issues I am never so much in awe of anyone, that I cannot speak. I just can't bear this sort of injustice. I have never required that *valiammaman* [maternal great uncle] spend even a single coin that he has earned from his own toils. I have only said that the money left in his hands by our ancestors for our prosperity and betterment should be used for our well-being. Kumminiamma and her children are not servants in this household! Why have they been cast aside so heartlessly? He did not provide either of her sons with the discipline of an English education. He paid no attention to Kalyanikutty's education. His actions are indeed cruel. Can such atrocities be justified? And now it seems as though he is going to raise our little Shinnan much as he would a young bull. I cannot let this happen; I will take him along with me and make sure he gets a proper education.

SHANKARAMENON: Education! It is incredible that you speak in these terms! What means do you have that can provide him with an education? Your monthly allowance is a mere Rs 50. What will you educate him with? If you invoke the karanavan's displeasure, the results can be disastrous. Go, and fall at his feet this very moment.

The minute Madhavan heard his uncle say 'If you invoke the karanavan's displeasure the results can be disastrous', it was Indulekha he thought of and his feelings found expression in his demeanour. However, he controlled himself instantly. Pacing gently up and down the room, he replied with a smile.

MADHAVAN: Displeasure? If I make a statement that is just, why should it annoy him? I am not afraid of his anger when it is unreasonable.

SHANKARAMENON: What insolence!
MADHAVAN: Insolence? I hardly know what the word means.
SHANKARAMENON: That ignorance seems to be the whole problem. You may have studied a little English, Appu, and become smart but that is no reason why you should forget our customs, traditions, and ways of life. Tell me, child, have you had lunch?
MADHAVAN: No. I felt very upset. Mother brought me some *palkanji*.

Just then Parvathiamma arrived with a little bit of palkanji in a silver dish.

SHANKARAMENON: Parvathi! Did you hear everything that *kuttan* said?
PARVATHIAMMA: Yes I did. It didn't sound good to me.
MADHAVAN: Let me have the palkanji.

Standing where he was, Madhavan gulped down two mouthfuls and turned to her, smiling.

MADHAVAN: So, are you displeased with me too, Mother?
PARVATHIAMMA: Of course, why doubt it? Anything that offends my jeshtan and my *ammaman* [maternal uncle] offends me too. Anyway, drink up your kanji, we can talk afterwards—it is almost noon. Why do you always leave your hair loose like this? Come here, I will tie it up for you. My goodness, what a lot of hair you have lost!
MADHAVAN: Mother, tell me, should Shinnan get an English education or not?
PARVATHIAMMA: That is a matter for your valiammaman to decide, isn't it, my dear? What would I know about such things? After all, he is the one who supported your education. He will probably support Shinnan's too.
MADHAVAN: And what if he doesn't?
PARVATHIAMMA: Then he need not be educated.
MADHAVAN: To that I cannot agree.
PARVATHIAMMA: Let me take that dish. I am going in, do come along soon for your meal.

Note

1. This line is a faithful translation of the original. Strangely there is no such mention of Madhavan in either of the Prefaces that O. Chandumenon wrote in December 1889 or May 1890.

chapter two

Indulekha

When I began writing this chapter, a fear that crept over me led me to the sad conclusion that I might lack the ability to describe beautiful heroines. But there is no escape; write I must and according to my ability. Indulekha is about eighteen years old, when this story begins. To me it seems easier to say something about the overall radiance of her form than to present in detail individual features. The various qualities which constitute beauty cannot be listed easily. In different situations, different combinations of features make a form beautiful. A dark complexion is generally associated with lack of beauty in a person. All the same, alongside a combination of other attractive features, a dark complexion can produce a radiant glow. (My readers should not presume from this that Indulekha is dark skinned.) Traditionally, a fair or golden-hued complexion is considered beautiful. Yet, even with a fair complexion some people do not appear beautiful. In my opinion, beauty is the result of an inner glow, of an inner radiance. In traditional Indian literature, jet-black hair and blue-black eyes are considered to be an important aspect of beauty. Yet while describing the quality of beauty in a woman, English poets generally speak of golden hair and light blue eyes—precisely what we in raw Malayalam speech derisively term 'cat-eyed'.

It seems to me that both precepts are valid. I am of the opinion that just as black hair suits our women and appears attractive on them, golden hair suits some European women. Light eyes can be very becoming and indeed lend a glow to people from Europe. I have found some European women with light blue eyes very beautiful. The beauty or ugliness of a body is the result of the impression that it creates in the mind, which in turn is the result of a combination of a person's features and complexion. That is why I feel that one cannot simply decide beforehand that if a woman has certain features or a particular kind of complexion, she will be beautiful.

If you survey some women from head to foot it may not be possible to fault any feature, yet overall, they may not seem attractive at all. On the other hand, others, if observed carefully, may have many faulty features but look extremely beautiful and appealing. For one to recognize beauty in a woman or to say that a woman is beautiful, her features should charm and attract both at first sight and in the thoughtful scrutiny of recall. At that time, when the features are recollected as a whole, the result should be an intense inner glow. A real beauty should not only captivate (the mind) at first sight, it should continue to fascinate and arouse a continuing desire to contemplate its form. It is such a woman that I consider a beauty. Indulekha is the epitome of such beauty in women. Let me make just one observation about Indulekha's complexion. Only by touch could one distinguish between her skin and the brocade border of the *mundu* which normally covered her midriff. It was impossible to tell by mere sight where the gold-threaded border of the mundu she normally wore ended and where her body began. The deep black of her locks, its length, abundance, and softness was most alluring. As for her lips, I wonder whether it is possible to see their likeness in women who are not Europeans. Her eyes—their length, their triple tone, their sparkle, the way she uses them on occasion, and the intense fire in them—can be described only by young men who have been subjected to their effect. In addition, she was at an age when her bosom was filling out. Is there a man invulnerable to the power of those growing breasts? Can anyone describe the bewitching beauty of this Indulekha!

I admit that it is impossible for me to relate the happiness, joy, excitement, confusion, devotion, ardent attachment, and pain that must have filled the minds of men as they beheld Indulekha's golden complexion, sparkling teeth stained delicately by chewing betel leaves, glowing lotus-like face, deep black hair, full bosom, slender waist, and so on.

Indulekha's education and manners matched her physical beauty. She was the daughter of a king from the house of Kilimanoor. Indulekha's father, the king, had passed away when she was only two and a half. She was barely three when her ammaman Kochukrishnamenon, the eldest son of her maternal grandfather Panchumenon, had taken her away to live in his household. Kochukrishnamenon was a dewan in the government service, drawing a salary of Rs 800. He was well educated in English, Sanskrit, and music. Until she was sixteen, Indulekha remained in his care and received a fitting education. She was taught English and trained in the finer details of Sanskrit drama. She received an advanced education in music and acquired skills in playing the piano, the violin, the veena, and other musical instruments. Besides this, she was taught to embroider and paint like the young ladies in Europe. Kochukrishnamenon, who was a brilliant person himself, longed to familiarize Indulekha with the education, knowledge, and customs generally taught to a young lady in England. It can be said that he saw to it that she learned as much as she could of all these accomplishments by the time she was sixteen. However, no one can be lucky all the time. By the time Indulekha was sixteen, Kochukrishnamenon passed away. Thereafter, she lived with her grandfather and mother in her grandfather's household Poovarangu.

It is impossible for me to convey through ordinary words, the quality and depth of the love that Indulekha's grandfather had for her. It could be because of Indulekha's natural good qualities, because she was his granddaughter and also because she had been dear to his beloved son. He had arranged for a two-storeyed bungalow for her. Indulekha's grandfather decided that she would not lack anything in any way because of her ammaman Kochukrishnamenon's untimely death.

As a result of her education and training that she got from her great and wise ammaman Kochukrishnamenon, Indulekha's daily routine, her practices, and behaviour were extremely charming and delightful. Though she knew English and had received an English education, she was keenly aware of her Malayali identity. Indulekha did not dislike Hinduism nor was she attracted to atheism. Fortunately, the contempt that sometimes some learned young people have for all others, had not in any way affected Indulekha. Bathing in the temple, marking her forehead with *kuri*, her way of dressing, her decorous speech, the respect she had for her mother, grandmother, grandfather and uncle, her friendship with those friends and neighbours, who had not learned English, her aesthetic sensitivity, and most of all the humility and lack of pride especially in the words she used, and in the way she behaved was a source of constant amazement to those who were acquainted with her. Anyone with a little intelligence would say that she was a model of how youngsters should learn to behave. Indulekha thus turned out to be a person who upheld her uncle's name and prestige.

The jewellery that Indulekha wore every day was minimal by the standards of the times. She owned quite a lot of jewellery given by her uncle, and she had also inherited what her father had given her mother, and those that her grandfather had given her. However, Indulekha was not enamoured of all this jewellery. It was at her mother, grandmother, or grandfather's insistence that she wore any jewellery at all on special days. She wore traditional engraved earrings, a locket on a cord-like gold chain around her neck, a flat gold chain that held a locket of diamonds, emeralds and, rubies below that, and on her both wrists were heavy Thanjavoor bangles. On her fingers were a few rings—these were the only ornaments she used daily. Though she did not care much for them, Indulekha took a special interest in her clothes. She changed twice every day, once in the morning when she had an oil bath and once in the evening when she had a bath but did not wash her hair. She was particular about the fine quality of the clothes she wore and was insistent that they should be freshly laundered. She always covered the upper part of her body with a gold-bordered white *melmundu*. She dressed in this manner every day. Though Indulekha was extremely sweet-tempered, there was no one in the taravad who was powerful enough to voice their opinion against her wishes or desires. Such was her competence and standing in the house. No one could fault Indulekha's manner or bearing.

My readers might think the name Indulekha to be quite incongruous when considered with the names of the other women in the novel. It is Kochukrishnamenon who started calling her Indulekha. The name decreed for the baby according to the horoscope was Madhavi. But, considering how gentle and beautiful she was, Kochukrishnamenon decided that she should be called Indulekha and so did everyone else eventually. However, when our story begins one person alone called her Madhavi and that was Madhavan. It need not be said that Madhavan and Indulekha could not help being in love with each other. Madhavan was extremely handsome, cheerful, wise, smart, and her grandfather's nephew. One can even say that in their heart of hearts they were already married to each other.

I doubt whether it is enough to say that when this story begins Indulekha and Madhavan had, in their heart of hearts, decided to marry. Then my readers might guess that they were in love. It is better to speak briefly and clearly about this matter than to leave it to speculation. Therefore, I shall say a little about what has happened thus far.

The noble Kochukrishnamenon was of the opinion that Indulekha herself should choose a suitable man as her husband after finishing her education. However, this grave man had not disclosed that to anyone. From the time the girl was ten or eleven, many worthy people had tried to learn Kochukrishnamenonpeishkar's opinion on this matter—but none of them succeeded.

A few days before his father's death, when Kochukrishnamenonpeishkar came on leave, bringing Indulekha to visit his father Panchumenon, the latter had observed that Indulekha was already fifteen. 'Should we not consider a *sambandam* for her?' he had asked his son, to which Kochukrishnamenon had answered: 'Indulekha has not completed her education; it is only after that that we need even think of such a thing as her sambandam. The responsibility vested in me as her uncle is to educate Indulekha and make her accomplished, and once this is done she will act appropriately herself.'

Though the elderly Panchumenon did not quite understand this answer, and was not very pleased with it, he did not press his son further on this matter.

While Indulekha was with Kochukrishnamenon, she met Madhavan frequently. By chance, Indulekha herself had heard her uncle tell people many a time that Madhavan was an extremely intelligent person. However, she had not heard him say more than that about Madhavan to anyone. No one was particularly sure whether he had decided that Madhavan would be a suitable husband for Indulekha.

Indulekha and Madhavan became extremely fond of each other when she moved to Poovarangu after her uncle's death. On the occasions when Madhavan came home from Madras, they spent a lot of time in each other's company. Indulekha and Madhavan began to fall in love. Indulekha did not let Madhavan know about her love for him as she did not want it to be a hindrance to his studies. Madhavan did not let her know of his love for her because he was a little shy and also because he doubted whether he would eventually get married to her. He had reason enough for his doubts. It was well known throughout Malabar that Indulekha was a gem of a woman. Madhavan knew this for certain from the letters that frequently came to Panchumenon, and from the discussions between various people at Poovarangu that men, including kings, wanted Indulekha. Hence, he felt that it was useless for a mere schoolboy like him to desire her. However, his love for Indulekha continued to grow. At home from Madras, daytime found Madhavan almost always with Indulekha. Quite unselfconsciously, they entertained themselves by reading, singing, playing the piano, and playing chess. Even then, each day by evening, when it was time for them to part, they felt that the days were short.

Most people were happy that Indulekha and Madhavan were in love because they were clearly suited for each other in their education and social status. Even then, many people had doubts whether Madhavan would get Indulekha as his *wife*. Anyone who knew the state of affairs in Malabar would be justified in entertaining such doubts. Many had heard from Panchumenon himself that even the Maharaja of Tiruvananthapuram was considering Indulekha as his consort; therefore, the doubt just mentioned was no surprise.

A little before this story begins, Madhavan took his BL degree examination and returned home immediately after. Madhavan used to play chess and spend time with Indulekha and gradually the intensity of his love increased so much that it became unbearable. Madhavan made up his mind: 'Which maharaja? What king? My Indulekha is my wife. If it is not to be I will not live.' During this time, Madhavan longed desperately to know how Indulekha felt. Though Indulekha loved Madhavan more than he loved her, she did not reveal her feelings to him. From her conduct Madhavan was unable to learn anything more than her constant willingness to play chess with him, laugh, and enjoy music with him. Since Madhavan was by nature friendly, his emotions for Indulekha found outward expression. To this Indulekha showed no aversion or objection, but no signs of her desire for him escaped her manner or speech.

One day during this time, while they were playing chess, Madhavan held the pawn without moving it and kept staring blankly at Indulekha.

INDULEKHA: Why are you not making a move? Why don't you play?

MADHAVAN: I don't at all feel like playing today.

INDULEKHA: You are a little slow in your game these days. But, maybe it is because you are worried about your examination results. What practical good can worry do? Please do not worry so much.

MADHAVAN: When the origin of disturbances cannot be stemmed, and when there is no capacity to block them, when reasons for them exist and there is no way of solving them—how can we control the mind?

INDULEKHA: You have to keep your mind under control. That is one of the virtues of a gentleman.

MADHAVAN: What is the virtue of a woman?

INDULEKHA: No woman has said that she is not feeling well enough to play now. Are you not the one who said that you do not feel enthused enough to play today?

MADHAVAN: But, Indulekha, your mind is under control.

INDULEKHA: I have not tried it. One must put that to the test only when one feels that it is not under control. I have never felt that my mind was not under control; there has been no occasion that made me feel that way.

MADHAVAN: If you always get whatever your mind desires, you are never troubled. You have always been able to get what you want, that is why you have had no occasion to put your mind to the test in this way.

INDULEKHA: My mind never longs for what cannot be achieved. I am extremely happy that this is a quality which is natural to my mind. Therefore Madhavan, what you said is correct. I have not had occasion to be miserable about anything that engages my mind.

MADHAVAN: Can it be like that always? If so, is it not because you have kept your mind disciplined?

INDULEKHA: Certainly not, if you have to keep your mind under control, you have to have courage and patience. My mind is calm even without the use of these things. Therefore, I think that the calmness of my mind is a quality that is natural to it.

MADHAVAN: Indulekha, have you never entertained thoughts about things that are not immediately possible?

INDULEKHA: I do not think so. However, I do not understand what you meant by immediately possible. I think only of practicable things.

MADHAVAN: Let me give you an example. Imagine a flower that is extremely beautiful and fragrant. Wouldn't you feel like touching it and experiencing its fragrance, Indulekha, even though you know you cannot acquire it easily? Would you desire it only if you can get it immediately, would you desire the flower only after you have thought at leisure about whether it is possible to get it, impossible to get it, possible to get it at the moment, or possible to get it at some future point of time?

INDULEKHA: If I realize that the flower is beautiful and fragrant, on seeing it I might rejoice. Unless I realize that it is feasible and appropriate to pluck it, I will not wish to hold it. That is one quality I do have.

MADHAVAN: Indulekha, what you have said just now and what I earlier said are the same. 'My mind will rejoice' actually means not only that you are attracted to it, but that in this rejoicing is also embedded the desire to experience the delight of the flower. However, then, you will reflect deeply about whether the wish is possible or impossible, and only then will you try to fulfil the wish. Indulekha, I think this is the gist of what you said just now. If this is correct it seems clear that you overcome your desires by sheer courage and patience.

INDULEKHA: I did not say that. Madhavan, you did not get what I said. First of all, the example that you gave of a flower itself is not appropriate. I shall make you understand what I meant with a better example. I am a young woman; I see a handsome young man. In my mind, I will not desire him before I am sure that that man is suited to be my husband. Here I do not use courage to hold back my mind after I have desired him. I think about wealth in the same way; I do not long for wealth unless it can be acquired lawfully. These are some of the good qualities that are natural to some people, whereas it is not like that for others. The virtue of the mind enters everywhere—what can be obtained, what cannot be obtained, where it is needed, where it is not needed. Now if the mind is acute, brave and intelligent, it will keep a check on itself. Therefore, if you belong to the latter type and if your mind has entered some impossible area, you will be able to retrieve it because you are an intelligent and clever person.

MADHAVAN: Indulekha, I don't agree with what you said. However, I am not going to argue with you over this matter anymore. Now I do not feel well enough (mentally) to argue with you as I used to.

INDULEKHA: I thought you were not inclined to play chess with me. I am surprised to hear that you are not even interested in talking to me.

MADHAVAN: Why do you say such things? I think I am an unlucky person—don't you consider it unlucky to be worried pointlessly?

INDULEKHA: Your ill luck is that you cannot stem that sorrow.

MADHAVAN: It will be useful for me if you tell me a remedy for that sorrow.

INDULEKHA: (laughing) If you tell me the reason for your sorrow I shall try to solve it. Come now, play, I am going to take your knight. You have spent enough time looking out saying you are sad. Will you be able to save your knight? Show me your skill.

MADHAVAN: Just a minute. I do not feel like playing. It will not work if I make a move now. Let me lie down on this couch. (Saying this, he put the pawn on the table and lay on the couch. Indulekha laughed, and sat down on a chair and started reading.)

MADHAVAN: What book is that?
INDULEKHA: *Shakuntalam.*
MADHAVAN: Where have you got to?
INDULEKHA: Why, do you want me to read aloud?

MADHAVAN: Please.
INDULEKHA: (reading a sloka)

> Kshamakshamakapolamananamura
> Kadinayamukthasthana
> Madya klanthara prakamavinatha
> Vamsauchhavi pandura
> Shochachya cha priyadarshana cha madana
> Klishteyamalakshyathe
> Pathranamiva shoshaneha marutha
> Sprushtalathamadhavi.

[Withered cheeks, sagging bosom, starved waist, drooping shoulders, pale and tortured by Kamadevan she appeared pathetic, and charming, like a wind-tossed jasmine creeper with faded leaves.]

MADHAVAN: Shiva, Shiva! I would have forgotten my sorrows if I had seen something like this.
INDULEKHA: How is it possible to see someone like Shakuntala now? Think deeply of Shakuntala, shut your eyes tight, and lie down; then maybe you will be able to dream about her.
MADHAVAN: Indulekha, though you are beautiful and scholarly, I think you are hard-hearted.
INDULEKHA: Yes, I am hard-hearted. Well, shall I read one more sloka from *Shakuntalam*?
MADHAVAN: Which one?
INDULEKHA: (reading another sloka)

> Anakhratham pushpam kisalayamalunam kararuhai
> Ranaviddham ratnam madhunavamanaswathitharasam
> Akhandam punyanam phalamiva cha thadrupamanakham
> Na jane bhoktharam kamihasamupasthasyathi vidhi.

[A flower that has not been smelt, a tender leaf that has not been nipped by a nail, a jewel that has not been pierced, fresh honey that has not been tasted, result of innumerable good deeds, her faultless figure is like these. I do not know who fate will bring as the enjoyer of all this.]

MADHAVAN: Isn't that a sloka which I should recite?
INDULEKHA: It is from *Shakuntalam*; anyone can recite it.
MADHAVAN: Some people's arrogance really surprises me.
INDULEKHA: Why?

MADHAVAN: Isn't it arrogance if somebody laughs when what is needed is compassion towards their fellow men? Is it not arrogance stemming from cruelty?
INDULEKHA: Yes, if you are laughing at them.
MADHAVAN: Aren't you laughing at me?
INDULEKHA: Do you want any English books? Let me get them for you.
MADHAVAN: I don't want to read anything.
INDULEKHA: Then read Bharthruhari.
MADHAVAN: I don't want to read anything, it is enough if you don't tease me.
INDULEKHA: Then let me play the veena for sometime, if you are distressed you will get some relief.
MADHAVAN: I don't want to hear you play the veena.
INDULEKHA: Then go to sleep; think of Shakuntala, if you would like to, keep this book of plays next to you. (Saying this, Indulekha approached Madhavan and asked: Don't you want the book?)
MADHAVAN: Why do you tease me so? What pleasure do you get out of it?
INDULEKHA: Is this what you call teasing? I am not sure. Anyway, if that is so I feel happy doing this and talking in this manner. Why don't you get up and play, Madhavan? Protect your knight; come on, get up.
MADHAVAN: I do not want any knight or any rook.
INDULEKHA: Then all you want is to lie down and think about Shakuntala. Isn't that so?
MADHAVAN: Yes, I want to do just that.
INDULEKHA: Okay. So be it then. Don't you ever go hunting these days? You don't take out your rifle, and I don't see you shooting. What is the reason for all this inactivity?
MADHAVAN: I do not feel like doing anything.
INDULEKHA: What is this that I hear? Are you going out of your mind or something?
MADHAVAN: Sometimes I think I am going mad.
INDULEKHA: Then shouldn't you try and find some remedy?
MADHAVAN: I should.
INDULEKHA: Let me inform your father immediately; yes I shall tell him. There he is. It is time for tea, shall I ask for tea for you too?
MADHAVAN: I don't want tea.
INDULEKHA: Do you want something to eat?
MADHAVAN: No.

INDULEKHA: Is something wrong with your stomach also?

MADHAVAN: I am ill all over.

INDULEKHA: This is a peculiar disease.

MADHAVAN: I too think it is a strange illness. Maybe it will be difficult to cure. I don't think I will ever have peace of mind again. Why don't you sit by me on the couch for some time? Or do you have a quarrel with that as well?

INDULEKHA: Yes, I am against it. You are a young man and I am a young woman. Can we play with each other as we used to in the past, as children?

MADHAVAN: What is wrong with sitting beside me on the couch?

INDULEKHA: I am against it. We shouldn't sit together at all now.

MADHAVAN: Now it is impossible to know whether a time will ever come when we can even sit together. Oh! What can be done?

INDULEKHA: Yes, it is not possible for anyone to predict the future.

MADHAVAN: (heaving a deep sigh) No one can say anything—that is how it is.

[A boy came in with tea and something to eat. Madhavan got up and walked away. He had not said anything like he had imagined he would.]

I feel intensely sad even to relate how Madhavan spent the rest of the day. He remained silent even when Indulekha laughed and frolicked. Sometimes, Indulekha asked, 'Why are you looking so glum?' Before Madhavan could reply, she would ask another question. One evening, when Indulekha was getting ready for her bath, Madhavan was with her in her room. Seated there he filled half a sheet of paper with his mental agony and left it on Indulekha's writing desk. Early next morning, he returned to Indulekha's *malika* and asked, 'I had left something in writing here, did you read it?' To this Indulekha replied, 'I am not certain of anything,' and asked Madhavan something else. Even if Madhavan appeared sad, it did not cause any change in Indulekha. She kept her love for Madhavan a secret.

On one moonlit night during that period, Madhavan was looking at the moon while he walked in the northern courtyard of the Poovarangu house. Seeing Madhavan from her room, Indulekha called out 'Madhava, Madhava!'

MADHAVAN: What is it?

INDULEKHA: Are you abusing the moon? This room also gets lots of moonlight. Do you have anything against coming up here?

MADHAVAN: I am not coming up. If you are against sitting on the same

couch together with me, aren't you against both of us being in the same room at night?
INDULEKHA: Yes, that is right; I am opposed to it. I said it without thinking. I shall come down to the courtyard.
MADHAVAN: You don't need to come down for me.
INDULEKHA: I will come down for my own sake.
MADHAVAN: I don't have anything against that.

Indulekha came down from her room upstairs and stood near Madhavan in the beautiful moonlight. In her hand was a string of jasmine which she herself had strung in the evening. When Madhavan saw Indulekha's face, lush hair and form in the fair moonlight, his mind began to whirl. Madhavan thought, 'Oh God, if this beauty loves me who will be as lucky as I am? If she does not, why should I live? It would be best to die now.'

As for Indulekha and her thoughts, they did not change in nature, if anything, they intensified. But she kept her thoughts to herself. One's mental agony can be reduced and lightened with outward gestures. If you are grief-stricken it is a great relief to cry out. Talking about your sorrow to a friend may soothe you. If you hide it, it is like trying to stem the flow of a stream which cannot be contained. It overcomes all barriers and finds expression. In the same way, it is good to laugh if you are happy or are feeling jovial.

As she looked at Madhavan's tender face in the moonlit courtyard, Indulekha found it hard to bear the clear mark of sorrow on it. Moonlight itself excites the mind and needless to say Indulekha was extremely disturbed to see Madhavan's attractive face so close to hers especially because they were intensely in love and alone.

But she showed no sign of her agitation, a state she was able to achieve through her patience and courage. Both of them stood and looked at the moon in silence for a long time.

After this, Indulekha recited a sloka:

swayram kairavakorakan vidalaya
nyunam mana khedaya
nambhojani nimilayan mrigadrisha
mmanam samunmulayan
jyolsnam kandalayan disho dhavalaya
nnambhodhimudwelayan
kokanakulayan thama kabalaya
nindhu samujrambhathe.

[The moon is rising. It helps the water lily buds open, fills human minds with sorrow, closes the lotus flower. It undoes the beauty of maidens, causes the jasmine to bud, lights the land, causes the sea tides to rise and fall. It brings sorrow to the *chakravaka* that swallows the darkness.]

MADHAVAN: I do not think that the writer of this sloka has correctly grasped all the qualities of the moon.

INDULEKHA: Why?

MADHAVAN: '*Mrigadrisham manam samunmulayan*' [that which undoes the beauty of maidens] if this is right there, why don't we see it here?

INDULEKHA: [laughing] Then I will recite another sloka:

*yaminikaminikarnakundalam chandramandalam
maranarachanirmanashanachakramivodhitham.*

[Like the ear drops of the young maiden night, the rising moon round as a perfect pestle makes ready the arrows of Kamadevan.]

MADHAVAN: I think these days Kamadevan's weapon is not being used on women.

INDULEKHA: Aren't women, poor things, actually cowards? Maybe Kamadevan was moved by pity and decided against it.

MADHAVAN: If that is so, I will say that Kamadevan is not only cruel but also a fool. If he does not use his weapons on women out of pity, what does he gain by using it on men? Why should he attack men without any reason?

INDULEKHA: Perhaps Kamadevan does this because he thinks men are strong and if he attacks them, they would inevitably attack women on their own.... Here, I have brought you a string of jasmine. I made it myself; I plucked the small lotus flower myself and threaded it as its locket. It is from the pond on the western side of Poovally. Madhava, it will look grand if you wear this mala in your hair. Here take this.

When Madhavan took the jasmine mala, Indulekha noticed that his hand was trembling.

INDULEKHA: Why is your hand trembling?

MADHAVAN: Isn't this Kamadevan's arrow? I shiver out of sheer fright.

Indulekha laughed.

MADHAVAN: (holding the lotus flower and looking at it)

shobhasarvaswamesham pradhamamapahritham
yathwaya lochanabhyam
madhwimadhuryasara thawa kalavachasa
mardhavam thwal prathikai
sthanabhramsho mahiyanapi cha virachitha
thwanmughaspardhinam vai
padmanam bhandhanathvam virama varathano
pishtapeshena kim syal.

[First, all the glowing wealth of these have been stolen with your eyes. In your words the sweetness of honey, in your body, all softness. That which competes with your face, their place too has been lost. You with a beautiful form, please stop choking the lotuses. What benefit do you gain by squeezing them thus?]

INDULEKHA: Good sloka—I want to learn it.

MADHAVAN: I will take a piece from this mala and keep it on my *kuduma*. It is more appropriate that you wear the rest of it in your hair.

INDULEKHA: Set aside questions of what is appropriate. Do what you like, Madhavan.

MADHAVAN: Would you agree to let me do what I like?

INDULEKHA: Do what you like as far as the mala is concerned.

Madhavan broke off a little bit from the mala and put it over his kuduma.

He held the rest of the mala and looked at Indulekha's face.

MADHAVAN: May I tuck this into your hair, Indulekha?

INDULEKHA: In my hair?

MADHAVAN: Yes.

INDULEKHA: With your hand?

MADHAVAN: Yes.

Indulekha stood there silently with a smile. Madhavan placed the flowers elegantly in Indulekha's hair. The moment he put it there—

INDULEKHA: This is wrong. You may be my grandfather's nephew and we may have been playmates from childhood, but we must remember that we are not children always.

MADHAVAN: When I placed this string in your hair, I did not do so as a child; it is a young man.

INDULEKHA: Then how could you touch me?

MADHAVAN: Didn't you see me touching you?

INDULEKHA: That is why I said it was wrong.

MADHAVAN: (with tears in his eyes) Why do you make it difficult for me? I do not wish to live in this world even for a moment, parted from you.

INDULEKHA: (suppressing her own deep sorrow firmly) Whoever asked you to part from me?

MADHAVAN: 'Part from you?' Are you using the words in the same sense as I did?

INDULEKHA: What meaning did you have in mind?

MADHAVAN: I used 'apart' in the sense that I should have the freedom and luck to be with you both by day and night.

INDULEKHA: It is getting late and chilly. Go in and sleep. Please come upstairs tomorrow for tea in the morning.

MADHAVAN: How can I sleep when my body and mind are throbbing as though they have been wounded?

INDULEKHA: For that you must take some medicine which will work to heal the wounds.

MADHAVAN: I have got a medicine for that—according to a certain formula. I will tell you the formula. Will you give me the medicine?

INDULEKHA: What is the formula?—let me hear it.

MADHAVAN:

indivarakshi thavathikshnakadakshabana
pathavrane dwividhamaushadhamevamanye
eekam thwadheeyamadharamruthapanamanya
dhuthumgapinakuchakunkumapankalepa.

[Lady with dark eyes, I think there are only two tonics for the wounds received from the intensity of your looks. One is drinking the nectar from your lips, the other is smearing the saffron from your full breasts.]

INDULEKHA: All right. It is a very good rule. Where will this medicine be available?

MADHAVAN: It is with you.

INDULEKHA: I cannot produce it now. It is very chilly. I am going inside. Go to sleep now—and don't lose your balance.

MADHAVAN: Tell me, will I get that medicine some time in my life? Say yes, once. I will consider myself a lucky man. Don't let me grieve like this— I just want to hear that word. Am I that lucky?

INDULEKHA: I feel terribly sleepy. I am going indoors.

Saying this, Indulekha immediately went up to her room.

Madhavan stood there, dejected, his eyes following Indulekha's path. Once in her room she stood looking at Madhavan through the window till he left the courtyard.

If I have to write about the way in which Indulekha and Madhavan behaved with each other I shall have to speak at length. Anyway, I am narrating these incidents which happened earlier since I wish to talk to my readers about one more encounter between them.

Since Madhavan thought of Indulekha all the time, his mind began to burn and smoke with an intensity hard to bear. One night he lay down trying to sleep—but couldn't. As he lay awake he thought; 'Why should I be so grief-stricken? If Indulekha were in love with me she would have become my wife long ago. Possibly she loves me, but I still doubt whether she is in love with me. More than that, there are so many men more suitable and richer, who desire her. She herself knows this. So, she might like to get acquainted with someone like that and then marry him. How is it possible to know a woman's mind? However educated she is, isn't mystery a woman's very nature? Then why should I be unreasonably distressed? I won't let myself grieve like this thinking about Indulekha. Early tomorrow, I must get my rifles and go hunting. Maybe my father will also come along. It has been many days since I hunted. This worry is about to destroy my manliness. I should not let it happen. My stupidity is causing me all this distress. I am young. High time Indulekha had a husband. I don't think she will wait for marriage till I get a good job. It is futile to hope for such a thing.' He firmly decided that he would not grieve, bravely shut his eyes, and decided to sleep. The moment he closed his eyes Indulekha's long eyes, her face with the rosy glow of a red lotus, her beautiful hair, and lips appeared in his thoughts. He stared, he saw nothing. Madhavan sat up and pretended to take heart, and decided firmly, 'I will not think about Indulekha!' Just then he saw a lady standing near his door.

MADHAVAN: Who is that?

'It is me. A mala has been sent from Poovarangu,' Indulekha's maid, and Ammu, entered Madhavan's room and gave him a fragrant champaka mala.

Madhavan took the mala and, looking at it, sighed deeply.

AMMU: She has asked you to come to her room tomorrow for tea. She insists that you come.

MADHAVAN: I am going out to hunt long before daybreak. Maybe my father also will come with me. Tell her that I will be back only after sunset.
AMMU: I will tell her that. If you want to see her early it will be possible. Now it is the time for *thiruvathirakuli*. My mistress gets up early in the morning and goes to the bathing place.
MADHAVAN: I should not visit women in the night. Tell her I will meet her the day after tomorrow in the morning.

Ammu smiled and said, 'I shall tell her so.' She went up to Indulekha's room and gave her the message.

When Ammu went back to Madhavan a second time he was holding the mala in his hand, enjoying its beauty. When he saw Ammu a second time, he asked her why she was there again.

AMMU: My mistress says she is stitching an exquisite cap. You can wear it when you go hunting. If you are reluctant to go to her room early in the morning, she says you can stand by the window in the courtyard, and she will give you the cap.
MADHAVAN: Then why couldn't she have sent it over now?
AMMU: Maybe the cap is not finished yet.
MADHAVAN: What, does she sit up and sew at night?
AMMU: Nowadays she sews and reads in the night, she doesn't sleep much.
MADHAVAN: What is the reason for that?
   'I don't know,' said Ammu, smiling shyly.
MADHAVAN: All right, you may go. Tell her I shall call out if I see the window open when I go out early in the morning.

Madhavan became thoughtful again as soon as Ammu left—so Indulekha also could not sleep. I am sure she is in love with me. I no longer have any doubts. Then why doesn't she show it? I see nothing but the playful side of her nature. Why? Thinking about this Madhavan sat up in bed and prepared the things he needed to take with him on the hunt. He took out and cleaned a good rifle, set aside the required cartridges, and told the servant that he wanted tea long before daybreak. He then went and lay down. At four o'clock in the morning he got dressed and taking one of his servants with him set out to hunt. He looked up as he passed Indulekha's room. He was fascinated to see her face, like the rising moon in the bright light above her window.

INDULEKHA: Why set off so early? If you have to kill animals don't you have to see them? How will you see in the darkness?

MADHAVAN: I have to travel some distance before I start hunting.
INDULEKHA: Oh! So your hunt is a very elaborate one, is it?
MADHAVAN: Yes, I am going for a great hunt. If I go on such an outing, I think I will get some consolation.
INDULEKHA: All right; when you came from Madras this time how many rifles did you bring?
MADHAVAN: Only one—'breach loader'.
INDULEKHA: I want to see it. Please send it up.

Madhavan's servant took the rifle upstairs at once.

Indulekha took it and kept it inside. Then she locked her door, asked her servant Ammu to light a torch and went downstairs for a bath; when she reached Madhavan, she said: Well let the 'breach loader' stay in my room. I haven't finished making the cap. Therefore, you can go hunting either tomorrow or the day after. Now please go and sleep comfortably.

MADHAVAN: What do you mean I can't go hunting?
INDULEKHA: You can't go today.
MADHAVAN: What is the reason for that?
INDULEKHA: The cap is not ready. That is the reason.
MADHAVAN: Did I say that I wanted a cap?
INDULEKHA: Did you say that you did not want it? When Ammu came yesterday you could have told her that you didn't want it.
MADHAVAN: Now I am saying that I don't want it.
INDULEKHA: Never mind. If you had sent word yesterday I would not have sat up and worked on it. Who will listen to you now if you say you don't want it, after you have made me work so hard on it?
MADHAVAN: I don't like all this childishness. What do you gain by troubling people?
INDULEKHA: I am a child. I feel you too are a child. So we can play together like we used to before.
MADHAVAN: Isn't it you who said just the other day that we shouldn't play childishly, and things like that?
INDULEKHA: I didn't look upon you as a child then.

She laughed and went for her bath. Madhavan walked about in the garden, dejected. It was bright daylight when Indulekha returned after her bath. Seeing Madhavan, she took him upstairs with her and invited him to tea. At first he refused, but gave in at Indulekha's insistence. They sat down in chairs placed a little away from each other.

INDULEKHA: Now it is not possible to go hunting today.
MADHAVAN: If you still enjoy your childish games, you should find another person to play with; I cannot bear this anymore.
INDULEKHA: What is it that you cannot suffer anymore—is it hunting?
MADHAVAN: I will tell you clearly what is troubling me.
INDULEKHA: Wait, wait, you need not tell me so clearly. I used to think you were very brave, but now when I see your behaviour I think I was wrong.
MADHAVAN: I have no courage left. You need not doubt that I am like any other person you see around here. I have never behaved in an indecent way. I have not fancied any woman before I saw you; that may be the reason for the intensity of this attachment. If you are going to vex me further, I have no intention of staying in this place.
INDULEKHA: So, if you go away to another place you will not think about these things, is that it? Does it mean that it is only when you see me that you are overcome with love for me?
MADHAVAN: What I just said doesn't mean that. It means that if I cannot be with you always as I wish to be when I am with you for even a short while, I do not want to stay here in my land and in my house.
INDULEKHA: All right, but if you are so deeply in love with me and I am not in love with you, will you still feel the same way?
MADHAVAN: I will never believe that you don't love me.
INDULEKHA: Then why this frustration?
MADHAVAN: What frustration?
INDULEKHA: Tell me what this frustration is.
MADHAVAN: I will. The reasons for this frustration are: one, you think that I have not reached a high position; second, you know that there are many wealthy men, many lords, and many kings who desire you.
INDULEKHA: Uptil now, I did not think you were such a fool. If I had been attracted to any of the men considered suitable or to these kings, I would have taken one of them as my husband. I am amazed at you for saying something so stupid. In such matters wealth is nothing to me and I have decided that the one I desire alone will be my husband.
MADHAVAN: Have you felt such desire for anyone till now?

INDULEKHA: Even if I have felt such desire, why should I tell a fool like you about it?

MADHAVAN: Why do you scold me so? Why do you do this to me?

INDULEKHA: That is enough. You are indeed a clown—you are sure that I am in love with you but even then you assume that just because kings and lords want me, I will accept one of them and go against my love and feelings. It is really a shame, you are so stupid. What a pity! You really thought I am such a simpleton? That is really strange. How could you be so fond of me then!

When he heard these words, Madhavan's eyes filled. My readers should think and decide for themselves whether these tears were the result of joy, respect, or sorrow.

INDULEKHA: Why do you weep when you are at a loss for words?

MADHAVAN: It is not because I don't have an answer. I simply don't feel like arguing all the time. I sat here because you insisted. You have not said a pleasant word to me after I came here, every word has been a quibble. In this land wherever Malayalam is spoken, women have the freedom as well as the opportunity to distress men; therefore, it is inevitable that they suffer.

INDULEKHA: How should I sweeten my words? Shall I drink some honey and then talk to you? Or maybe you should drink some honey before I talk to you; then you will experience a certain sweetness. When you talk stupidly and I retort, who will agree that the words of the one who retorts are not at all sweet, that they are sour, etc. What did you say about the women of the region where Malayalam is spoken—that they are capable of assailing their men?

MADHAVAN: It is not quite that. The women of this region are not faithful to their husbands like women of other lands. They take and discard husbands as they please, they have other freedoms also. Therefore, what I said was that the women of this region have a certain arrogance.

INDULEKHA: Really! Remarkable words! Is this your regard for Malayali women? Considering that you are well educated and knowledgeable, this is indeed surprising. A Malayali woman who is intelligent will reply like this: 'What did you say? Malayali women are not faithful to their husbands? Atrocious! Plenty of Malayali women are devoted to their husbands, just as women in other kingdoms are. Innumerable women show their devotion. Besides, if a woman is not devoted to her husband, does that make her an adulteress? Do you then mean to say that all the women in this region—or the majority of them—are adulteresses? If you say so, I will not believe it; that is certain; that is for sure. Adultery is inevitably practised in many different places and by many different races. However, if you think that just because we Nair women are unlike Nambuthiri women, who lead a cloistered life without talking to other people and without being educated; because we do not live like beasts, we are labelled adulterous or not devoted to our husbands, nothing can be more faulty than this. Think about the position of women in countries like Europe or America. Isn't education, knowledge, and freedom for women and men in these countries similar to what Malayali women experience? Are all these women adulterous? In this region, if a beautiful woman is educated, all the men who converse and spend time with her are immediately thought to be her lovers. Tell me—how true is this? If a woman who has learnt music sings, and if some men listen to her at the same time, fools like you will think that all of them are her paramours, and those men will also pretend so. If you yourselves are like this, how can we help it? If you men were self-respecting and assertive, would you tolerate women of your caste being insulted like this? A woman can, without forsaking her devotion to her husband, be entertained by and freely enjoy certain matters with other men. She can also think independently. I am really amazed, Madhavan, that you also, like many other misguided people, think that the beautiful women of Keralam have only adultery in mind when they entertain and enjoy themselves in this way.

In my opinion, it is when women are not free and are raised like caged animals that they are likely to become adulterous. Is a cow or a dog ashamed of adultery? By this I don't mean to say that educated and knowledgeable people will never think of adultery. Even educated people can sometimes think peculiarly and behave in an odd manner. When some stupid people say that these are a consequence of education and knowledge, I am astounded. Education and knowledge are important ways of destroying such unacceptable behaviour. Madhavan, one fault you find with us is that we take and discard husbands as we please— there may be some ill-bred women who behave like this. However, our freedom to do thus is remarkably commendable—this freedom is missing even in Europe. I have read that some brilliant people in Europe and some very great men in America are of the opinion that women should have this freedom at all times. How many husbands and wives suffer great sorrow regularly both in India and in Europe because they don't have this freedom. Instead of misusing it, if it is used where it is essential, it can be useful for both men and women. Also, how many women in this region of Keralam actually disown their husbands even though they have this freedom? How many husbands abandon their wives? If you can make an exact count of such matters occurring between wives and husbands in Keralam for the past ten years, you will find that it may not have happened even once in a thousand cases. Occasionally such an event might take place somewhere. There will be reasons for it too; rarely does this happen without provocation or simply due to the imprudence of either the husband or the wife. However, it is indeed a pity to insult us by saying that it is a regular feature among Kerala women. This independence is really a good thing, though it should be used only when it is necessary. Sometimes, some people might misuse it carelessly and because of that they might get a bad name, but that is not the fault of the freedom itself. It is the foul result of misusing the freedom. If you are displeased with me, certainly I will not allow you to accuse all womenfolk.'

MADHAVAN: I do not think that it is good for a husband and wife to have the right to sever their relationship whenever they feel like it. If such is the situation, the relationship between them will be one based only on mutual consent. I do not feel any inclination towards such a relationship or consider it praiseworthy.

INDULEKHA: (laughing) Then you may not be interested in the kind of relationship between a man and woman that we have in our region. Is that not so?

MADHAVAN: Not at all.

INDULEKHA: If that is the case, didn't you say that you would like to go off to some other country? Please do so, that would be best for you.

MADHAVAN: That is exactly what I am planning to do. Are you agreeable to such a move?

INDULEKHA: Why do you need my consent?

MADHAVAN: If you will agree to be my wife, this our land will be heaven for me.

INDULEKHA: But you were of the opinion that the relationship between a man and woman here was not a serious one? Then why do you desire it?
MADHAVAN: That does not apply to you and me.
INDULEKHA: Quite right; very well said.

While they were conversing in this way, Indulekha's mother came upstairs and began teasing them, so Madhavan's private conversation and his day's hunt both stood cancelled.

I will now recount the story in brief.

It became extremely difficult for Madhavan to bear his sorrow; one could say that he became indifferent to food and sleep. Not only that, he stopped going to Indulekha's rooms as frequently as he used to. One day, while Madhavan's mother (Parvathiamma) was talking to Indulekha, Madhavan's name was mentioned by chance. 'Madhavan seems to have some kind of worry.'

INDULEKHA: There could be a good reason for that.
PARVATHIAMMA: I don't know of any reason. He is not eating; for both lunch and dinner taken together he is hardly eating an *uri* of rice, he does not drink either milk or tea. His companions say that he doesn't sleep at all at night. I really don't know, maybe he is going to fall sick.
INDULEKHA: I will talk to him. Please ask him to come here.

When Parvathiamma told this to Madhavan, he went to Indulekha's room.

INDULEKHA: Why have your visits here become so infrequent?
MADHAVAN: I don't feel like coming here.
INDULEKHA: Do you feel ill when you do?
MADHAVAN: I don't feel well at all and the feeling increases when I come here. I am ill all the time.
INDULEKHA: I am going for a bath. Please rest on the couch and read the newspaper. I shall return immediately. Then we will talk.

Madhavan lay on the couch. He didn't touch the newspaper.

'What on earth has the newspaper done?' While Indulekha was laughing and asking such a question on her way downstairs, she noticed a servant going up to Madhavan with a telegram for him. Believing that it might be some news of his examination, Indulekha unhesitatingly opened the telegram and was extremely happy on reading it. Running upstairs, she said, 'You have cleared the BL examination.'

MADHAVAN: All right, good.

That was all he said. Neither did he take the telegram from her nor did he utter a word after that, nor did he stir. He just lay there with an intensely sorrowful expression, looking at Indulekha's face, moonlike in its brilliance. Studying Madhavan's face, Indulekha was troubled. However, she suppressed her anxiety with great courage.

INDULEKHA: What is all this! You looked grieved? Such distress when you get information that you have cleared the BL examination with a first class and first rank! How amazing that you lie like this and so indifferently. Amazing indeed!

MADHAVAN: Whether I clear my BL examination or not, it is all the same to me.

INDULEKHA: Let me go and give my *valiachan* [grandfather] and both our mothers the news about your success in the examination. At least they will be happy.

MADHAVAN: Why do you take all this trouble? I shall go and tell them at leisure. What is the hurry?

INDULEKHA: I will go this moment and tell them. Don't you want to read the telegram? Look!

MADHAVAN: I don't think I want to read it. I don't feel any great joy at having passed this examination.

INDULEKHA: Why?

MADHAVAN: Because I am in such torment.

INDULEKHA: Tortured because you have passed the BL examination?

MADHAVAN: If (only) I had known earlier that you had such a stony heart....

INDULEKHA: If you had? Why don't you complete what you were saying?

MADHAVAN: Yes, if I had known—

INDULEKHA: If you had known what?

Indulekha went and stood closer to Madhavan.

MADHAVAN: If I had known I would not have come to such intense grief and destruction.

INDULEKHA: Intense grief and destruction?

MADHAVAN: How can you be so hard-hearted?

INDULEKHA: Wait, I will speak about that when I return. I want to tell valiachan and our mothers myself about your BL examination results. I am on my way, and will run to tell them. Please stay here. Should you be sad when you get news that you have cleared an exam?

MADHAVAN: You need not trouble yourself so much for me, I am not at all happy that I passed this examination. I have just one prayer—that my life and my body should soon be separated. When I am in the throes of death, what is an examination?

The moment he said this, tears coursed incessantly down his face.

When Indulekha saw Madhavan in this condition, her heart was intensely grieved—one can say it burnt down. Exhausted by her intense grief and the love which she could not suppress at that moment, she drew close to the couch, held Madhavan's extremely attractive face close to her beautiful body, and, sighing deeply, kissed him on his lips.

'My dearest husband! Why do you grieve like this? I have regarded you as my husband for the last two years. My mind, my body and my whole self are yours. You should be what you want to be and remain happy. I have not desired anyone other than you—and will not desire anyone else.' Saying this, she rested for a minute on his chest. She wiped away his tears and stood up.

Madhavan had heard only the first few words clearly. He had become ecstatic, sunk in the ocean of bliss, and turned deaf and blind. It was some time before he regained his senses.

MADHAVAN: Now you can go and tell everyone the news that I have passed my BL examination. I desire to live in this world (provided) you share with me all the prosperity and good fortune that will come to me in this life, and that has now become possible for me. I am an extremely lucky man; there is no doubt about it. Now it is more appropriate for you to speak about my success in the examination.

This was the secret moment when in their innermost hearts they promised themselves to each other.

Panchumenon was aware that Indulekha and Madhavan were well matched and that Madhavan alone would be the person who would be Indulekha's husband. Though he was not exactly pleased about this state of affairs, he had not shown his displeasure either.

chapter three

An Angry Man's Oath

The quarrel that took place between Panchumenon and Madhavan, recounted earlier, nearly blinded Panchumenon with anger. By nature he was rather short-tempered and also traditional. He was the karanavan of the wealthy Chambazhiyot Poovally taravad. Both the earlier karanavars of the taravad had been employed as dewans. Even before that, the Chambazhiyot Poovally taravad had been a prosperous one. In time, the reputed members of the taravad acquired great wealth and it became an important household. However, in-between, great losses also took place and their wealth diminished considerably.

At the time of this story, the taravad possessed land which yielded 28,000 *para*s of paddy and orchards which gave a *paatom* of Rs 15,000 annually. From this they could save Rs 5,000 a year after all their expenses. It is not possible to say that this was a small sum. The earlier karanavars had been wealthy and capable, and the present ones were forced to follow the pattern established by them. As a result, there was heavy expenditure; there were two rest houses that fed the Brahmins and the workers twice a day, and then there was the cost of maintaining the Bhagawathi temple and other places that had been set up for various ceremonies.

Earlier, generous allocations were made towards meals and oil baths for the servants and the like and although miserly by nature, Panchumenon could not avoid spending freely. After all this, he succeeded in saving Rs 5,000. He was extremely reluctant to spend even a *kasu* of these savings. Despite that, he gave away Rs 35,000 worth of other wealth and money to his daughter Lakshmikuttyamma (Indulekha's mother) and her mother Kunjikuttyamma. When they were not in Madras, Indulekha, her mother, and Kunjikuttyamma lived in the house called Poovarangu with Panchumenon and son Govindankuttymenon. The house had two or three malikas with ponds, a bath house, temples, and rest houses near it. The huge and important Poovally taravad, stood two hundred to three hundred *vara* away from Poovarangu. However, both shared a compound wall.

At the time of our story, Panchumenon was seventy years old. While one of his uncles was the dewan, he was supposed to have been the tahasildar. It was thirty years since he had left all that.

In appearance, he was rather fair, balding and quite stout—three teeth missing in his upper jaw and five in his lower jaw; eyes bloodshot; above his mundu he wore a thick waist chain; around his neck a *rudrakshamala* set in gold; on his head a woollen cap; and in his hand a stick with its knob covered with silver. It sufficed to say that these were his ornaments.

Though he had been employed earlier he did not have any knowledge of English. And even though he was simple and considerate, he was born hot-tempered and, at this time, both old and ill, his permanent emotion was anger. It was only with Indulekha that he never lost his temper. Perhaps, this was because of her qualities or perhaps because of his extreme fondness for his deceased eldest son, Kochukrishnamenonpeishkar. Knowing his temper and fearing that he might lose it, he rarely went up to Indulekha's malika. However, he did not allow a day to pass without enquiring at least two or three times about her welfare. It is doubtful whether anyone in Poovarangu or Poovally, except Indulekha, had seen a day pass without being scolded by Panchumenon. The quarrel between him and Madhavan took place in the taravad at six in the morning. As soon as it was over, he stalked out in a temper and returned to his own residence, Poovarangu. The first person he set eyes on as he reached the front of the house, was Lakshmikuttyamma.

PANCHUMENON: That rascal, that untouchable, that wicked man! Do you know how he insulted me?
LAKSHMIKUTTYAMMA: Who?
PANCHUMENON: Madhavan.
LAKSHMIKUTTYAMMA: What! Madhavan insulted you!
PANCHUMENON: Yes, Madhavan himself!

Panchumenon then greatly exaggerated whatever Madhavan had said and won Lakshmikuttyamma over. By then Kesavannambuthiri had come out from the house and had overheard all that was being said.

PANCHUMENON: (to Kesavannambuthiri) I won't give Indulekha to this sinner. Lakshmikutty, why aren't you saying anything?

LAKSHMIKUTTYAMMA: What should I say?

PANCHUMENON: You are still attracted by Madhavan's good looks, aren't you? Why don't you say something? Despicable, despicable, all of you are despicable people! You should have your heads chopped off.

LAKSHMIKUTTYAMMA: How is it that I find Madhavan attractive! I don't have anything to say about all this.

PANCHUMENON: I have; and I will say it. By my Shriporkillibhagawathi, I swear that I will not give Indulekha to Madhavan!

The minute he made this oath, Panchumenon began to feel sorry. He knew extremely well how determined Indulekha was and about her intelligence and strength of purpose. He was also aware of the love between Madhavan and Indulekha. 'If this is the case, how valid will this oath be? If it doesn't work out, how demeaning it will be for me,' thought Panchumenon and sat down on the threshold of the house for some time. Then a thought struck him. He asked somebody to call Kesavannambuthiri. The moment the Nambuthiri came and sat on the threshold, Panchumenon moved close to him and spoke to him in an undertone.

PANCHUMENON: The other day *thirumannassu* [your respected self] was talking about Moorkillatha Nambuthiri. I remember you had mentioned that he had heard about Indulekha and had remarked that he would consider it worthwhile if he could start a sambandam with her. Is he good looking?

KESAVANNAMBUTHIRI: Tremendously attractive! His is the colour of fine gold. His complexion will certainly be lighter than Indulekha's. I have never set eyes on a man like him. And as for his wealth, there is no necessity to discuss that.

PANCHUMENON: If Indulekha meets him and gets acquainted with him, do you think she will accept him?

KESAVANNAMBUTHIRI: (holding the *poonul,* his sacred thread) I can swear— the moment she sets eyes on him, she will be captivated. Shiva! Shiva! This is an auspicious thing. How can I even attempt to speak about it! See him first, then you will begin to realize his position in life.

PANCHUMENON: Is it possible for you to bring him here once?

KESAVANNAMBUTHIRI: Surely, I'll get him here.

PANCHUMENON: Do you think that with his arrival, Indulekha will lose her craze for Madhavan?

KESAVANNAMBUTHIRI: (holding the poonul again) By this Brahmin, Indulekha's craze for Madhavan will disappear. I don't have any doubts about that.

Panchumenon smiled in great happiness.

PANCHUMENON: Then send him a letter. Let him come. Don't write anything foolish. You know the kind of person Indulekha is; later we shouldn't lose face. Just write to the Nambuthiri that he should come and stay here for a few days.

KESAVANNAMBUTHIRI: It is through Bhagawan's blessing that you could think of this. Bhagawan's blessing! Indulekha's tremendous luck! Her taravad's good fortune! Your good luck! A very auspicious time for me. I will write the letter immediately.

PANCHUMENON: Take care to word the letter carefully. Indulekha is a very stubborn girl who has studied English. Whatever anyone says has no effect on her. With his good looks and clever ways, the Nambuthiri should be able to win her over; that is the need of the hour.

KESAVANNAMBUTHIRI: If Indulekha does not become the Nambuthiri's wife soon after, the sun will travel northwards, from the south.

PANCHUMENON: Are you quite sure? Is the Nambuthiripad so desirable?

KESAVANNAMBUTHIRI: Of course! I have no doubts. I will write immediately.

PANCHUMENON: Yes, yes if that is so, then go ahead.

chapter four

A Separation

MADHAVAN: Mother, please get everything ready for me. At daybreak I have to set off for Madras. Is my father inside?
PARVATHIAMMA: Have you decided to go?
MADHAVAN: Why doubt it? I am going.
PARVATHIAMMA: When your father left for his house in the morning, he said that you should go over and meet him.

Madhavan left immediately for his father Govindapanikkar's house.

Govindapanikkar was an intelligent, good-natured, and sympathetic man. Since he did not have a family of his own—and therefore no related expenses—he was also a man with a lot of money.

GOVINDAPANIKKAR: *Kutta,* have you bathed?
MADHAVAN: Yes, I have.
GOVINDAPANIKKAR: And are you going off to Madras tomorrow?
MADHAVAN: If you agree, I hope to go tomorrow.
GOVINDAPANIKKAR: If you want to go, you should certainly do so. Don't ask the karanavan for your travel expense. I will give it to you. Look, I have got you a pair of *kadukkan.* Here they are.

He gave Madhavan a pair of fine ruby kadukkan worth about Rs 500.

GOVINDAPANIKKAR: I had decided that I would give you a present if you cleared your BL; this is it.
MADHAVAN: They are beautiful indeed. I will come back here and have lunch

with you. But first I have to write a letter to Madras. The post is about to be cleared. I will return as soon as I have finished the letter.

Madhavan left for his house. When he had almost reached, he saw Ammu, Indulekha's maid, coming out of the house and walking towards him.

MADHAVAN: What is the matter, anything unusual?
AMMU: My mistress has gone to the bath house. She asked you to go over if you have the time.
MADHAVAN: Is that so? I shall do that. Who else is there in the bath house?
AMMU: There is no one else.
MADHAVAN: Well, go ahead.

When Madhavan entered the bath house, Indulekha was removing her *thoda* and preparing to apply oil on her skin. As soon as Madhavan came in, she replaced the thoda and, smiling, stood looking at Madhavan's face. Without hesitation Madhavan drew Indulekha to himself with both hands, and embraced her. In answer, Indulekha tenderly kissed Madhavan. The moment she finished kissing him, she murmured 'Let go'—'let go'.

MADHAVAN: I am leaving for Madras tomorrow.
INDULEKHA: I heard about that. There are still fifteen days left for the high court to open. Then why are you going tomorrow? Why are you going to Madras in such a hurry? Is it because grandfather is angry with you?
MADHAVAN: Was an oath taken here yesterday?
INDULEKHA: Yes, but do you know that the discussion and decision took place without consulting me!
MADHAVAN: Madhavi, why should anyone ask you? Shouldn't you conduct yourself according to valiammaman's wishes?
INDULEKHA: Yes, I should do as he wishes and that I certainly will do. However, in certain matters I can only do as I wish. Unfortunately, this matter of the oath is one of those.
MADHAVAN: My dear, valiammaman will throw you out if you say such things.
INDULEKHA: Didn't he throw out my husband yesterday? Let him throw me out tomorrow.
MADHAVAN: If your husband doesn't have the means to support you....
INDULEKHA: The protection that God provides for people who are thrown out of their house will suffice for me too. Why should we delay matters?

Isn't it best for us to let people know, according to custom, about our intention and go ahead with this matter?

MADHAVAN: We have wedded each other in our heart of hearts. Even uncle agrees with the proposal. Whoever expected such a quarrel to take place? Things have taken a difficult turn now.

INDULEKHA: What is the difficulty? There is nothing of the sort. If you are prepared to take me to Madras tomorrow with you, I am willing to come.

MADHAVAN: That would be foolish. Only God knows the heartache I go through when I am separated from you. However, it will pain me more if people think badly of my beloved; so please be patient. I received a letter from Gilham *sayiv* a few days back. He had said that there would be an assistant's job falling vacant and he had asked whether I was willing to take it. I expressed my willingness. I do not know how long it will take to make the appointment. The moment I get it, I will return. Then Madhavi, you can be with me in Madras. Even though both of us are wealthy and even though my father will give me all the money that I need, without a job of my own I do not think either of us will consider it feasible, to take my dearest to Madras.

INDULEKHA: What is in your hand, a roll of paper?

MADHAVAN: That is a present which my father just gave me. A ruby kadukkan. Look....

Indulekha took the ornament and looked closely at it.

INDULEKHA: First-rate ones; sit there—let me put them on for you.

Madhavan sat down. Indulekha fixed the kadukkan in Madhavan's earlobes. When Madhavan started to get up—

INDULEKHA: Please sit down. Let me, with my own hands, knot this kuduma too. Only if that is tied up on one side will the kadukkan and the face set each other off well.

After knotting the kuduma, Indulekha stood gazing at Madhavan's face. He realized that the kadukkan suited him extremely well from the way Indulekha, after pausing for a minute and sighing deeply, kissed his cheeks continuously. While the two were talking and enjoying each other's company, Lakshmikuttyamma came to the entrance of the bath house and asking 'Who is talking inside?' entered.

LAKSHMIKUTTYAMMA: You have lost all shame. You appear as though you are mad. Govindapanikkar has sent someone to look for you. Did you say that you would go there for lunch? Then how could you come and sit here in the bath house amusing yourselves? Indulekha, are you not hungry today? Crazy children! Kuttan, I heard that you are going off tomorrow.

MADHAVAN: What is the time?

LAKSHMIKUTTYAMMA: Ten-thirty.

MADHAVAN: Shiva! Shiva! I had to send off a letter. I have missed the post and Father will be angry. I will meet you (both) before I go.

Saying this to Lakshmikuttyamma, he rushed straight to his father's house. His father was seated with a plantain leaf before him, waiting for his meal. A leaf had been readied for Madhavan also.

GOVINDAPANIKKAR: Kutta, where have you been all this while?

MADHAVAN: I was talking to someone and I got a little delayed. You should have had your lunch. What a pity! You are used to lunching early and today, because of me, you are delayed.

GOVINDAPANIKKAR: Why don't you say that the delay was caused by you and Indulekha? I won't punish you. You are not the only culprit. Oh! You have already put on the kadukkan? It must be due to Indulekha's enthusiasm. Is that not so?

Madhavan hung his head in embarrassment, and started his meal. As soon as he finished, Govindapanikkar called him inside, sat him down on his lap, and kissing him on his forehead said—

GOVINDAPANIKKAR: Are you grief-stricken about Indulekha? If so, then let me say, it is unnecessary. I know that girl well. To this day I have never seen a child as intelligent as she. I am more amazed at the range of her intelligence and firmness of her mind than I am at her beauty. You need not doubt that she will ever accept anyone other than you in this life. This decision cannot be changed on any account, not just by Panchumenon, but, even if she is encouraged by God Brahma himself.

Madhavan didn't say a word, but caressing his father's hand, continued sitting on his lap.

GOVINDAPANIKKAR: Are you taking Shinnan with you this time?

MADHAVAN: I want to take him with me. However, I thought I would first find out what you thought about it.

GOVINDAPANIKKAR: Do what you think is right. If you are taking him with you I will meet all his expenses.

MADHAVAN: Father, why should you? Shouldn't valiammaman necessarily do that?

GOVINDAPANIKKAR: If he doesn't give...I don't think he will give....

MADHAVAN: If he doesn't give—

GOVINDAPANIKKAR: There is no need to quarrel. By nature Panchumenon is both hot-tempered and unintelligent. If you fight, people will not wait to find out the reason for the fight before ridiculing everyone involved. You should fear what they say.

MADHAVAN: I really regret that I am the cause for this unnecessary expenditure on your part.

GOVINDAPANIKKAR: What expenditure is this for me, kutta? Though I do not have as much wealth as your taravad has, because my expenses are so slight, I have as much wealth left over as you have. I am prepared to spend all that for your benefit and to satisfy your desire. Take Shinnan along with you. However, ask your karanavan before you do that, although it is not necessary for you to ask for permission. You can send the child's father, Shinu*pattar* to tell him. You should also bid farewell to your valiammaman. If he decides to quarrel, come away quietly.

MADHAVAN: All right, I will do as you say, Father; I will return in time for the night meal. But please, eat at the usual time—do not wait for me.

While they were talking, Shinupattar came to meet Govindapanikkar. Walking up to the house, he stood outside in the *purathalam* and coughed to attract his attention.

GOVINDAPANIKKAR: Who is there?

SHINUPATTAR: It is me—Shinupattar.

GOVINDAPANIKKAR: You can come in. I myself shall break the news to this person.

The moment Shinupattar entered—

GOVINDAPANIKKAR: Please sit down, Swami!

SHINUPATTAR: Who is that—is it Madhavan? What is all this? The karanavan is very angry; I don't know whether he is angry with me. A short while ago, on my way back from the temple, I caught sight of him on the road. He did not talk to me at all. I have never seen him so furious. This has happened once or twice before. There were reasons good enough on those occasions, but I could not understand the reason for his anger this time.

MADHAVAN: Aren't you Shinnan's father? Isn't that a good enough reason?

Both Govindapanikkar and Shinupattar laughed.

GOVINDAPANIKKAR: Swami, you should go now to Panchumenon. When you meet him, tell him that kuttan is taking Shinnan to Madras and that we need only his permission to do so. I have decided to bear the cost of his education. You need not tell him that.

SHINUPATTAR: Oh no! Is that so? I will tell him now. Let me tell him that it is I who am going to send the money for Shinnan. Let me also get a little bit of respectability! He might get angry with me. If he abuses me I will also do so.

GOVINDAPANIKKAR: Don't pick up a fight. About the expenditure, say what you want to. But, I would advise you not to lie about it.

SHINUPATTAR: That is no lie. I will say exactly that.

Madhavan looked at his father and smiled. Then Madhavan's father and Shinupattar shook their heads and smiled. Shinupattar repeated, 'I will say exactly that.'

Shinupattar left immediately. He went to Poovarangu and stood in the purathalam.

PANCHUMENON: Who is there?
SHINUPATTAR: It is me—Shinu.
PANCHUMENON: Why have you come here now?
SHINUPATTAR: I have something to say.
PANCHUMENON: What is it? Speak up.
SHINUPATTAR: I am going to give my son Shinnan an English education.
PANCHUMENON: Do you know English?
SHINUPATTAR: I will spend the money and educate him.
PANCHUMENON: You! Educate him!
SHINUPATTAR: I am going to send him to Madras.
PANCHUMENON: You send him to whichever *rashi* you like—send him to the scaffold if you want to.

SHINUPATTAR: You don't give English education from a scaffold. It is not a punishment.

PANCHUMENON: What is this I hear, *komatti* pattar? What did you say, you impolite fellow? Did you come here to abuse me because that impudent Madhavan sent you here? Step down from here—step down. Is anyone around? Send this fellow out! Throw him out.

'If I am a komatti, why did you allow your sister to have a sambandam with me?' Saying this almost in a whisper, the pattar ran down and left.

As decided, the next day, Madhavan and Shinnan left for Madras at daybreak. Since Panchumenon's anger had heightened, Madhavan did not venture to bid him farewell.

chapter five

Panchumenon's Anger

Panchumenon could not suppress his anger as Shinnan was taken to Madras without his permission and also because of Shinupattar's insolent words. He scolded everyone he met and lashed out whenever he could. First he wanted that Chatharamenon be summoned. The simple and extremely patient Chatharamenon arrived and stood before Panchumenon humbly; he was terrified.

PANCHUMENON: You bastard, you impudent fellow, did you send Shinnan to Madras? You!

CHATHARAMENON: Madhavan has taken Shinnan to Madras along with him.

PANCHUMENON: Without your permission?

CHATHARAMENON: He did not ask me for any special permission.

PANCHUMENON: You rascal! Tell me, did he take him with your permission or without your permission?

CHATHARAMENON: I was not against it.

PANCHUMENON: Why didn't you stop him? Didn't you know that this was against my wishes? Then why didn't you prevent it?

CHATHARAMENON: Father said he had asked you for permission before he took him.

PANCHUMENON: Which father? Komatti? From the day that wretched komatti was allowed to enter the taravad, only evil things have happened here. What did that komatti tell you?

CHATHARAMENON: Gopalan told me that Father had taken permission.

PANCHUMENON: Send for Gopalan.

This Gopalan was hasty, stupid, and young. Obedient to the order, Gopalan approached the karanavan.

PANCHUMENON: What did your father, komatti, tell you? Did he say that I agreed to send Shinnan to Madras?
GOPALAN: My father is not a komatti—he is a pattar.
PANCHUMENON: What did you say, you insolent boy?

Panchumenon immediately got up and slapped Gopalan a few times.

GOPALAN: Don't hit me without reason.
PANCHUMENON: What will you do? Didn't I hit you now? What happened? Did you prevent it?

By then Shankaramenon had run up to them. He caught hold of Gopalan, pulled him back and pushed him away.

PANCHUMENON: Shankara, everything here is amiss. I think it is because of *kaliyugam*. Didn't you get to know how that rascal Madhavan insulted me. At an ill-fated moment, I gave him an English education; this is the unfortunate result of that. That apart, now this brat, Gopalan, who doesn't know west from east is answering back. Shouldn't I break his teeth?
SHANKARAMENON: Nowadays it is better not to talk to children. They are growing up without any respect for elders. I do not say anything to these youngsters.
PANCHUMENON: You are the one who is teaching them to be like this—without respect for others. Anyway, Chathara, from now you need not look after the property at Cheruthuruthikalam. Clear up all related matters immediately. Show me all the accounts—I want it done this moment.
CHATHARAMENON: I will do everything according to your orders, valiammaman.
PANCHUMENON: You rascal! Will you obey valiammaman's orders? Aren't you the komatti's son? That is why you have become so wretched. If you need something you can't get it without my permission. His self-assured father will give Madhavan what he wants. Govindapanikkar does not have other relatives to support. That is why Madhavan is so haughty. What can the komatti, your father, give you? Only the *pappadam* and plantain left over from the feast—is that not so? What else does the komatti have? Why are you so arrogant, you rascal of a boy! Why don't you speak?

CHATHARAMENON: Valiammaman, I am dependent on you for everything.
PANCHUMENON: Then why are you also insolent, like Madhavan? Who is meeting Shinnan's expenditure?
CHATHARAMENON: Gopalan said it is my father.
PANCHUMENON: (to Gopalan) Is that so?
GOPALAN: Yes, Father is the one who gave the money.
PANCHUMENON: Father! Your father Palghat komatti, that beggar of a cook. Where did he get the money from?
GOPALAN: My father is not a komatti.
SHANKARAMENON: No need to be so insolent.

Panchumenon stood up to beat him. Shankaramenon tried to appease his uncle's anger by coming between them, and also got a few blows.

PANCHUMENON: Shankara! We must get back all the land which is in Gopalan's custody. I won't give this rascal even one kasu.
GOPALAN: I have already let out all the plots of land you gave me for supervision to *kudiyanmar*s [bonded labourers] for a year. They will vacate it only after a year.
PANCHUMENON: Won't you vacate it?
GOPALAN: It is those rascals who should leave first!
PANCHUMENON: Won't you vacate the land? Do you want to see how I make you do it?
GOPALAN: I will see how you make me vacate!
PANCHUMENON: Will you or not?
GOPALAN: I don't have any property with me.
PANCHUMENON: You thief—why are you lying? Do you mean to say that I have not entrusted any property to you?
GOPALAN: I didn't say you have not entrusted me with land. I said I have entrusted that land to others for a year.
PANCHUMENON: Why are you giving me false arguments?

Saying this, Panchumenon got up to hit him again. Gopalan ran away and the old man pursued him and they ran all over the courtyard. Finally, when they were crossing the courtyard door, Panchumenon tripped and hurt his knees.

Shankaramenon rushed to pick him up. In his anger, Panchumenon started to run again but Shankaramenon restrained him firmly and calmed him down.

PANCHUMENON: Narayana! Look at the power of the times. The strangeness of kaliyuga! I hurt my legs running after this rascal of a boy. I have to suffer all this. No land which yields even a little bit should be given to Kummini and her insolent children. Everything should be taken away today itself, Shankara. Let them just eat here in the manner of slaves and servants.

Still furious, Panchumenon marched towards Govindapanikkar's house, to give him a good scolding too. He met Shinupattar on the way.

PANCHUMENON: What did you say the day before yesterday from the malika?
SHINUPATTAR: What is it? I don't remember anything.
PANCHUMENON: Komatti! Don't you remember?
SHINUPATTAR: Why do you use such derogatory words about Brahmins?
PANCHUMENON: Brahmin! You are not a Brahmin. What did you say now?

Shinupattar lost his temper.

SHINUPATTAR: When you said the child is going to be sent to the scaffold, I told you that that is not how English is taught.
PANCHUMENON: Henceforth you need not step into my house.
SHINUPATTAR: All right. I won't enter your house.
PANCHUMENON: You shouldn't be seen in the *oottupura* or in the temple.
SHINUPATTAR: That is not done according to your orders. A Brahmin can go to all the oottupuras and all the temples.
PANCHUMENON: Will you enter my oottu and my temple without my permission? Let me see how you will.
SHINUPATTAR: What is there to see? I will definitely go in. If you prevent me I shall lodge a petition against you.
PANCHUMENON: What did you say, you komatti?

Panchumenon advanced towards the pattar. The commotion made Shankaramenon come running. Gesturing to Shinupattar to go away, he went up close to Panchumenon and began consoling him.

PANCHUMENON: I shouldn't see this Shinupattar anywhere here. He will even give a petition against me! Ill-mannered lout! Cruel fellow! Sinner! As a young pattar he worked with the dewan, this komatti. In my folly I allowed him to make a sambandam with the family. He has sired two or four insolent children, exactly like him. Because of them, I had cause to fight with my own darling nephew Madhavan.

On remembering 'my own darling Madhavan', this simpleton of a man choked and tears rose to his eyes.

SHANKARAMENON: Madhavan is not really disrespectful. He said something foolish in a fit of anger.

When he heard Shankaramenon saying 'said something foolish', Panchumenon's anger flared again.

PANCHUMENON: You are a dumb ass! A fool, a vagabond! He spoke without thinking? Well, let him find out what happens. I will have my revenge on him for hurting me like this. He will repent, in great sorrow he will come and beg for my forgiveness. His father's money and common grass are the same to me.

Panchumenon hobbled towards Govindapanikkar's house leaning on his walking stick. Shankaramenon did not follow him. He was quite intelligent and knew that the extremely sharp Govindapanikkar would not pick a quarrel with Panchumenon. Very respectfully, Govindapanikkar asked Panchumenon to take a seat, and then he too sat down.

PANCHUMENON: Look what Madhavan has come to! Did you get to know all the details?
GOVINDAPANIKKAR: He has become very arrogant these days. If youngsters receive an English education, they become insolent. Moreover, if they have cleared some examination and such things and happen to live in Madras, they think no end of themselves. I heard that he used some questionable words while speaking with you. I did not like it one bit. I did not ask him about this matter—what is the use of questioning him?
PANCHUMENON: If you don't question children, it is unfortunate for them. If you don't scold them, they will lose track of what they are doing and will have no sense of purpose.
GOVINDAPANIKKAR: That is right, that is right, what your highness says is correct, there is no doubt about it. If we let them be, children will get spoilt.
PANCHUMENON: See Panikkar, when I was young—when I was the same age as Madhavan—if I appeared before my valiammaman, I did so trembling. If at all he questioned me about something, I used to stare at him, unable even to answer. Whenever I saw valiammaman, I was

so frightened that he might as well have been a lion. Even now when I think of him, I feel a sort of fear. Let me tell you a story, this happened when he was alive. I had a friend in this area—he was a Muslim—named Kunjalikutty. You are not acquainted with him. He has been dead for many years now. At that time he was roughly my age. He presented me with a pair of chappals when he returned from a place he had gone to with his father, on some business—I kept it a great secret. When I went out in the evening from Poovally, I would wrap the chappals in a mundu or something, and slip out of Poovally. Only after I had gone some distance, would I slip them on and continue walking. On returning home, I would remove my chappals and smuggle them in; this was a regular practice. One evening, I had wrapped them as usual in my mundu and was walking back, when I saw valiammaman standing in front of the house. He was the ammaman of the dewanjiammaman who had died recently, a very sharp person. When he saw me he asked, 'What have you got there, all wrapped up in your hand?' In great fright I stood there, silently. Ammaman stepped down into the courtyard and gripped me by the hand. He asked me to unwrap the packet in the mundu. He saw the chappals. 'Have you become so insolent as to wear chappals, you rebel?' and gripped my kuduma and dragged me to the front of the house and started beating me. Narayana, Shiva, Shiva! After that there was no end to the beatings I got. He beat me many times with his hand. Even then he could not control his anger, so he went inside and got a cane and began beating me again. Look here, what you see on this thigh, this big mark is a mark left from that beating. I cried aloud. Those were the days when the dewanjiammaman was at home. When he heard the cries in Poovarangu, he came running and pulled valiammaman aside. He took me to Poovarangu, and massaged me with oil. I was bedridden for fifteen or twenty days. Ammaman ordered that my chappals be burnt; accordingly, they were burnt to ashes. From then to this day I have not worn chappals. When I see a pair I get frightened.

Think of the youngsters of today—Madhavan walks about only in chappals. Those days, even dewanjivaliammaman did not walk inside the house with chappals. I myself have seen Madhavan wearing chappals and walking about in the house sometimes. If children become lawless like this, what will we do? There is no greater stupidity than educating children in English. Indulekha would have been a better

girl if she had not received an English education. But what is it that
can be done? Most unfortunately certain accidents happen. Observing
the people who are English-educated, those who have not learnt
English have also taken to their ways. That impudent boy Gopalan,
that komatti Shinu's son, what insolent words he used against me
just now in Poovarangu. I was furious. I thought I would give him a
proper beating, so I chased him. But I fell down and hurt my knee.
These are the effects of *kaliyugavybhavam*.

GOVINDAPANIKKAR: Yes, these are the evil effects of the times. This is a
very good example of that. Otherwise, you would not have fallen down
and hurt your knee.

PANCHUMENON: I don't know Govindapanikkar, whether you remember
this. But once your karanavan beat you very hard. I am the one who
came running and calmed him down. Your ammaman Narayanapanikkar
was a very powerful man. One day during Onam, he saw you playing
on the stage meant for the kathakali performance in the temple
compound, with a few other children. Whereupon he began beating
you in the compound itself. He continued beating you till you came
here and continued even after that. He beat you really badly. Hearing
your cries I ran up and consoled you. Afterwards you did not loaf
around during that Onam season—do you remember this?

GOVINDAPANIKKAR: I remember it only as if it were a dream. I don't
remember it very clearly.

PANCHUMENON: You were hardly fourteen. The respect that we had for our
elders at that time can never be found these days. The children of
today, the moment they get some English education, become egotistic.
We people are not educated at all. They think that we are complete
fools. We can only term this kaliyuga. One day, some time ago, I saw
Indulekha reading a book. My girl, I asked her, what is the story of the
book? She told me the story in Malayalam. When I heard that story I
was struck numb.

GOVINDAPANIKKAR: What was the story about?

PANCHUMENON: Oh the story! I shall tell you. She herself said it was fiction.
However, just think and tell me how it will spoil children if they read
such stories. I do not remember the entire story so clearly. One sayiv
(she told me his name, I don't remember it now) had a daughter. She
decided to marry the sayiv's nephew. The nephew and the girl's father
were not on good terms with each other and thus the father did not

permit the marriage. Instead, he devised some tricks and got this nephew married off to another girl. After that he brought home many suitable young men to get his daughter married. The girl did not approve of anyone. She remained stubborn, and insisted that she would not marry. Finally, out of sheer mental agony the father died. This is the gist of the story. Look, Govindapanikkar, what will happen if girls read these kind of stories?

GOVINDAPANIKKAR: If they read such stories it is going to have a terrible effect on them. Terrible! What hope is there? We gave them an English education and now we can do nothing about it. When was this story told?

PANCHUMENON: Many days back.

GOVINDAPANIKKAR: What is the necessity of reading all this—can't they read the Ramayanam or Bhagavatam.

PANCHUMENON: That is what I too say. There are so many volumes of books in our literature at Poovally. No one touches them. All the volumes which are on *aalekham* [palm-leaf manuscripts] have disintegrated beyond repair. I had told Madhavan long ago to dust them and keep them clean—he has not done so yet.

GOVINDAPANIKKAR: Can't Indulekha clean them?

PANCHUMENON: She is contemptuous of aalekham volumes. Do you think these people will touch anything other than printed books? It is the height of kaliyuga—what else can one say?

GOVINDAPANIKKAR: Yes, it is the height of kaliyuga, I cannot say anything else.

PANCHUMENON: After being educated in the English manner, I wonder, will they convert to Christianity?

GOVINDAPANIKKAR: I too am afraid of this. What can be done if these corrupted minds get converted? Isn't the king English? Who will listen to our woes?

PANCHUMENON: All right, all right, the reason that you have given is a good one. In spite of that we should do what we have to. After that let whatever is likely to happen happen. You should ask Madhavan in detail about the quarrel which cropped up between us some time back.

GOVINDAPANIKKAR: I have decided to ask him. Let him come back from Madras.

PANCHUMENON: Panikkar, you should question him when he returns from Madras.

GOVINDAPANIKKAR: I will ask him—do not have any doubts about that.
PANCHUMENON: If both of us get angry with Madhavan, that should be enough to cow him down. This kind of audacity towards me is because he thinks that you will be there to support him.
GOVINDAPANIKKAR: There is no doubt, he will mellow down.
PANCHUMENON: In addition to this, Panikkar, I have another plan. You are a very intelligent person—let me share it with you. Madhavan has a wish: he wants Indulekha to be his wife. Indulekha too wishes the same, I think. I am going to prevent this. For one thing, they are not suited to each other as far as their age is concerned. Further, it is not appropriate for Madhavan to start a sambandam so early. It is better for Indulekha to begin a sambandam with some rich lord. Therefore, I have decided to hand her over to a rich man. He will come here very soon. But, it will be a difficult job to talk to her and get her to agree—she is very stubborn. I would like you to take an active part in getting her to agree to this. What do you think of my plan?
GOVINDAPANIKKAR: I will certainly do that but I do not know who the lord is.
PANCHUMENON: He is the Nambuthiripad from Moorkillatha *mana*. It seems he is very wealthy.
GOVINDAPANIKKAR: All right, let him come.
PANCHUMENON: Did you know the expenditure for Shinnan is going to be met by Shinupattar. Where does he get so much money from? I am not going to give even a kasu towards that. In addition, I am going to ask for all the land in the custody of Kummini's children. Let me see how these good-for-nothings will educate him! Let me see.
GOVINDAPANIKKAR: Yes, let us see.
PANCHUMENON: You should not give them money, or help them in any way.
GOVINDAPANIKKAR: What do I gain if I help them financially?
PANCHUMENON: That is exactly what I am telling you.

Thereupon, Panchumenon went back to his house without quarrelling and cursing. However, he had spelt out clearly his secret plans to Govindapanikkar.

Within two days Panchumenon's anger cooled a bit. But his wish that Indulekha's sambandam with the Nambuthiripad should be conducted immediately intensified as time went by.

chapter six

Panchumenon's Anxiety

One night, while Panchumenon was sitting in the *thekkini* to have his evening meal, he noticed that Kesavannambuthiri who had finished his, was about to go back inside. Seeing this, Panchumenon asked him to sit down for a while. Kesavannambuthiri sat on a low seat near him.

PANCHUMENON: Have you not sent word? What has happened? Is there no reply as yet?

KESAVANNAMBUTHIRI: I sent a message immediately. The messenger brought back the news that the Nambuthiri was not at home and would be back only after four or five days. Today, early in the morning, I sent a second message. If he has returned I think he should be here tomorrow.

Panchumenon sent someone to call Lakshmikuttyamma. She came and stood close to her father.

PANCHUMENON: Lakshmikutty! Have you told Indulekha this news?

LAKSHMIKUTTYAMMA: What news?

PANCHUMENON: Look, just look at the girl's cheek! Didn't you get to know all about the news? You should be beheaded! I should kick out all these criminals!

LAKSHMIKUTTYAMMA: What is all this, Father? No one has given me any news. Why are you getting angry with me for no reason?

KESAVANNAMBUTHIRI: Lakshmikutty is not aware of all this. I have not told her anything. You had asked me to keep the matter a secret; therefore, I did not tell anyone anything.

PANCHUMENON: Oh, then that is all right. I thought your highness must have told Lakshmikutty everything today. (Looking at Lakshmikuttyamma) Child, that is why I lost my temper with you. Anyway, let that be. Now give me your opinion: I have decided on a sambandam for Indulekha with Moorkillatha Nambuthiripad. Do you think Indulekha will like that?

LAKSHMIKUTTYAMMA: How can I tell you now whether Indulekha will be convinced or not?

PANCHUMENON: This is what I call cheek! Your highness, can't you see how impudent this girl is?

KESAVANNAMBUTHIRI: Why can't you ask Indulekha herself? That would be better, wouldn't it?

PANCHUMENON: Your highness is a crass idiot! Who is going to ask Indulekha? If Lakshmikutty asks her she might give a reply. Lakshmikutty! Have you heard anything about this Moorkillatha Nambuthiripad?

LAKSHMIKUTTYAMMA: No.

PANCHUMENON: Your highness should tell her. Make her aware of all that she needs to know about him.

KESAVANNAMBUTHIRI: Certainly, I will do that.

Panchumenon finished his dinner and started rinsing his hands. A servant came with a letter for Kesavannambuthiri.

PANCHUMENON: Is that a reply to the letter you had sent earlier?

KESAVANNAMBUTHIRI: Yes, yes, it is.

PANCHUMENON: Let me hear you read that letter. Please read it slowly.

Kesavannambuthiri read the letter aloud.

'I got your letter and was happy to note the contents. I shall reach there in time for my regular bath. Cherusseri will also come with me. I have heard more about Indulekha than what the Nambuthiri has told me. I am eager to see her. Rest in person.'

PANCHUMENON: Good! It is not yet time for Indulekha to retire. Your highness should also come with me. We will both go to her room. Let me try and talk to her a little bit about this, then we will learn what she thinks.

When Kesavannambuthiri and Panchumenon entered Indulekha's room, she was lying on a couch, reading *Shakuntalam*. She rose immediately.

Kesavannambuthiri sat down on a chair and Panchumenon on a couch. Patting her on her back gently, he asked:

Child, what are you reading? Are you reading some fiction like you said you were, earlier?

INDULEKHA: No. I am reading *Shakuntalam*, Grandfather. The print in this book is very bad. It is difficult to read.

PANCHUMENON: Why don't you buy a better book? Where will you get it? I will give you the money now.

INDULEKHA: I don't know whether a good print of this book is available at all. I will find out and let you know, Grandfather.

PANCHUMENON: My dear, you should get one in large print.

INDULEKHA: (smiling) Isn't that difficult, Grandfather? It will cost a lot of money. Another thing, I do not even know whether this book is available in large print.

PANCHUMENON: What is it that you don't know?

INDULEKHA: Big type for printing.

PANCHUMENON: I don't know anything about all this. If you don't have the typescript you may buy that also.

Indulekha smiled.

PANCHUMENON: Both of us came here to tell you something, my dear. If everything were to be as it was in the past, you need not have known anything about it. You would know about it only when the event took place. However, now since this is kaliyuga we are a little frightened. That is why we have come here to inform you—(turning to the Nambuthiri) your highness, please tell her.

INDULEKHA: Grandfather, you may proceed according to the practices of the old times. I have not been affected by *kali* at all. I want to know about matters only when they take place.

KESAVANNAMBUTHIRI: (to Panchumenon) All right, all right. Good answer. Enough, that is enough. Now we will go to sleep.

PANCHUMENON: If something untoward happens at the time of the function .... Shouldn't we ensure that such a thing doesn't happen?

INDULEKHA: Since we don't know what problems will arise, how can we resolve them?

PANCHUMENON: See, how the new logic of her education is showing!

INDULEKHA: How does new logic show, Grandfather? Didn't I speak in Malayalam?
PANCHUMENON: Yes, my dear, don't I know your versatility?
INDULEKHA: What is the versatility in this? Grandfather, I don't understand what you are saying.
PANCHUMENON: (to Kesavannambuthiri) If we argue with her, we will not be able to sleep today. Why doesn't your highness talk of the matter we came to speak to her about. Tell her clearly.
KESAVANNAMBUTHIRI: Indulekha has understood everything.
PANCHUMENON: That might be true, but shouldn't we know what she's thinking?
KESAVANNAMBUTHIRI: That we need to know only when the event takes place. She herself said so, didn't she?
PANCHUMENON: Why is your highness saying something so idiotic? Ask, ask her!
KESAVANNAMBUTHIRI: We have arranged a sambandam for you.
INDULEKHA: Who decided that?
KESAVANNAMBUTHIRI: Your grandfather himself.
INDULEKHA: All right, then let him decide.
KESAVANNAMBUTHIRI: Is this agreeable to you, Indulekha?
INDULEKHA: Is consent necessary for something that has already been decided upon?
KESAVANNAMBUTHIRI: We want to know whether this is agreeable to you or not.
INDULEKHA: If that is so, shouldn't you have found out beforehand and then taken a decision?
KESAVANNAMBUTHIRI: It is not something that you, Indulekha, need to know before it is decided.
INDULEKHA: This is difficult indeed. 'It is a matter about which you need not know anything; you should know only when it takes place.' Then why worry about my consent after you have decided everything?

Panchumenon's anger rose when he heard these words. However, seeing the resolution on Indulekha's shining moon-like face he became calm. He was silent for a while. Then:

PANCHUMENON: This is getting quite complicated. Let Lakshmikutty ask her about this tomorrow. Let us go and sleep now.

Saying this, Kesavannambuthiri and Panchumenon came away. Panchumenon went into his room and anxiously told his wife about Indulekha's stubbornness.

KUNJIKUTTYAMMA: If you scold her appropriately she will not be so insolent. It is because you are so tender towards her that she is defiant. You shouldn't love children so much.

PANCHUMENON: I am not frightened of anyone in this world except Indulekha! If she gets angry I cannot bear it. What shall I do?

Regretting, indeed cursing the oath he had angrily made, the old man fell asleep.

I shall end this chapter only after talking a little about the conversation that took place between Kesavannambuthiri and his wife in their room at the same time.

When Kesavannambuthiri entered his room he saw his wife sleeping. He sat on the bed and woke her up by caressing her gently.

I have not said anywhere in this book about this Kesavannambuthiri. One cannot say he had a great deal of property but he was a reasonably rich man; he had invested his share of the money in a cotton mill. Though he was not exactly good to look at, he was not ugly either. He was dear to the Moorkillatha Nambuthiripad, and also dependent on him. He was not married to a woman of his community (meaning he was not the eldest Nambuthiri in his family). It was not very often that he went and stayed at his *illam*. He ate in the home of a Brahmin which was close to the *sathrasala* of Poovally. He had a *kuttipattar* [young Brahmin attendant] and two personal servants. He was a simpleton, about whom the following statement would be very apt: 'Even if great people are fools they are termed simple.' He was a decent and well-behaved person who loved his wife intensely. He always remembered that he was very lucky to have got such a wife. He woke up the sleeping Lakshmikuttyamma thinking that he would talk to her about the sambandam that had been arranged for Indulekha with the Nambuthiripad from Kannazhi Moorkillatha mana.

KESAVANNAMBUTHIRI: Lakshmi! Lakshmi! Are you already asleep? It is not even nine o'clock.

Lakshmikuttyamma opened her eyes and sat up.

KESAVANNAMBUTHIRI: Why do you sleep so much?

Panchumenon's Anxiety

LAKSHMIKUTTYAMMA: Have you chewed your betel leaf yet? See, I have prepared it and kept it ready for you on that silver plate on the table.

KESAVANNAMBUTHIRI: Oh, all right, I shall take it now.

Putting the betel leaves in his mouth, he sat down on the bed.

KESAVANNAMBUTHIRI: Don't you want to listen to the news about our meeting with Indulekha?

LAKSHMIKUTTYAMMA: Hasn't Indulekha gone to sleep yet? These days that girl sits up and reads for a long time in the night. I don't know whether she will fall ill because of this. Apparently, light from a kerosene lamp is not good for the eyes.

KESAVANNAMBUTHIRI: Who told you all this nonsense? You are talking about kerosene oil! That is good oil. The cotton mill is lighted up with kerosene oil lamps. How can I tell you how crowded it is! I am interested in taking you there and showing you all those wonderful things.

LAKSHMIKUTTYAMMA: What are those wonderful things?

KESAVANNAMBUTHIRI: Shiva! Shiva! Narayana! Narayana! What should I tell you? The intelligence of these Europeans is really amazing. Lakshmi, if you saw that you would be astounded. It is really a miracle. What you hear as the famous cotton mill is, in fact, an iron wheel. That wheel makes all the thread. What rotates the wheel is smoke. Smoke—smoke—just plain smoke. However, the smoke doesn't hurt our eyes as it does when it comes from the kitchen. That company has a big tail which goes up—a tail like a flag-post. They say that is for the smoke to go up, but I am a little doubtful about that. There are some tricks inside all this. The clever Europeans wouldn't let out the secret. If there is nothing like that, do you think that the iron rods and needles will obey—there is some trick behind this.

LAKSHMIKUTTYAMMA: Why don't any of you get to know what the trick is all about?

KESAVANNAMBUTHIRI: If we ask about that the engineer will shoot us down. Oh no! We shouldn't ask anything. However, when we all go there, he takes us near the engine and tells us a lot of lies. Even children will not be taken in by what he says. But we do not show that—we pretend that we understand everything.

LAKSHMIKUTTYAMMA: I think what your highness said about the smoke turning the engine is utter stupidity. Some days ago, Indulekha had told me a few things about trains. She told me that machines of this sort run with the power of steam; and that smoke by itself does not have the power, and because it is always seen together with fire we happen to see smoke where there is fire, though it does not have any purpose or use.

KESAVANNAMBUTHIRI: It may be like that for trains—the cotton mill works on smoke. Maybe under that flag-post, there might be some other trick. I have no doubt about it. Govindankutty or Madhavan must have told Indulekha about all this. These Britishers won't tell these innocent boys how exactly everything works. They will be made to believe something stupid and they will think that that is the truth and repeat the same to the women and others. They won't tell them any factual details. You have to convert to their faith before they tell you anything.

LAKSHMIKUTTYAMMA: I don't know all that—smoke doesn't have any power, that's all I know.

KESAVANNAMBUTHIRI: Why do you talk like that? Smoke is very powerful. Isn't the smoke from a sacrifice powerful? I have one more doubt: I wonder whether this is a sacrifice which is made to propitiate some gods. Who knows, there may be some gods or wheels kept inside the flag-post. Maybe this sacrifice is endearing to those things. Maybe this company works because these have been propitiated, who would know—only Narayanamurthy [God].

LAKSHMIKUTTYAMMA: Then why don't you find out?

KESAVANNAMBUTHIRI: Lakshmi, what are you saying? Do you think the Britishers will allow it in this life? If they permit such activity won't they lose their power? Will they ever let us know the details about the working of these tricky things, like the train or the telegraph system? They will not do it ever. For instance, to set up this cotton mill, have the Britishers spent even a little bit of money? No—it is the local people's money. Even then, what is the use? Has this knowledge been imparted to a single person? Huge amounts of money have been taken and the work for the thread factory was done in England. Then they brought it here and set up the company. If you look at the company it is big and beautiful. Now a white man is managing the company with smoke and making thread. When we see the way the company functions we are amazed. Aren't we local people stupid? Otherwise, couldn't the parts of the thread factory have been assembled in Kozhikode.

What was the objection? Isn't it our money? Shouldn't they do as we want them to? But we can't say all this to the Britishers. They took about one and a half lakh rupees and made all the parts of the cotton mill in their own country and brought it here in a ship. They are very intelligent. How stupid we are!

LAKSHMIKUTTYAMMA: All right, will there be some profit in this?

KESAVANNAMBUTHIRI: Everyone says there will be, definitely. Many people have given money; we will know in two or three years. It would have been very good if the Englishmen taught us all the tricks.

LAKSHMIKUTTYAMMA: Don't you see the Englishmen teaching the people, what else should they do now? Maybe we do not have the intelligence to learn.

KESAVANNAMBUTHIRI: Really, my Lakshmikutty, do you really believe this? They do not teach all this in school. If that were so it would have been good. All that they do at school is spoil our children. They will prevent the children from entering the temples, bathing if they become impure, or applying holy ashes and sandalwood paste to their foreheads and stop them from respecting their teachers and elders, and giving due respect to Brahmins. Then they will teach the children unnecessary and useless stories and ask them to take some examinations and add some letters to their names to give them respectability through that. What is the use of all this? How are express telegrams made? If we ask any child who has learnt English about how trains run, they won't be able to say anything about it, just like you and I. When one child learns English he becomes ashamed of all the people at home. English education is good only for that.

LAKSHMIKUTTYAMMA: It is not like that. Some time back, Indulekha told me in detail about how a train runs. I understood that clearly. I think all these children know a great deal more than us—maybe it is because they know more about things that they are ashamed of us. One day Madhavan told me about the telegraph. I found it fascinating.

KESAVANNAMBUTHIRI: Let Indulekha drive a train and I will accept it.

LAKSHMIKUTTYAMMA: How can that be? First of all there should be a train. Then she should learn how to drive it. The people who drive trains are like daily-wage workers. They do not know the mechanism like our English-educated children know.

KESAVANNAMBUTHIRI: What a pity! You, Lakshmikutty, are a simpleton. You shouldn't trust these Europeans. They claim that they do not have any magic and strategies. Some time back when I went to Kozhikode I went for a ride on the beach with a king in a vehicle. We saw a small bungalow near the beach. When I asked what it was, the king said that it was the place where the Britishers offer their secret worship, that place is called the church. If anyone speaks about the secret worship in that place to outsiders, the British have ordered the person beheaded. They performed this secret worship, pleased the goddess and got the whole country under their control; they have incapacitated our kings. Even then they just tell us that they have no magic or other secret ways. Isn't this really something?

LAKSHMIKUTTYAMMA: Can local people join this beheading church?
KESAVANNAMBUTHIRI: I don't know that, I don't think they will let us join.
LAKSHMIKUTTYAMMA: I am feeling sleepy.
KESAVANNAMBUTHIRI: I too feel sleepy.

Lakshmikuttyamma went off to sleep. Nambuthiri also went to lie down. Only then did he remember that he had woken up Lakshmikuttyamma to talk about his conversation with Indulekha and about the Nambuthiripad, and that so much of time had been wasted talking about the cotton mill—the simple-hearted Kesavannambuthiri felt that this was utter foolishness.

chapter seven

Kannazhi Moorkillatha Manakkal Surinambuthiripad

Ordinarily there is no need for an author to wonder at the very outset whether the story under preparation or the incidents and the people depicted in it will cause unease or ill will. However, this is a new kind of story in Malayalam. Therefore, suspecting that some of my readers might mistake some of the incidents found in the book to be my thoughts, or included for some ulterior motive, I think it is necessary to discuss the problem a little here.

In this chapter, as well as in the coming chapters, I find it necessary to recount the story of a Nambuthiripad who is both fickle and a womanizer. Among Malayalis, I respect Nambuthiris more than any other group. Among them I know extraordinarily brilliant and capable people and I also have a few good friends. Any caste has people who are clever or stupid, brilliant or foolish, good or bad. It is so among Nambuthiris as well. The Nambuthiripad who appears in this story is a dimwit. However, my readers will understand why I lack the spite to make fun of the commendable people that Nambuthiris are and of the eminent position they hold in this region, when they get acquainted with one Cherusserinambuthiri who is smart and has an excellent sense of humour.

In English novels, the characters who figure in this type of story are European men and women who occupy different positions in life. Some of these books talk about living and great Europeans in a derogatory manner or make fun of them; or they may depict such people in a laudable way. However, no one in Europe has any quarrel or disagreement about the way in which these presentations are made in the stories when they are done without any ill will. Therefore, I think that no one should be offended by the things that are said in this book.

The letter that Kesavannambuthiri read out to Panchumenon was from this very Nambuthiripad.

Kannazhi Moorkillatha mana was a famous household in the land. In wealth and nobility it was said to be unequalled. Among the noble Nambuthiripads in this mana, Surinambuthiripad was the second one, but because the *apphan* [uncle] Nambuthiripad was old and ill, Surinambuthiripad was the one entrusted with the care of all the matters of the mana. At the time of this story, he was forty-five years old. As he had been preoccupied with the management of the household from a young age, he did not receive an education. He was a bachelor and by nature a libertine. Even though the elder Nambuthiripad, his brother, had tried hard, he had resisted marriage. Two of his younger brothers were already married. Making this an excuse he whiled away his time taking Nair women as wives. I am not even going to attempt a head-to-foot description of him. Even though he was fair-skinned, one can say that he was not in the least bit handsome or good looking. However, one could not say that he was disfigured. In this region there are sure to be a lakh or more of people who look like this. There was nothing special about any of his features—his features were neither attractive nor greatly disfigured. However, it is necessary to dwell especially on two or three matters that concern his physique and nature. When he smiled it looked as though his mouth stretched to his cheeks and beyond; his nostrils were well shaped but looked as though they were not big enough for his face; as for his gait, it looked as though a crow was hopping about. Since I have said at the very beginning that he was a libertine, there is no need to say anything further about this aspect of his character. If men who are rich are unduly attracted to women, there is no need to speak further. All their thoughts and actions definitely have something to do with these matters. It is only in name that Surinambuthiri looks after the matters of the mana—the work was really done by the caretakers, who worked for a monthly payment. As some of them were smart, one can say that the affairs of the household were managed quite well. Surinambuthiri was naïve, but because of his poor character, not many people considered him to be so. Like many rich people who have no wisdom or learning, he too had a high opinion of himself. The servile caretakers in his employ had convinced him that he was a capable person, and the women he lived with made this stupid man believe that he was as handsome as Manmadhan. Repeated flattery had gone to his head and he considered himself a great person. Prostitutes, sharp and wicked enough to extract money, would tell him about the elegance of his handsome body. The simpleton really believed all these absurdities; he was proud to think that they were his real qualities. Even though he was forty-five years old, there was no limit to his pride. One day, a woman said, 'Your slave cannot bear to not see you even for a single moment.' This left a deep impression on his mind. 'Your slave considers it very lucky to join her body to your respectable body. Who desires money? Everyone has money. Does everyone have this honourable physique?' So some other woman had said and he remembered this like a line from the scriptures.

At that time, Govindannambuthiri from Cherusseri illam was his companion. It is not possible to talk of another person with the same taste and cunning. He had studied grammar and acquired a good grasp of it; he was knowledgeable in music; both his face and body were handsome. Never have I conversed with a man of such distinction. I can say with conviction that no one else in the story has his distinction in taste. Cherusserinambuthiri was not at all devious. However, if he found any person who deserved to be made fun of, one can say that he did so mercilessly. Only very dull people were unafraid of his barbs. Only a person who did not have even the faintest sense of his cruel wit would be unafraid of him. He was no friend of Surinambuthiripad; he had only contempt for him. However, it could not be expressed openly. Surinambuthiripad, a prominent person among the Nambuthiris, was famous for his wealth and nobility. How can one openly disrespect him? The Nambuthiripad was fond of anyone who praised him. If one did not proclaim that he was extremely handsome and capable, the Nambuthiripad, thus displeased, would be hostile towards him. It was difficult for him to understand whether the praise was sarcastic or not.

Govindannambuthiri was a very close friend of Narayanannambuthiripad, the very capable younger brother of Surinambuthiripad. However, when he visited Moorkillatha mana it was difficult for him to talk to his friend. Surinambuthiripad used to summon him immediately to his room upstairs and to take leave of him was very difficult. This was the nature of the relationship between Surinambuthiripad and Govindannambuthiri. If anything that Govindannambuthiri said was not to the Nambuthiripad's liking, he would get offended. Afraid that there might be attacks, Govindannambuthiri praised him sarcastically. Therefore, Cherusserinambuthiri had no choice but to praise him. Another thing about the Nambuthiripad was that he was crazy about kathakali. He was well versed in this art and had great taste. He would not be satisfied even if he were to watch kathakali for 365 days a year, and if there had been more days he would have willingly done the same. His younger brothers were more capable than he; however, in his opinion, they were fools.

The Nambuthiripad was massaging himself with oil in the bath house when Kesavannambuthiri's letter was brought to him. The moment he read the letter, he sent for Cherusserinambuthiri. Govindan who was in charge of the *vettilapetti,* rushed off to call Cherusserinambuthiri. He was an intelligent boy, but also a rascal who knew all about his master's character and who had a measure of his merits and demerits. However, he also respected and loved the Nambuthiripad. When Govindan reached Cherusseri illam, Govindannambuthiri had finished his meal and had come out to the front of the house and, in order to play chess, was carving pawns from the stem of the banana plant.

CHERUSSERINAMBUTHIRI: Why Govinda, why have you come in such a hurry?

GOVINDAN: You have been ordered to come.

CHERUSSERINAMBUTHIRI: Has the Nambuthiripad finished his meal?

GOVINDAN: No, he is in the bath house being massaged with *ulappenna.*

CHERUSSERINAMBUTHIRI: What is the urgency? Is there anything special coming up?

GOVINDAN: There is a letter from Chambazhiyot from Karuthedathu Kesavannambuthiri. As soon as he read it he gave orders to call you.

CHERUSSERINAMBUTHIRI: All right, I understand what it is. I will come. Let me change my mundu.

Saying this he went indoors.

Twenty days back, Cherusseri had gone to Chambazhiyot with Kesavannambuthiri. He had met Indulekha and Madhavan at that time and had liked them. He had come away saying he would return soon. When Cherusseri was leaving, Kesavannambuthiri had said that it would be suitable if a sambandam could be started for Indulekha with Surinambuthiripad; he had asked Cherusserinambuthiri to help, but Cherusseri had said that it was not possible for him to make any such effort.

After Cherusserinambuthiri returned from Chambazhiyot, he had told Surinambuthiripad's clever younger brother Narayanannambuthiripad a little about Indulekha. Cherusseri had not breathed a word about Indulekha to Surinambuthiripad. In this way, our Cherusserinambuthiri was already acquainted with Indulekha.

Since Govindan had come with a message for him, Cherusserinambuthiri went inside to change into a clean mundu. Coming out he said, 'Govinda, now we will go,' and they set off.

On the way, Govindan said to Cherusserinambuthiri:

Your slave thinks that your highness has understood the reason for the orders to call you. If you have not, I shall tell you.

CHERUSSERINAMBUTHIRI: Please tell me.

GOVINDAN: It seems that there is a beautiful lady in Chambazhiyot, in Poovally where Kesavannambuthiri has a sambandam. The letter is about the decision of his highness to have a sambandam. I think you will have to go with him to Poovally.

Cherusserinambuthiri listened to all that Govindan told him with a smile. Finally:

CHERUSSERINAMBUTHIRI: Govinda! Won't you also come if we have to go?

GOVINDAN: Your slave will definitely come. The person who brought the letter now, told me that your highness has seen the girl. I do not know whether that is true.

CHERUSSERINAMBUTHIRI: I have seen her. Did the person who brought the letter also give you all the details about the sambandam?

GOVINDAN: No—that his highness himself told me. Your slave has not read the letter. His highness said another thing—this is not like the other sambandams. The girl (he mentioned some name—Chandrabhama or Chitralekha was the name that he said) will be brought back to the mana the day after the sambandam begins. He has declared that apphan shall be told and his permission taken.

When he heard this, Govindannambuthiri could not do anything but laugh; so he laughed aloud. Though Govindan did not know exactly why Govindannambuthiri laughed, he too laughed with him. Then both of them hurried to the mana.

As soon as Govindan was sent off to call Cherusserinambuthiri, the Nambuthiripad finished his bath and meal, and thinking hard of Indulekha and enjoying the thought, he emerged and stood in front of the house. At that time, the person who transacted business for the mana, Thassanmenon, came to the Nambuthiripad and stood by him.

NAMBUTHIRIPAD: Today I don't have time for anything. Thachu, you go.
THASSANMENON: You have to attend to these matters.
NAMBUTHIRIPAD: Whatever you say, today I just don't have the time.
THASSANMENON: The day after tomorrow the case may be filed. It is essential that I speak to you about that now.
NAMBUTHIRIPAD: Whatever it might be—I just don't have the time to listen to anything.
THASSANMENON: A document has to be filed in the court. A representation has to be given for that. I have written and brought the representation, you have to endorse it.
NAMBUTHIRIPAD: Today is Saturday—Thachu, don't you know that I don't sign any documents on Saturday? Then why do you come and disturb me like this?
THASSANMENON: If the document has to be filed, it has to be presented on Monday, otherwise the case will not be admitted.
NAMBUTHIRIPAD: Let it be. Isn't there a court of appeal?
THASSANMENON: If the representation is not filed, it will be rejected by the court of appeal too.
NAMBUTHIRIPAD: This is really a calamity—if I put you in charge of something, why do you come and disturb me like this?
THASSANMENON: Is it possible for your slave to sign the representation?
NAMBUTHIRIPAD: Today is Saturday: I will not sign on any representation. Don't you remember, Thachu, I signed a complaint on a Saturday and that case was not successful.
THASSANMENON: This is not a complaint, it is a representation.
NAMBUTHIRIPAD: Whatever it is I won't sign it today, that is for sure. Thachu, go and bathe.
THASSANMENON: I think in this case the witness will have to appear.
NAMBUTHIRIPAD: Me? Is it me?
THASSANMENON: Yes.
NAMBUTHIRIPAD: What is all this! Even if the case is lost I won't go to court. Have the summons come?
THASSANMENON: The summons have come. A reply was sent as though you were not here.
NAMBUTHIRIPAD: Who is this rascal who dared give my name as a witness!
THASSANMENON: This is about the complaint against Ullathil Panchumenon.
NAMBUTHIRIPAD: Who is Ullathil Panchu? What is this? Have we filed a case against him?

THASSANMENON: Haven't you, to ask him to vacate the Cherpatte threshing floor?

NAMBUTHIRIPAD: All right, all right—I was a little bewildered. Didn't you say some time back that a court order has been passed on that?

THASSANMENON: Your slave hasn't told you anything of the sort. Panchumenon has staked a claim to it—he argues that four or five bits of the mana land are his.

NAMBUTHIRIPAD: Panchu did that? Is he such a wicked person? I didn't know this. Send somebody and ask Panchu to come here. Let me talk to that wicked person. If he is so evil, we should forbid him access to the pond, the well, the temple, and everything else. Then he will come running behind me like a dog. Thachu, you should have told me about this matter earlier.

THASSANMENON: I don't think any of this will be fruitful. Panchumenon has brought an English barrister.

NAMBUTHIRIPAD: If an Englishman comes, what do I care?

THASSANMENON: He is a capable person.

NAMBUTHIRIPAD: We will also give our case to an Englishman. It would be nice if it was Mackshaman who has the cardamom estate. We have a cordial relationship. Thachu, go and tell him the details.

THASSANMENON: The Englishmen who have leased the hills can't take up these matters.

NAMBUTHIRIPAD: Don't be insolent. That sayiv will do anything for me.

THASSANMENON: All right. Then your slave will arrange everything accordingly. If you do not sign the document now, the case will be rejected on Monday.

In this manner when Thassanmenon's and Nambuthiripad's argument about signing and not signing had waxed, Narayanannambuthiripad emerged from the house and somehow got the Nambuthiripad to sign the document. As soon as he marked his signature, he said, 'Why isn't Cherusseri coming?' and walked to the gatehouse where he waited for Cherusseri to arrive. Meanwhile, he recalled Indulekha's beauty and was soon lost in thought. As he was standing thus he saw Cherusseri and Govindan walking towards him. Even before they had come up the steps, the Nambuthiripad shouted out.

NAMBUTHIRIPAD: (calling out loudly) Cherusseri come quickly—come quickly! How slowly you walk! Why can't you walk faster? Don't you want to hear the news? A letter has come from Chambazhiyot from

Karuthedam. Have you heard about a girl called Indulekha? You said something about your going there, was she there at the time? She is beautiful, isn't she?—just like Damayanti! I am going to enter into a sambandam with her. This is not like my earlier sambandams, I am bringing her over here. It seems she knows English and other things— I have never met a woman who knows English. She is extremely beautiful. She is like Damayanti—that is what I heard.

By the time he had finished saying this, Cherusserinambuthiri had drawn close.

CHERUSSERINAMBUTHIRI: If that is so, there is need for a Nalan. And Nalan will be Nambuthiri himself.

NAMBUTHIRIPAD: Cherusseri! Stop all this teasing! I am growing old. That girl is just fifteen years old. What beauty do I have? Don't talk about that—shouldn't we leave at once?

CHERUSSERINAMBUTHIRI: Shouldn't we talk about that? Is forty-five years an age? If you are handsome at twenty-five, where will your looks disappear when you are forty-five? Don't say such things, I don't think the women of this place will lose their fascination for you even when you are eighty.

NAMBUTHIRIPAD: Have you met Indulekha? Cherusseri, didn't you go there with Karuthedam some days back?

CHERUSSERINAMBUTHIRI: I have met Indulekha.

NAMBUTHIRIPAD: Is she beautiful?

CHERUSSERINAMBUTHIRI: She is a beautiful girl.

NAMBUTHIRIPAD: Some people say that she knows English, does she?

CHERUSSERINAMBUTHIRI: I have heard people say that she knows English.

NAMBUTHIRIPAD: If women learn English they lose their sense of cleanliness: that is a big drawback.

CHERUSSERINAMBUTHIRI: I feel that if they learn English, their sense of cleanliness increases—when I saw Indulekha I felt that.

NAMBUTHIRIPAD: What is it...do you have any association with Indulekha? If you have, you can tell me before I associate with her—I don't have any objection to your telling me about it. Why is it that when I listen to your words Cherusseri, I feel you are associated with her, are you?

CHERUSSERINAMBUTHIRI: What association?

NAMBUTHIRIPAD: A relationship with Indulekha.

CHERUSSERINAMBUTHIRI: It is criminal to say this. I don't have the temperament for such things. Besides, Indulekha is an intelligent girl, she is not like ordinary Nair girls. You will find out when you meet her. That girl might be perplexed when she sees your physique and the nature that goes with it. It is unlikely that she will be fascinated by anyone else.

NAMBUTHIRIPAD: Please don't praise me on my face, Cherusseri. Am I so handsome? I don't think so.

CHERUSSERINAMBUTHIRI: That is how your highness should feel, but you don't expect me to agree!

NAMBUTHIRIPAD: Cherusseri, have you seen Neelattu Lakshmi?

CHERUSSERINAMBUTHIRI: I have not seen her.

NAMBUTHIRIPAD: Have you seen Puzhayattu Paru?

CHERUSSERINAMBUTHIRI: No.

NAMBUTHIRIPAD: Then you must have met Koppattu Kummini. Some time ago when there was a singing session, Cherusseri, you were here. Who is better—Koppattu Kummini or Indulekha?

CHERUSSERINAMBUTHIRI: I did not actually see the face of the girl who sang that day.

NAMBUTHIRIPAD: All right, so who is the most beautiful among the women you have seen?

CHERUSSERINAMBUTHIRI: Indulekha.

NAMBUTHIRIPAD: Any doubt about it?

CHERUSSERINAMBUTHIRI: No doubt about it.

NAMBUTHIRIPAD: Then it is my luck.

CHERUSSERINAMBUTHIRI: Yes, it is.

NAMBUTHIRIPAD: Is there anything more pleasurable for a man than the pleasure he gets from a woman!

CHERUSSERINAMBUTHIRI: If you decide that the greatest pleasure is the pleasure a woman gives, there is nothing beyond it.

NAMBUTHIRIPAD: Cherusseri, how do you view it?

CHERUSSERINAMBUTHIRI: That is not how I see it.

NAMBUTHIRIPAD: Your opinion seems to be that the pleasure given by a woman is not unparalleled.

CHERUSSERINAMBUTHIRI: I am not saying that there is no pleasure beyond the pleasure that a woman can give—that is all.

NAMBUTHIRIPAD: Then why is everyone so snared by the pleasure a woman can give?

CHERUSSERINAMBUTHIRI: All I can say is that to be so captivated and troubled by it is sheer stupidity.

NAMBUTHIRIPAD: Cherusseri, these days you have become quite an *advaiti*. I am crazy about women.

CHERUSSERINAMBUTHIRI: And they about you.

NAMBUTHIRIPAD: Is that the reason why I'm also so crazy about them?

CHERUSSERINAMBUTHIRI: Certainly, why doubt it?

NAMBUTHIRIPAD: Recently something funny happened. Cherusseri, do you want to hear about it? I had gone to Mackshaman sayiv to talk about the hill ranges. His wife (Govindan told me that her name is *mathamma* sayiv [madam]) was seated in a chair quite some distance away from where the sayiv was and reading a paper. From the moment I approached and sat by the sayiv till I got up to leave, that lady was glancing furtively at me.

CHERUSSERINAMBUTHIRI: Must have been fascinated by you, I have no doubt about it. What else could she do but ogle you?

NAMBUTHIRIPAD: Listen—finally I don't know whether it was after sensing the mathamma sayiv's inclination that Mackshaman laughed and said something in English to her. She also laughed and said something in reply. Immediately that idiot Mackshaman, without understanding the situation, said, 'I think I should introduce my wife to you. I hope that will not displease you?' I felt like laughing. But I didn't. 'Oh! surely, I will only be too happy about it,' I said. Immediately Mackshaman rose and brought her over. She stood by me. I didn't stand up. She sat down by me, extended her hand like the sayiv extends it; I also extended my hand and she caught hold of it. I felt a shiver pass through my whole body.

CHERUSSERINAMBUTHIRI: She must have felt it even more.

NAMBUTHIRIPAD: I held on to her hand for a while longer. I felt fascinated by her form. That idiot Mackshaman was watching and standing by, smiling. I took off the diamond ring which I was wearing on my small finger, not sure whether Mackshaman would be pleased. I glanced at his face briefly. That idiot said, 'Oh! Your gift to my wife? I have no objection—you can do so.' Boldly, I put the ring on the mathamma sayiv's finger. She took it and smiled. 'It is a good ring,' she said in English. Mackshaman translated the sentence. By then, Cherusseri, my fascination for her had increased manifold.

Kannazhi Moorkillatha Manakkal Surinambuthiripad

CHERUSSERINAMBUTHIRI: It must have heightened her's, I have no doubt about it.

NAMBUTHIRIPAD: Listen—after that mathamma sayiv stood and extended her hand towards me.

CHERUSSERINAMBUTHIRI: That is an important sign of her inclination. Perhaps she could not bear to continue seated, looking at you. She must have got up and left immediately, isn't it?

NAMBUTHIRIPAD: Yes—after holding my hand once more she left.

CHERUSSERINAMBUTHIRI: You didn't see her after that—did you?

NAMBUTHIRIPAD: No.

CHERUSSERINAMBUTHIRI: She must have been extremely fascinated by you. Sayiv was with the two of you; that is why I think she got slightly ruffled and went away. Otherwise, she would have flirted with you a little bit more.

NAMBUTHIRIPAD: Cherusseri, you are an intelligent person. This is why I'm so fond of you. What you say is true. That woman was fascinated by me and I by her. But I didn't pursue it any further because our scriptures do not permit associations with such women; there was no other problem.

CHERUSSERINAMBUTHIRI: You shouldn't go against the scriptures. I am amazed when I think of your intellectual capacity. Even though you wanted her intensely, knowing that this desire was against the scriptures, you courageously decided against it.

NAMBUTHIRIPAD: Sometimes I am quite bold in these matters. I confounded Koppattu Kummini a lot. Want to hear that story?

CHERUSSERINAMBUTHIRI: I have heard you narrating it once before. I remember it clearly even now. It is from that day that I started to believe that you are quite a daredevil.

NAMBUTHIRIPAD: However, the complexion of these English women is special indeed. What is Indulekha's complexion like?

CHERUSSERINAMBUTHIRI: It is a golden complexion.

NAMBUTHIRIPAD: Is it better than my complexion?

CHERUSSERINAMBUTHIRI: Why do you ask me that? Your complexion is different.

NAMBUTHIRIPAD: Now Cherusseri, you are making fun of me. Is my complexion better than Indulekha's?

CHERUSSERINAMBUTHIRI: Your question amazes me—why do you want to talk about something which is obvious?

NAMBUTHIRIPAD: True...Cherusseri, you have seen me, you have seen Indulekha also—you know my inclination for romance and beauty. Taking all this into consideration, do you believe that that girl will be enamoured by me? I will go along with your conclusions.

CHERUSSERINAMBUTHIRI: Why question me like this? It is a shame! I had already made up my mind on this matter. On seeing you, I don't think that girl will be able to resist her desire for you even for a minute. I am sure that with her insight, the moment she sees you, she will understand what type of a person you are. Thereafter, should I tell you what will follow? And you are asking, will that girl be captivated? What a question! When are you planning to leave?

NAMBUTHIRIPAD: Tomorrow morning. I will feel better if you, come with me and with us will come two kuttipattars, the caretaker Narayanan, six servants, and Govindan. Cherusseri, you will sit with me in the palanquin for the day's journey. To bring Indulekha back with us, we should take another palanquin, carried by eight people.

CHERUSSERINAMBUTHIRI: That can be taken later, there is no need to take it now. There are six or seven palanquins in Indulekha's house.

NAMBUTHIRIPAD: All right. Cherusseri, go and inform apphan.

CHERUSSERINAMBUTHIRI: How will we go tomorrow? Ramapanikkar's kathakali has been arranged here.

NAMBUTHIRIPAD: Was that for tomorrow? All right, if that is the case, let him perform. We will go as planned. Let the youngsters watch it. When we get back we will have two or three more performances. Indulekha can see them as well.

CHERUSSERINAMBUTHIRI: Ramapanikkar said that he has to leave definitely by the day after tomorrow.

NAMBUTHIRIPAD: Then shall we postpone the trip to the day after tomorrow?

CHERUSSERINAMBUTHIRI: I think that is better.

NAMBUTHIRIPAD: No—the performers will come next year also.

CHERUSSERINAMBUTHIRI: As you wish. I shall discuss the matter with the performers.

Surinambuthiripad's inclination for kathakali and for Indulekha clashed, saddening and disturbing him.

NAMBUTHIRIPAD: I wrote that I would reach there tomorrow.

CHERUSSERINAMBUTHIRI: When did you send the letter?

Kannazhi Moorkillatha Manakkal Surinambuthiripad

NAMBUTHIRIPAD: I was in the bath house and sent a person to call you, Cherusseri; it was then that I sent a reply to Karuthedam.
CHERUSSERINAMBUTHIRI: So what is the problem? Send a letter now saying that you are coming only the day after tomorrow.
NAMBUTHIRIPAD: Is it right at the beginning of the relationship, to cause Indulekha mental agony or worry? She will be waiting, thinking that I would reach tomorrow.
CHERUSSERINAMBUTHIRI: Indulekha will neither worry nor be in agony. I will take the responsibility. What is the difficulty if you shift tomorrow's journey by a day? You are a man with varied interests; do you think that everything will work out exactly as planned?
NAMBUTHIRIPAD: All right—then I shall see the performance by Raman. I have decided that. Then please go and tell apphan now and bring back the answer.
CHERUSSERINAMBUTHIRI: I shall do that.

Saying this, Cherusserinambuthiri went into the house. His friend Narayanannambuthiripad was standing in the southern room. They looked at each other and laughed. Narayanannambuthiripad had understood everything—about Indulekha's beauty, her good qualities, her self-determination, competence, her education, and about a suitable husband for her. Cherusserinambuthiri had given a clear account of Madhavan and his situation to Narayanannambuthiri. So his elder brother's urgency and agitation in this matter, left him nonplussed.

NARAYANANNAMBUTHIRIPAD: Has the journey been arranged for tomorrow?
CHERUSSERINAMBUTHIRI: Tomorrow it is the kathakali; the day after, seeking Indulekha for marriage.
NARAYANANNAMBUTHIRIPAD: I feel a little doubtful about what you told me, Cherusseri. When I see him showing off, I feel that with Karuthedam's assistance he might bring Indulekha over here.
CHERUSSERINAMBUTHIRI: It is because you haven't seen that girl and Madhavan. That is why you are so sure. I haven't seen another Malayali girl like Indulekha. I have no worry whatsoever on this count. I'm only nervous about how much she will snub the Nambuthiri.
NARAYANANNAMBUTHIRIPAD: What are you saying—Karuthedam has written so definitely. Will he write like this without consideration?
CHERUSSERINAMBUTHIRI: Let that be. Why should we argue so much about

something which is going to be confirmed in a day or two? I have to see apphan Nambuthiri. Where is he?

NARAYANANNAMBUTHIRIPAD: In a room upstairs. Why do you want him— is it to let him know about this matter?

CHERUSSERINAMBUTHIRI: Yes. (He went upstairs to tell apphan Nambuthiri and returned to Surinambuthiripad's room.)

NAMBUTHIRIPAD: Cherusseri, you are the one who causes all these impediments. What is so noble about kathakali? Why couldn't we have started tomorrow itself?

CHERUSSERINAMBUTHIRI: Just now, I went and told apphan Nambuthiri that we are going the day after tomorrow and took his permission. Is it right to go tomorrow?

NAMBUTHIRIPAD: My meeting with Indulekha is getting delayed. Where is the need to say all this? Now I have to be patient till the evening, two days hence.

CHERUSSERINAMBUTHIRI: As a temporary salve for this sorrow, from now until the time of the performance think of the fun you will have watching kathakali. Then thoughts of Indulekha will not disturb you. We leave immediately after. Then you can think exclusively of Indulekha. And as you sit thinking deeply about her you can also glimpse her. Now that you have decided on something, don't be depressed about it.

NAMBUTHIRIPAD: Cherusseri, have your dinner here and let me lie down for a little while.

Thus the Nambuthiripad went to rest a while and Cherusserinambuthiri went to Narayanannambuthiri's room.

chapter eight

An Arrival from Madras

Panchumenon, Kesavannambuthiri, and all the caretakers were waiting in the front room for the grand arrival of the Nambuthiripad from Moorkillatha mana. This was the day following the events recounted in the sixth chapter. *Paladapradhaman,* big pappadams, and sugar had been prepared as part of a grand meal. A letter had been despatched informing them that he would not be setting out that day, but that he would reach in time for lunch the next day. However, the messengers had stopped somewhere on the way since night had fallen and reached Poovarangu only in the morning. Panchumenon and others were awaiting the arrival of the Nambuthiripad. As soon as the letter was read, the karanavan walked into the house, the Nambuthiri went for a bath, and the others who had assembled went their separate ways. A while later, Indulekha came to the front of the house on her way to her bath. So did her mother.

LAKSHMIKUTTYAMMA: My dear child, why do you keep awake burning the kerosene lamp for so long? How long did you read after my father came away?

INDULEKHA: Not for long. I went to sleep soon after. Mother, *kochammaman* [younger uncle] has not yet come. Didn't he write to say that he would be here yesterday?

LAKSHMIKUTTYAMMA: That is right, maybe he will come today. Or I don't know whether Madhavan has asked him to stay back.

While they were talking thus, they saw Govindankuttymenon and his servants entering with their luggage. The previous day Govindankuttymenon had arrived by train and on the way had stayed at the rest house belonging to Poovally. He had set out that morning, and had just reached the house.

INDULEKHA: There, kochammaman is coming!

With a smile she stepped down into the courtyard and walked towards him. Lakshmikuttyamma also stepped down with her.

GOVINDANKUTTYMENON: Indulekha, are you alright?

INDULEKHA: I am, now! Kochammaman, didn't you write and say that you would come yesterday? We were looking forward to your arrival.

Soon Lakshmikuttyamma, Govindankuttymenon, and Indulekha went inside together. Govindankuttymenon had a bath, took his meal and went to meet his father at his house. When he returned, he went up to his mother's room and greeted her and his elder sister before going upstairs to Indulekha's room.

Shouldn't I tell my readers a bit about Govindankuttymenon? I need to say something. He had an incisive mind. However, one might suspect that his manner lacked humility. But he was not fickle-minded in any way. Whoever was acquainted with him respected him tremendously. He was delicately built. Like his distinguished elder brother who had passed away, he loved Indulekha more than anyone else in the world.

When she saw her ammaman approaching, Indulekha rose and smoothed the cover on the couch, and waited for him to sit down. Govindankutty seated himself. Indulekha served him tea which she herself had lovingly made and brought a variety of snacks in a silver plate and placed it on a small table by him. Then in response to her ammaman's command, she sat in a chair placed by the table.

GOVINDANKUTTYMENON: Madhavan has reached Madras safely and without any difficulty. He will soon start earning Rs 150 in the secretariat. Indulekha, have you finished reading the novel which I gave you? Do you understand it well?

The moment he uttered Madhavan's name and mentioned that he was going to get a job, Indulekha's beautiful lotus-like face shyly went through a series of changes reflecting shades of bashfulness. The intelligent Govindankuttymenon knew that such a thing would happen. He realized that there was nothing that Indulekha would be more glad to hear but knowing how shy she would feel to talk about Madhavan, he gave her all the news without making her ask for it. Then he moved on to other matters, allowing her to regain her poise.

INDULEKHA: The novel is interesting. I read the whole book.

GOVINDANKUTTYMENON: Your mother said that you read long in the night. There is no need to exert yourself in this manner.

INDULEKHA: I don't fire myself out and I don't read for long in the night. A while back I happened to sit up and read *Shakuntalam*. And that day for some reason Grandfather and Kesavannambuthiri came up here. My mother knew about this because they told her. I don't read at all in the night.

There is no need to say that Govindankuttymenon had heard about Panchumenon's oath from Madhavan. He learnt through the letter, written by Govindapanikkar to Madhavan after Panchumenon and Govindapanikkar had talked to each other, that Panchumenon was trying hard to forge a sambandam with Surinambuthiripad. However, when Indulekha mentioned this, he asked with a teasing smile, 'Why did they come to your room that day?' Indulekha's water-lily-like eyes filled with tears.

GOVINDANKUTTYMENON: Where are your brains? If people behave in a funny way, shouldn't you laugh? Why are you so disturbed? If you are planning to cry, I won't ask you anything more about it.

INDULEKHA: All right, I won't cry.

Immediately she talked about the conversation they had had that night. Govindankuttymenon laughed a lot. He also thought highly of his niece's intelligence and respected her for it.

INDULEKHA: It seems that this Nambuthiripad is coming tomorrow.

GOVINDANKUTTYMENON: (laughing loudly again) Let him come. Father told me about this matter.

INDULEKHA: Kochammaman, what was your answer?

GOVINDANKUTTYMENON: I said nothing. I stood there listening as though I was not interested in anything. I have not seen Madhavan's father. I should go to his house.

Govindankuttymenon got up to leave.

INDULEKHA: I don't know what is going to happen tomorrow.

'Nothing is going to happen,' Govindankuttymenon laughed and went towards Govindanpanikkar's house.

chapter nine

The Coming of the Nambuthiripad and Other Things

The moment the kathakali performance was midway, Surinambuthiripad got up from the couch and called Govindan.

NAMBUTHIRIPAD: Govinda! I am leaving now. Aren't the palanquin bearers sleeping here? A little while ago I saw them seated among the audience in chairs. Go and look for them—go quickly and bring them here.

Govindan went in search of Cherusserinambuthiri. He went to the gatehouse only to find that the Nambuthiri had gone to bed. But he had not yet fallen asleep.

GOVINDAN: It's an order—you have been sent for. We are leaving for Chambazhiyot immediately. Everyone is busy calling out to the palanquin bearers and others. Hurry up.
CHERUSSERINAMBUTHIRI: What a nuisance! How will we make our way along dangerous roads in the dark? We should not leave now; that is for certain.
GOVINDAN: That you yourself should command and arrange.

Cherusserinambuthiri immediately went towards the Nambuthiripad's room. He was standing there looking rather excited. Fifteen fine zari-edged upper cloths, ten or twenty different types of a particular kind of mundu, a number of different rings, a box made of solid silver studded with gold, rolls of betel leaves made in gold, a vessel with a silver handle to store water, a travel lamp with a silver chain, lids of silver, a gold watch with a gold chain which could be worn around the neck, dresses made from woven gold, cups, a gold vessel to hold sandalwood and holy ash, a mirror with a case of gold, a rosewater spray made of gold, bottles of perfume, and various other things were spread on the table. The Nambuthiripad was walking up and down in his room calling out, 'Raghava, Shankara, Koma, Rama, asses—all of you are sleeping; thieves—not even a single person turned up for the kathakali performance.' When Cherusserinambuthiri reached the house, he was calling out thus from his upper-storey rooms, and jumping up and down like a caged civet causing a lot of commotion.

NAMBUTHIRIPAD: Good, this is good punishment for everyone! Cherusseri, you should be in charge. Shouldn't we leave? You will get a lot of time to sleep after you get there.

CHERUSSERINAMBUTHIRI: What is all this! Won't it be difficult to travel in the middle of the night on this dangerous road over such a long distance? Hadn't we decided to leave only after daybreak?

NAMBUTHIRIPAD: If I in my enthusiasm tell you, Cherusseri, about an auspicious matter, you make it into an inauspicious one. We should go now, we should leave this moment. Cherusseri, you can sleep in the palanquin. You don't have to worry about danger on the way; let the palanquin bearers do that! Let four people brandish lighted torches. We should leave now.

Cherusserinambuthiri was very reluctant to set off just then. Many hills and two ferries had to be crossed. He also knew that it was not going to be fruitful to say anything to this excited person. The clever Nambuthiri struck upon a plan to prevent that night's journey. Let's see, I won't let him start tonight in this enamoured state, he thought, and thus making a definite decision, he replied to the Nambuthiripad.

CHERUSSERINAMBUTHIRI: Oh, all right. We will start now. I am ready.

The Nambuthiripad was very happy. Everyone busied themselves getting ready with a great bustle and much noise. When the *chenda* and *maddalam* rose to a crescendo, it was almost impossible to hear anyone speak. Seeing the arrangements that were taking place, and the frenzied activity of the caretakers and servants (from the attic to the room downstairs), an onlooker might wonder if the mana had caught fire. Cherusserinambuthiri walked up to the table to look at the special things readied and placed on it. That too pleased the Nambuthiripad. It always pleased him if people praised or admired his ornaments, upper cloths, or betel nut cases.

NAMBUTHIRIPAD: Cherusseri, look at that—that silver box—I don't think you have seen it before.

Cherusseri had seen the box a thousand times.

CHERUSSERINAMBUTHIRI: I don't really remember where I have seen this. Such fine workmanship. Was it made in this region?

Cherusseri knew that the box had been made by a silversmith who lived nearby. But he knew that his question would delight the Nambuthiripad.

NAMBUTHIRIPAD: No, it was not made here. Who can craft such a thing here? A modala from Mysore gave it to me as a gift, when I rented out the mountainside to him.

CHERUSSERINAMBUTHIRI: A Mysorean modala?

NAMBUTHIRIPAD: Yes.

CHERUSSERINAMBUTHIRI: Must be a *mudaliar*.

NAMBUTHIRIPAD: He can be called a *mussaliar* [Mappila priest]. Look at the upper cloth on the top of the pile—it is special. It is made in a region called Bamcross. Quite expensive. A sayiv called Meghadantan, who rented the cardamom estate, had it woven for me.

Cherusseri looked at the cloth with an expression of surprise.

CHERUSSERINAMBUTHIRI: Where did you say this was woven?

NAMBUTHIRIPAD: A country called Bamcross.

CHERUSSERINAMBUTHIRI: Wherever is that country!

NAMBUTHIRIPAD: It is in the south-west of England. Meghadantan told me that in that area it is day for six months and night for six months.

Putting down the cloth after examining it, Cherusseri slowly picked up the gold mirror and in an intensely astonished tone said, 'A very special mirror.'

NAMBUTHIRIPAD: A gift from the younger raja of Cochin last year during the *pooram* festival in Trichur.

Cherusseri remembered very clearly that the Nambuthiripad had not gone for the pooram last year.

CHERUSSERINAMBUTHIRI: A special mirror surely.

He put the mirror back in its place. Stroking his beard, he smiled gently.

NAMBUTHIRIPAD: Why did you smile, Cherusseri?
CHERUSSERINAMBUTHIRI: Nothing special.
NAMBUTHIRIPAD: Hey, tell me. Why did you smile? Tell me, tell me.
CHERUSSERINAMBUTHIRI: It doesn't matter—there is nothing to be said. I feel I should have shaved yesterday. But I don't have to worry about shaving in this journey. The person who should shave and look handsome is Indulekha's husband. It does not matter how his companions appear. The thought made me smile. That is all.

The Nambuthiripad had not shaved for more days than Cherusserinambuthiri. He had a few grey bristles also. Cherusseri made these announcements after noticing all this. The Nambuthiripad took the mirror and looked at himself.

NAMBUTHIRIPAD: This is punishment! Good you reminded me, Cherusseri. I would have messed up everything! Shiva, Shiva! It is even grey: I am an old man, Cherusseri!
CHERUSSERINAMBUTHIRI: I don't think so.
NAMBUTHIRIPAD: Then you don't want me to shave?
CHERUSSERINAMBUTHIRI: That is your wish.
NAMBUTHIRIPAD: Shall I get it done now in the light of a lamp?
CHERUSSERINAMBUTHIRI: Shaving at night is not permitted, especially because we are going on an auspicious journey. I feel that it would be better to do without the shave.
NAMBUTHIRIPAD: That cannot be. I will shave after daylight, but then, how can I go before having a bath?
CHERUSSERINAMBUTHIRI: No, you shouldn't go before bathing.
NAMBUTHIRIPAD: We will go after I've taken a bath.
CHERUSSERINAMBUTHIRI: Then isn't it better that we go after breakfast?
NAMBUTHIRIPAD: So be it.
CHERUSSERINAMBUTHIRI: Let me make arrangements for all that.

Cherusseri came down happily. The Nambuthiripad went off to his room to sleep.

As decided, the next morning after breakfast, around eight-thirty, the Nambuthiripad, Cherusseri, and the retinue started on their way.

The people at Poovally had been intimated that the Nambuthiripad would reach in time for a bath, and so they made arrangements for a grand meal for the second time. Panchumenon and Kesavannambuthiri together waited without their morning baths till twelve o'clock. Finally Panchumenon began to get a little restless.

PANCHUMENON: What is this, your highness! I am going for my bath. I think this Nambuthiripad is not at all dependable.

KESAVANNAMBUTHIRI: This is really sad! I have never seen anyone else who is so dependable. If you knew about the matters he is concerned with, you wouldn't say so. Shiva, Shiva! He is busy there. Only if you visit the mana you will know. Managing land on the side of the mountain, the elephants, the weekly rent, the renewal of a lease, there are so many such matters! Shiva! Who is there to do all this except him? Recently they had a gold chain made for an elephant—it is very special.

PANCHUMENON: Is it made of solid gold?

KESAVANNAMBUTHIRI: Yes, of solid gold.

PANCHUMENON: It is the power of money.

KESAVANNAMBUTHIRI: Yes, it is the power of money.

PANCHUMENON: I don't know whether this girl is going to put us all to shame.

KESAVANNAMBUTHIRI: You need not fear that—let her talk for a while with the Nambuthiri. Then she herself will insist on this sambandam.

PANCHUMENON: Right, right. Yes, it is only when I hear your words that I feel happy again—all right. Let me go off for a bath. It would be proper if your highness waited for a little while.

KESAVANNAMBUTHIRI: Certainly.

Kesavannambuthiri's words gave Panchumenon intense pleasure. ('If Indulekha talks to the Nambuthiripad she will make him her husband.') Good—this is a good plan. Kesavannambuthiri and I want this very much. The girl is a little stubborn. But Kesavannambuthiri says she will be charmed when she meets the Nambuthiripad. Therefore, the letter was sent. Let him win her over. If she still does not yield, I'm not responsible for it. I would say that it was because the Nambuthiripad was incompetent and couldn't overcome her resistance. Other than that, what can I do! I have only vowed that I won't hand her over to Madhavan—I haven't vowed that I will give this girl to the Nambuthiripad. If the Nambuthiripad is capable, let him make her his wife. If that doesn't materialize, we should look for another person. This was how Panchumenon thought the matter over and debated with himself contentedly, as he went off to bathe. However, he also felt that he should talk to Kesavannambuthiri once again about it and make it clear to him; only then could it be clarified and settled. As soon as he had finished brushing his teeth, he returned to the front of the house. He saw Kesavannambuthiri seated there, hungry, a faded smile on his face.

KESAVANNAMBUTHIRI: Why did you return without bathing?
PANCHUMENON: Nothing. I have to add something to what I said earlier. I have to say something urgently to Govindankutty.

Drawing Govindankuttymenon close to him:

PANCHUMENON: Kutta, I told you yesterday about a sambandam for Indulekha. I have to say one more thing to Kesavannambuthiri about that matter in your presence. I have only promised that I won't give Indulekha to Madhavan. I have not said that I would give her to the Nambuthiripad. Only if she consents, will this sambandam take place and I have let Kesavannambuthiri know that. I am not the one to let a sambandam take place that is against Indulekha's wishes. If it doesn't take place, I am not answerable to him. I am saying this now—I am saying this in front of you.
KESAVANNAMBUTHIRI: I will be responsible for everything. It is enough if the Nambuthiripad arrives here, that is all I wish for.

Hearing this the old man went for his bath, his mind at rest.

GOVINDANKUTTYMENON: (to Kesavannambuthiri) It is almost one o'clock. Why have you not broken your fast this morning?
KESAVANNAMBUTHIRI: They will come now. I can hear a humming—can you?
GOVINDANKUTTYMENON: Yes.

Saying this Govindankuttymenon went indoors.

It is difficult to narrate the commotion at the arrival of the Nambuthiripad. Eight people for the palanquin, six for the litter, those who were bearing these as well as those who were walking along to relieve the bearers, had been ordered to hum together. Fourteen people humming together in one voice. Two to four people crying out 'hey, hu, fo, fo, hu-hu' at the fore. This cry was the royal sign of the Nambuthiripad. It was with this festivity that the palanquin arrived at the courtyard. Though Cherusserinambuthiri alighted at the gate itself, the litter bearers kept humming until they had entered the courtyard. Everyone who lived in Panchumenon's taravad and in his own house, all of them, both young and old (excepting Indulekha and Govindankuttymenon) pushed each other around as though a battle was taking place. In every part of the house, everyone, according to his ability, and the availability of space, stood gaping at the arrival. The women stood in the rooms upstairs, pressed against the window, men and managers—all of them forgetting their meal—thronged in front of the house, taking care to keep Panchumenon in front of them. Kesavannambuthiri stood in the courtyard welcoming them and waiting to help the Nambuthiripad out of the palanquin. Manager and servants rushed into the courtyard; those who worked in the kitchen looked out of the kitchen window and through holes in the walls so that only their eyes could be seen; the servant women stood behind some banana trees, or peeped out from behind a fence. Hearing these sounds of celebration and the shouts of people calling out, the wayfarer Brahmins who were sleeping after a meal, waiting for the sun to go down a little to resume their journey, jumped up with a start and ran to the edge of the pond. They quickly occupied different places on the doorstep, treetops, at the entrance and in whichever place they could sit, even as they tied up their tufts of hair. 'What is this? Who is this?—like an earthquake,' people asked jostling each other. Needless to say, those living close to Chambazhiyot Poovally house thought that they had been hit by an earthquake. The moment the palanquin reached the courtyard, Kesavannambuthiri opened its door. Immediately, a golden statue jumped out from within. Yes, a golden statue—surely a golden statue! A cap of gold, a golden coloured dress covering the body, and the border of the sash, all gold. On the feet, a pair of footwear set with golden globules, gold rings on all ten fingers, and as though this was not enough he had draped an upper cloth of gold over himself; in his hand he held a small mirror in a gold cover—to look at himself frequently; gold-gold-gold all over! What can one say about the glow which exploded in the sunlight when the Nambuthiripad alighted from the palanquin at one-thirty. For a full metre all around him, the very sunlight glowed in hues of gold. The moment Panchumenon saw all this, the old man felt that what Kesavannambuthiri had said was going to be true. Indulekha would run after this Nambuthiri; she would run—there was no doubt about it! Soon after he had stepped out of the palanquin, everyone stood in stunned silence for half a minute. The Nambuthiripad, aware that everyone was enamoured by his dress, stood unmoving in the sun for half a minute. He peered about to see if Indulekha was standing near the door; he did this two or three times as though he was peeping in. Immediately, Panchumenon and Kesavannambuthiri together gestured, showing the way and leading this golden statue to the front of the house. They sat him down on a huge chair which had been readied for him.

NAMBUTHIRIPAD: I have heard about Panchu.
PANCHUMENON: I am greatly honoured that you have come here.
NAMBUTHIRIPAD: Karuthedam, please sit down—where is Cherusseri?
CHERUSSERINAMBUTHIRI: I am here.
NAMBUTHIRIPAD: Sit down...please do sit.
CHERUSSERINAMBUTHIRI: I will.
NAMBUTHIRIPAD: Why aren't you sitting? Karuthedam? Sit down.
PANCHUMENON: I don't know why your royalty was late in coming—maybe you haven't had your meal.
NAMBUTHIRIPAD: It is over, we ate in the morning. I couldn't start as planned because of a mountainside controversy. I was late, a little bit, so I started after breakfast.

Cherusseri laughed to himself thinking that shaving off his beard was the great work of the mountainside.

PANCHUMENON: Your slave had thought that you may be busy with various matters.
KESAVANNAMBUTHIRI: Hadn't I told you?
PANCHUMENON: There is no need to wait any longer for your bath. Didn't you have your breakfast quite early?
KESAVANNAMBUTHIRI: Everything is ready for a bath.
NAMBUTHIRIPAD: Oh! Karuthedam, I think you haven't had your bath.
KESAVANNAMBUTHIRI: No.
NAMBUTHIRIPAD: Then we will go and have a bath.

All of them started towards the bath house.

While the Nambuthiripad was seated there he had peeped indoors about seven or eight times. And he doubted whether the one or two women he saw was Indulekha. After everyone had gone for a bath, Panchumenon came inside and sat down for his meal.

PANCHUMENON: (to his wife) The Nambuthiripad is a great man.

KUNJIKUTTTYAMMA: I have never seen anyone like this before. Indulekha's horoscope is certainly marvellous. What the astrologer said some time ago has come true. He had said that she would get a great man as a husband very soon.

PANCHUMENON: Did Indulekha see the Nambuthiripad—was she here downstairs?

KUNJIKUTTYAMMA: She did not come downstairs. She must have watched from upstairs.

PANCHUMENON: You should find out. Did Lakshmikutty see him?

KUNJIKUTTYAMMA: She stood with me inside and looked at him for a long time. Then she went to her room.

PANCHUMENON: This sambandam will take place, that is for sure.

KUNJIKUTTYAMMA: If this sambandam does not take place it is our ill luck.

PANCHUMENON: I feel it will certainly take place.

KUNJIKUTTYAMMA: If this does not take place, no greater calamity can befall us.

PANCHUMENON: I have no doubt—it will happen.

KUNJIKUTTYAMMA: I too have no doubts. Indulekha is not a stupid girl.

PANCHUMENON: Anyway, we will know soon enough. I firmly believe that she will definitely agree. Go quickly and try and talk to her—then we will know for certain.

KUNJIKUTTYAMMA: I will go immediately.

chapter ten

A Letter from Madras

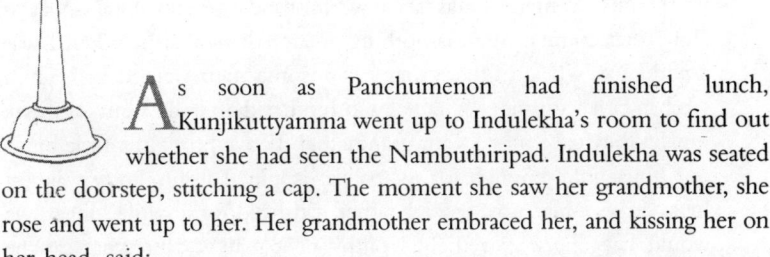

As soon as Panchumenon had finished lunch, Kunjikuttyamma went up to Indulekha's room to find out whether she had seen the Nambuthiripad. Indulekha was seated on the doorstep, stitching a cap. The moment she saw her grandmother, she rose and went up to her. Her grandmother embraced her, and kissing her on her head, said:

KUNJIKUTTYAMMA: My dear, a great fortune has come your way! Did you see the procession?

INDULEKHA: Why, was there a festival in the temple? Why didn't you call me, Grandmother? How many elephants were there? I didn't hear the music or the drums.

KUNJIKUTTYAMMA: Not the temple procession! The Nambuthiripad's procession!

INDULEKHA: (the glow on her face faded as she moved away from her grandmother's embrace) I didn't see it.

KUNJIKUTTYAMMA: You didn't guess? Even after all this festivity?

INDULEKHA: What festivity? I didn't see anything!

KUNJIKUTTYAMMA: If you sit upstairs with your door shut, stitching away, what will you see? The Nambuthiripad is worth seeing. He is very handsome. Clothes of solid gold! My dear, I am sixty years old and I have never seen anyone like this. He is at his royal meal—as soon as he has finished he will come here. In fact, I think he will come upstairs to see you. Cherusserinambuthiri, who was here a while ago, has also come with him. He is reluctant even to sit in the Nambuthiripad's presence. The wealth of his household defies description. Even the chain that tethers the elephant is made of gold. Make sure everything is neat and tidy when he comes upstairs.

INDULEKHA: This place is never untidy at anytime. Why is he coming upstairs—what reason does he have to see me?

KUNJIKUTTYAMMA: What other reason could he have to come to our house? He has come because he has heard about you. My dear, take care to talk to him politely. I have been waiting eagerly for a very long time to set my eyes on a great man arriving as your husband. I now believe I've had the opportunity. Nothing more fortunate can happen to my child. If women become prosperous, they will make their taravads prosperous. Women should take good husbands—eventually it is wealth alone that counts; there is nothing greater than wealth. When I was a child I was beautiful, so many handsome men wanted to begin a sambandam with me. My father and mother didn't allow any of them. Finally they gave me to your grandfather. I have brought a little bit to our household, enough for us to live happily. Lakshmikutty was not lucky in a similar way. If your father had lived for a while longer, we would have been extremely wealthy people now. But what can be done about that! We didn't have that kind of luck. And now the young girls in our taravad will become wealthy. But nobody as wealthy as you, my dear! In our taravad there has never been as fine a sambandam as the one you have now. That is why I said it is luck.

INDULEKHA: Is that so? Has the Nambuthiripad begun a sambandam with me? How is it that I don't know about it?

KUNJIKUTTYAMMA: Now...now...it is as though the sambandam is already over! After coming all the way, how can a great person like him go without a sambandam? You must be mad to think otherwise. If this Nambuthiripad doesn't begin a sambandam who will?

INDULEKHA: All right Grandmother, whatever you say. Let me go and sleep for a while.

KUNJIKUTTYAMMA: My dear, you shouldn't sleep during the day. Let me bring you that gold necklace with *thali*s embedded with emeralds, and that thoda studded with precious stones. When the Nambuthiripad comes up here on his royal visit, you should meet him wearing fine jewellery.

INDULEKHA: I will not wear any such thing, that is for sure. But now I want to rest for a while.

KUNJIKUTTYAMMA: My dear girl, even if you don't wear any jewellery it is all right—you do not need ornaments. When the Nambuthiripad comes, you should speak to him charmingly so that he is attracted to you.

Kunjikuttyamma then went downstairs while Lakshmikuttyamma came up. Indulekha and Lakshmikuttyamma exchanged glances and smiled.

LAKSHMIKUTTYAMMA: There was such festivity with the coming of the Nambuthiripad. In my opinion, the man is a complete fool. He will soon be coming up to this room.

INDULEKHA: Let him.

LAKSHMIKUTTYAMMA: He will say that he wants a relationship.

INDULEKHA: With whom?

LAKSHMIKUTTYAMMA: With you!

INDULEKHA: As soon as he comes in?

LAKSHMIKUTTYAMMA: (laughing) Maybe! Yes, I think he will say it immediately.

INDULEKHA: If he says it like that, my servant Ammu can answer him.

LAKSHMIKUTTYAMMA: If Madhavan also were here it would have been such fun.

LAKSHMIKUTTYAMMA: (seeing the change that came over Indulekha's face the moment she heard Madhavan's name) Oh! ho! my dear child, your life is already in Madras, there is no doubt about it. I think you are very troubled. Don't worry. God will allow only that to happen which is good.

INDULEKHA: My mind is not troubled greatly. Is there absolutely no news from Madras?

LAKSHMIKUTTYAMMA: Govindankutty did not say anything in particular.

INDULEKHA: Has Cherusserinambuthiri also come?

LAKSHMIKUTTYAMMA: Yes, he too has sat down for his meal. Let me go now. Get ready for a battle with the Nambuthiripad!

Saying this Lakshmikuttyamma went downstairs.

Indulekha was extremely happy when she heard that Cherusserinambuthiri had come. Though they had been acquainted for only five or six days, both Indulekha and Madhavan were impressed by his intelligence, taste, and amiability. However, at that point Indulekha felt a little indisposed to see him. Earlier when she had met Cherusserinambuthiri, Madhavan had been with her. Indulekha was aware that he knew and was happy about the understanding between them. It was likely that he was also aware of the reason behind the Nambuthiripad visit. She felt a little uneasy because she thought that Cherusseri might feel contempt for her. But assured that the contempt would soon fade away, she went inside to try and sleep.

After some time she saw her servant Ammu come in with a paper in her hand.

INDULEKHA: What is it, Ammu?
AMMU: This is a letter from Madras. Kuttanmenon master asked me to give it to you.

She handed Indulekha the letter.

Indulekha took the letter anxiously and stood up to read it. There were two letters. One was opened. I am transcribing it below:

At eight o' clock in the night, the day Kuttan left, I got a letter from Gilham sayiv confirming my appointment in the secretariat. I have joined work today. I hope Kuttan and others are keeping well. I will take a week's leave and come over on the train that leaves the day after tomorrow or the day after that. I request you to give the letters enclosed to my father and Madhavi.

How should I let you know of Indulekha's happiness the moment she read this? A difficult task. Tears of joy filled her eyes quite naturally. Then she opened the letter and read it again. The contents of this letter need not be made public. After Indulekha read that letter she did some ridiculous things. First I thought I wouldn't recount them but then I decided to describe them because some (reader) might be of the opinion that because of my partiality for her I am not telling the story truthfully. After reading Madhavan's letter, Indulekha kissed it over and over again. She then opened her letter desk, put the two letters inside and locked it. She then sent Ammu to find out whether Govindankuttymenon had had his tea. He told Ammu that he was just going over to see Indulekha.

Lakshmikuttyamma heard from Govindankuttymenon that Madhavan had got a job. Overjoyed, she came upstairs and met Indulekha. She was even happier when she saw how happy her daughter was.

LAKSHMIKUTTYAMMA: Succeeded, hasn't he?
INDULEKHA: God's blessing—that he got a job so quickly.
LAKSHMIKUTTYAMMA: What about the oath then?

INDULEKHA: Let that be. I shall go very soon to Madras, Mother—you won't object, will you?
LAKSHMIKUTTYAMMA: I do not have any objection to my daughter going anywhere with Madhavan. My poor dear, for how many days have you been distraught. Even then, I fear that Father will be displeased.
INDULEKHA: You need not worry about that, Mother. My grandfather is a very simple man. He is also very fond of me. If I fall at his feet and cry he will listen to me and accept the fair request I place before him—I am convinced about that.

As they were talking thus, Madhavan's mother (Parvathiamma) came upstairs.

PARVATHIAMMA: What is it my dear, has Madhavan got a job yet?
INDULEKHA: A letter has come saying that he has got a job. It is your luck. He has got a good job very quickly.
PARVATHIAMMA: From now Madhavan has to live in Madras. That is the only reason for my sorrow.
INDULEKHA: He won't have to live there for long. There is a probability that he will soon get a better job and come back to this place.
PARVATHIAMMA: If so, it will be good. My God! For how long have I been living away from my child!
INDULEKHA: Now you can go and live in Madras.
PARVATHIAMMA: Me alone?
INDULEKHA: I too will come with you.
PARVATHIAMMA: Oh, that would be very nice. But for no reason Madhavan has started a quarrel with valiammaman.
INDULEKHA: So will you or will you not come with me?
PARVATHIAMMA: God! Let God make that possible. My son will not need greater luck than that. But then there is this difficulty.

Just then they saw Govindankuttymenon coming up. Lakshmikuttyamma and Parvathiamma went downstairs. Govindankuttymenon was also delighted to see Indulekha visibly happy. They stood without speaking for some time. Then:

GOVINDANKUTTYMENON: Indulekha, prepare to leave for Madras. Didn't you read that Madhavan will set off from there either tomorrow or the day after?

Indulekha stood there silently, saying nothing. In her happiness, she flushed and paled by turn. Though Govindankuttymenon was also happy, he was a little troubled when he thought of his father's oath. Govindankuttymenon had no doubt that Madhavan would go off with the girl. So he was not at all worried about Indulekha. He was worried about how to make it all possible with the consent of his ageing father. However, his demeanour did not reflect even the slightest anxiety.

GOVINDANKUTTYMENON: The Nambuthiripad has come, didn't you hear about it?

INDULEKHA: Yes.

GOVINDANKUTTYMENON: My father said something very appropriate about this matter. It gave me great happiness.

INDULEKHA: What did he say?

GOVINDANKUTTYMENON: This sambandam will take place only if you are so inclined. He will not try to force you into it. He said this to both Kesavannambuthiri and me; so Indulekha, you need not worry at all.

INDULEKHA: If that is my grandfather's wish, why did he bring him here?

GOVINDANKUTTYMENON: That is to test whether Indulekha would be attracted to him upon seeing him.

Govindankuttymenon went back to his room. As he was going downstairs he said, 'If there is a letter to be sent to Madras, seal it and send it down. I shall post it with my letter.'

It is very painful for me to tease Indulekha. Even then I'm not concealing any part of the story. Why did someone so intelligent as Indulekha behave so stupidly? I cannot refrain from asking! As soon as Govindankuttymenon went downstairs, Indulekha reopened the letter box and taking out the letter expressed her joy. She then put it back into the box and locked it up.

Happiness made her too weak to lie down, sit, or stand and she felt exhausted. Govindankuttymenon wrote a letter to Madhavan, and placing it on the table, went to meet Madhavan's father at his house.

Govindapanikkar was sitting in the fore region of the house. He smiled when he saw Govindankuttymenon.

GOVINDANKUTTYMENON: *Jeshta*, didn't you see the arrival of the Nambuthiripad?

(Govindankuttymenon addresses Govindapanikkar as *jeshtan*.)

GOVINDAPANIKKAR: No, I didn't. I heard the humming of the palanquin bearers. I am just going to Polpayi*kalam*. For the time being if I stand here, it is not going to be auspicious. Your father might send a man for me. Then he will ask me to think further about the Nambuthiripad's sambandam. I do not want to get involved, so I will stay over today and tomorrow and come back only the day after.

GOVINDANKUTTYMENON: I too shall come along. I cannot bear the Nambuthiripad's vulgar displays—I shall also come.

GOVINDAPANIKKAR: But please inform your father. Otherwise he will get angry with me.

Immediately, Govindankuttymenon sent a man to his house and had his clothes and other things brought over and set off for Polpayikalam. Having arranged with a man to inform his father if he asked about him, Govindapanikkar and he set off together.

chapter eleven

What People Said about the Nambuthiripad

MUTHU: (from inside the *oottupura*) How grand! Hey, I have never seen anyone costumed like this Nambuthiripad. What a fancy gown! What a cap! The cloth draped over his gown must be quite expensive. Certainly a wealthy man. And handsome too.

SHANKARASHASTRI: What did you find handsome? The drape, or the gown? I thought his face was exactly like that of a horse.

MAANU: You are always jealous. The Nambuthiripad's face like that of a horse? What a shame! From which angle did you see it? I was standing close, almost touching the palanquin. The Nambuthiripad has the complexion of burnished gold! A very handsome man! As for that gold chain about his neck, I have never seen anything like it.

SUBBUKUTTY: Eh! That is not a chain meant for the neck; it is the chain of a watch. He must have tucked the watch somewhere into his waist.

SHANKARASHASTRI: Whatever his complexion, or however many chains he may wear, his face is that of a horse.

MAANU: I think Shastrikal has gone mad. All of us think that there is no one as handsome as this Nambuthiri. Isn't that so, Shinu? Subbukutty, what do you say? What do the rest of you think?

SUBBUKUTTY: We all think that he is handsome.

SHANKARASHASTRI: I don't care what you think. He has the face of a horse.

A WAYFARER PATTAR: Don't know when the ceremony is going to be held.

SUBBUKUTTY: Heard that it is tomorrow.

SHANKARASHASTRI: Who told you?

SUBBUKUTTY: Somebody did.

SHANKARASHASTRI: Don't slow down that wayfarer. (To the wayfarer) Hey! Go and enquire at the house. Don't believe anything that this man says.
A PATTAR WHO ENTERED THE OOTTUPURA: The ceremony is this very day. There is going to be a quarter rupee each for Brahmins, and half a rupee each for Nambuthiris.
SHANKARASHASTRI: Who told you all this?
THE PATTAR WHO HAD JUST ARRIVED: Someone mentioned it at the bath house.
SHANKARASHASTRI: (to the wayfarer) Go and find out.
THE WAYFARER: If it is today, shouldn't they be preparing for the meal now? I don't see any bustle.
SHANKARASHASTRI: It may not be today.
KRISHNA THE ASTROLOGER: Shouldn't the horoscopes be matched?
SUBBUKUTTY: What does a horoscope matter when there is money? Wealth is everything. How is it possible that they will not match?
KRISHNA THE ASTROLOGER: If they had given us some money, I would have said that the match is perfect, that they are especially suited to each other. Who among the Nairs really cares about horoscopes? The Nambuthiripad has come here secretly. He has sambandams in a hundred places.
SHANKARASHASTRI: If he has come secretly, he has to look for another person.
SUBBUKUTTY: I heard that you, Shastrikal, went to Poovarangu some days ago to read *Shakuntalam* there. At that time you must have got a sense of that girl's grit—people who have studied shastram are all stupid in the same way.
MUTHU: If the Nambuthiripad presents her with a ring, a hundred Indulekhas will agree.

Without replying, Shankarashastrikal got up and walked to the temple. This Shastrikal was a good friend of Madhavan's and a very learned man. He knew Indulekha well and knew that her intellect was special. Therefore, what he heard made him uncomfortable. In Shastrikal's opinion, Madhavan was the most suitable man for Indulekha. 'If this sambandam takes place, it will be a real pity! Sometimes things like this do happen because of the importance given to wealth—what can be done? There is nothing in the world that can vanquish wealth.'

Deep in thought and feeling very sad about all this, Shastrikal went up to the temple gatehouse, spread out his upper cloth, and lay down to sleep.

Shastrikal had problems even there: a few minutes later a crowd had assembled in the gatehouse. *Warrier* and a *maraan* were the ones to emerge.

WARRIER: (to Shastrikal) What are you doing here, Shastrikal swami! I think today at Poovarangu there is no reading of plays and such things. There is a crowd at the bathing place. The Nambuthiripad is at his royal meal. Shastrikal, did you find out whether the sambandam will take place today itself?

SHASTRIKAL: I did not find out anything. Let me sleep for some time.

By then the priest Embranthiri, a few Nambuthiris and pattars were seen entering through the door of the northern gateway, shouting like a gang of raiders. The talk was all about the Nambuthiripad himself.

EMBRANTHIRI: The Nambuthiripad is a very handsome man. I saw him. I wonder how old he is?

ONE NAMBUTHIRI: He must be at least fifty years old.

ANOTHER NAMBUTHIRI: Chi! He is not that old. He must be forty or forty-five at the most.

ONE PATTAR: Never mind his age, Indulekha will agree. What clothes, what bearing—can't even imagine it! I have not seen clothes such as these even on the Lord of Ananthashayanam.

ANOTHER NAMBUTHIRI: These clothes, appearance, and plenty of money—that's all he has. The Nambuthiri is a man unduly fond of women; he is not dependable or even capable. Why are they giving Indulekha to that lecher? Is the sambandam taking place today?

EMBRANTHIRI: Yes, we will ask Shastrikal and make sure. Shastrikal is an acquaintance of Indulekha. Eh! Shastrikal, asleep during daytime, are you? Don't sleep, wake up.

Shastrikal had shut his eyes and was lying down as if he were asleep. When he could no longer ignore the Embranthiri's persistent calls, he sat up.

EMBRANTHIRI: Is Indulekha's sambandam today?

SHANKARASHASTRIKAL: I do not know about any sambandam.

Thereafter the Shastrikal rose and walked away.

The people at Poovally also had much to say about the Nambuthiripad.

KUMMINIAMMA: Chathere, I haven't seen anyone as impressive as this. I was dazzled by him.

CHATHARAMENON: You were dazzled by his clothes!
KUMMINIAMMA: I don't know. I haven't seen an appearance such as his ever in my life. I remember having seen valiammaman, the Dewanji, but he didn't carry himself with such aplomb. Just think of Indulekha's luck; she is smart. Even so, when I think of Madhavan I feel sad.
CHATHARAMENON: Why?
KUMMINIAMMA: There is nothing to be sad about. If such a great man makes an offer, Madhavan shouldn't object. Even so, it does sadden me to think of him.
CHATHARAMENON: Mother, you are mad. This Nambuthiripad won't get Indulekha in this birth. Indulekha is for Madhavan. This is all a fancy game for valiammaman.
KUMMINIAMMA: You are mad.

The opinions expressed in the kitchen, bathing house, near the bank of the pond and so on were also divided.

On the bank of the river, one youngster said to another: 'Hey, what is the name of this Nambuthiripad?'

'It seems it is *Kannil Mukillatha Vasuri** Nambuthiripad.'

'That's not a pleasant name, that is for sure.'

'It is not name that matters but money. It seems the chain of the elephant in his mana is made of gold. Then what does it matter if he doesn't have a nose—or has smallpox?'

'So what if he has such wealth. Indulekha has rejected Madhavan and I have lost my respect for her. Madhavan is the right husband for her.'

'Does Madhavan have elephant chains made of gold? How stupidly you talk! Women value wealth above all.'

'It's been an utter waste of money that Kochukrishnamenon had her tutored in English. What is so special now about her English education? That too is only for money.'

'What will Madhavan say when he comes to know of this?'

'Madhavan's fury will rise like Shishupalan's. But what good will that do? Indulekha will continue to be happy with the noseless, pock-marked Nambuthiripad.'

*Kannil Mukillatha Vasuri Nambuthiripad: a cruel black description which means the noseless, pock-marked (disfigured) Nambuthiripad.

'This Nambuthiripad's illam is indeed appropriately named. Some time back I saw him from close quarters. I could not even see his nose. His face is like an overturned pot. Chi! Why is it Indulekha's fate to be so? His money and rubbish are the same to me. If I were Indulekha's ammaman, like Govindankuttymenon there, I would not have given her to this pock-marked fellow.'

'And if Indulekha wants it?'

'Then there is no help for it. Do you think Indulekha would be willing? I heard that this is taking place at the insistence of Panchumenon.'

'Why can't that Panchumenon just die? Must he remain alive to curse and injure the people in the household? It is a pity that such an ugly person is to wed Indulekha!'

'There is still time to decide. Do you think Indulekha will consent? What if she does not?'

'Panchumenon will beat her and drive her out of the house. Besides, Madhavan is not here. This is the most fitting sambandam for her in this birth. It seems there is nobody in the kingdom as rich as he is. Who needs anything else? Isn't Madhavan still a school boy?'

'I have heard that Madhavan and Indulekha are very fond of each other.'

'All that will just disappear. If Madhavan ever had a *shukradasha* [good period] it is over.'

'Let whatever is to be, be.'

Saying thus, one of the men went off to bathe and the other to his house.

In Poovarangu, people spoke about the Nambuthiripad in different ways. I mentioned to you earlier that after Indulekha received the letter from Madras she was overjoyed and excited. Some servants who did not know the reason for her excitement thought that it must have something to do with the arrival of the Nambuthiripad. Kunjikuttyamma's maidservant went upstairs for some work. She saw Indulekha, who smilingly asked her:

'What is it, Paru? Doesn't the man you have sambandam with visit these days?'

PARU: He has been staying at another place for six or seven months. He has another sambandam there—Kandaranair told me.

INDULEKHA: All right, shall I fix up a sambandam for you with another man?

PARU: I don't want anyone. The *thali* on my neck is broken. For four months my neck has been bare. I reminded my *valiamma* [senior mistress] many times—she doesn't get it repaired for me. What shall I do!

When she heard the maid's sorrowful story, Indulekha opened one of her boxes and took out a thali from it worth Rs 8 or Rs 10, threaded it on a string, and gave it to Paru.

INDULEKHA: Here, wear this thali. Now you need not be sad because you haven't got a thali.

Paru wept with joy. She took the thali and immediately on reaching the ground floor, joyfully told everyone about the gift she got. Kunjikuttyamma saw that Paru was wearing a new thali.

KUNJIKUTTYAMMA: Where did you get this thali from?
PARU: When I went upstairs, *cheriamma* [young mistress] gave it to me.
KUNJIKUTTYAMMA: Indulekha?
PARU: Yes.
KUNJIKUTTYAMMA: Why is Indulekha so happy today? What is the reason for her good mood?
PARU: Great happiness. How can she not be happy, valiamme, when such a lord comes seeking a sambandam with her?

While they were talking thus, Shankarashastrikal came up to Poovarangu to see Indulekha. Kunjikuttyamma saw him and called out.

KUNJIKUTTYAMMA: Shastrikal, why have you come now?
SHASTRIKAL: Nothing special. I just came to see if I could meet Indulekha.

Kunjikuttyamma knew that Shastrikal was a good friend of Madhavan.

KUNJIKUTTYAMMA: Don't go there now. The Nambuthiripad and the others are due to arrive now. It would be better if you were to go back to the temple.
SHASTRIKAL: Let it be so. The Nambuthiripad must have decided on a sambandam.
KUNJIKUTTYAMMA: Why, don't you approve of it, Shastrikal? Who else would be a more suitable husband for Indulekha?
SHASTRIKAL: True, true.
KUNJIKUTTYAMMA: Indulekha is also very happy. She has been waiting for a long time to see the Nambuthiripad. The girl is excited; Paru here went upstairs without a thali and look, she gave Paru a really good one. She is very happy. Initially I was a bit nervous but with

the blessings of God and our ancestors everything has turned out well.

SHASTRIKAL: Why were you anxious at first?

KUNJIKUTTYAMMA: Oh that—don't you know? Madhavan and Indulekha are very much in love. I thought it would be very difficult to separate them. Govindankutty's father was also a little anxious. Now, none of us have that fear. How much better this Nambuthiripad would be than Madhavan! Don't you think so?

SHASTRIKAL: Infinitely better. Infinitely better. I'm leaving now.

Shastrikal walked away, unhappily. He passed by the Nambuthiripad making his way in a jubilant procession to Poovarangu. The golden attire of the Nambuthiripad dazzled him. He sat down, deep in thought at the base of the peepul tree.

'What a pity! In this matter I don't think there is any room for much doubt. How sad Madhavan will be! How has this great sinner Indulekha become so hard-hearted? How terribly hard-hearted! What will these wretched Nair women not do! They think that whoever has more money should be their husband! How could I even for a moment have thought that this good-for-nothing girl's intelligence was similar to Madhavan's. What a shame! But what can be done?'

While he was mulling over things thus, Govindan, the one in charge of the betel leaves box and another boy approached and stood by the peepul tree.

SHASTRIKAL: Are you the people who came with the Nambuthiripad?

GOVINDAN: Yes.

SHASTRIKAL: How many days is the Nambuthiripad going to stay here?

GOVINDAN: Today and tomorrow definitely. I think the day after tomorrow he will take leave. He will take her with him.

SHASTRIKAL: What will he take?

GOVINDAN: His wife.

SHASTRIKAL: Is the sambandam today itself?

GOVINDAN: Most probably, otherwise it could be tomorrow.

SHASTRIKAL: The Nambuthiripad has not gone in for a *veli*, has he?

GOVINDAN: His two younger brothers, their lordships, have gone in for a veli.

SHASTRIKAL: Is the Nambuthiripad a capable person?

GOVINDAN: Extremely. There has not been anybody like him in that mana.

He is also very powerful. The fact that his lordship has come here and is taking up this sambandam is great luck for this taravad and Panchumenon. He doesn't often visit Nair houses like this.

Saying this Govindan walked away. The boy sat down.

SHASTRIKAL: (to the boy) Where do you come from?
THE BOY: Govindarajapuram.
SHASTRIKAL: For how long have you been with the Nambuthiripad?
THE BOY: It's been six years, but till today he has not given me a salary. Once I protested and he gave me Rs 50, but took it back after two days. Since then, he has not given me anything. If I had got something I would have left. When I ask for money, he says he will pay with interest. He is very attracted towards women. He has got about twenty sambandams now. One woman for two months; he doesn't look after the matters at the mana at all. That boy Govindan said that the Nambuthiripad doesn't go to Nair houses. It's a lie—he will visit wherever there is a woman. At no time does he have any money. Two or three Mappilas are ready to lend him money at Rs 5 interest for every hundred. This stupid man will write off anything in his hurry to get money. Soon he will write off his property. Is it an insignificant matter that he wastes money like this? For this journey, he had to borrow Rs 300 at Rs 5 interest for a hundred. He is mad about women.
SHASTRIKAL: All right, don't say anything against your master. I did not ask you anything about these things. I am going to take a bath.

Shastrikal went to the pond and the boy to the rest house for Brahmins.

chapter twelve

Conversation between Indulekha and the Nambuthiripad

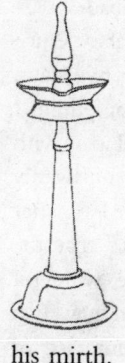

As soon as the Nambuthiripad finished his bath and his meal, Kesavannambuthiri told him what Panchumenon had said earlier. Cherusserinambuthiri was also with him. Suppressing his mirth,

CHERUSSERINAMBUTHIRI: That is how it should be. '*Kavitha vanitha chaiva swayamevagatha vara*'. (Poetry and women should come of their own accord; only then it is worthwhile—this is the rule.). As to whether Indulekha will come or not I have not the slightest doubt.
KESAVANNAMBUTHIRI: There can't be two opinions on this. Let's go there now, it is four o'clock.
NAMBUTHIRIPAD: All right. Cherusseri! I shall wear a gown. I felt that the gown I wore earlier sat rather well on me. When I got out of the palanquin, it seemed to glow in the light of the sun.
CHERUSSERINAMBUTHIRI: Naturally, that cloth of gold was Rs 95 for a measure, wasn't it? That's what you should wear now.

Wearing the gown, cap, upper cloth, rings, and the gold-studded chappals, the Nambuthiripad alongwith Cherusseri, Kesavannambuthiri, and the servants arrived at the front of Poovarangu house. Panchumenon immediately escorted him indoors and seated him on a huge chair and stood by silently.

NAMBUTHIRIPAD: Is Indulekha's room adjacent to this?
PANCHUMENON: If your slave may say so—yes; the western door of the southern room opens onto her malika.

'Then I shall proceed regally to that room,' said the Nambuthiripad. Before Panchumenon could ask where he was, Kesavannambuthiri himself rushed in saying 'I shall let Indulekha know', and ran to her malika. At that time Indulekha was writing a letter. When she saw the Nambuthiri she rose rather hastily and asked, 'What is the matter?'

KESAVANNAMBUTHIRI: He has expressed his wish to see you. Your grandfather and he are waiting downstairs—shall I ask them to come up?
INDULEKHA: Let them come.
KESAVANNAMBUTHIRI: He is a great Nambuthiripad. I hope you will be careful how you speak to him, Indulekha.
INDULEKHA: I don't know how I should speak. I have no idea; it would be best if he didn't come to see me at all—that will be better.
KESAVANNAMBUTHIRI: Why shouldn't he come? Speak your mind.
INDULEKHA: That is what I have also decided.

Kesavannambuthiri went downstairs to call the Nambuthiripad.

Indulekha planned how she would write humorously to Madhavan about the many things after her meeting with to the Nambuthiripad. She took the half-written letter and other things and put them away in the letter box. She then came out to the purathalam and stood there holding on to a support like a child standing up to take an examination. Meanwhile, Kesavannambuthiri asked the Nambuthiripad to go up (to Indulekha's room). Panchumenon went up with him only till the southern room.

KESAVANNAMBUTHIRI: Indulekha does not know how to speak according to the established custom and manner.
NAMBUTHIRIPAD: Having learnt so much English, doesn't she know even this? Even Meghadantan sayiv addresses me in the established manner. Never mind, if she agrees to be my wife, I will teach her all that. Let her speak in any manner now.
KESAVANNAMBUTHIRI: Yes, that is right. You are very wise!
NAMBUTHIRIPAD: The moment she becomes my wife everything will be as I wish.

Then, making a lot of noise, he went up the stairs. On reaching the veranda he saw that gorgeous gem—Indulekha—leaning against the balustrade. He felt as if lightning had struck his eyes. Dazed, he stared and continued staring at the beautiful Indulekha. So strong was her magnetism that he stood motionless for a minute or two. 'I have never seen beauty like this—it is really my great luck. She will lust after me. From now I will not go to any other woman. Other than her, I shall not even think about another woman. That's for sure.' Thus thought the Nambuthiripad on coming back to himself and indeed upon seeing Indulekha's figure.

Indulekha gazed at the Nambuthiripad steadily. She wasn't staring; Indulekha didn't know how to stare. Kesavannambuthiri immediately pulled out a chair for the Nambuthiripad to sit on it. Then he left. The Nambuthiripad could not take his eyes off Indulekha. She too kept looking at him. Finally:

NAMBUTHIRIPAD: When I came you were downstairs—weren't you? I thought I saw you.

He stretched his lips and smiled widely.

INDULEKHA: I wasn't.

The 'I' startled the Nambuthiripad. A Nair lady had never spoken to him like that, but dazzled by Indulekha's beauty, the Nambuthiripad ignored these minor irritations.

NAMBUTHIRIPAD: Didn't you come downstairs at all?
INDULEKHA: No, not at all.
NAMBUTHIRIPAD: Why didn't you?
INDULEKHA: There was no reason.
NAMBUTHIRIPAD: I could not come on the day that was first decided upon. I sent a letter—didn't you see it?
INDULEKHA: No.
NAMBUTHIRIPAD: Didn't Karuthedam show it to you?
INDULEKHA: No, he didn't.
NAMBUTHIRIPAD: Karuthedam is a big idiot. The day I decided to set out, Makshaman sayiv, who leases the cardamom estate, arrived without warning. The estate had been leased for Rs 8000—because of that I couldn't come on the appointed day. My meeting with you kept getting delayed. I have heard so much about you that I feel I already know you. Indulekha, you must be the daughter of Karuthedam before his sambandam with your mother.
INDULEKHA: Whose daughter? Karuthedam Nambuthiri's? No I am not, I am King Ramavarma's daughter.

NAMBUTHIRIPAD: Yes, yes—that is what I said.
INDULEKHA: If that is so, it is all right.

The Nambuthiripad wondered what he should say next; there was something that he should have said. After a while:

NAMBUTHIRIPAD: Reports of your beauty have made me quite powerless.
INDULEKHA: I can't understand why you felt so vulnerable.
NAMBUTHIRIPAD: I've ignored the matters of the mana.
INDULEKHA: That's really worrisome. Am I the person who prevents you from attending to the matters of the mana? What is the reason for this?
NAMBUTHIRIPAD: Yesterday Cherusseri recited a sloka. I have a desire to recite it to you, Indulekha. I heard that you have been tutored in English. Will you understand a Sanskrit sloka?
INDULEKHA: It will be very difficult.
NAMBUTHIRIPAD: If you wish to be fluent you should read a lot in that language.
INDULEKHA: Yes.
NAMBUTHIRIPAD: I will recite a sloka. See if you can understand it. If not, I shall explain it to you.
INDULEKHA: It is very doubtful whether I'll understand the meaning.
NAMBUTHIRIPAD: Then I will explain it to you.

The Nambuthiripad thought of a sloka to recite. He could remember only one or two. Since his knowledge of the language was not very sound, he was prone to making blunders and forgetting words and lines. After much thought he could remember only half a sloka.

NAMBUTHIRIPAD: *Astham piiyushabhava sumathigarajarala hari prasidha.* I can't remember the rest. Do you know Cherusseri? He said that you know him. We are always together. He is the one who recites the slokas. I find it very difficult to remember all this. Anyway, where is the time for remembering slokas when one is so busy with everyday matters! But the sloka that I recited is very special. Why—why are you so startled? Let me try again: *Aastham piiyushabhava sumathigarajarala ithi prasidha.*
INDULEKHA: (laughing) You need not trouble yourself, recite when you remember it.

NAMBUTHIRIPAD: Chi! Let me try and finish the sloka. *Aastham piiyushabhava sumathigarajarala ithi prasidha.* O-ho, got it, got it. *Thallabhopayaghinnapicha garalaharo hethurullasabhava.* I cannot remember the next two lines at all. No use trying to recollect them. *Aastham piiyushabhava....* Oh, did I forget it again? This is a real problem. Oh ho no, I got it. *Aastham piiyushabhava sumathigarajarala ithi prasidha. Thallabhopayaghinnapicha garalaharo hethurullasabhava.*

After repeatedly trying, he confessed he couldn't remember any further. He walked out to call Karuthedam. Kesavannambuthiri was waiting at the stairwell and came running.

NAMBUTHIRIPAD: Karuthedam, go to Cherusseri and get the complete sloka of *Aastham* on a palmyra. Do it quickly.

Kesavannambuthiri ran off. He found Cherusseri sitting on a chair in the *nalukettu*. By then Kesavannambuthiri had himself forgotten the word.

KESAVANNAMBUTHIRI: Cherusseri, the Nambuthiripad has asked me to get you to write a sloka for him. Please write it down quickly. Here is the palmyra and the writing tool. The sloka? What is it...oh, let me see, yes, yes, I remember. The beginning of the sloka is *Asiil*. Please write it quickly.

Cherusseri took the palmyra and wrote:

Aasiddasaratho nama suryavamshedha parthiva
Bharyasthisroni labdhvasau thasu lebhe
na santhathim.

[There was a king called Dasharatha who was born in the clan of Surya. Though he had three wives he did not beget any children.]

Kesavannambuthiri took the palmyra and ran upstairs. The Nambuthiripad could not read even a word without his spectacles. However, he thought that wearing spectacles in front of Indulekha might not give a favourable impression of his youth. So he asked Kesavannambuthiri to read it. Kesavannambuthiri too couldn't read very well without spectacles. Nevertheless, he proceeded to obey orders.

KESAVANNAMBUTHIRI: *Aasi–dasa–ratho–namasu–ryavamshe–dhaparthiva.*

Conversation between Indulekha and the Nambuthiripad

By then Indulekha was collapsing with mirth.

NAMBUTHIRIPAD: Nonsense! This is not the sloka. I know the first line. Write it down.

He made Kesavannambuthiri write what he had said earlier. With the palmyra Kesavannambuthiri went to Cherusserinambuthiri a second time.

KESAVANNAMBUTHIRI: Cherusseri, you are always playing a joke. You did not write the sloka which the Nambuthiri had asked for. See, I have brought it written on a palmyra. Please write the whole thing.

Cherusserinambuthiri took the palmyra and looked at it. 'Oh-Oh! Is it this sloka? But didn't you say that *"Asiil"* was the first word?' He corrected the mistakes in the first two lines of the sloka and wrote out the third and fourth line. Kesavannambuthiri rushed upstairs again. The Nambuthiripad asked him to read it.

KESAVANNAMBUTHIRI: This is a big sloka. It will not come out well if I read it. Indulekha is here and she has a sound knowledge of words. Indulekha, please read it.

INDULEKHA: No, that's not true but I too know the sloka. You need not take so much trouble. I shall recite it.

Saying this and to get rid of him, she recited:

> *Aastham piiyushalabhassumughi garajara mrityuharee prasidha-*
> *sthallabhopayachinthapi cha garalajusho hethurullakhathaya*
> *Nochedaloladrishtiprathibhayabhujagii dushtakarma muhusthe*
> *Yamevalambya jive kathamadharasudha madhurimapyajanan.*
>
> [Lady with a beautiful face, it is well known that one who acquires the eternal amrit can ward off poison, old age, and death. Even the thought of acquiring it works towards a cure of a person who has been poisoned. I have to depend on you even while suffering the intensity of your look and its torturous effects. How can I live without enjoying the sweet nectar of your lips?]

NAMBUTHIRIPAD: A very special sloka, isn't it?
INDULEKHA: Yes.
NAMBUTHIRIPAD: Karuthedam, go and sit downstairs.

KESAVANNAMBUTHIRI: I shall get some betel leaves.

Saying this he went downstairs.

NAMBUTHIRIPAD: Indulekha, do you have a passion for kathakali?
INDULEKHA: Passion for what?
NAMBUTHIRIPAD: Kali—about kali.
INDULEKHA: Till now I have not been obsessed with anything.
NAMBUTHIRIPAD: I'm crazy about it—very crazy.
INDULEKHA: (laughing) Yes, that is true. There is no doubt about that.
NAMBUTHIRIPAD: Have you heard about this earlier?
INDULEKHA: No, I've heard about it just now.
NAMBUTHIRIPAD: You've learnt about it from me?
INDULEKHA: Yes.
NAMBUTHIRIPAD: There was kathakali performed at the mana. Raman's portrayal of *dashasyan* is done very well. Indulekha, have you heard about Raman? He is called Sudrar Ramapanikkar. He boasts a lot but his body and the stage effects are superb. From now on, you can watch a performance daily. Yesterday I watched a *strivesham* too. In recent times I haven't seen anything like it. Do you know of a boy named Raghavan? If he were to shave, his face would look exactly like yours. Do you have performances here often?
INDULEKHA: No.
NAMBUTHIRIPAD: How many years is it since you watched kathakali?
INDULEKHA: Four or five years.
NAMBUTHIRIPAD: Shiva-Shiva! Four to five years! Such a wealthy house and it is four or five years since a performance of kathakali took place in this house. It is surprising! That is what will happen if you do not know enough about it. Panchu also has only so much knowledge about it. So who can blame you?
INDULEKHA: Yes, I agree.
NAMBUTHIRIPAD: Indulekha, do you know English?
INDULEKHA: I have studied a good deal of it.
NAMBUTHIRIPAD: Can you talk to Englishmen?
INDULEKHA: I can talk to anyone.
NAMBUTHIRIPAD: I have heard quite a lot about you. But meeting you has gone beyond all my expectations. I must say I'm lucky.
INDULEKHA: Why?

NAMBUTHIRIPAD: Seeing you is luck indeed.

INDULEKHA: I wouldn't know why you consider yourself lucky just to see me.

NAMBUTHIRIPAD: Don't you understand even if I tell you so many times?

INDULEKHA: I can understand only as much as you tell me. How can I understand what you have not told me? When you said you are lucky I understood that, but you did not answer why you consider yourself lucky. So, how could I understand what you meant?

NAMBUTHIRIPAD: Getting a chance to meet you is my luck. And I am all admiration for your ability to argue. I have a feeling you wish me to publicize this, as if beating a drum.

INDULEKHA: There is no drum here. I am not at all interested in your drumming.

NAMBUTHIRIPAD: You are indeed very entertaining; this is how we should spar. You might have heard about me.

INDULEKHA: No.

NAMBUTHIRIPAD: Have you not heard of me at all?

INDULEKHA: No.

NAMBUTHIRIPAD: Don't you know anything about me?

INDULEKHA: No.

NAMBUTHIRIPAD: So you did not know about my arrival?

INDULEKHA: Yesterday someone said that you were coming.

NAMBUTHIRIPAD: You did not make enquiries about me?

INDULEKHA: No.

NAMBUTHIRIPAD: Why didn't you?

INDULEKHA: There was nothing to ask—that is all.

NAMBUTHIRIPAD: I hope you know the reason for my coming?

INDULEKHA: No.

NAMBUTHIRIPAD: What? Don't you know even that?

INDULEKHA: No.

NAMBUTHIRIPAD: I came here only to see you.

INDULEKHA: Yes, that could be the reason.

NAMBUTHIRIPAD: I am in sole charge of all the property matters of the mana.

Pretending to look at the time, he pulled out the watch tied to the end of the mundu. He said it was five o'clock.

INDULEKHA: Oh! Then it is time for my evening prayer.

NAMBUTHIRIPAD: No, it's not yet time for that. Don't you want to look at this watch?

He extended the watch to Indulekha who showed her appreciation for it.

NAMBUTHIRIPAD: Meghadantan sayiv presented this as a gift when I gave over some land for Rs 75,000.

Indulekha laughed very loudly when she heard Meghadantan sayiv's name. She returned the watch to him. Her laughter and attitude convinced the Nambuthiripad that she had started to fall in love with him. She, in turn, was thinking that she should write about this to Madhavan.

Nambuthiripad's desire for Indulekha increased. Then this stupid impatient man said:

NAMBUTHIRIPAD: My wish is to be with you always, Indulekha.
INDULEKHA: I think that is a desire which will not be fulfilled.

At that moment, Kesavannambuthiri came upstairs with a silver platter on which were arranged betel leaves and other things.

INDULEKHA: I have to bathe and then go to the temple. Kesavannambuthiri, do sit here.

She hurried downstairs. But her parting look hit Kesavannambuthiri as though someone had dealt him a blow with a heated iron rod. He stood there helplessly holding the tray feeling ashamed of himself. The Nambuthiripad was not very happy with the situation—even then he sat there chewing betel for quite some time and walked about and looked at all the things in the room. He saw a lot of books—and decided that it was a mistake to teach women English.

KESAVANNAMBUTHIRI: (to the Nambuthiripad) Indulekha goes to the temple without fail every evening. She is very particular about it.
NAMBUTHIRIPAD: I'm sure she will return soon. Shall we sit here till she comes?
KESAVANNAMBUTHIRI: I don't think we need to do that. At nine o'clock, after dinner, we can come here and listen to Indulekha sing. Isn't that better?
NAMBUTHIRIPAD: Yes, that sounds better.

Both of them went downstairs.

When the Nambuthiripad was upstairs with Kesavannambuthiri observing the things in the room, Indulekha was engaged in a conversation with Cherusserinambuthiri. When she came out into the nalukettu through the room to the south, she saw Cherusserinambuthiri seated in a chair, all alone in the southern room. The moment he saw Indulekha, he rose and advanced towards her with a smile. She too was extremely happy to see him but she didn't know what to say. That was the state of her mind. However, the resourceful Cherusseri dispelled Indulekha's discomfort immediately.

CHERUSSERINAMBUTHIRI: I didn't even hope that I would be able to meet you today. I have no part in this prank. I am innocent; please don't misunderstand me.

When she heard these words, Indulekha's mind was at rest and she could speak.

INDULEKHA: Why didn't you come upstairs as well? Is it because you know me and have some affection for me? When I heard that you had come I was very happy.

CHERUSSERINAMBUTHIRI: When the Nambuthiripad came upstairs he didn't ask me to accompany him. My situation is that of a companion. That is why I thought I shouldn't come up without being asked. Anyway, I was going to come up tomorrow morning. It is my luck that I have been able to see you now. I heard that Madhavan is getting a salary of Rs 150. I am very happy about it.

The moment she heard Madhavan's name, the sparkle came back to her eyes and she felt a little bashful. Cherusserinambuthiri saw the way she bent her head and smiled, and he was extremely happy. He respected Indulekha's feelings.

INDULEKHA: I have received a letter saying that he will be here in two days' time. Maybe this time when he goes back....

She broke off and stood there shyly.

CHERUSSERINAMBUTHIRI: When Madhavan goes back you will also go with him, won't you?
INDULEKHA: (with a smile) Yes.

CHERUSSERINAMBUTHIRI: I will come with you both. My blessings and wish is that you and Madhavan should have a long life together as man and wife.

Suddenly tears filled his eyes. Anyone with ordinary intelligence would wish that the extremely beautiful Indulekha should marry only the very handsome Madhavan. It is not surprising that the scholarly Cherusserinambuthiri felt so. He knew that besides their striking physical appearance, their learning, intelligence, and good conduct made them so well suited to each other.

When the Nambuthiri spoke thus, Indulekha's eyes too filled with tears and she became speechless.

INDULEKHA: We look forward very respectfully to your blessing always.
CHERUSSERINAMBUTHIRI: Has he written about the exact date of his arrival?
INDULEKHA: Some time next week, that is what he writes. It is already two or three days since he wrote. That means he might arrive the day after, or three days hence.
CHERUSSERINAMBUTHIRI: I don't know when I will be travelling back from here. The Nambuthiripad has not announced any plans. Hasn't he come here to stay?

At this both of them laughed.

INDULEKHA: Why did you send the *Shriramodantha* sloka some time back?

They laughed again.

INDULEKHA: It is my good fortune that you also came along with him. I will go to the temple and come back. If you are not leaving in the morning, after breakfast you should surely come upstairs.
CHERUSSERINAMBUTHIRI: I don't think there will be a return in the morning.

Indulekha laughed and left for the bath house.

Cherusserinambuthiri sat down again. Then came the sound of pacing and wooden chappals clacked upstairs. Indulekha's words and the hurried manner in which she had left did not please the Nambuthiripad at all. However, he was happy that at nine o'clock he was to go upstairs a second time to hear her sing. He immediately descended to the nalukettu to meet Cherusseri.

Conversation between Indulekha and the Nambuthiripad

NAMBUTHIRIPAD: Why Cherusseri, are you bored sitting all alone? Why didn't you come upstairs? Indulekha is very beautiful—very beautiful indeed. I have never seen a woman like her. Shiva-Shiva! What exquisite beauty! And so much of it—amazing.

CHERUSSERINAMBUTHIRI: Indulekha would never have seen a man like you. She too must have been amazed. From the start, I was sure of that.

NAMBUTHIRIPAD: Why Cherusseri, didn't you recite a sloka recently—something about how Ravanan was crazed when he saw Rambha. Please recite that sloka.

Cherusseri recited the sloka:

Iyam bala leeladaragamanalolalakabhara
Chalachelachola pihithakuchashaila vidhumukhi-
Lasalphala mala nipathadalijaala vishamitha-
Smarajwala vrilamapaharathi niilabjanayana.

[Young girl whose curls move in time with her gentle step, the swirl of her clothes and her rising bosom, moon-faced one, forehead glowing, a swarm of bees smothering your garland, volcanic passion and lotus-like eyes, you dispel all feelings of shame.]

NAMBUTHIRIPAD: Please write down that sloka on a palmyra leaf.

Kesavannambuthiri quickly brought a palmyra leaf and a stylus. Cherusseri wrote down the sloka and gave it to the Nambuthiripad. Holding that palmyra leaf he sat there for a long time. Just then he caught sight of Indulekha's mother (Lakshmikuttyamma) walking through the northern room of the nalukettu. I don't think I need to tell you that Indulekha's mother was a very beautiful woman. She was only thirty-five years old. The moment the Nambuthiripad saw the lady, he turned to Kesavannambuthiri. 'Who is this lady who just passed by, Karuthedam?'

Kesavannambuthiri felt a great fear within himself. Lakshmikuttyamma was his favourite wife. And he knew the ways of this Nambuthiripad. He became a little perturbed.

KESAVANNAMBUTHIRI: She is Indulekha's mother.
NAMBUTHIRIPAD: Oh-Oh! she is your wife, isn't she?
KESAVANNAMBUTHIRI: Yes.

NAMBUTHIRIPAD: I need to meet and talk to her, call her here.
KESAVANNAMBUTHIRI: I have no objection. When you come to hear Indulekha sing you can talk to her—isn't that better?
CHERUSSERINAMBUTHIRI: No, it is better to talk now. What can you talk about when Indulekha is singing?

Cherusserinambuthiri was tickled by the Nambuthiripad's desire to talk to Lakshmikuttyamma and Kesavannambuthiri's confusion at that. 'This is what should happen to him; let silly Kesavannambuthiri be a little agitated.' That is why he intervened. The Nambuthiripad was extremely pleased.

NAMBUTHIRIPAD: What Cherusseri said is correct. I want to meet and talk to her now itself. We can all go to Karuthedam's room and sit there, Karuthedam doesn't have any manners. Shouldn't he have invited us to his room before this, Cherusseri?
CHERUSSERINAMBUTHIRI: Certainly. We can go right now—can we not, Karuthedam?
KESAVANNAMBUTHIRI: Yes, why not?

Kesavannambuthiri got up with a tragic expression, and with him went the Nambuthiripad.

NAMBUTHIRIPAD: Why aren't you coming, Cherusseri?
CHERUSSERINAMBUTHIRI: I shall sit here. But if you wish I can come with you.
NAMBUTHIRIPAD: Then why don't you sit here? Karuthedam and I will go.

When the Nambuthiripad and Kesavannambuthiri entered the room, Lakshmikuttyamma was not there. Indulekha's maid Ammu was sitting there, chopping betel nut. Ammu was very beautiful and Indulekha was very fond of her. She was about twenty-five years old and was not really from the class of domestics. Indulekha had ordered her to wear clean clothes always, a gold neck ornament studded with rubies on a white thread and plain thodas in her ears. It is needless to say that because of her contact with Indulekha she had acquired a greater sense of cleanliness. When the Nambuthiripad stepped into the room, it was Ammu he saw. He took her to be Indulekha's mother.

NAMBUTHIRIPAD: Is your wife so young? Karuthedam is indeed very lucky.

Is this Indulekha's mother? She looks as young as Indulekha. It is indeed surprising! What a miracle! How old is she? Why don't you turn towards us? Why do you stand there? Lakshmi! Come closer to me. Your daughter is not so shy. Are you shy because of Karuthedam? Come here.

KESAVANNAMBUTHIRI: She is not Indulekha's mother—she is Indulekha's maid. Indulekha's mother has gone out somewhere.
NAMBUTHIRIPAD: I was confused. Karuthedam, go and call her.

Kesavannambuthiri went out. Ammu tried to slip out with him.

NAMBUTHIRIPAD: Stand there, wait—let me ask you something. You are Indulekha's servant, aren't you? You are indeed a woman of taste, you shouldn't be a servant. You are extremely beautiful. Wait a while, wait, wait.
AMMU: Your slave is late, going upstairs.
NAMBUTHIRIPAD: Do you have a sambandam?
AMMU: No.
NAMBUTHIRIPAD: What a pity! You are doing all the work in this house and ill-treating your body. Come here—what are you holding...betel leaves and nuts?
AMMU: No, just chopped areca nut.
NAMBUTHIRIPAD: Does Indulekha chew betel leaves?
AMMU: Sometimes.
NAMBUTHIRIPAD: Does Indulekha have any love affairs? Please tell me secretly.
AMMU: Love affairs?
NAMBUTHIRIPAD: Any adulterous affair—adulterous affair.
AMMU: Adulterous affair?
NAMBUTHIRIPAD: Secret affairs—secret affair.
AMMU: Your slave doesn't know anything.
NAMBUTHIRIPAD: When I take Indulekha away with me, surely you must come along with her.
AMMU: Yes, I will.

She laughed and went out.

Kesavannambuthiri, stunned, went looking for Lakshmikuttyamma. He saw her returning from the temple. Shamefacedly he went up to her.

KESAVANNAMBUTHIRI: He says he wants to see you and is sitting there in the room. Why don't you go immediately?
LAKSHMIKUTTYAMMA: What a nuisance! Has he turned his attentions to me now?

KESAVANNAMBUTHIRI: It is not that. Aren't you Indulekha's mother; wouldn't he want to see you once? Isn't it natural? What is wrong if he wishes to see you?

LAKSHMIKUTTYAMMA: Nothing; let it be so. I shall make an appearance.

Lakshmikuttyamma began walking behind Kesavannambuthiri. She saw Ammu step out of the room laughing. Lakshmikuttyamma waited at the door of the room. Kesavannambuthiri went in.

NAMBUTHIRIPAD: What is it, hasn't she come?

KESAVANNAMBUTHIRI: Yes, she has come; she is standing here.

NAMBUTHIRIPAD: You can come inside, come inside. I saw Indulekha and wished to see her mother too.

Lakshmikuttyamma stepped in and stood partly hidden behind the door.

NAMBUTHIRIPAD: What is it, Karuthedam, why don't you have a lamp? Ask for a lamp.

He asked for a lamp to be placed near the door; it was done. Then he looked straight, diagonally, and slantingly at Lakshmikuttyamma's body and desired it intensely. Kesavannambuthuri's perplexity and sorrow multiplied.

NAMBUTHIRIPAD: It is your luck, Karuthedam—immense luck. One can't say she is a greater beauty than Indulekha. Your name is Lakshmikutty, isn't it?

LAKSHMIKUTTYAMMA: Yes.

NAMBUTHIRIPAD: Really—Lakshmidevi herself—I intend to call you Lakshmidevi from now. Say something, Karuthedam?

What could Kesavannambuthiri say! Only that his situation was unenviable. It occurred to the simple-minded man that this ill luck would deprive him of his livelihood.

If only he had fully realized Lakshmikuttyamma's verve and smartness, he would not have had any cause to feel so perplexed. What was he to do?

NAMBUTHIRIPAD: She is Lakshmidevi—what do you say, Karuthedam? You are indeed lucky. A man who is as rich and powerful as I am could not effect such a situation till now.

KESAVANNAMBUTHIRI: I think it is time to go for *uuku*.

Conversation between Indulekha and the Nambuthiripad

NAMBUTHIRIPAD: Not yet. Lakshmikutty, bring that lamp here. Let me look at my watch.

Kesavannambuthiri took the lamp to him. It did not please the Nambuthiripad at all. He had desired that Lakshmikuttyamma should bring the lamp but he remained silent. He looked at his watch and observing that it was only six-thirty, began talking again.

NAMBUTHIRIPAD: How old are you, Lakshmikutty?
LAKSHMIKUTTYAMMA: I am in my thirty-fifth year.
NAMBUTHIRIPAD: You are quite young. How very lucky, Karuthedam. How did you manage to get in here?

Kesavannambuthiri's heart started pounding! 'O God, will this scoundrel go off with my wife? And I invited all this trouble upon myself! If he doesn't get Indulekha, will he go off with her mother?' Such thoughts troubled Kesavannambuthiri intensely.

NAMBUTHIRIPAD: Lakshmikutty, your sambandam before this was with a king from Kilimanoor, wasn't it?
LAKSHMIKUTTYAMMA: Yes.
NAMBUTHIRIPAD: It is after this sambandam that you, Karuthedam, got the lucky break, isn't it? Why don't you say something, Karuthedam?
KESAVANNAMBUTHIRI: It is getting late for uuku.
NAMBUTHIRIPAD: It is not late; it is quite all right if you do it at seven o'clock. Ask Govindan to bring my silver box here.

Govindan brought the silver box and placed it in front of the Nambuthiripad.

NAMBUTHIRIPAD: Lakshmikutty, you may look at this silver box.

When Lakshmikuttyamma stepped forward to take the silver box, her figure came into full view.

NAMBUTHIRIPAD: Miracle—miracle—surprise. It is a surprise indeed. Amazing! Karuthedam is particularly lucky. She is very beautiful! Karuthedam, you are very taken up by her, aren't you? Is there any doubt about it? How is it possible for anyone not to be taken up by her? She is indeed Lakshmidevi herself. Is that betel box nice?
LAKSHMIKUTTYAMMA: Very nice.

NAMBUTHIRIPAD: If you want you can take it.
LAKSHMIKUTTYAMMA: I don't think I am free to do that.
NAMBUTHIRIPAD: You are very good at repartee. This is how you should be. No wonder Indulekha is so beautiful. But she does not have this dexterity with words, that is for sure. How old is she?
LAKSHMIKUTTYAMMA: This is her eighteenth year.
NAMBUTHIRIPAD: Then you gave birth at seventeen!
LAKSHMIKUTTYAMMA: Yes.
NAMBUTHIRIPAD: No more children after that?
LAKSHMIKUTTYAMMA: No.
NAMBUTHIRIPAD: Perhaps you are not happy now.
LAKSHMIKUTTYAMMA: I don't have any problems.
NAMBUTHIRIPAD: The king was a very capable person, wasn't he?
LAKSHMIKUTTYAMMA: Yes.
NAMBUTHIRIPAD: What a pity! It is very difficult for a woman to get a husband whose ability matches hers. Men too face the same problem. Each one should be able to find someone suitable—that is what is special. Or it would be very sad. Why aren't you saying anything, Karuthedam?
KESAVANNAMBUTHIRI: I think it is seven o'clock.
NAMBUTHIRIPAD: Not yet. How many years has it been since you began a sambandam with her?
KESAVANNAMBUTHIRI: Almost six years.
NAMBUTHIRIPAD: And you don't have any children?
KESAVANNAMBUTHIRI: That's right.
NAMBUTHIRIPAD: Your luck amazes me. Some time back Cherusseri recited a sloka. It speaks about a man's jealousy when he sees another man's wife. I cannot remember the sloka; please call Cherusseri here.

Kesavannambuthiri went to call Cherusseri. Cherusseri was waiting for the Nambuthiripad to arrive for the uuku.

CHERUSSERINAMBUTHIRI: What is happening? It is almost seven o'clock.
KESAVANNAMBUTHIRI: My dear Cherusseri! Why should I talk about my stupidity! I think the Nambuthiri won't ever come out of that room. What can I do! I can only say that it is my ill luck.
CHERUSSERINAMBUTHIRI: Why is he calling me now?
KESAVANNAMBUTHIRI: I think it is to recite a sloka.
CHERUSSERINAMBUTHIRI: What a punishment! Now what sloka is there to recite? All right, I will come.

Cherusserinambuthiri went inside with Kesavannambuthiri.

NAMBUTHIRIPAD: Cherusseri, didn't you recite a sloka a few days back, about a man who became despondent on seeing another's wife? Please recite that.

CHERUSSERINAMBUTHIRI: About a man who became despondent on seeing another's wife? Which sloka is that? I don't remember.

NAMBUTHIRIPAD: Chi! There is no need for bewilderment. I shall tell you: it is about the moon shamelessly looking at a woman's face and another brazen man who stood gazing at her right in front of her husband.

CHERUSSERINAMBUTHIRI: (smiling as he recites the sloka)

Kim bruvasthawa poornachandramahathim nirlajjathamiidrishim
Yathwasyamukhamandale sathi bhava napyajjihiithe pura
Aavismrithya kimethadukthamadhuna yathadrishim sundarim
Bhunjanasya puro vayamcha purusha ithyasmahe nisthrapa

[O full moon, must you also rise in the east when her fair face is already there. Ah! We are indeed shameless to desire a woman who is another man's wife.]

NAMBUTHIRIPAD: Yes, this is the sloka. Lakshmikutty, do you comprehend the turn of the phrases?

LAKSHMIKUTTYAMMA: I read a few poems when I was young.

NAMBUTHIRIPAD: Cherusseri is a good scholar, a learned person. He is also very entertaining. Karuthedam does not even have an iota of sense about the turn of phrases. Even then he is very lucky indeed.

KESAVANNAMBUTHIRI: I don't have a flair for words. It is getting very late for uuku, very late indeed.

NAMBUTHIRIPAD: Then we will go. We will return to listen to your daughter sing. I hope to see Lakshmikutty also at that time.

Once again he looked hungrily at Lakshmikuttyamma's face and then stepped outside. On their way out to the pond, they saw Panchumenon.

NAMBUTHIRIPAD: Panchu is indeed fortunate. I saw Indulekha and Lakshmikuttyamma too. Apparently there is a competition between them as to who is more beautiful. It is Karuthedam's luck. Both of them are indeed very beautiful.

Panchumenon was not very happy with these words. One could say he was a little angry. Even so he kept it all to himself.

PANCHUMENON: Now it is time to go for the uuku.

NAMBUTHIRIPAD: Yes; after the uuku we can have our meal and return quickly.

When the Nambuthiripad and the Nambuthiris entered the courtyard, Panchumenon beckoned Kesavannambuthiri. Kesavannambuthiri stepped back. Panchumenon and the Nambuthiri entered the nalukettu together.

PANCHUMENON: Was Indulekha impressed?

KESAVANNAMBUTHIRI: She will be convinced. How can she not be impressed?

PANCHUMENON: We can talk about what will happen later—has it happened?

KESAVANNAMBUTHIRI: That cannot be decided at the moment. She will be convinced; there is no doubt about it.

PANCHUMENON: It is not possible for me to believe what you are saying. I was quite flustered initially but now I think the Nambuthiripad is an utter fool.

KESAVANNAMBUTHIRI: He is very rich; shouldn't we think of that?

PANCHUMENON: Indulekha will not consider all that. I think this hope of ours is in vain. The Nambuthiripad doesn't even know how to talk. Why must he give me a detailed description of how beautiful Indulekha and Lakshmikutty are? His speech is made up of words that have no connection.

KESAVANNAMBUTHIRI: They are all great people; they can say anything.

PANCHUMENON: If he says whatever he wants to, he will have to listen to many things. I don't quite like all this. What did Indulekha say?

KESAVANNAMBUTHIRI: She did not say anything in particular.

PANCHUMENON: What about the Nambuthiripad?

KESAVANNAMBUTHIRI: He did not say anything in particular. I am getting late for my uuku. I shall come and tell you everything after my meal.

PANCHUMENON: There is nothing to say. This alliance won't take place, that is all. Why did you behave in this nonsensical way?

So saying, Panchumenon stepped inside and Kesavannambuthiri went to the bath house.

While Kesavannambuthiri and Panchumenon were talking to each other, the Nambuthiripad and Cherusseri, who were on their way to the bath house also had a conversation.

NAMBUTHIRIPAD: Cherusseri! I am enamoured of Indulekha's mother than Indulekha herself. Her swift repartee is admirable. And to look at? Didn't you see her, Cherusseri?

CHERUSSERINAMBUTHIRI: I saw her, she is beautiful. In the matter of age too she is very suitable.

NAMBUTHIRIPAD: Do you mean to say that Indulekha will not suit me?

CHERUSSERINAMBUTHIRI: I won't say that. It is for you to decide.

NAMBUTHIRIPAD: Are we sure about Indulekha? Did Panchu say anything to you?

CHERUSSERINAMBUTHIRI: Why should Panchu say anything? Isn't it certain?

NAMBUTHIRIPAD: That is how it should be, but....

CHERUSSERINAMBUTHIRI: Why, do you have any doubts?

NAMBUTHIRIPAD: It is only my extreme fascination which makes me so insecure.

CHERUSSERINAMBUTHIRI: All that is only on account of your fascination. You are bewildered in a matter that need not cause any doubt. That is all that need be said.

NAMBUTHIRIPAD: Let this Indulekha matter rest. Think of Lakshmikutty's situation—look at Karuthedam's luck.

CHERUSSERINAMBUTHIRI: That is what I was thinking of telling you. Karuthedam's luck is indeed great.

NAMBUTHIRIPAD: Is Karuthedam married? Has he got into a veli?

CHERUSSERINAMBUTHIRI: No.

NAMBUTHIRIPAD: Can't this good-for-nothing go and get into a veli?

CHERUSSERINAMBUTHIRI: That good-for-nothing may not get into a veli.

NAMBUTHIRIPAD: He will only insist on sticking close to Lakshmikutty.

CHERUSSERINAMBUTHIRI: That's right.

NAMBUTHIRIPAD: And the fact is Lakshmikutty is not even attracted to him. I could see that instantly.

CHERUSSERINAMBUTHIRI: Must you speak in such detail to me who am well versed with your great intelligence? Can any woman feel attracted to another man after meeting you?

NAMBUTHIRIPAD: Lakshmikutty is a little attracted to me.

CHERUSSERINAMBUTHIRI: I have no doubt about that.

NAMBUTHIRIPAD: How do we plan that?

CHERUSSERINAMBUTHIRI: Plan what?

NAMBUTHIRIPAD: To satisfy that attraction.

CHERUSSERINAMBUTHIRI: Aren't there lots of tricks for that? Just stop seeing Lakshmikutty.

NAMBUTHIRIPAD: What on earth are you saying? Cherusseri?

CHERUSSERINAMBUTHIRI: Didn't you come here for Indulekha?

NAMBUTHIRIPAD: Yes, but after coming here I am also enamoured of Lakshmikutty.

CHERUSSERINAMBUTHIRI: But can you have a sambandam with both the mother and the daughter? Is that decorous?

NAMBUTHIRIPAD: I will have a relationship with Indulekha herself. But—

Just then Kesavannambuthiri arrived at the bath house and the Nambuthiripad decided to keep quiet. After the uuku he stood in the moonlight in the holy courtyard of the temple. All memories of Lakshmikuttyamma fled. What had affected him deeply surfaced now. The Nambuthiripad had never seen a woman like Indulekha before. Pure libertine that he was, he was always attracted to beautiful women, but while standing calmly in the moonlight his thoughts were only of the young Indulekha. Thinking over and over again about her, he called Govindan and gave him the palmyra which had the sloka about Ravanan who was enamoured of Rambha.

NAMBUTHIRIPAD: Go, give this palmyra to Indulekha herself in her room and say that I gave it to you.

Govindan immediately took the palmyra to Indulekha's room upstairs. She had just finished her meal and was going up to her room.

GOVINDAN: My lord has sent a letter. He has ordered that it should be delivered here.

INDULEKHA: (with extreme anger even though she understood the matter) Which lord? What letter?

If you had seen the touch of anger on Indulekha's face, you too would agree that anger made her face glow.

GOVINDAN: This is the revered letter of the Moorkillatha thamburan.

INDULEKHA: He has no business writing to me. Tell him I won't accept it.

Thereupon she immediately went to her room.

Govindan felt ashamed of himself. Hiding the palmyra in the fold of his mundu, he returned to the Nambuthiripad.

The Nambuthiripad was standing with a group of people in the holy ground of the temple. Seeing Govindan, he called out loudly, 'Govinda! Did you give Indulekha that letter?'

Govindan was very uncomfortable. He hesitated, not knowing what to answer. Finally he said he had given it to her, and left quickly fearing that there might be more questions. Since he knew the Nambuthiripad would later go to the bath house for an oil massage, Govindan went there. Taking the palmyra from the fold of his mundu, he said very quietly in an aside to the Nambuthiripad:

GOVINDAN: Earlier your slave told you a lie that I had given your revered letter. Kundalekha did not accept the letter. Your lordship has no business to write to Kundalekha, she said, and that she won't accept your revered letter. I lied earlier because there were other people with you.

NAMBUTHIRIPAD: You are a great fool! She is not Kundulekha—her name is Indulekha. But it is good you lied: this is why I like you.

GOVINDAN: That Kundulekha....

NAMBUTHIRIPAD: Fool—don't say Kundulekha again, say 'Indulekha'.

GOVINDAN: Yes—your slave made a mistake. That Indralekha....

NAMBUTHIRIPAD: You stupid fool! Silly fool! She is not Indralekha, say 'Indulekha'.

GOVINDAN: Your slave—(yes) your slave thought she was a very insolent person.

NAMBUTHIRIPAD: All right, did you meet Indulekha's mother? A startling face, eh? A very beautiful person. She is attracted to me. She is Karuthedam's wife.

GOVINDAN: Then what about Indulekha, isn't she attracted to you?

NAMBUTHIRIPAD: Indulekha has learnt English and other things and she has certain mannerisms. Her mother is not like that. She is very good at repartee. Didn't you bring that silver box with you?

GOVINDAN: Your slave brought it back long ago.

NAMBUTHIRIPAD: Good boy! You have a sense of humour! This is why I am so fond of you, Govindan. I told Lakshmikuttyamma to accept the silver box. To which she said she was not against it. For some time, I was worried that if you left it there she might have taken it and kept it.

GOVINDAN: Hasn't your slave been living by your grace? Doesn't your slave know all this?

Talking animatedly like this with Govindan, the Nambuthiripad began preparing for a good scrub and bath.

While the Nambuthiripad was oiling himself in the bath house, a conversation took place between Kesavannambuthiri and Cherusserinambuthiri on the veranda. For many reasons Kesavannambuthiri was sad. Without any warning, the Nambuthiripad had asked to see his wife. There was no doubt that his wife was beautiful. In his opinion the Nambuthiripad was also very good-looking. Then the Nambuthiripad was very rich—high-born too. What if Lakshmikutty was attracted to him? Panchumenon would surely allow it, there was no doubt about that. The Nambuthiripad would express his desire for a sambandam. Wasn't he a great person? My God! What will I do if Panchumenon sends for me and says that I shouldn't object to it. What difference does it make whether I agree or not? The matter will be effected. I can go back to my illam. If Shudra women are cultivated as partners, dangers like this are inevitable. This simpleton Kesavannambuthiri continued to think for long and hard. Then his thoughts moved to Lakshmikutty's face and body once again. 'Oh my dear, will some danger like this befall me?—No, that won't happen. After seeking a sambandam with Indulekha, how can he expect a sambandam with her mother? It can't happen.' He decided to be brave but his mind kept wavering. 'I have already told this Nambuthiripad that there will be music at nine o'clock. What if Indulekha doesn't sing at that time? What if she doesn't play on the veena? I will be so embarrassed.' He found Cherusserinambuthiri sitting next to him while he was thus mulling over these questions.

CHERUSSERINAMBUTHIRI: What is it, you look anxious?
KESAVANNAMBUTHIRI: (with a watery smile) I am not. What anxiety?—There is no reason for anxiety.
CHERUSSERINAMBUTHIRI: Then why are you so preoccupied?
KESAVANNAMBUTHIRI: Nothing at all, I was thinking of today's singing. It is past eight-thirty.
CHERUSSERINAMBUTHIRI: Do you see any obstacles?
KESAVANNAMBUTHIRI: What obstacles can there be? Tonight at nine o'clock Indulekha will sing. You too can come upstairs. She occasionally sings after dark; sometimes she also plays on the veena. It is only very rarely, only on certain days, that there is no singing. It is impossible that there won't be any singing today. We will also go and listen to it. Indulekha will have no objection. Aren't the Nambuthiripad and the others here?
CHERUSSERINAMBUTHIRI: If there is any singing, I too will come along and listen.
KESAVANNAMBUTHIRI: There will be singing—there is no doubt about it.

Kesavannambuthiri had doubts about this. Even then this simpleton continued to believe that the routine would not be disturbed. He did not have the courage to ask Indulekha, let alone look at her. Kesavannambuthiri was in a fix. Finally—

KESAVANNAMBUTHIRI: Tonight, there will be singing. Aren't Surinambuthiri and the others here?
CHERUSSERINAMBUTHIRI: Why are you perplexed, Karuthedam? There will be singing, we can listen to that—isn't that certain?
KESAVANNAMBUTHIRI: Cherusseri, do you doubt it?
CHERUSSERINAMBUTHIRI: What! What doubts can I have? You were the one who arranged all this.
KESAVANNAMBUTHIRI: Chi! Chi! I didn't arrange anything. What can I arrange? Indulekha will also play on the veena today, like she plays on the veena every night. You can listen to it then, that is all that I told Surinambuthiri.
CHERUSSERINAMBUTHIRI: So be it. Then, why are you anxious about it?
KESAVANNAMBUTHIRI: I am not anxious—I am not at all anxious. However, I am a little doubtful whether Surinambuthiri will misunderstand what I told him. No music tonight—that is impossible.
CHERUSSERINAMBUTHIRI: Leave that alone. Did Indulekha show how attracted she was when she saw Surinambuthiri? Let me hear that story.
KESAVANNAMBUTHIRI: Indulekha?
CHERUSSERINAMBUTHIRI: Yes, Indulekha.

You should have seen Kesavannambuthiri's face. Had he been stabbed in the face with a dagger it would not have drawn a drop of blood. For a long time he merely stood there, speechless. Finally—

KESAVANNAMBUTHIRI: Indulekha in love—in love—what, I can't understand anything. It has become very clear to me that I cannot understand the character of women who have learnt English. Panchumenon is one person who is not scared of anyone in the three worlds but he is so frightened of this girl that he shivers with nervousness. Surinambuthiri is indeed a very great man. I thought she would submit at least when she saw him. Now I realize it was wrong to think so. I do not know the ways of the English, Cherusseri. I have seen only one sayiv who works in the yarn company.

On hearing this, Cherusseri laughed loudly for a minute.

CHERUSSERINAMBUTHIRI: Will Surinambuthiri get Indulekha? Tell me that.
KESAVANNAMBUTHIRI: It is not yet possible to say anything with certainty. I can tell you that only after tonight.

The Nambuthiripad joined them after his bath. He was not feeling very cheerful when he thought of the rejected sloka. Even then his mind kept turning to Indulekha's figure. If she is disgusted, let it be. We can find out at nine o'clock. It is enough to look at her, there is no need to talk even—this is what the Nambuthiripad thought. After their meal he and the others went to Poovarangu.

NAMBUTHIRIPAD: Cherusseri! Now there is no need for the gown, only the upper cloth is needed, isn't that so?
CHERUSSERINAMBUTHIRI: Yes.
NAMBUTHIRIPAD: Govinda, you take the silver box with the gold bubbles on it and the rose-water sprayer made of gold. Place it before the audience.
KESAVANNAMBUTHIRI: The singing will be accompanied by the veena. Here it is done seated on a chair, not on mats.
NAMBUTHIRIPAD: This is the danger of you teaching English to women. Does anyone sit on a chair and sing? What is all this? You tell Panchu that tonight Indulekha should sit on a mat of woven grass and sing—Karuthedam, you tell him that.
KESAVANNAMBUTHIRI: Certainly.

On reaching the nalukettu, the Nambuthiripad sat on a chair. Kesavannambuthiri slowly went up to Indulekha's malika and saw that the door of the veranda was firmly shut. I cannot express the sorrow and the perplexity that Kesavannambuthiri experienced at that time. First he thought of calling out to her. The simple-minded Brahmin did not have the courage to do that. Immediately he went into the house to his wife's room. She was lying down preparing to sleep.

KESAVANNAMBUTHIRI: Lakshmikutty! Lakshmikutty! I feel humiliated.

Lakshmikuttyamma got up.

LAKSHMIKUTTYAMMA: What is the matter?
KESAVANNAMBUTHIRI: I invited Surinambuthiri here thinking that today

there would be music as there is every day but Indulekha has latched the door of her room and gone off to sleep. What will I tell the Nambuthiri?
LAKSHMIKUTTYAMMA: You should tell him what has happened. What else can you do? I told you because I thought there would be singing like every day—I don't think there is singing today; Indulekha has shut the door to her room and has gone off to sleep. So let the singing take place tomorrow. What is so shameful in this?
KESAVANNAMBUTHIRI: But in order not to displease the Nambuthiripad I told him that Indulekha will sing tonight. If she doesn't, something disastrous will happen. Lakshmikutty, you should come upstairs and call Indulekha.
LAKSHMIKUTTYAMMA: That is some punishment. I will never call her down. Why, don't you know Indulekha? It is better for the Nambuthiripad to turn in for the night. What is he troubling himself so much about?
KESAVANNAMBUTHIRI: Chi! It shouldn't be like that. Then let me tell Panchumenon and see what happens.
LAKSHMIKUTTYAMMA: Yes, do that.

Kesavannambuthiri went in search of Panchumenon who was in the nalukettu talking to the Nambuthiripad. Kesavannambuthiri stood in the south room and signalled to Panchumenon without the Nambuthiripad seeing him. Panchumenon went inside. When he was told the details, the angry Panchumenon declared that he wouldn't do anything. He strode right back and continued talking to the Nambuthiripad. Kesavannambuthiri stood in the south room, helpless.

NAMBUTHIRIPAD: Where did Karuthedam go? Can't find him at all. It is past ten o'clock. Wasn't the performance arranged for nine o'clock initially?

When he heard this, Kesavannambuthiri made his presence known and jumped out of the room like a devil.

PANCHUMENON: Everything has been arranged for you in the rooms above the gate. Your slave is old. It is difficult for me to stand for so long.

Saying this he went inside.

The Nambuthiripad felt a little angry to hear that his sleeping arrangements had been made in the outhouse. 'Anyway we are going to sleep only after the singing and everything. By then it will be two or three o'clock in the morning. Till then I can sit with Indulekha.' This thought made him very happy.

NAMBUTHIRIPAD: What is the delay, Karuthedam?
KESAVANNAMBUTHIRI: There is no delay.
NAMBUTHIRIPAD: Then let us go to the room. Cherusseri, you can listen to some songs and then go back and sleep.

Kesavannambuthiri stood there unable to talk for a long time and finally:

KESAVANNAMBUTHIRI: I think Indulekha is ill: she has gone off to sleep. The door to her room is shut.
NAMBUTHIRIPAD: Karuthedam, can't you call her? Go and call her.
KESAVANNAMBUTHIRI: I called her.
NAMBUTHIRIPAD: Call loudly and see.
KESAVANNAMBUTHIRI: I called loudly.
NAMBUTHIRIPAD: Then what happened?
KESAVANNAMBUTHIRI: She didn't open the door.
NAMBUTHIRIPAD: Did she say she had some physical illness?
KESAVANNAMBUTHIRI: Yes.
NAMBUTHIRIPAD: Did she say she can't sing?
KESAVANNAMBUTHIRI: She did.
NAMBUTHIRIPAD: Then we could have sat upstairs and talked. Won't she open the door?
KESAVANNAMBUTHIRI: She said she won't open the door.
NAMBUTHIRIPAD: Go once more and find out.
CHERUSSERINAMBUTHIRI: It wouldn't be right to do that; she will get better by tomorrow. She might have a headache or something like that. We will meet tomorrow after food. That is better.
KESAVANNAMBUTHIRI: Yes, that is better.
NAMBUTHIRIPAD: Karuthedam, your wife doesn't sing?
KESAVANNAMBUTHIRI: No, she too has gone to sleep.

The Nambuthiripad and Cherusserinambuthiri went upstairs to the gatehouse. The Nambuthiripad was not at all sleepy. Thinking only of Indulekha, he went about like a mad man. Finally he called Govindan and asked him to prepare betel leaves.

GOVINDAN: You did not sleep your royal sleep yesterday also. Some time back I heard the clock strike twelve. Your slave is wondering whether you might fall ill or something.

NAMBUTHIRIPAD: You fool! How will I feel sleepy, sitting so near her, when that Indulekha is sleeping in that malika.
GOVINDAN: Then why didn't you order that your rooms be arranged in that malika?
NAMBUTHIRIPAD: There is no use giving such orders. Indulekha is like the English in her manners. One has to find out whether it is convenient before going in. It is all very peculiar! If that girl were not so beautiful I would have insulted her and come away. How insolent she is! Her speech and manner are not proper. She talked to me as she would to an equal. I think she wanted to sit down in my presence. But I did not allow her to do that. I also did something stupid. When I met her I was immediately captivated, and not thinking of my situation I said something silly and undignified to her. I wonder whether she wants to harass me and get some money out of me. When I gave her the gold watch I saw her looking greedily at it. So, I took it back immediately. She cannot do this so prematurely with me. I wonder if she refused to take the sloka because I took back the gold watch, but then I will give her that watch. I feel a great desire for her, Govinda. I have never felt such desire before. When I see her again I have decided to be very serious. I am not feeling well—my mind is not at peace either. I feel I shouldn't have come. To return without Indulekha will be very shameful. I came because of the letter that great fool of a Karuthedam wrote; now I think it is time to proclaim the purpose. Shame, shame—it is a great shame.

Govindan heard all this very calmly. He prepared the betel and giving it to the Nambuthiripad stood in the customary way and started saying:

GOVINDAN: Your slave has something to tell you. If you are agreeable, I will open my mouth.
NAMBUTHIRIPAD: Tell—tell. I do not feel sleepy at all.
GOVINDAN: Indulekha has got some other man. She is very fond of him. Your slave feels that she is a woman of bad character. Then her haughty manner is also too much. She will find it difficult to adjust at the mana with her English customs and manners. It will be difficult to change her ways. There is a very good girl here in Poovally who is Panchumenon's niece. Your slave saw her coming to the temple and going back. She doesn't know any English. Everyone says that she is good-natured. So it seems to your slave that you should try for that. The rest is left to your highness' inclination.

NAMBUTHIRIPAD: Ha—you are a clever one! Govinda! You are a clever fellow. Very smart fellow—intelligent fellow! Now my illness has vanished. This girl does not know English. That's for sure, isn't it?

GOVINDAN: Absolutely nothing at all. She is a simpleton—fine character. When you were having your royal meal, there was a Shinupattar who was very active, she is his daughter.

NAMBUTHIRIPAD: All right, is she beautiful?

GOVINDAN: She is very beautiful.

NAMBUTHIRIPAD: Then I am agreeable to that. If I carry off this headstrong Indulekha forcefully from here, she won't behave herself for even two days.

GOVINDAN: What you say is true.

NAMBUTHIRIPAD: Then call Shinupattar immediately.

GOVINDAN: There is no need for any hurry. We'll wait till morning.

NAMBUTHIRIPAD: Then can I see the girl in the morning?

GOVINDAN: You can see her for a prolonged span of time.

It was morning by the time this talk with Govindan ended. Even then the Nambuthiripad slept for a long time out of tiredness.

chapter thirteen

Second Conversation between Indulekha and the Nambuthiripad

The Nambuthiripad probably dozed for about half an hour. On awaking, he called Govindan and made him repeat everything. He felt happy and at ease.

NAMBUTHIRIPAD: Where is Cherusseri sleeping? Has he woken up?
GOVINDAN: He's gone for a bath. He slept in the room south of this one. Please don't mention to Cherusserinambuthiri what your slave said right now.
NAMBUTHIRIPAD: Why?
GOVINDAN: Your slave feels that you should speak only after you gauge the situation.
NAMBUTHIRIPAD: Clever boy! You are indeed very clever. Then let this matter be a secret. I shall meet Indulekha once again today and if she does not immediately fall in with our plan we can conduct the other matter and depart immediately with *her* early in the morning. Let people know about it only after we leave. Then we don't stand to lose anything. Therefore, keep this matter an absolute secret. Lie to everyone that it is Indulekha herself who is being taken away after the sambandam. If Indulekha herself is agreeable we can actually take her, isn't that so?
GOVINDAN: Yes.
NAMBUTHIRIPAD: Then I should see the girl. How can we manage that?
GOVINDAN: Your slave shall go and find out. She will come to offer worship at the temple. You can see her then.

NAMBUTHIRIPAD: Brilliant child! Clever boy! Go and find out.

Govindan found Kalyanikutty bathing in the women's bath house and he ran back to the Nambuthiri to report this. The Nambuthiripad rose hurriedly and went to the pond. He was dressed very simply in a silk mundu with *kara* [narrow border] tied at chest level, and wooden sandals.

My readers' knowledge about Kalyanikutty is limited to reading her name in the Preface. You would know that this girl is Shinupattar's daughter and thirteen years old. She is a very good-looking girl with a charming face but don't imagine that she has even a hundredth of Indulekha's beauty—that is one story, and this is an entirely different one. Kalyanikutty was a girl raised purely in the traditional Malayali way. She knew how to read and write, and could sing a little. She had a little education and was quite pretty to look at. In Malabar, it is a fact that some women have given birth at the age of thirteen. One can only say for Kalyanikutty that her body showed signs of maturity. She was an extremely shy and simple girl. She had just wiped herself dry and untangled her wet hair with her fingers when the Nambuthiripad walked straight up to her. The moment she saw him, she stepped aside. She had no idea that this was the Nambuthiripad. Hadn't she seen him the previous day looking like a statue of gold? Thinking that it was somebody she didn't know, Kalyanikutty moved back into the bath house. And the Nambuthiripad! Was he a person to give up so easily? Definitely not. He went in, looked directly at her and called back to Govindan, 'a very good girl'. Govindan rushed him out because he saw Cherusseri coming out after a bath. The Nambuthiripad found himself standing face to face with Cherusseri.

CHERUSSERINAMBUTHIRI: What is this? Is it time for your bath?
NAMBUTHIRIPAD: Yes.
CHERUSSERINAMBUTHIRI: So early?
NAMBUTHIRIPAD: Yes.
CHERUSSERINAMBUTHIRI: Then why did you come out of the bath house?
NAMBUTHIRIPAD: To relieve myself.
GOVINDAN: An elaborate bath is better in the other bath house.
NAMBUTHIRIPAD: Then we will go there. Cherusseri, proceed to the temple and say your prayers.

Pretending to be preoccupied, the Nambuthiripad marched towards the bigger bath house with Govindan.

Second Conversation between Indulekha and the Nambuthiripad   131

Cherusseri was not convinced by all this. The Nambuthiripad usually got up at eight o'clock and bathed after ten. Before that he cleaned his teeth and other things. Today was quite different. It looked as though he had just jumped out of bed. Why did he rush out of the women's bath house? Why did Govindan hurry him to the other bath house? He suspected that there was something behind all this. Cherusserinambuthiri walked for some distance. When he looked back, he saw a girl coming towards the temple: he understood everything. Someone informed him that she was Panchumenon's niece. The clever Cherusseri realized what was going on. He decided to speak to Indulekha about this and sat down to pray.

NAMBUTHIRIPAD: (to Govindan) I'm completely convinced. I am extremely happy. I do not want that self-assured one who has learnt the language of those who eat beef. Kalyanikutty is a very nice girl. Her age is extremely special. Nowadays, I desire women of this age. Govinda! Go immediately and do your best. Why should we go and see Indulekha now?

GOVINDAN: Do not talk like this. Have you forgotten what you said earlier? Let everyone think that it is Indulekha who is being taken away. Isn't that what you wish? Now if you change your mind—the secret will be out.

NAMBUTHIRIPAD: Ha—you are indeed smart—smart! I won't say a word. Do what you think is right. Go and arrange everything. But there is a problem. When I see Indulekha I may go mad and feel I don't want any other woman. What can be done? I will be at peace only if I don't see her. That is why I said that.

GOVINDAN: Your highness should stand firm on his decision. Aren't there many women in this world for whom just a glimpse of you would be enough!

NAMBUTHIRIPAD: Hah! Smart fellow! I shall be bold. Indulekha and a blade of grass are the same to me. Go now and implement our secret plan.

Govindan went away wondering whom he could entrust the work to. He lacked the courage to tell anyone. His crafty plan was that the others should get to know of this matter only after the Nambuthiripad had left Poovarangu.

The Nambuthiripad had an early meal and arrived at Poovarangu to meet Indulekha. Here I must say something positive about him. Even though Cherusserinambuthiri tried hard to trick him into a confession, he kept fast to the advice given by Govindan and didn't let a single word escape him. After his meal, when he was walking on the veranda in a leisurely manner, he had a conversation with Shinupattar who was present in the manner of a server.

NAMBUTHIRIPAD: Why Shinu, if all the arrangements are made today, couldn't we leave early tomorrow morning?
SHINUPATTAR: Certainly. Everything is ready.

Shinupattar did not know what had taken place in Poovarangu. After the quarrel with Panchumenon who had threatened to have him beaten up if he were seen anywhere near Poovally house, Shinupattar had not entered Poovarangu. So, he knew nothing about the happenings at the house.

NAMBUTHIRIPAD: Everything has been arranged. The only thing to be ascertained is whether it is today. It should be fixed for today itself.
SHINUPATTAR: Any auspicious event should be arranged immediately.
NAMBUTHIRIPAD: Is there a palanquin here for Indulekha?
SHINUPATTAR: Four or five palanquins are ready.

The Nambuthiripad went to Poovarangu after this conversation with Shinupattar. Exactly like a bell around a crow's neck, Shinupattar added more to whatever the Nambuthiripad had said, and talked about it near the temple, near the pond, and in the *madom*. Quite a few Nambuthiris and Pattars had assembled for a small function that day in the temple and Shinupattar spread the news that Indulekha's sambandam would take place that night. A certain Shankarashastrikal felt very unhappy when he heard this. He had heard Govindan lying to the Nambuthiripad about giving Indulekha the palmyra. Shastrikal had been sure then that things had been decided according to what Kunjikuttyamma had told him the previous evening. Shinupattar's news confirmed all his fears and he sighed deeply! 'What a shame! For a long time I thought that she was an intelligent woman. Even a dimwit can tell that the Nambuthiripad is a fool besides being a womanizer. Is it possible that Indulekha hasn't realized it? Even if she has—she decided to give up Madhavan and become the wife of the silly horse-faced Nambuthiripad. The brilliant Madhavan—like Manmatha and intensely in love with her—what a pity! There is no justification for this other than that such a decision must be prompted by the desire for money.' After his meal he decided to meet Govindapanikkar. On his arrival, he found out that he had gone to

Polpayikalam the previous evening and would return only the next morning. Shastrikal fell asleep on the steps of the veranda.

I had said that after his meal, the Nambuthiripad had come to Poovarangu. Cherusserinambuthiri and Kesavannambuthiri were with him. The moment he reached the nalukettu the Nambuthiripad sat on a chair and Kesavannambuthiri went up to Indulekha's malika to let her know about the Nambuthiripad's arrival.

Kesavannambuthiri did not have the courage to ascend the steps to Indulekha's malika. Several times he went up halfway and came down again. Observing these antics through the window of her room, his wife Lakshmikuttyamma felt very sad. Immediately she went to the well of the stairs and called out to him.

LAKSHMIKUTTYAMMA: What are you doing? You are frightened of Indulekha, aren't you? I shall go and tell her. I don't think she will object very greatly if the Nambuthiripad wants to see her by day. Let me go and tell her.

Kesavannambuthiri felt greatly relieved. He blessed his wife and stood in the stairwell.

When Lakshmikuttyamma went upstairs Indulekha was relaxing, reading Madhavan's letter.

INDULEKHA: What is it, Mother? The Nambuthiripad is coming up to see me. Isn't that right?

LAKSHMIKUTTYAMMA: Yes, my dear daughter. You need not fear that great fool Nambuthiripad at all. Yesterday he came to my room and how absurdly he behaved! Even my father has lost respect for him. But we should be polite. He will leave today or tomorrow. Talk politely with him, play the piano for a little while. Why should it be known that we insulted a Brahmin? Let him visit you.

INDULEKHA: I do not wish to insult him or anyone else in this world in any way. But when someone tries to insult me, I won't stand around without parrying it. If that Nambuthiripad had talked to me decently yesterday I would have sung or played the veena whenever he wanted. Mother, do not think that I am haughty. Am I not a human being? I am not a thing without feelings! If the Nambuthiripad will speak courteously, let him come. I will sing or play the veena. But if he comes upstairs thinking that he has to make me his wife and says something indecorous, he will have to return more insulted than yesterday.

LAKSHMIKUTTYAMMA: That this Nambuthiripad is a great fool is well known. Do we get angry with mad men, dear?

INDULEKHA: As in the other castes, among the Nambuthiris too there are very intelligent people. Mother, converse with Cherusserinambuthiri for some time and you will say Nambuthiris are very clever people. I don't enjoy entertaining mad men. If mad men talk foolishly I will not listen to them patiently, that is certain.

LAKSHMIKUTTYAMMA: All right, shall I let him know that he can come?

INDULEKHA: Let him come if he must. If he talks to me like he did yesterday I shall behave with him exactly as I did before.

The simpleton Kesavannambuthiri stood like a statue at the bottom of the staircase, his face turned up, waiting for Lakshmikuttyamma to descend.

KESAVANNAMBUTHIRI: Is it time, shall I ask him to come?

LAKSHMIKUTTYAMMA: Let him come. Just tell him that he shouldn't talk nonsense to Indulekha like he did yesterday. Otherwise, today will be a repetition of yesterday.

KESAVANNAMBUTHIRI: All right, shall I ask him to come now?

LAKSHMIKUTTYAMMA: Yes.

This time when Kesavannambuthiri went up to the malika, the Nambuthiripad was not irritated.

He was actually thinking of a strategy. 'Yesterday when she saw me, she must have felt that I was vulnerable. Today she should feel that I am in control. What is there in her to be so enamoured of? Why should I, such a noble man, be enamoured of a strong-willed girl who has learnt the language of the beef-eaters. Is there a girl who cannot be bought? How many women have I kept as wives! How many have I discarded! How many more am I going to keep! It is a great drawback to be so enamoured of this girl. I will show her today. I will put on a manner. A superior air! When I stand, sit, look, talk or don't talk, or don't look, Indulekha should be scared out of her wits—let her watch out. If she is haughty I shall not give in an inch. That girl will shiver with fright and fall at my feet.' The Nambuthiripad smiled feeling jubilant.

Cherusserinambuthiri observing the Nambuthiripad's various antics wondered how troublesome all this would be for Indulekha. He felt a mixture of anger and sadness thinking that someone so high born and rich should behave so foolishly. 'It is a great pity! A man who is so wealthy and from such a high caste, does not wish to cultivate a suitable woman as his wife; instead has relationships with prostitutes. His misdeeds are draining his intellect and ability. Why can't he give up his antics and get pleasure in its purest form.' Cherusserinambuthiri sat feeling extremely sad.

NAMBUTHIRIPAD: Cherusseri, you might think that I am enamoured of many women.

The question made Cherusseri a little angry.

CHERUSSERINAMBUTHIRI: Men will always be enamoured of women. But it is not always good to be so.
NAMBUTHIRIPAD: What is so bad in being enamoured?
CHERUSSERINAMBUTHIRI: There is a lot in it. When a man and a woman share mutual love, their attraction is positive. But attraction without love is just a craze—a craze which can be disastrous.
NAMBUTHIRIPAD: Is the love that Ravanan felt for Rambha out of place?
CHERUSSERINAMBUTHIRI: That you should find out from Rambha. I do not know whether Rambha responded to Ravanan's love.
NAMBUTHIRIPAD: Oh! Ravanan got Rambha.
CHERUSSERINAMBUTHIRI: He might have.
NAMBUTHIRIPAD: Isn't that fulfilment?
CHERUSSERINAMBUTHIRI: I am not saying that a love that is out of place will not be fulfilled. It is not necessary for a woman to be in love with a man to live with him.
NAMBUTHIRIPAD: No?
CHERUSSERINAMBUTHIRI: No.
NAMBUTHIRIPAD: I don't understand what you are saying. You just said that misdirected love won't materialize.
CHERUSSERINAMBUTHIRI: I didn't say any such thing. Thieves and burglars sometimes get away with things. In the same way one can possess a woman or a man without love. But when the other doesn't respond to your love, it is base to try and win it by force.
NAMBUTHIRIPAD: What is low about it?
CHERUSSERINAMBUTHIRI: It does not have any substance, any value. A woman or a man who acts like that is like an animal—like a cow or a dog.

NAMBUTHIRIPAD: Then why did Ravanan love Sita? Isn't it said in the Ramayana that Sita was not attracted to him?

CHERUSSERINAMBUTHIRI: Precisely. Ravanan wanted Sita. He knew that Sita did not love him. So he tried very hard to make her love him—it did not work. Then he began to hate Sita and this destroyed him. However, we must remember that though Ravanan had many faults he never forced himself on Sita.

NAMBUTHIRIPAD: Then if I am attracted to a woman I can do all that Ravanan did.

CHERUSSERINAMBUTHIRI: If you decide to go through the hardships that he endured, and if you have his strength!

NAMBUTHIRIPAD: Let's say a man sees a woman and is very enamoured of her. But that the woman does not return the same feelings. How is that man to satisfy his desire?

CHERUSSERINAMBUTHIRI: What do you mean by enamoured? If you mean 'desire' then shouldn't a man courageously overcome his desire when he realizes that the woman is not attracted to him?

NAMBUTHIRIPAD: Why should I suppress the desire? Shouldn't I find out whether I will get her?

CHERUSSERINAMBUTHIRI: You should find out whether she will fall in love with you. If you don't get her love, give it up.

NAMBUTHIRIPAD: Even if it is attainable without her necessarily being attracted towards me?

CHERUSSERINAMBUTHIRI: Didn't I say that such people are like animals?

NAMBUTHIRIPAD: What you are saying is sheer stupidity! Why should a man consider whether the woman is enamoured of him or not?

CHERUSSERINAMBUTHIRI: I will explain. It is a man's pleasure to know that he has sexually pleased a woman. In the same way a woman should say that she had pleasure with a man only when she has given pleasure. If such feelings are to be fulfilled there has to be intense love between the two of them. Otherwise, if a man desires pleasure from a woman, he is like a beast—if the desire is fulfilled it can only be said that they performed some antics.

NAMBUTHIRIPAD: Self-restraint! That would be punishment indeed. If this is so, one man cannot have pleasure with many women—that is for sure.

CHERUSSERINAMBUTHIRI: Yes, ideally it is one woman for one man. That is the natural rule of creation.

Second Conversation between Indulekha and the Nambuthiripad

NAMBUTHIRIPAD: How many wives did Sri Krishnan have?
CHERUSSERINAMBUTHIRI: I do not know.
NAMBUTHIRIPAD: He had sixteen thousand and eight wives. What do you think of Sri Krishnan? Do you think he was a man of taste or not?
CHERUSSERINAMBUTHIRI: If he had sixteen thousand and eight wives and he was a human being like us, I will say he was not a man of taste at all and I would also say that he was a libertine. However, the very book from which we learn that he had so many wives, also tells us that he was not a human being. Sri Krishnan held up the Govardhan mountain with his left hand like an umbrella, saving the cows and the cowherds; and he brought to life those who had died by poison, and did many other things which are not humanly possible. I doubt whether the afore-mentioned rules which apply to ordinary human beings apply to a body that has the capacity to do all this.
NAMBUTHIRIPAD: If a man loves a woman, the woman too will love the man. I have shared pleasure with many women. All these women were charmed by me. Cherusseri, don't you know anything about this? Why are you talking in this strange way?

Cherusseri laughed. He felt very sad because he was left with a lingering sense of the ridiculous.

NAMBUTHIRIPAD: Don't you think that all women are enamoured of me?
CHERUSSERINAMBUTHIRI: I am not saying anything about your highness. I am talking about ordinary mortals.

At that moment Kesavannambuthiri came running to inform him that Indulekha would see him.

NAMBUTHIRIPAD: Wait—wait for some time. What is the hurry? Shouldn't we consider my convenience?
KESAVANNAMBUTHIRI: Certainly. Only when it is convenient for you.

Kesavannambuthiri was a little surprised—what is all this? What an unpredictable person! Before he could finish thinking all this, the Nambuthiripad started speaking.

NAMBUTHIRIPAD: We will go now. Karuthedam, you need not come, I alone shall go. Cherusseri, lie down here and sleep.

The Nambuthiripad in all seriousness draped the upper cloth over himself and went up to the malika. Indulekha was standing against the doorway like a prisoner who had been brought to the court to be questioned. The Nambuthiripad stepped out into the purathalam and saw Indulekha. The moment he saw her, this fool's bravado deserted him. He grinned and thought to himself 'Shiva-Shiva! In this birth I cannot do anything but sit with you, you beautiful woman! What a face! What complexion! What hair! What eyes! Shiva-Shiva! Narayana! Everything is gone, everything is gone. No determination. No courage. Where did Devendran's courage go when he saw the maharishi's wife?—When Ravanan saw Rambha?' He sat on the chair and somehow gathering courage said emphatically:

NAMBUTHIRIPAD: 'To a courageous man, a blade of grass and a beautiful woman are the same.' Indulekha, do you know of such a saying?
INDULEKHA: (laughing out loudly) I have heard it now. It is a very good saying.

Indulekha's laughter lent a certain expression to her face. The Nambuthiripad's carefully cultivated air of seriousness vanished. He forgot all his decisions and was captivated by Indulekha.

NAMBUTHIRIPAD: Please laugh aloud once more. Did they also teach you to laugh? The way you laugh is very beautiful. Please laugh once more.

Indulekha, tired of laughing, went inside to wash her face.

NAMBUTHIRIPAD: This is indeed bad! It looks as though it is not even possible to talk like yesterday. Then why did you ask me to come?
INDULEKHA: Please wait. I shall be with you soon.

She washed her face and came outside again.

NAMBUTHIRIPAD: How old are you, Indulekha?
INDULEKHA: Eighteen.
NAMBUTHIRIPAD: How old do you think I am?
INDULEKHA: I do not have the capacity to calculate age, when I see a person. Therefore it is not possible for me to tell.
NAMBUTHIRIPAD: Can't you even make a guess?
INDULEKHA: It may not be correct.
NAMBUTHIRIPAD: An approximate guess?

Second Conversation between Indulekha and the Nambuthiripad

INDULEKHA: If you want me to say something, I will say it. I think you have crossed fifty years.

NAMBUTHIRIPAD: Chi! What nonsense! You think I am past my youth. Have I crossed fifty? Can't you tell when you see youth in full bloom?

INDULEKHA: Didn't I tell you that I can't tell a person's age?

NAMBUTHIRIPAD: At eighteen you still can't spot a young man?

INDULEKHA: I don't know what you mean by 'young'.

NAMBUTHIRIPAD: It is because you have learnt English that you do not understand anything at all.

INDULEKHA: It is possible that that is the reason.

NAMBUTHIRIPAD: I haven't had a veli.

INDULEKHA: Well, that's good.

NAMBUTHIRIPAD: My younger brother married to have a family. I spend my time in great comfort. If Nambuthiris get married in their own community it marks the end of their comfort. I have never had a wife. Say something, Indulekha.

INDULEKHA: When your highness wishes to talk what can I say to interrupt?

NAMBUTHIRIPAD: Do you want to hear the sloka which I sent yesterday? I shall recite it.

INDULEKHA: No need—please don't trouble yourself.

NAMBUTHIRIPAD: That's no trouble. Isn't reciting slokas an enjoyable pastime?

INDULEKHA: I don't know.

NAMBUTHIRIPAD: You feel like that because you have studied English.

INDULEKHA: Maybe.

NAMBUTHIRIPAD: Studying English is fatal for the finer feeling of love.

INDULEKHA: That is true.

NAMBUTHIRIPAD: Indulekha, you have a fine sense of love.

INDULEKHA: I don't think so.

NAMBUTHIRIPAD: Have you read the poem called 'Nala'?

INDULEKHA: No.

NAMBUTHIRIPAD: Aren't women supposed to learn this poem? Shall I recite a sloka from that poem?

INDULEKHA: There is really no need to trouble yourself.

NAMBUTHIRIPAD: What is all this! Whenever I prepare to recite a sloka why do you call it a trouble?

INDULEKHA: Because it is troublesome.

NAMBUTHIRIPAD: Gem-studded thodas suit you better.

INDULEKHA: Is that so?

NAMBUTHIRIPAD: Do you have ear-studs set with gems?
INDULEKHA: No, I don't.
NAMBUTHIRIPAD: I shall get a pair made. I have some very special gemstones with me.
INDULEKHA: There is no need and occasion for you to make a pair for me.
NAMBUTHIRIPAD: I came here because a letter was sent to me.
INDULEKHA: Yes, I know that.
NAMBUTHIRIPAD: Panchumenon said Karuthedam wrote a letter. I came because of that.
INDULEKHA: Yes.
NAMBUTHIRIPAD: He invited me to visit here for a sambandam.
INDULEKHA: With whom? With Kesavannambuthiri?
NAMBUTHIRIPAD: Don't joke, I am extremely unhappy.
INDULEKHA: Yes.
NAMBUTHIRIPAD: Is it all right if I am unhappy?
INDULEKHA: Isn't that what you said?
NAMBUTHIRIPAD: What is this big box? Is it a music box?
INDULEKHA: Yes.
NAMBUTHIRIPAD: Can you play it?

Indulekha opened the box and started playing the piano.

From the two conversations, my readers might get the impression that Indulekha's attitude was ambivalent. The day before, Indulekha had not understood his character and situation as she had done today. A very well-placed man had come to carry her off. Yesterday her contempt and anger was intense at the fact that she was going to be tested. Today the situation had changed. Indulekha had learnt that her grandfather did not have a good opinion about the Nambuthiripad and that he would not want her to be tested by this Nambuthiripad. She realized from the Nambuthiripad's words that the Nambuthiripad himself had come to believe that he wouldn't get Indulekha. Not just that, when Indulekha assessed his low intelligence she could not help but feel sympathetic towards him.

When she started playing the piano, many people gathered below her malika. Like earlier times, Kesavannambuthiri stood near the stairs like a guard and said, 'Nobody need go up, there is no need to go up.' Those who were driven away like this started cursing Kesavannambuthiri and others.

ONE PATTAR: What is all this fuss about? During daytime, can't one enter

the room where a husband and wife are sitting together to listen to some music?
NAIR: Maybe the Nambuthiripad doesn't like other people coming into the room. Why should we upset him?
PATTAR: What does the Nambuthiripad stand to lose if someone else happens to listen to Indulekha singing?
NAMBUTHIRI: Isn't she a new wife? That is how it will be.

Just then Shankarashastrikal arrived at the temple. He saw a great bustle, people talking, and heard the piano from Indulekha's malika. He asked for Govindankuttymenon. Learning that he had gone with Govindapanikkar to Polpayikalam, Shankarashastrikal, overcome with intense sorrow, went off and lay down in the temple. He decided to leave for his native place that very day.

The music continued for ten minutes.

NAMBUTHIRIPAD: You can stop now. You must be tired. How long can you work with those tender hands?

Indulekha looked at him contemptuously.

The Nambuthiripad asked for his silver box and gold rose-water sprayer. After these were brought he turned to Indulekha and said:

NAMBUTHIRIPAD: Look at this box. Is it well made?

Indulekha looked at the box and the rose-water sprayer after taking them in her hands and expressing her appreciation returned them to him.

NAMBUTHIRIPAD: If you want them, they are yours.
INDULEKHA: No, I don't want them.
NAMBUTHIRIPAD: I have no objection to your having them.
INDULEKHA: I don't want them.
NAMBUTHIRIPAD: I don't desire any woman other than you, Indulekha.
INDULEKHA: So be it.
NAMBUTHIRIPAD: Oh! Are you agreeable to that?
INDULEKHA: I am.

Nambuthiripad smiled and stood up. He jumped up at once.

INDULEKHA: What antic is this?

NAMBUTHIRIPAD: Antic? Great luck has come my way. I should be dancing. Haven't I got Indulekha, didn't I get what I wanted?
INDULEKHA: You shouldn't talk like this. I will never be your wife in this birth. Even if you desire me, it is not going to work. If you speak in this manner again I will not see you. I have much to do.

Saying this, Indulekha went in. The Nambuthiripad immediately went downstairs.

By the time he reached the end of the staircase, he had already consoled himself with the thought of Lakshmikuttyamma and the girl he had seen later. He searched for Govindan and had a private chat with him. The following are the details:

NAMBUTHIRIPAD: What is it, Govinda? Is everything arranged?
GOVINDAN: Your slave has not told anyone anything. Your slave thinks that your highness should call on Panchumenon to talk about this in secrecy.
NAMBUTHIRIPAD: Then call Panchu, I shall tell him. I am certain about the matter concerning Indulekha. She will not be my wife in this birth at all.
GOVINDAN: Shiva! Shiva! What insolence! I haven't heard of such pride in women before. Your slave prays that tomorrow we can stand before her with Kalyani.
NAMBUTHIRIPAD: Yes. You are clever! Call Panchu.
GOVINDAN: It is better to sit in the gatehouse. I shall bring him there secretly.

Govindan went in search of Panchumenon.

The Nambuthiripad called Kesavannambuthiri and told him that there were certain important things that needed to be discussed. He asked him to be seated in another room. This was also one of Govindan's tricks. Kesavannambuthiri sat there looking rather sorrowful and fell asleep after some time.

When Govindan went in search of Panchumenon it was past three o'clock. Panchumenon was resting after his meal. Govindan stood outside the room and spoke to Kunjikuttyamma. Kunjikuttyamma went in and woke her husband. Angry at being woken up:

PANCHUMENON: You good-for-nothing, why are you troubling me?
KUNJIKUTTYAMMA: The Nambuthiripad is calling you.
PANCHUMENON: The Nambuthiripad! Stupid Nambuthiripad! Troubling us

all for no reason. Can't this good-for-nothing go away? I have never seen an ass like Kesavannambuthiri.
KUNJIKUTTYAMMA: There is no need to get upset. Indulekha and the Nambuthiripad spoke amicably to each other today. Till now there was music and laughter in the malika. Great enthusiasm. Indulekha is very happy, it seems.
PANCHUMENON: (sitting down very slowly) Was there music? When?
KUNJIKUTTYAMMA: When you went to the field on the eastern side.
PANCHUMENON: I didn't hear all that. Let me go and find out everything.

Saying this, the old man went happily with Govindan to the gatehouse.

chapter fourteen

The Nambuthiripad's Wedding

NAMBUTHIRIPAD: Panchu, I wish to speak to you in private.
PANCHUMENON: I can't imagine what it might be. I am at your command!
NAMBUTHIRIPAD: You should make it possible.
PANCHUMENON: Well, if it is possible, why should your slave have any objection?
NAMBUTHIRIPAD: It is possible.
PANCHUMENON: The decision can be made once the command is given.
NAMBUTHIRIPAD: I want to start a sambandam tonight with your niece Kalyani and before daybreak tomorrow I wish to proceed to my illam with her. Indulekha is not at all fascinated by me. Today, she told me in no uncertain words that she will not be my wife. I saw Kalyanikutty this morning, and I'm convinced that this is the best way out. The sambandam should take place tonight or I will be humiliated.

When Panchumenon heard this, he was very surprised. He stood still without saying a word. Then he laughed.

PANCHUMENON: Isn't this a little complicated? Let me think about it.
NAMBUTHIRIPAD: No, that is not possible. Panchu, you should not humiliate me. You should send me off honourably. I am already in a tricky position.
PANCHUMENON: Let me find out.
NAMBUTHIRIPAD: There is nothing to find out. If you permit, everything is possible.

PANCHUMENON: I shall get back to you soon.
NAMBUTHIRIPAD: Let this be a secret. People should get to know only after I leave.
PANCHUMENON: I will keep it a secret.

Panchumenon walked down from the room upstairs. What a story! He headed straight for his room, wondering what he should do now.

He was invited to start a sambandam with Indulekha and he is taking Kalyanikutty away! Won't this look ridiculous? And the butt of ridicule will be the Nambuthiripad. Indulekha had made it clear that she didn't want this idiotic Nambuthiripad. So he has decided to have a sambandam with Kalyanikutty and take *her* away. This is not an insult to Indulekha, nor to Kalyanikutty. Though a fool, he's a great man, is he not? And rich! Had Indulekha wanted him Kalyani could never have made this sambandam. Again, isn't a sambandam with this Nambuthiripad an asset to the taravad? Therefore, it was better to give his permission. 'Anyway, I shall consult my younger brother Shankaran on this,' he thought. He then called out for his wife.

KUNJIKUTTYAMMA: What is it? Isn't what I told you correct?
PANCHUMENON: (laughing) Yes, yes. Ask someone to fetch Shankaran.
KUNJIKUTTYAMMA: I shall send someone, but will the sambandam take place today?
PANCHUMENON: (laughing) Today itself.

Kunjikuttyamma immediately despatched a person to fetch Shankaramenon, she told all the servants and the maids and whoever she saw, that it was Indulekha's sambandam that night. The news spread everywhere. When Shankaramenon did not turn up, Panchumenon himself went to Poovally house in order to search for him. Just then Shankarashastri came to Poovarangu to take leave of Panchumenon as he had decided to go to his village.

Shankarashastri was the shastrikal who had been appointed by Panchumenon to recite the Ramayana every day. One didn't know why he wished to return to his village. Was it because he was disillusioned by Indulekha's decision? Well, whatever the reason, he had decided to go. At Poovarangu it was Kunjikuttyamma he met.

SHASTRIKAL: Where is he?
KUNJIKUTTYAMMA: He has gone to Poovally. Indulekha's sambandam has

been fixed for tonight, Shastrikal. Why aren't you doing anything about that? I didn't see you here at all.

SHASTRIKAL: I don't feel well. I am going back to my village. By the time the moon sets, I hope to reach our oottupura and probably sleep there tonight.

KUNJIKUTTYAMMA: Today is the day for Indulekha's sambandam; you can't go!

SHASTRIKAL: I must go right away. Please tell him (Panchumenon) I will be back in seven or eight days. Until then I have arranged with Annatharavadyar for the recitations and other things.

KUNJIKUTTYAMMA: I shall tell him.

Back at the temple, Shastrikal decided to leave at seven in the evening with two Nambuthiripads who had urgent business to finish. From Chambazhiyot, the railway station is at quite a distance. Since moonlight brightened his path he decided to walk half the way.

By the time Panchumenon found Shankaramenon it was almost six o'clock.

PANCHUMENON: Where were you, Shankara?

SHANKARAMENON: I was in the field planting the coconut saplings. I do not appreciate your handing over the responsibility of the compound to Unnikitta. They are not turning over the soil fast enough. The saplings have been planted too close to each other.

PANCHUMENON: We shall talk about all that later. Do you want to listen to a bit of news?

SHANKARAMENON: What is it?

PANCHUMENON: That Nambuthiripad wants to take away our Kalyanikutty after a sambandam.

SHANKARAMENON: What is all this?

PANCHUMENON: He just sent for me and told me so.

SHANKARAMENON: Ammama, what did you say to that?

PANCHUMENON: I haven't said anything definite. I thought I would discuss it with you and then decide. Shouldn't we get Govindapanikkar—send somebody!

SHANKARAMENON: Govindapanikkar has gone to Polpayikalam with Govindankutty for a hunt. They will return only tomorrow.

PANCHUMENON: His craze for hunting is a little excessive. Why did he drag that boy with him? I think Govindankutty has also become like

Madhavan. This is the result of teaching these good-for-nothing children English. Anyway, what do you think of this sambandam?

SHANKARAMENON: Whatever you wish.

PANCHUMENON: Even if the Nambuthiripad is a fool, he's a noble man, isn't he? His sambandam will be an asset to our taravad—there is no doubt about that. My only unease is that this sambandam is for someone who belongs to the family of Kumminiamma.

SHANKARAMENON: Do not worry about that. The girl is meek.

PANCHUMENON: It is the boys who are troublesome. All right, are you agreeable to it, Shankaran?

SHANKARAMENON: I am agreeable to whatever you would like to do.

PANCHUMENON: Then you should go to the Nambuthiripad and let him know about it.

SHANKARAMENON: Hasn't it been decided that it should take place today itself?

PANCHUMENON: (laughing) That is what the Nambuthiripad said. If it is over and done with today, he will go off from here tomorrow. So let it be today itself.

SHANKARAMENON: I shall tell Kesavannambuthiri.

PANCHUMENON: The Nambuthiripad told me this story in great secret. You need not tell Kesavannambuthiri about this now. But send for Govindan, who is with the Nambuthiripad.

Shankaramenon went to the part below the gatehouse and told Govindan the news. It was already seven in the evening. Govindan immediately went into the room where the Nambuthiripad was seated like a tiger waiting for its prey.

NAMBUTHIRIPAD: What is it Govinda? Has everything been arranged?

GOVINDAN: Yes. Everything has been arranged, don't delay your bath. Everyone is agreeable to this matter. But you should not talk about it to anyone. I have made it known to everyone that the sambandam is with Indulekha.

NAMBUTHIRIPAD: Will anyone believe it?

GOVINDAN: Immediately after your bath you must give gifts to the Brahmins. After that they will disperse and carry the news outside that the sambandam is with Indulekha.

NAMBUTHIRIPAD: You are indeed clever. But won't Karuthedam and Cherusseri come to know about this matter?

GOVINDAN: They do suspect but do not know for certain. Let the gifts be given after your bath.

NAMBUTHIRIPAD: Where is Cherusseri?

GOVINDAN: He has gone to the temple or some other place. Your slave didn't see him.

NAMBUTHIRIPAD: What about Karuthedam? I had told Karuthedam to sit right here.

GOVINDAN: He woke up just now and is sitting in the south room chewing betel.

NAMBUTHIRIPAD: Then let us go and bathe.

Saying this he made Govindan hold the portable brass lamp and went downstairs. Kesavannambuthiri also went with him. When they reached the front of the temple they saw Shankarashastrikal with two other Nambuthiris. They had just had their dinner and were waiting in the courtyard to go to the station. The Nambuthiripad was acquainted with one of the Nambuthiris.

NAMBUTHIRIPAD: O—ho! Kilimangalam, when did you arrive? Where are you going at this time of the night?

KILIMANGALAM: I am going to the court on an urgent business. Otherwise I wouldn't have started off without meeting you. I heard that you had come. I was very happy. I will come and see you soon.

NAMBUTHIRIPAD: Kilimangalam, have you seen Indulekha?

KILIMANGALAM: No.

NAMBUTHIRIPAD: You can come to the mana and see her. I shall start from here early in the morning.

KILIMANGALAM: You must be taking her with you?

NAMBUTHIRIPAD: Yes. Is there any doubt about that?

KILIMANGALAM: That is exactly how it should be. No one can match your luck. I will come to the mana very soon and meet her.

As soon as this conversation was over, Shastrikal and the Nambuthiris went to the rest house to sleep.

The Nambuthiripad finished his bath immediately and invited the Brahmins to the madom and gave them gifts. Two hundred Brahmins received their gifts and dispersed.

In the meantime, Shankaramenon told Kalyanikutty's mother Kumminiamma to make arrangements. The news made Kumminiamma extremely happy. She informed Parvathiamma immediately. Parvathiamma was overjoyed for two reasons. She went up at once to Indulekha's room where she found her talking to Cherusserinambuthiri. The moment Indulekha saw Parvathiamma coming in, she stood up. Parvathiamma told her that she had something very personal to tell her. Both of them went further into Indulekha's quarters.

PARVATHIAMMA: Did you hear the news?
INDULEKHA: No; what is it?
PARVATHIAMMA: The Nambuthiripad has decided to begin a sambandam with Kalyanikutty tonight.

Indulekha laughed a great deal and for a long time. Upon recovering her breath:

INDULEKHA: Who told you all this?
PARVATHIAMMA: Shankara jeshtan came to Poovally and conveyed the message. Everyone was busy arranging the west room, laying the cot and the mattress. Ammaman was sitting at the back. He asked for the lamps and other things to be taken from the room.
INDULEKHA: Has Kalyanikutty been informed of this matter?
PARVATHIAMMA: I have not seen her. I do not know whether *jeshtathi* [elder sister] has told her. She seemed extremely happy.
INDULEKHA: It is a pity! Shouldn't that girl be informed when a sambandam is going to be started for her? Why don't you go now? I will see the Nambuthiripad off and come to Poovally immediately.

Smiling, Indulekha went to the veranda outside.

INDULEKHA: Your highness, did you hear some news? The Nambuthiripad wishes for a sambandam with Grandfather's niece, Kalyanikutty, tonight.
CHERUSSERI: (laughing) God's grace! If he hadn't got Kalyanikutty he would certainly have had a sambandam with the maid. What a pity! When a man doesn't have reason and pride what good is he at all! If the news is correct, the return journey will take place early tomorrow morning. By the time Madhavan reaches here I will be home. In case you plan to go to Madras the day after his arrival, let me know through a letter. I will come to Madras. Let good fortune follow you hard and fast, you and Madhavan.

Cherusseri then took leave of Indulekha and arrived at the madom. The Nambuthiripad had finished distributing the gifts and was seated on the veranda chewing betel leaves.

Kesavannambuthiri was still very perplexed thinking of the gifts that had been given, the Nambuthiripad's conversation with Kilimangalam, and the singing in the afternoon. He was unable to make sense of anything. The moment the Nambuthiripad settled on the veranda, Kesavannambuthiri took Cherusserinambuthiri indoors.

KESAVANNAMBUTHIRI: What is all this, Cherusseri? I do not understand anything. Where were you all this while?
CHERUSSERINAMBUTHIRI: I was in Indulekha's malika.
KESAVANNAMBUTHIRI: What is happening? Today gifts were given and there is talk of a sambandam. Has Indulekha agreed?
CHERUSSERINAMBUTHIRI: There *is* a sambandam today, but not for Indulekha.

Kesavannambuthiri's heart missed a beat. Feeling faint he sat down and drank a whole pot of water. Now he understood the reason he had been made to stay in the room and the secret conversation between Panchumenon and the Nambuthiripad. Quite sure that his wife Lakshmikutty was lost to him, and struggling with intense and unbearable pain he looked at Cherusseri. Cherusseri was determined that Kesavannambuthiri should learn a lesson.

CHERUSSERINAMBUTHIRI: Why are you looking at me? Karuthedam, you are responsible for all this!

The remark convinced Kesavannambuthiri that he had lost his wife.

KESAVANNAMBUTHIRI: I did not think of any of this, Cherusseri. I am a simple man. I will not stay here for another moment. I am returning this minute to my illam, never to return.
CHERUSSERINAMBUTHIRI: Can you leave without asking the Nambuthiripad?
KESAVANNAMBUTHIRI: I will not speak to him in this birth. Nor shall I step into Moorkillatha mana. I am not a dependent of this Nambuthiripad. I had no idea that he was such an insensitive and thoughtless person.
CHERUSSERINAMBUTHIRI: Karuthedam, do you remember you asked me to take the initiative about Indulekha's sambandam and I said that it was not possible for me?
KESAVANNAMBUTHIRI: I do remember, and very clearly. Cherusseri, you are

a brain. If I had a hundredth of your intelligence, none of this misfortune would have befallen me.

CHERUSSERINAMBUTHIRI: Do you understand now that if you interfere in matters that are not your concern, you will bring trouble only upon yourself?

KESAVANNAMBUTHIRI: I understand perfectly well, Cherusseri! Anyway, I cannot stand here and be a witness to this sambandam. Let me call the servants.

CHERUSSERINAMBUTHIRI: Karuthedam, what objection do you have in witnessing this sambandam?

KESAVANNAMBUTHIRI: Punishment—a good punishment! I may not be as intelligent as you are, but don't think I am such a fool.

CHERUSSERINAMBUTHIRI: What is all this? How can you be a fool if you are present when the Nambuthiripad begins a sambandam with Kalyanikutty?

Kesavannambuthiri gaped in astonishment.

KESAVANNAMBUTHIRI: For Kalyanikutty? Is the sambandam with Kalyanikutty?

CHERUSSERINAMBUTHIRI: Yes, with Kalyanikutty.

KESAVANNAMBUTHIRI: Shiva! Shiva! Narayana! Narayana! I was very perplexed! Shiva! Shiva! Cherusseri, you made me intensely unhappy.

CHERUSSERINAMBUTHIRI: I did not make you unhappy. What did I say? Did I say that the sambandam was for a particular person? Did you ask me, Karuthedam? No, I just said that the sambandam was not for Indulekha. What can I do, if you are unhappy believing that the sambandam is for your wife?

Kesavannambuthiri's breathing became normal. Both of them went to the Nambuthiripad and together they headed for Poovarangu where they sat talking to Panchumenon for a long time. Then all four, with the servants, went to Poovally. According to custom, the Nambuthiripad washed his feet and entered the house, went to the western room and lay down on the special silk bedspread. Then like a live pig that is brought to its pen, the womenfolk of the house brought poor Kalyanikutty and pushed her into the western room, securely locking the door from the outside. The sambandam was over. Ever alert, Govindan got all the palanquin bearers together, and stood waiting outside ready to leave. He also warned everybody accompanying the Nambuthiripad that should anyone ask on the way, they were to say that it was Indulekha herself who was being taken away after the sambandam. Just a little before dawn, Govindan stood outside the door of the western room and coughed, trying to wake up he Nambuthiripad. Immediately everyone in the house woke up. Panchumenon and Kesavannambuthiri arrived from Poovarangu. The girl was locked into a palanquin. The Nambuthiripad got into his palanquin. Kesavannambuthiri deciding to follow the Nambuthiripad on his journey, got into a litter and Cherusseri, smiling, got into his. They all set off with a lot of noise and loud cries.

chapter fifteen

A Calamity

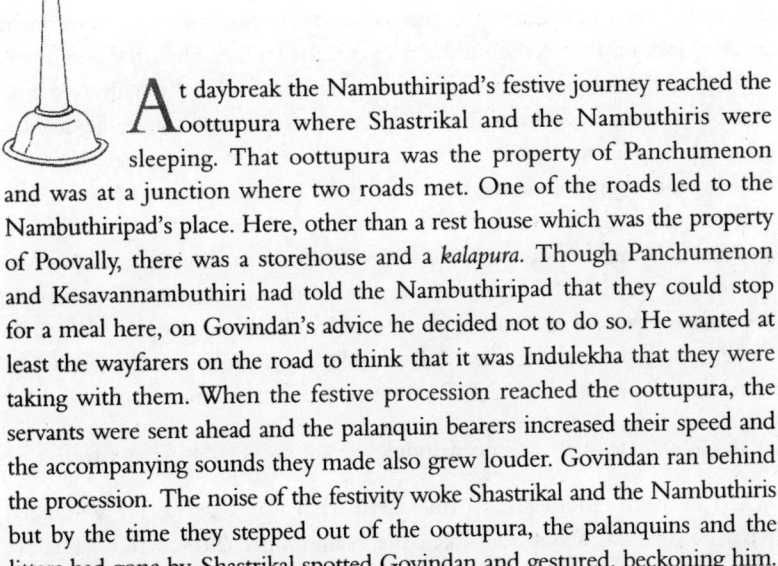

At daybreak the Nambuthiripad's festive journey reached the oottupura where Shastrikal and the Nambuthiris were sleeping. That oottupura was the property of Panchumenon and was at a junction where two roads met. One of the roads led to the Nambuthiripad's place. Here, other than a rest house which was the property of Poovally, there was a storehouse and a *kalapura*. Though Panchumenon and Kesavannambuthiri had told the Nambuthiripad that they could stop for a meal here, on Govindan's advice he decided not to do so. He wanted at least the wayfarers on the road to think that it was Indulekha that they were taking with them. When the festive procession reached the oottupura, the servants were sent ahead and the palanquin bearers increased their speed and the accompanying sounds they made also grew louder. Govindan ran behind the procession. The noise of the festivity woke Shastrikal and the Nambuthiris but by the time they stepped out of the oottupura, the palanquins and the litters had gone by. Shastrikal spotted Govindan and gestured, beckoning him.

SHASTRIKAL: What is it, Govinda! This is the oottupura and there are rooms reserved for him. Wasn't it better to stop by and have a meal?
GOVINDAN: That is what Kesavannambuthiri and others said. My lord and Cherusserinambuthiri were also of that mind. But someone was very adamant that that person should reach the mana and have a meal there itself. That person is stubbornness itself!
SHASTRIKAL: Who are you talking about—Indulekha?
GOVINDAN: Yes.
SHASTRIKAL: She is not stubborn but evil.

GOVINDAN: She is evil! About that I have no doubts. What can be done! My lord is greatly in love with her. Indulekha too feels the same towards him. From now onwards we are Indulekha's slaves—what are we to do!

SHASTRIKAL: Indulekha's love is a love for amassing wealth—she knows no other love.

GOVINDAN: There's no doubt about that. I'll make a move now. The palanquins have far outstripped me.

Govindan ran after the procession. Shastrikal and the Nambuthiris took the road to the railway station.

As his letter said, Madhavan took the train from Madras the day before the sambandam took place. On the day of the festive journey, he got down at 11 o'clock in the morning at the railway station where Shastrikal and others were heading to catch the train to their native place. Near the railway station were two or three madoms that served meals. Tired and hungry he decided to eat there. He expected to reach the rest house by evening where he could rest for the night and arrive home the next day in time for the meal. (He had brought only one servant with him. Shinnan and another servant were in Madras while he was on leave for eight days.) At the madom he found one or two wayfarer Nambuthiris and some pattars conversing. These people were the ones who had had food in the Chambazhiyot temple. They were staying there because they hadn't been able to get the morning train. All of them had eaten and were gossiping when Madhavan entered.

ONE NAMBUTHIRI: It is indeed Indulekha's luck—that is what I feel.

When he heard Indulekha's name, Madhavan was startled. He wondered what all this was about and asked the Nambuthiri, 'Which Indulekha are you talking about?'

NAMBUTHIRI: A girl named Chambazhiyot Indulekha. Why, do you know her?

MADHAVAN: What is the luck that has befallen Indulekha? I'd like to know.

NAMBUTHIRI: Yesterday was Indulekha's sambandam.

Madhavan stood for a moment like a tree struck by lightning. He tried to speak, but couldn't. After a whole minute he could only stammer:

MADHAVAN: Who?—who?—who is it who has begun a sambandam?

Seeing Madhavan's countenance, all the Nambuthiris were perplexed. They stared at each other.

MADHAVAN: Who?—who? speak up. What are you trying to keep back? Why can't you tell me? Who has begun a sambandam? I must know.

ONE NAMBUTHIRI: What is it, you seem quite disturbed? Why are you so angry? We don't know the details.

MADHAVAN: If you don't know, you shouldn't say anything without knowing for certain.

ONE PATTAR: What are you going to do? Will you punish us?

MADHAVAN: Are you testing me?

Madhavan then advanced threateningly towards the pattar. Just then, another Nambuthiri intervened. 'Hey, you shouldn't be angry. Sit down. He seems to have just got off the train. Maybe he is coming from Madras. You can tell from his face that he is tired. Sit down. Then we will talk.'

MADHAVAN: Who did you say has had a sambandam with Indulekha? I want to know that.

PATTAR: It is the Moorkillatha Manakkal Nambuthiripad.

MADHAVAN: When did the sambandam take place?

PATTAR: It must have been yesterday. We came away early. The sambandam was decided for last night. We know that for certain.

MADHAVAN: How do you know for certain?

PATTAR: The people in the temple said this. Your relative by marriage, Shinupattar, also told me.

Madhavan sat down lifelessly on the veranda.

An old Brahmin woman, who sold meals in the madom, seeing this extremely handsome boy in such a baffled state, immediately came outside and laid out a mat for him. 'Please sit on this. If you drink some buttermilk it will ease your weariness. Shall I bring some?' she asked. Madhavan was deaf to all her entreaties. He sat down on the floor, and after some time said to no one in particular, 'I want some water to drink.' A Nambuthiri gave him some water and then unrolling his mat he lay down on it. Seeing the sorrow of this tender boy, all the people in the madom grieved equally. After some time, he began to read the letter that his father Govindapanikkar had written about the Nambuthiripad's sambandam. This is what he had written: 'The karanavan and Kesavannambuthiri are trying very hard to fix up a sambandam for Indulekha with the Moorkillatha Manakkal Nambuthiripad. This Nambuthiripad is very wealthy. Even then I don't think the sambandam will come about. My child, you need not worry about this at all.' Madhavan put the letter back in the box and lay down again to think.

'Can it ever happen? It is not possible for such a thing to happen. However, I didn't get any letter from Madhavi about this Nambuthiripad. She has never delayed writing to me. It could also be due to other things. However, Shinupattar won't speak irresponsibly! What is all this! Maybe this is how a woman's mind works. The Nambuthiripad may be more capable than I. Maybe he is smarter and more humorous. Indulekha might have fallen in love with him. Ammaman might have compelled her.' One moment he would think like this and the next moment he would deny everything. 'Can my Madhavi ever desire another man even for a moment? What a fool I am! Chi! Somebody made up a story and these people believed it. But they got this news from Shinupattar.' While Madhavan lay there with his mind oscillating thus, some wayfarers stopped by. They lived near the place where the Nambuthiripad lived. They were people who had witnessed the Nambuthiripad's festive journey. One of them was telling another, 'On the way we saw a festive journey.' The moment Madhavan heard this his body was rocked by shock waves and an unpleasant sensation swamped his body and mind.

ONE NAMBUTHIRI: What is the festivity? Whose journey is it?
THE NAMBUTHIRI (who had consoled Madhavan earlier): Don't ask anything. That person lying there will quarrel again.
ANOTHER NAMBUTHIRI: What is all this! Can't we talk? Let him quarrel—what was the festivity about, tell us.
ONE OF THE WAYFARERS: It was the journey made by the Moorkillatha Manakkal Nambuthiripad. The girl from Chambazhiyot whose sambandam was over yesterday was in one palanquin, his eminence in another, Cherusseri Govindannambuthiri in one litter, Karuthedam Kesavannambuthiri in another litter, lots of servants with swords and shields, crying and calling out. What festivity!
THE NAMBUTHIRI (who had answered earlier to another Nambuthiri): Look, he's got up—now he will quarrel. Look at the way he's standing.
MADHAVAN: No—I won't quarrel at all.

Saying this he began pacing the courtyard of the madom. Just then he saw Shankarashastrikal and the others going into the madom on the south.

Madhavan called out. Shastrikal turned back and was greatly perplexed. 'My ill luck! Has this also come to me so quickly! How will I face this boy? What shall I tell him? I am a great sinner.'

SHANKARASHASTRIKAL: Yes, it is me.
MADHAVAN: What I heard here about Madhavi, is it all true?
SHANKARASHASTRIKAL: Yes.

The 'yes' struck him like lightning. Madhavan's face and body darkened and seemed to shrivel like Nalan becoming disfigured by the snake Karkodakan's bite. He did not say anything to Shastrikal. To the east was a big pond and a peepul tree with a cemented seat at its base. He walked towards that. Shastrikal followed him. Madhavan did not notice Shastrikal following him. He stood leaning against the tree for almost half an hour, blind and numb. A certain calm settled on him. Turning he saw Shastrikal standing near him but could not stem the flow of tears. Shastrikal also wept. Poor Shastrikal was sadder than Madhavan and couldn't utter a word. Finally, Madhavan himself felt that this was degrading. Wiping his tears, and mustering up courage, he spoke to Shastrikal:

MADHAVAN: Why are you sad, Shastrikal? Such things happen in the world.

Shastrikal could not speak at all. His voice trembled and eyes watered. This Brahmin was very educated and also had a fine sense of humour, but Indulekha's cruelty and its effect on Madhavan saddened him profoundly. Madhavan was very fond of this Shastrikal as was Indulekha.

MADHAVAN: Why are you needlessly unhappy? Then, for Madhavi—no for Indulekha—this is a happy time. Your friends, Indulekha and I, are not sorry. Then, why are you sad about me?
SHASTRIKAL: Henceforth, Indulekha is not worthy of my love. I hate her.

At this, Madhavan's eyes filled again. He stood wordless.

MADHAVAN: Why should you blame her so much? This must be the obstinacy of my ammaman.
SHASTRIKAL: But it looked as though she and the Nambuthiripad were very fond of each other, with matching temperaments. The Nambuthiripad? A great fool who is known the world over for his folly. He has the face of a horse.

MADHAVAN: Enough, enough. I don't want to hear all this. I am going back to Madras by the evening train.
SHASTRIKAL: I think that is best. Then shouldn't you eat quickly?
MADHAVAN: I don't feel like eating.
SHASTRIKAL: But you must. If you don't wish to eat in the madom, I shall bring your food here. There is no one around and it is quite cool also.
MADHAVAN: Then bring me some rice after you finish.

Shastrikal went off to eat. Madhavan sat under the peepul tree and began thinking. He decided to do something. That you will read in this story further.

After his meal he boarded the train. He did not allow Shastrikal to accompany him.

The next day as soon as he reached Madras he went to meet Gilham sayiv. He had not gone to the court that day but was in his office and Madhavan's card surprised him. He had taken leave for eight days just two days ago saying he was going to Malabar to get married. When Madhavan came in, Gilham sayiv understood that something terrible must have happened. Gilham sayiv was very fond of Madhavan and had decided to take Madhavan into the civil services. The intense sorrow and the journey to and fro had ravaged Madhavan's face. If he had not sent his card in, the sayiv would have found it difficult to recognize him.

GILHAM SAYIV: Madhavan, what is this? Was there a death in your family? Why did you return so quickly? Your face and manner show that something is very amiss—please sit down.
MADHAVAN: Nobody in my family or among my friends has died, but I am in great mental agony. I don't hesitate to tell you this because I know you are very fond of me.

The moment he heard this, the clever sayiv could more or less comprehend what the matter was. He remembered that Madhavan had taken leave for his wedding. Something must have happened. If Madhavan wished to recount it, he had no problem listening. But knowing that he would be embarrassed the sayiv did not ask for an explanation.

GILHAM SAYIV: I don't need to know the reason right away. You can tell me later at your leisure. But if you want me to do anything for you I would be happy to do so.

MADHAVAN: I am going to ask you to give me a year's leave. I want to travel in the country.

The sayiv thought for a while and replied:

GILHAM SAYIV: If you have an emotional problem, there's nothing like travel to clear it. Your views about travel to clear the mind have convinced me, especially because after your education you have not travelled anywhere. We, in foreign countries, after leaving the university, travel and only then work. Which country are you planning to travel in? If it is possible, you should go to Europe. However, it's winter the next three months, and an unhealthy time. After that, it is very pleasant weather. But where do you plan to go immediately?

MADHAVAN: If it is not advisable to go to Europe, I will travel in north India and Burma and see some places.

GILHAM SAYIV: Then I think you should take leave for only four months. If you want more leave write to me, I will extend it. I can see that you are very tired. Quick. Go and eat something.

Saying this, the sayiv rose and gripped Madhavan's hand. 'May you be blessed by auspicious events. May all your sorrows end and let me see you well.' When he said this, there were tears in the eyes of both men.

Madhavan came back immediately, bathed, and made a pretence of eating. He then wrote a letter to his father and sent Shinnan and the two servants with the letter to Malabar. The next day in the evening he took the train to Bombay.

The story I have to tell you now is a pitiable one. It is more painful than what I have written until this point. However, I cannot but write about it.

Shinnan and the two servants found themselves in the Chambazhiyot oottupura by midday the next day. They stayed the night there and reached Chambazhiyot by ten o'clock the next morning. Shinnan and one of the servants went to Poovally and the second servant went to Govindapanikkar's house. He and Govindankuttymenon were seated, chatting, and when he saw the servant Govindapanikkar asked him whether Madhavan had also come. 'Kuttanmenon master has not come—there is a letter,' said the servant.

Govindapanikkar felt a little uneasy. 'He is not ill or anything, is he?' After the servant had assured him that Madhavan was not ill, he opened the letter and read:

I got all the news from Shankarashastrikal and the others. You and I had the same opinion about Indulekha. But I don't blame myself too much for being so misguided about her. No one can measure the range and pattern of human hypocrisy. As I am very upset mentally, I am setting out on a tour of the country. If I feel well after some time I shall come and see you and mother. Father, you need not worry about me. Don't ever imagine that I will commit suicide or any such stupid deed. I will return after my tour is over. However, when that will be I have no idea. I am fully aware of how dear a son I am to you and my mother. Whatever I might write, I know you will be upset. But think of my mother, and don't reveal the full extent of your sorrow. If you, my father, show even a bit of sorrow, my mother will be very sad. I am leaving Madras tomorrow.

To make my father aware of all this,—Madhavan.

The moment Govindapanikkar read the letter he cried,'Oh, my God! My dear child! You have left me and run away.' Saying this he beat his breast and fainted. Govindankuttymenon immediately read the letter and understood everything. He then sprinkled some water on Govindapanikkar's face. The moment he regained consciousness, Govindankuttymenon said in great anger.

GOVINDANKUTTYMENON: What has Madhavan done? A pity—a pity! Though so intelligent he has acted like this. What a great pity! When you fainted I wondered whether Madhavan had died. You are grieving unnecessarily, not because you are not intelligent and perceptive but because of your intense love for Madhavan. After all, what has happened to Madhavan? He felt sick at heart and has decided to go on a tour of the country. And he has informed you. What is there to worry about so much? There are trains all over India—if he were going to Europe, that too can be managed comfortably. If we spend a little bit of money we can get to know his whereabouts. But we ourselves will go in search of him.

GOVINDAPANIKKAR: I will have a meal only after I leave Malabar—there is no doubt about that.

GOVINDANKUTTYMENON: So be it. I will also accompany you. You are grieving without any reason! If Madhavan's mother sees you sorrowing like this, how will she bear it?

By the time this much was said, Indulekha was seen coming up to the house in clear sunlight. Immediately Govindapanikkar wiped his tears and got up.

Indulekha's face was the colour of blood after walking in the sun. Her hair was undone and was sweeping the ground. 'What is the news from Madras?' Behind her, Indulekha's mother, grandmother, Parvathiamma, and four or five servants could be seen. It was quite a crowd.

INDULEKHA: What is the news from Madras? Tell me.

GOVINDANKUTTYMENON: Indulekha, go inside. You need not be upset; there is nothing to worry.

PARVATHIAMMA: Oh! Where has my child gone? Oh-Oh-I can't continue living for another moment.

INDULEKHA: Shinnan told me that he had brought a letter. Where is that letter?

Govindapanikkar gave the letter to Indulekha.

The moment she read the letter she rushed into the house, threw herself on the bed and began wailing. Parvathiamma's cries became unbearable.

'My dear son, when will I get to see you again? There is no child, God knows, like my son. Why should I continue living, God? My child, who will look after you? Knowing that I don't have any other children, you still left me like this and went away—my dear child! Oh my God!'

She began beating her breast violently. No one had the courage to say a word to this mother.

By then Shankaramenon, Chatharamenon, and others arrived from Poovally.

SHANKARAMENON: (to Parvathiamma) Why are you crying like this? Nothing has happened to Madhavan.

The moment he said this, Shankaramenon also started crying. He was extremely fond of Madhavan.

SHANKARAMENON: (wiping his tears) In ten days time Madhavan will come back. Wherever he is, we will go and bring him. Then why are you grieving?

PARVATHIAMMA: If you are going I will also come with you. I cannot sit around without my son. That is certain.

SHANKARAMENON: All right, Parvathi can also come. Go to Poovally and sit quietly there. Get up—everything will work out well. No harm will befall Madhavan.

GOVINDAPANIKKAR: Parvathi, go now. I am going with Govindankutty this moment in search of Madhavan. Within ten days we will come back with Madhavan. You need not grieve at all.

They consoled Parvathiamma and sent her to Poovally.

Nobody had the courage to tell Indulekha anything. Finally, on the insistence of Govindankuttymenon and Shankaramenon, Govindapanikkar went in to console Indulekha.

GOVINDAPANIKKAR: (to Indulekha) Why are you grieving? Nothing has happened for us to grieve like this. If you continue to grieve, the journey Govindankutty and I have decided to undertake in search of Madhavan will have to be cancelled.

When she heard this, Indulekha sat up.

INDULEKHA: Have you decided to go in search for him?
GOVINDAPANIKKAR: Certainly, I am going.
INDULEKHA: He must have embarked on a voyage by now. What then?

At that moment Govindankuttymenon stepped into the room.

GOVINDANKUTTYMENON: Why, can't we get a ship to England? You need not worry about anything. If we are alive we will bring Madhavan back with us.

Saying this Govindankuttymenon called his mother and together they went to Poovarangu to get ready for the journey.

INDULEKHA: (to Govindapanikkar) Who could have caused all this havoc? I don't know of anyone who is against me and Madhavan.
GOVINDAPANIKKAR: There's been some misunderstanding. It is rumoured that the days when the Nambuthiripad listened to songs in your room, he slept there those two nights. I heard people say that in Polpayi. Didn't Shastrikal also say something foolish to Madhavan? What can be done! It is our ill luck—I won't come back without seeing my child. If I don't meet him I will die.

When he said this tears flowed from his eyes.

INDULEKHA: Do not grieve, you will surely meet him. All of us will be happy. However, my main worry is that even though he knew my character very well he decided so quickly that I am a person without inner strength. That is a grief I cannot bear.

Saying this Indulekha wept.

GOVINDAPANIKKAR: This time when Madhavan was leaving for Madras I had myself spoken to him about your competence and other qualities. It is unfortunate that he did not remember that conversation. There is no point grieving in this manner. Let me prepare fully for the journey.

He consoled Indulekha somewhat, and sent her back to Poovarangu with her mother Lakshmikuttyamma. Govindapanikkar consoled his wife for a while and got ready to go. Panchumenon was very happy when he heard the news. 'All this will happen to a rebel like him.' However, he had not clearly understood the reason for Madhavan's going away. He had made a faint guess that it might be because Madhavan was frightened of Panchumenon's vow. When Govindankuttymenon took leave of Panchumenon, the latter was not pleased at all, but knowing fully well that any expostulation would be ineffective, he nodded his assent. That night, after dinner, Govindapanikkar and Govindankuttymenon, with four servants, set out in search of Madhavan.

chapter sixteen

Madhavan's Tour of the Country

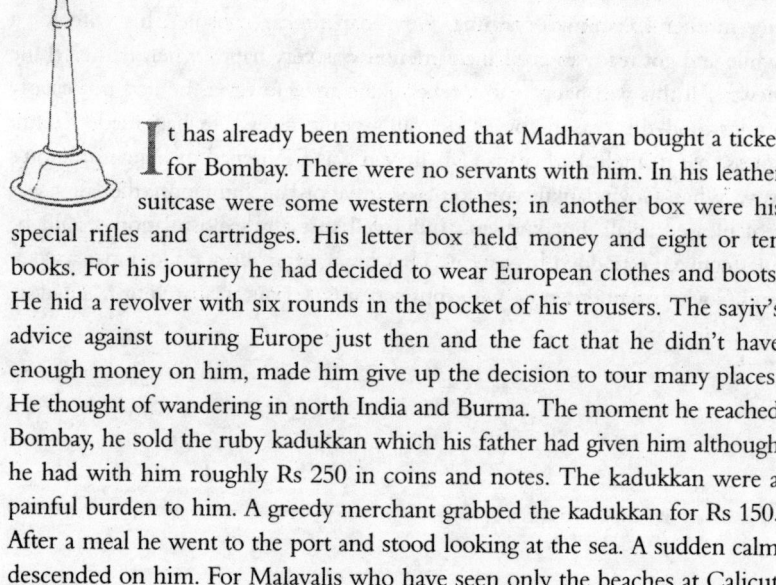

It has already been mentioned that Madhavan bought a ticket for Bombay. There were no servants with him. In his leather suitcase were some western clothes; in another box were his special rifles and cartridges. His letter box held money and eight or ten books. For his journey he had decided to wear European clothes and boots. He hid a revolver with six rounds in the pocket of his trousers. The sayiv's advice against touring Europe just then and the fact that he didn't have enough money on him, made him give up the decision to tour many places. He thought of wandering in north India and Burma. The moment he reached Bombay, he sold the ruby kadukkan which his father had given him although he had with him roughly Rs 250 in coins and notes. The kadukkan were a painful burden to him. A greedy merchant grabbed the kadukkan for Rs 150. After a meal he went to the port and stood looking at the sea. A sudden calm descended on him. For Malayalis who have seen only the beaches at Calicut and at other places, it is impossible to imagine the features of the Bombay port. All the merchant and battle ships sailing to England or coming to India first dock at Bombay. There are huge ships which fill the place. All the grand people who come from England disembark here. In the same manner, people from India headed for England embark for their voyage here. Practically all the special cargo which comes from England to India is first unloaded in this great port. Need I say anything more about the greatness of such a place?

The view of the harbour in the evening is incomparable. I am sure such beauty cannot be seen anywhere else in India.

The beach is dotted with colourful carriages, white as foam, black as rain clouds. Some are saffron, some vermilion, and others of mixed hue. These are pulled by six or four or sometimes only two horses. They look picturesque and glitter and mesmerize the eyes in the yellow sunlight. You see them stopping near the shore, with people seated inside and taking in the sea breeze. You see people walking along or lounging on beautifully carved seats by the sea shore. Then there are the faces of eminent men, beautiful women, and the glowing flower-like faces of small children. Their enjoyment of the scene is a beautiful sight. Those big steamers—English, French, and German—stand there in a row as if unable to decide which is greater among them. You stand there watching as their giant chimneys shoot up columns of smoke into the sky while the ships disappear over the horizon. It is fascinating to watch ships gradually revealing their size as they near the shore. In the port one finds people ready to embark on a voyage with their families. Blessing them and bidding them farewell are their grieving kith and kin. At another place, an eager husband embraces a dearly loved wife who has been lonely in England for a long time. He then puts her in a limousine and drives her off in great happiness. In yet another place are children who have been reunited with their parents after four or five years. The parents hold them close and kiss them, weeping tears of joy. Above all there floats soothing music from the band, entertainment for listeners. And infusing life into all these sights is the everlasting and indescribable glow of the sunset. Madhavan stood there amazed. He felt like a man who has cleared all his debts and was now free to do as he wished. His impulse was to sail away in one of the ships he saw in front of him. By eight o' clock, he was on the *Merina* which was sailing that night to Calcutta.

In times of misfortune nothing auspicious occurs. Madhavan had not ascertained when the ship was likely to touch the shores of Calcutta. This ship had to stop at many ports before it reached Calcutta. In two days' time, Madhavan had got over his desire for a sea voyage. Not just that, he had started to feel physically ill. Nine days later the ship reached Malabar. How do I speak about Madhavan's despondency when he saw the shore of Malabar through binoculars? Thinking of his parents filled his eyes with tears. There was a reason for this vulnerability. He had a slight temperature and there was a boil on his thigh. It was difficult to get up or walk about. Moreover, he had no taste for the food served on the ship and could not find a face that he liked.

Other than a few bearded Muslims, and Europeans who looked at him with great contempt, there was no one else on the ship. He did not even have a servant. It was at this time that the ship came to a port at Keralam. When he looked through a tube he saw his country very clearly. 'What a pity!

'God! You have put me in such a difficult situation.' Immediately he thought of Indulekha. Even if he were dead he decided that he wouldn't step into Keralam, and lay down on his bed. The ship was moving very slowly. I will hasten my narrative now. Twenty-three days after its departure from Bombay, the ship reached Calcutta. When he got off the ship Madhavan was completely cured of his bodily ills. This comfort and well-being must have been due to the fact that he had begun enjoying the sea breeze and the food on the ship. Even then, the moment he set foot on firm ground, he exclaimed, 'Oh! what a blessing. I am on firm ground again.' The city of Calcutta amazed Madhavan. The reasons for the amazement I do not wish to recount. After he had been in Calcutta for two days, he went to see the park (where the animals are put on show). He walked around and saw many interesting sights.

He was standing near an iron cage with a cheetah inside. Just then, four very expensively dressed people came up and stood near him. It was feeding time for the cheetah, so all of them stood close by to watch this activity. The caretaker opened the first door of the cage and put some meat in. There was some confusion and the door was left open. Immediately the cheetah leapt out of the cage. The four of them took to their heels. At that instant Madhavan pulled out his revolver and fired a shot. The cheetah lunged at him. He fired a second shot and the animal lay dead. Immediately all the brave ones who had fled returned. One of them took Madhavan's hand and said in English, 'Brilliant boy—brilliant boy!' Then he spoke in the following manner:

'Aren't you from Malabar?'

(There was a reason for this question. In the fight with the cheetah, Madhavan's headgear fell off revealing his long kuduma. Seeing the kuduma, the man guessed that Madhavan was from Malabar. He had been acquainted with some Malayalis while he was in Madras.)

MADHAVAN: Yes.

'When did you come to this place?'

MADHAVAN: Two days ago.

'Where are you staying?'

MADHAVAN: In a hotel.

'You must have come to see the country?'

MADHAVAN: Yes.

'I have great respect for people from Malabar. Your youth, handsome figure, and immense courage have impressed all of us. I am a businessman and householder in this land. My name is Babu Govinda Sen. This is Gopinath Banerjee and he is my partner in business. And here is Babu Chitraprasad Sen. He is my younger brother and this young man, Kesabchandra Sen is my son, employed in the government service at Bombay. If you do not have any engagements for the days you are here in Calcutta, please accept our invitation to stay at our bungalows. My son is going away in a week's time to Bombay. If you are planning to return to Malabar by that time both of you can easily and comfortably travel together till Bombay.'

Madhavan's heart melted at these kind words spoken with such humility and in very good English.

MADHAVAN: I accept your hospitality. I don't have any relatives or people I know in this land. I'm fortunate that you feel this regard for me though there is no reason for it.

They reported the matter of the dead cheetah to the keeper of the park. Then the Babus and Madhavan got into a very special open carriage, which was standing by yoked to four handsome horses, and drove off to the house of Babu Govinda Sen.

Babu Govinda Sen and his younger brother Chitraprasad Sen were prominent among the millionaires of Calcutta. Their bungalow was named *Amaravati*. It stood in the midst of a beautiful garden. Madhavan was spellbound to see four or five very large and very white bungalows with their *gopuram*s touching the sky. He had never seen bungalows of such height. From the moment he entered the big gates of these bungalows, everything was a matter of great surprise for him. He felt that this could be the great Devendra's Amaravati. He could not see any detail on which money had been wasted thoughtlessly. Huge statues on either side adorned the gateway. Leading from it was a semicircular gravelled path to the entrance of the house, flanking which was an intricately worked copper wire mesh on which a charming creeper in full bloom had entwined itself. Near the entrance, a few feet away, were artificial ponds lined with captivating marble carvings. Who will not be attracted by this? If I were to speak of all the things in *Amaravati*, I would have to write four or five books like the one I am writing now. Madhavan felt as though he was in a land of fantasy. He saw nothing that did not fascinate him intensely. He was amazed by the things that had been collected and placed elegantly in every room. Numerous were the green velvet beds with gold or silver thread work; carved chairs and couches lined the great and spacious rooms.

There were a variety of tables patterned after English designs with marble, white stone, special wood, and ivory. There were numerous standing mirrors framed in gold which were 12–18 feet in height. All the lovely objects in the room were reflected and appeared double their size in these mirrors, thus startling those who were not used to them.

Around four or five hundred silver tubes encased in clear glass were suspended from the ceiling reflecting many colours. Carved crystal chandeliers hung in a wide circle, held up with silver chains suspended from intricately carved wooden ceilings. Inside, bright lamps—green, yellow, golden—glowed luminously. Then there were wall-set lamps, as they were called in English, fixed to the wall in their patterned glass cases. Some were gilt-edged and had shapely handles set into the wall. There were numerous other lamps with crystal hangings in white, blue and yellow. Some were painted in this colour and varnished in such a way that they decorated the grand walls. In some places, the floor was covered with silk carpets, in other places set with finely crafted marble slabs. Grand wooden staircases in the shape of a lotus or of a winding snake led to the upper storey. Statues painted in white, green, and yellow with gilt necks and bases stood all along the staircase. The rooms had grand interiors with expensive silk curtains at the windows and in doorways; mattresses, pillowcases, quilts of silk and velvet with silver and golden borders. Who can describe the things that Madhavan saw!

Who would not be charmed by the grand upper storeys girdled by balconies structured one above the other! After five or six storeys were the terraces. The floor of some of these terraces had been laid in pure glass; at other places a mixture of porcelain and glass was used to carve out patterns of leaves and flowers. Some were laid out in delicate mother-of-pearl. Sometimes beautiful silken mats covered the floor. On four sides of the terrace stood a curtain-like fence, its beauty inexpressable. In other places, water, pumped up from a very deep source with the help of machines, spouted through the mouths of exquisitely crafted animals in glass and marble—a source of intense happiness to the senses. I don't think I have the ability to describe in detail the things that were seen by Madhavan in *Amaravati*. Therefore, I shall cut short my description.

Besides the balconies, Madhavan was also delighted by the pools, the luxurious gem-studded cots, libraries, and gardens. He felt that he had been transported to another world with comforts unseen and unheard of so far.

Madhavan accepting the invitation of Govinda Sen, lived very comfortably for eight to ten days in this heaven-like *Amaravati*.

It has been more than twenty days since Govindapanikkar and Govindankuttymenon started on their journey. My readers ask me about them but I have very little to say. 'All over India there are trains and telegrams, then why is it so hard to locate Madhavan?' Govindankuttymenon who was so certain when he set out, was suddenly at a loss. Even if there are trains, steamboats, or whatever, without luck man cannot achieve anything. He was very sure of this. The moment they reached Madras they went and met Gilham sayiv who reassured them and informed them that Madhavan had gone to Bombay. They rushed straight to Bombay. From Bombay they went to Kasi where Govindapanikkar fell ill. So they had to stay there for ten days. For no obvious reason, Govindankuttymenon had a hunch that Madhavan might have gone to England. Like a pair of madmen, they rushed back to Bombay. After several days of painstakingly careful enquiries they came to know that a young man with a kuduma had boarded a ship. Immediately, from the post office they secured a list of the people who had sailed for England from there. Madhavan's name was not on any of those. They wondered whether Madhavan had registered a different name. That did not seem very likely. Little people, how insignificant your lives are! Madhavan's name was listed in the book of travellers to Calcutta, but in another place. Govindankuttymenon however had no intention of looking there. What could be done?

Intelligence must be coupled with luck, or it is difficult to achieve anything.

Govindapanikkar fell ill on his return to Bombay. They decided to travel to Calcutta and from there to Burma after some days.

Many ideas occurred to Govindapanikkar. He thought of using newspapers. The rumours regarding Indulekha's sambandam had been published in some newspapers but Madhavan must have been suffering on the ship. Whatever be the reason, it was certain that Madhavan did not see those newspapers.

chapter seventeen

How Madhavan was Found

Madhavan lived for almost ten days in great comfort in the *Amaravati* bungalow which rivalled the heavenly Amaravati. He accepted the hospitality of Babu Govinda Sen who was as rich as Kubera. Four days before Madhavan mentioned taking leave of them, Govinda Sen's son, Kesabchandra had returned to Bombay after his vacation. The same day Babu Gopinath Banerjee had also left for a place where his company had a branch. Madhavan announced that for the time being he was not going back to Malabar, and that he was planning to travel in Burma, Kasi, Allahabad, Agra, Delhi, and Lahore for two months. Kesabchandra and Gopinath Banerjee both made Madhavan promise that on his return journey he would stop for a couple of days at the place where Gopinath Banerjee's company had a branch office; and if he happened to go via Bombay, stay with Kesabchandra there for two days. Four days later Madhavan told Govinda Sen that he was taking leave of them. Babu Govinda Sen was unsurpassed in wealth, humility and benevolence.

In this book I have referred to Panchumenon and the Moorkillatha Nambuthiripad as extremely wealthy people and in one or two places about the latter also being an eminent person. Now I will speak of Babu Govinda Sen also as a wealthy and affluent person. However, my readers should not imagine that their wealth was of the same order. There is a vast difference between a wealthy person in Madras state and one in Bengal. The difference can be found in the way wealth multiplies. In Madras a person who has five lakhs is a great lord. In Bengal a man who has five lakhs is a wealthy man, but only of the fourth class. There, a wealthy man with five crores is a reasonably well-off lord. A person who is considered very affluent in Bengal would be worth around fifteen crores. Govinda Sen and his younger brother Chitraprasad were foremost among the people who were worth more than fifteen crores.

When it was time for Madhavan to depart, Govinda Sen felt extremely sad.

GOVINDA SEN: We have grown so fond of each other that your going away is a matter of great sorrow to me. But it cannot be helped. When I think of your qualifications, your good will, your abilities, as I know of them, I am convinced that you will secure a valuable job in the Madras government. Next year my son may be taken on through the civil service examination. I don't wish him to be in a government job. But that is his interest. Being a householder, looking after affairs of the home and business are things he is also committed to. I hope all your worries are resolved soon. I will pray that you enter the civil services and also that you rejoin your beloved family.

Saying this, Govinda Sen held Madhavan close and embraced him. As parting gifts, he presented him with a specially made gold watch and gold chain, a silk suit woven with gold thread, and a letter box carved in ivory and silver. Then Govinda Sen drove Madhavan in his carriage to the railway station from where he was going to board the train to the place where Gopinath Banerjee had his branch office. By the time the train was ready to leave, there were tears in both men's eyes.

MADHAVAN: For some inexplicable reason you, who are so fortunate and capable, felt a certain respect and sympathy for me. I will always consider this meeting my good fortune. A person blessed like you are cannot desire anything from an ordinary person like me. I can do nothing for you. I do not wish that you should ever need me. However, I want you to believe that the memory of your warm affection will be with me till the end of my life. When I return home, I shall write and give you all my news.

GOVINDA SEN: I desire your well-being exactly as I desire the well-being of Kesabchandra.

Govinda Sen was at a loss for words. He made a note of Madhavan's address both in Keralam and in Madras. When he got into the train he gave his photograph to Madhavan.

Govinda Sen left, feeling rather sad. The train moved. Madhavan had bought a ticket to Gopinath Banerjee's place. As he had given his word to Gopinath, he could not leave without meeting him.

Madhavan was so preoccupied he did not notice his surroundings. The train arrived at a big station from which point Gopinath's house was a distance of 68 miles. Madhavan ate some snacks. Soon the train started again. At the next station, a handsome young man opened the door of the coach and looking straight at Madhavan asked in English whether anyone had any objection to his getting in. Madhavan replied that he had no objection. The rest of the passengers said nothing, perhaps because they did not know English. This handsome man sat next to Madhavan in the train.

He was very good-looking and his dress and demeanour attractive. He appeared to be a Muslim. His long hair was cut straight, a little above his shoulders. He had an impressive moustache; he also had what is called sidelocks in English, neatly trimmed. His colouring was a shade of ripe lemon. He wore a cap heavily embroidered with gold thread. The cap, the black hair around it, the glowing face, and the moustache together made a very attractive picture. He wore a coat of glittering white velvet that stopped four or five fingers below the knees and had closely placed buttons down the front. From the neck to waist, the coat was woven in gold. On his feet he wore green silk socks and shining boots; round his neck hung a golden watch and a chain. An intense fragrance of lavender or roses clung to him. The moment he sat down, this very delightful person took out a cigar from his gold-coloured cigar case. He offered a cigar to Madhavan. When Madhavan said that he did not smoke, he asked Madhavan whether he had any objection to his smoking. Madhavan said he had no objection and the young man immediately began to smoke. After some time, he turned to Madhavan: 'Where are you coming from? Where are you going? I don't think you have travelled in this area before.'

MADHAVAN: I am coming from Calcutta and am going to meet a friend. My country is Malabar—in Madras state. I came here to travel and see north India. It is my luck that I had the opportunity to meet you.

THE HANDSOME MAN: Yes, indeed, I feel the same way about you. Do you have a friend or anyone else travelling with you; or, are you alone?

MADHAVAN: I am alone.

THE HANDSOME MAN: I see. I am a sub-judge in Allahabad. I am going home to meet my father. My father is a famous painter. He does not want me to work. But I chose to do so. I have a ticket for the first class. My wife and two children are in the first-class compartment. I get bored in the train, so at every station, I get out onto the platform and walk about. It is quite dull to travel for long distances in the train. The moment I saw you, I felt like talking to you. I could make out that you knew English. I am very pleased. My name is Sher Ali Khan. I guess you have a BA degree.

MADHAVAN: Yes.

SHER ALI KHAN: Let me tell you one more thing. You have got a BL too; isn't that so?

MADHAVAN: (smiling) Yes.

SHER ALI KHAN: I too am a graduate. How many days do you intend to stay with your friend?

MADHAVAN: Just a day.

SHER ALI KHAN: If you don't have any particular plans, we could travel together to my place. Haven't you come to travel in this country? It is not necessary that you should travel to a particular place first. You could stay in my house for a week, see all the interesting things there, and then travel to any other place of your liking.

MADHAVAN: I have decided to see a friend. That is why I said I have to go to his place first.

SHER ALI KHAN: I gathered that you have no one in this place. Who is your friend?

MADHAVAN: Gopinath Banerjee. I got to know him recently in Calcutta. He invited me before he left Calcutta. I am responding to the invitation.

SHER ALI KHAN: Oh! Misra Gopinath Banerjee is a close friend of mine. He is my father's friend too. I have not seen him for quite some time. He is a very good person and a great trader. I am glad to know that you are his friend. If that is the case, I will give you a letter for him. I will invite him too. It would make me very happy if both of you visited my place together. I am on four months' leave. Come along at any time within these four months.

MADHAVAN: Certainly, I would like to come.

As they were talking thus, the train reached another big station. One cannot describe the crowd in that station. It was dusk by this time. The platform was overflowing with people and luggage. Even if you shouted, another person would have found it difficult to hear you. The moment the train came to a halt, Sher Ali Khan took hold of Madhavan's hand and stepped out on to the platform calling out loudly, 'Peon! Peon!'

A huge, bearded Pathan in a coat, pagri, and sash got down from another compartment. 'Sahab,' he said with great respect and walked up to the sub-judge.

SHER ALI KHAN: Get into the train and guard his belongings. We will go to the refreshment room [the room where snacks and other things are kept ready for the sayivs].

'Yes sahab,' he answered and went inside and stood guard there.

The sub-judge held on to Madhavan's hand and entered the refreshment room, joking.

SHER ALI KHAN: What shall we eat?
MADHAVAN: Whatever you like.
SHER ALI KHAN: You do not have any objection to wine and meat?
MADHAVAN: I have no objection.
SHER ALI KHAN: All right. Boy! Boy!

The boy responded with a loud 'Yessar.'

SHER ALI KHAN: Mutton chops, cutlet, bread, cheese, sherry; bring all this.

Saying 'Yessar' he ran off to fetch the order.

The sub-judge and Madhavan sat down. The sub-judge then decided to bring his son along. 'He is sitting in the first-class compartment with his mother. He was crying insistently, wanting to come out with me. He won't eat his food without me. I will be back in a minute.' He took a look at his watch and said, 'There are still fourteen minutes for the train to leave.' He then went to fetch the child. Madhavan was extremely happy and sat there awaiting his arrival. As ordered, the steward brought one thing after the other and arranged it. Madhavan waited for the arrival of the sub-judge. Five minutes were over–six–seven–eight–nine–it was ten minutes. Madhavan wondered what was wrong. The butler, who was standing by, pointed out that there were only four minutes left and that the food was getting cold.

Madhavan set off in the direction of the first-class bogie. He opened the doors of all the bogies, and called out loudly, 'Mr Sher Ali Khan, sub-judge, Sher Ali Khan, sub-judge!' No one replied. Madhavan was taken aback. When he returned to his own bogie, he found that none of his things were there. The peon as well as the sub-judge had disappeared. Some of the travellers in the bogie who did not know English made Madhavan understand through gestures that all the things had been taken away by the huge peon. Again Madhavan, not knowing where and why, ran about distractedly on the platform like a mad man. By then the train had started moving. It is difficult for me to relate correctly and convincingly Madhavan's perplexity and sorrow. All his things were lost except the clothes he was wearing, a small change of two rupees, a watch he always wore and a railway ticket. Among the things which went, the most expensive ones were the gold watch and the chain, one very expensive letter box made of ivory and the special silk shirts Govinda Sen had given him. Poor fellow! That simpleton Madhavan stood on the platform for a long time. He had also missed his train. The sub-judge from Allahabad had looted him.

This great thief who passed by the name of Sher Ali Khan had grabbed plenty of money many times in this manner. He and his friends had seen Madhavan in the evening at the station where they got down to have snacks. They figured that he was new to the place. With his companions, Sher Ali Khan decided to cheat Madhavan.

Wondering what could be done, Madhavan ran to the stationmaster's room.

MADHAVAN: See, all my things have been stolen. I am from another country. Kindly help me!
STATIONMASTER: Go and tell the police.
MADHAVAN: I cannot find any policeman.
STATIONMASTER: What can I do?
MADHAVAN: I am from another region.
STATIONMASTER: What can I do about that?
MADHAVAN: I don't know anyone here.
STATIONMASTER: What can I do about that?
MADHAVAN: If you do not help me, I am helpless.
STATIONMASTER: Go and tell the policeman. Porter, show this man a policeman. If there are no policemen here, show him the police station.

No policemen could be found on the platform. When they went to the police station, the door was shut. In that area they do not have the policemen of British India. This robbery also took place in an area outside British India. The hotel butler followed Madhavan. 'The things that I prepared for you come to one and a half rupees—if you wish, eat them but give me the money.'

MADHAVAN: I did not demand anything. That thief ordered it. Why should I give the money?

BUTLER: You ordered it, you should give the money.

Saying this he continued to follow him.

As he could not find any policemen, Madhavan returned to the railway station and approached the stationmaster again.

MADHAVAN: Can't find any policemen.
STATIONMASTER: What can I do about that?
BUTLER: (to the stationmaster) This person came to the hotel and ordered the things. After they were made, he refused to pay for them.
STATIONMASTER: (to Madhavan) Why are you not paying?
MADHAVAN: If you order me to do so I will give him all the money I have. However, you should do something for me. Am I not a human being who is in a terrible predicament? You should help me and send a telegram (by wireless) to my friend.
STATIONMASTER: It is already past six o'clock. Who is your friend?
MADHAVAN: Mr Gopinath Banerjee—I am going to meet him. Please send him a telegram right away.

The moment he heard the name 'Gopinath Banerjee', the stationmaster's attitude changed. This stationmaster was very close to that millionaire. Numerous types of goods were shipped through the station each day for him. He received a lot of money from him as gifts. And not just that, once, when the stationmaster was in danger for being arrested for some error, the timely intervention of Gopinath Banerjee averted it. For the stationmaster, Gopinath Banerjee was like God himself. The moment he heard the name, he jumped up.

STATIONMASTER: Are you Gopinath Banerjee's friend? Are you going to meet him? Porter, bring this man a chair. Please sit down. I will despatch a telegram this very moment. I have just sent a reply to one of his telegrams. Gopinath Banerjee would be at the railway station near his place now. You just need to write out the telegram for me.

Madhavan immediately drafted the telegram and gave it to the stationmaster.

The stationmaster said that he would get the reply in five minutes and sent off the telegram. He had some tea and eats brought in for Madhavan and also sent for a policeman immediately, doing everything that was required. The hotel butler who asked for money was nowhere to be seen. Barely half an hour later the reply telegram arrived. It was addressed to the stationmaster and read as follows:

I got the telegram from Madhavan of Malabar. He is a person who is very close to my heart. You should do everything that is necessary for him and make him comfortable and give him accommodation for tonight. The last train from here has already left, or I would have come there this very evening. You should tell Madhavan not to worry at all. Do everything necessary for him and stay with him till I arrive. I will be there by the first train tomorrow. Inform the police immediately. Madhavan need not know all this; simply do what is necessary.

The stationmaster's respectful attitude towards Madhavan and his prompt action after receiving the telegram were things that even a king may not have enjoyed.

He sent for the police immediately. A big room in a hotel, with a mattress and furniture were arranged for Madhavan's stay. In fifteen minutes the chief policeman arrived with a few attendants. The chief officer, a Muslim in a very elaborate outfit, made his enquiries with the stationmaster.

CHIEF OFFICER: Whose things were robbed? How much wealth was lost?
STATIONMASTER: A king from Malabar is here. Things worth a lakh of rupees have been stolen. This king is a friend of Gopinath Banerjee. He is inside—he is a great king. He himself sent a telegram to Gopinath Banerjee. I also got a reply. Look here.

Saying this he showed the telegram to the chief officer.

Madhavan overheard everything and though he was in low spirits, laughed loudly when he heard the stationmaster saying that he was a king from Malabar and that he had lost things worth a lakh.

The police officer read the telegram, nodded once, and said to the stationmaster:

POLICE OFFICER: I want to meet this king. I must take down all the details about the injustice.

The stationmaster went in and after he told the police officer that he could step in too, the huge Mussalman officer entered very respectfully and salaamed Madhavan. He then stood before Madhavan as though about to go through a drill.

Madhavan rose from the chair immediately and held his hand saying, 'I am happy to be acquainted with you.' He sat him on a chair close by and talked with great humility. The officer looked at Madhavan with pleasure and reverence.

OFFICER: I am very sad about all the trouble caused to you, O king! I shall try my best to get a clue as to who has perpetrated this great wrong.
MADHAVAN: I am not a king.

When he heard this, the stationmaster felt irritated—small wonder that this stupid one's things were stolen—he said to himself.

MADHAVAN: I am not a king. I am a Nair from Malabar and employed in the government.
OFFICER: All right, how many of your things have been stolen?
MADHAVAN: I cannot say accurately.
STATIONMASTER: Lots of things have gone. Lots and lots.
MADHAVAN: Roughly things worth Rs 2000 might have gone. The costly things were given to me as gifts by Maharaja Shri Govinda Sen when I was coming away from Calcutta. I am not sure of their value.
OFFICER: Is Govinda Sen also your friend?
MADHAVAN: Yes.
OFFICER: Could you please tell me the details of the things stolen.

Madhavan spoke in detail about the incident. For ten minutes the officer stood without moving or talking, like a meditating yogi. He then smiled and looked at the principal peon standing near the door. He pretended he had got all the details.

OFFICER: Without the slightest doubt, this robbery took place with the knowledge of the butler.
STATIONMASTER: There is no doubt about it.
MAIN PEON: I'm sure of it.

The peons looked at each other surprised that their chief had found a clue to the robbery. They stood there looking at their chief as though they had received their orders a bit late.

MADHAVAN: I don't think there is a chance that the hotel butler knows anything about it.
STATIONMASTER: (angrily) You need not do anything related to this matter. Let the officers find a clue. These people are admirable in sniffing out clues for almost anything. Let them do their work.

MADHAVAN: All right, I won't say anything more about it.

The chief officer sent for the hotel butler who came in, and stood before the officer, trembling with fright.

OFFICER: Where have you stored the things you stole from him? Produce them!
BUTLER: Me? Whose things? Have I stolen something?
OFFICER: (to one peon) Beat up that dog!
BUTLER: Ayyoh!
OFFICER: Again!
BUTLER: Ayyayoh, Ayyayoh! I do not know anything.
OFFICER: Beat him up thoroughly—you donkey. You have no strength? Beat him up, beat him, beat him on the head!
BUTLER: Ayyoh! Appa! Appapa! Appapa! Dead—dead—I am dead—My God! I have been killed!
OFFICER: Beat him up—Beat him up again, kill him.
BUTLER: Appa! I want some water—I am about to die.
OFFICER: Pull his arm behind him and bind it up tightly and haul it upwards. Let another peon pull his leg forward.

When orders were executed:

BUTLER: (unable to suffer the pain) Ayyoh! Ayyoh! I will bring the stolen goods—I will bring them.
OFFICER: Where have you kept them?
BUTLER: I have kept them somewhere. Please untie and release me!
OFFICER: Where?
BUTLER: Ayyayoh! I have kept them in the room where I sleep. Please let me go!
STATIONMASTER: (to Madhavan) See—the thief, he is the one who stole it. You are very kind-hearted. We will see the things now.

Madhavan was not at all convinced. He believed that the butler had owned up because he could not bear the pain! The butler went in and never emerged again. How could he produce things that were not with him? More enquiries were made. Many porters and daily-wage earners were beaten up because there was no clue at all. By then it was nearly twelve o'clock and the officers said they would come back when it was light and left.

Gopinath Banerjee arrived by the first train the next morning. He asked for all the details about the robbery. Nothing was clear. He left the officers and others to make enquiries and returned to his native place with Madhavan. A telegram with all these details was sent to Govinda Sen. The reply telegram that Gopinath Banerjee received is reproduced below.

I am indeed sorry to hear about the misfortune that Madhavan has met with. For Madhavan's tour of North India and to meet all the expenses for him to return to Madras a sum of two thousand should be entrusted to him. However, the money need not all be handed over at once. Let what he needs immediately be given to him as ready cash. The rest he might carry in cheques which can be encashed in the banks at Allahabad, Agra, Delhi, and Lahore. Send our Bairam Khan with Madhavan on his journey and let him be his companion till he returns from Bombay. He is a veteran traveller. Tell Madhavan not to worry about the theft.

The respect and reverence Madhavan felt for Govinda Sen when he read the telegram can be estimated by my readers. Even then Madhavan felt it a great grievance that he should allow Govinda Sen to spend even a coin on him, and said thus to Gopinath Banerjee.

MADHAVAN: The enormously generous Govinda Sen! May he live long and for the good of the people in the world! I have decided to return to Madras. I will come back and meet you and respected Govinda Sen some time in the future. Just now I only need the money for my fare from here to Madras.
GOPINATH BANERJEE: If it is so, stop with me for four or five days before you go. Only then will I find it acceptable.

Madhavan stayed back for four or five days.

In the previous chapter I mentioned that Govindapanikkar and Govindankuttymenon were in Bombay. Govindapanikkar had not recovered fully from his illness. The journey to Burma was scheduled for that day, the next day, or the day after: it had not been fixed. One day as things were in this state of uncertainty, Govindankuttymenon was enjoying the breeze near Bombay esplanade, when Babu Kesabchandra Sen passed by. Kesabchandra thought that Govindankuttymenon's face had the same outlines as Madhavan's. He retraced his steps and asked Govindankuttymenon:

KESABCHANDRA: Which country do you belong to?
GOVINDANKUTTYMENON: I am from the country of Malabar.
KESABCHANDRA: I felt so when I saw you. Do you know somebody called Madhavan in Malabar?

Govindankuttymenon started. Waves of happiness, sorrow, and surprise hit him at the same time. Immediately—

GOVINDANKUTTYMENON: Where is he? I am a relative of his. It is almost two months since he left his country. His father and I have been searching for him but our progress has been very slow. It is eight or ten days since we reached here.

Kesabchandra Sen gave him the details.

KESABCHANDRA: Now he must have left Calcutta. However, I will send a telegram to my father and see if his whereabouts can be traced.

Together they walked to the telegraph office and sent a telegram. After that Kesabchandra Sen went with Govindankuttymenon to meet Govindapanikkar. He brought both of them over to his house.

Around eight o'clock at night the reply telegram arrived: 'Madhavan has left Calcutta. He must be with Gopinath Banerjee. There is no need for his father to worry about him. He will return safely.' This was the reply. As soon as he got this telegram, another was sent to Gopinath Banerjee asking whether Madhavan was at his place. A reply to that arrived the next morning. 'Madhavan boarded a train for Bombay at six o'clock last evening. He is not ill. The moment he arrives he will come over and meet you.'

How should I narrate the happiness that Govindapanikkar and Govindankuttymenon felt when they read the telegram?

The day Madhavan's train was to reach Bombay, Kesabchandra Sen waited at the station with a vehicle to welcome him. But Kesabchandra decided to play a practical joke on Madhavan. He asked Govindapanikkar and Govindankuttymenon and their people not to come to the station. By the time Kesabchandra reached the station, the train had already arrived. Madhavan alighted from the train and saw Kesabchandra. They shook hands and both got into the vehicle, reached the bungalow and sat on the veranda. Madhavan related all that had happened after Kesabchandra left Calcutta.

KESABCHANDRA: That is fine then, you have made the acquaintance of a sub-judge in Allahabad. How does it matter if you lost a little money? You got a very good friend!

Both of them laughed a lot.

KESABCHANDRA: What is your plan now? Isn't it better to return to Malabar?

MADHAVAN: No, I am not returning to Malabar. However, I will go to Madras tomorrow and return in eight or ten days.
KESABCHANDRA: Are you going only up to Madras and then coming back? Why don't you go to Malabar also? You can meet your father and others.

The mention of his father greatly saddened Madhavan. However, when he thought of the other matter he cursed inwardly.

MADHAVAN: I have a great wish to see my father. I don't think it will be possible now.
KESABCHANDRA: It is time for us to eat. Don't you want to have a bath?
MADHAVAN: I do.

Saying this, Madhavan got up.

KESABCHANDRA: I have invited two of my friends for a meal to keep you company. I think you will be happy to meet them.
MADHAVAN: Your friends are my friends also. I am indeed happy that you have invited them.

Madhavan went in for a bath. Immediately Kesabchandra called Govindapanikkar and Govindankuttymenon to the dining room and seated them at the dining table. He too sat down. After some time, when he saw Madhavan emerging, bathed and dressed, he got up and brought him to the dining room.

KESABCHANDRA: Here, I invited these two people who are sitting here, do you know them?

Madhavan looked. Should I say anything more of what happened? 'Oh! I am so fortunate I met you, Father!' Govindapanikkar too got up and embraced Madhavan. 'Oh! my dear boy! You have caused me so much sorrow.'
Kesabchandra left them together for a while.
After all the embracing and weeping was over, Govindapanikkar asked Govindankutty to send a telegram home. 'I am not sure whether his mother and that girl are not dead by now.'

MADHAVAN: Which girl? Which girl is there to die of sorrow for me?
GOVINDANKUTTYMENON: My niece Indulekha. Madman! What a story this is! The antics you have been upto!

Madhavan was quite stunned to hear this. He felt numb all over.

GOVINDAPANIKKAR: My dear boy, what a pitiable thing you did. You hurt your mother, that girl, and both of us so much. You came home, heard a lie and simply turned around and went away. We heard all the details. It is a pity! Maybe you were going through an inauspicious period. It should be over by now.

Madhavan found it difficult to utter even a word. He just sat down.

Kesabchandra came in and saw all this, but he did not ask Madhavan anything. Everyone began eating. Madhavan also pretended to eat. After the meal was over, Govindankuttymenon sent a telegram with all the details to Malabar.

After Kesabchandra had retired to another room:

GOVINDAPANIKKAR: Why is it my dear boy, that you do not say anything?
GOVINDANKUTTYMENON: How can he talk after acting so stupidly?
MADHAVAN: Father! When I hear all this, I feel I am listening to stories from the *Arabian Nights*.
GOVINDAPANIKKAR: This is a good story. You made Indulekha grieve for you. I doubt whether your mother is alive, she was so devastated.

Madhavan put his head down and wept.

He decided to stay with Kesabchandra Sen that day, and go to Malabar by the next day's train.

When Govindapanikkar, Madhavan, and Govindankuttymenon sat in the high terraced house in that special moonlight enjoying the breeze, a conversation took place between them. In the next chapter I have shared some of its important details with my readers.

chapter eighteen

A Conversation

As Govindapanikkar, Madhavan, and Govindankuttymenon sat talking in Babu Kesabchandra Sen's palatial house in the snow-like moonlight, Govindapanikkar initiated the conversation reported below.

GOVINDAPANIKKAR: My children, in my opinion the new type of English education that makes you knowledgeable is beneficial in many ways. But it also has one or two defects. The good qualities that you naturally possess are destroyed and you become spoilt. This is a matter of great sorrow to me. Let me explain this. First, as you all know, in this world there is plenty of natural good and evil. Considered carefully, in course of time, you will understand these concepts. But you youngsters, not yet mature, read certain types of books, learn certain things, and are perplexed by them. You think that you can talk about them and ignore our customs, religion, and its workings. Secondly, because of this, the respect, trust, and love which you always owe your relatives and teachers is gradually being destroyed. In most cases, these emotions no longer exist. When I think about what you have just done, Madhavan, I am inclined to believe that you were able to do so because of the knowledge and ideas which your English education has afforded you. When you decided to run away from home, you did not spare even a thought for your father and your mother. *You* felt uneasy and so you ran away from home. Not for a moment did it occur to you how much your mother and I would grieve over this. The reason for such an attitude is your lack of love and respect for us. You don't trust us and all this is due to your studying English, I would say. First of all, people should have the right kind of trust in God and faith in God. That trust, and the fear of God, lead to faith and respect for your elders. If you do not have faith in God, how can you have faith in elders?

MADHAVAN: What a pity! I am extremely sad that you, my father, have misunderstood me so much. Even if I had not received an English education, I would have reacted in the same manner. Aren't there people who have run away but who have not had an English education?

GOVINDAPANIKKAR: In these matters it is none other than educated people like you who cause their parents grief in this cruel manner. Your new knowledge and modern thinking has caused much harm. You mindlessly ridicule the many good deeds that we Hindus perform and the merits we acquire as a result. This contempt for positive ways of thinking is a result of English education. If the knowledge and wisdom which men have, stand in the way of their thoughts about God, that knowledge and wisdom are useless. If your ancestors have accepted a particular religion, you should also have faith in that religion. You are of the opinion now that Hindu religion is meaningless. I have not seen you going to the temple these days, Madhavan. Govindankutty also does not go. You mark yourself with sandalwood paste just for the name's sake. I do not think you apply the holy ash at all. It is indeed a pity that you have turned out this way.

MADHAVAN: Father, you need not be sad about that at all. I am not an atheist. After having thought about many things I believe that God exists. I have not decided that I won't go to the temple. If I get holy ash I have no objection to using it on my forehead and arms. However, I am not so certain about the connection between sandalwood paste, holy ash, temple, and God. If you can make me understand that, I will consider going to the temple and applying holy ash.

GOVINDAPANIKKAR: What is your opinion, Govindankutty?

GOVINDANKUTTYMENON: I think that men think less of God as worldly knowledge increases. Religion is what each man has made. Each person has the right to think about its positive and negative aspects. It is wrong to say that we should follow whatever our ancestors have followed without thinking about its good and bad aspects.

GOVINDAPANIKKAR: English education encourages you to talk like this. Does God exist or not, Govindankutty?

GOVINDANKUTTYMENON: I do not believe that there is a special power called God. I know that the world has come into existence naturally; it will develop and be destroyed in a like way. I do not see something called God or the power that is a special being. Then how can I believe that it is there?

GOVINDAPANIKKAR: My God! Have you gone a step beyond Madhavan? He at least has a feeling that God exists—that is some relief. You do not have even that! Didn't you both go to the same school? Then why do you have such different opinions? All I can say, my dear children, is that your attitude is very strange.

GOVINDANKUTTY: Yes; I don't see any reason to think that there is a God.

MADHAVAN: All right, Father, I would like to hear your opinion about the necessity of going to the temple and applying sandalwood paste or holy ash in the name of God.

GOVINDAPANIKKAR: I will tell you although I don't know whether it will convince you. Still, let me try. The temple has been built for us Hindus to revere God. Even though God is everywhere and fills up all places, ordinary people do not have that kind of theological knowledge. In order that they too have thoughts about God and revere him, our excellent ancestors made these arrangements a long time ago. The customs of temples, the rituals to be conducted, the kind of obeisance to be made, and other particulars were all decreed for this purpose. Smearing sandalwood and holy ash when we do obeisance to God are practices according to certain rules. This is the connection.

MADHAVAN: I understand the relationship between temples, holy ash, and sandalwood paste. But what is their link with God?

GOVINDAPANIKKAR: All right, that is where the danger is. Didn't I say that the temple is where we worship God?

MADHAVAN: Yes; what you said, Father, is that our wise ancestors set up places called temples, so that ordinary people would have thoughts of God and revere him. Aren't temples meant for those who think of God only when they go there and otherwise are devoid of faith? People who think of God and revere him without applying sandalwood paste and holy ash need not go to the temple. And from what you said, Father, going to the temple is an empty action that has been introduced by wise people for those without wisdom. It seems to me that there is no real connection between the temple and God.

GOVINDAPANIKKAR: I think that only the greatest of sages, who do not need to eat and sleep, who are free from other deceptions of the world, and who are almost divine, need not go to the temple. For people who live according to the laws of the world, temples, idols, and other things help us to revere and remember God.

MADHAVAN: Like you said, Father, there aren't many men who have become like God or escaped the deceptions of the world. Man is an animal whom God has created to live according to the laws of the world. So man will never have the strength to flee its hold. If some people pretend that they have the power, it is utter foolishness. And if some people believe that there is truth in their pretence, that too is downright false. I shall accept that some are free from the hold of the world if you, Father, show me those who do not have desire and anger or who do not yearn for food and sleep. My firm belief is that such people do not exist. All people are similar in their ordinary behaviour. Education and knowledge bring about differences. However, in the everyday detail of behaviour there cannot be many variations. Therefore, as you said Father, there can't be too many amongst us who have given up food, sleep, and other things. Again as you said at the beginning, if temples have been built for the use of the ignorant, shouldn't only those who want to worship God go there? I agree that God is seen in every creature and that he has the power of creation and destruction in him. If I were convinced about this, wouldn't it be dishonest on my part to go to the temple and worship the idol there?

GOVINDAPANIKKAR: From the way you speak, my dear boy, it sounds as though it is very easy to have thoughts of God. Shiva! Shiva! Just because you say that God is everywhere, can you thereby decide not to go to the temple? My dear boy, do you mean to say that there is no one who has escaped the clutches of worldly customs?

MADHAVAN: Unless diseased, all are inclined to eat, sleep, and form attachments.

GOVINDAPANIKKAR: Shiva! Shiva! I have heard enough. There are sages who have overcome these fancies.

MADHAVAN: I don't believe there are such people.

GOVINDAPANIKKAR: My dear boy, you are a total atheist.

MADHAVAN: I am not an atheist—I believe that God exists.

GOVINDAPANIKKAR: What about sages?

MADHAVAN: People are not like what you said, Father. Whether sages or ordinary people, there are not many of the kind you mentioned.

GOVINDAPANIKKAR: I have seen a yogi who ate nothing other than seven grains of black pepper every day and seven curry leaves. He does not even drink water.

GOVINDANKUTTYMENON: He must be a very smart pretender. He has deceived you. I have no doubt about it.

GOVINDAPANIKKAR: He lived with me in a madom for nine days without eating anything.

GOVINDANKUTTYMENON: You jeshtan, you did not see him eat anything. He convinced you that he had ceased to eat. That's all. It is not possible for men to live without food. It is a scientific reality. Then what is the use of saying such stupid things?

GOVINDAPANIKKAR: This is the difficulty in talking to 'English people'. You do not believe anything we say. What can we do? I can promise you that that yogi did not have anything to eat other than what I mentioned. He would bathe very early in the morning and do his yoga. Till noon he chanted his prayers sitting in the midst of sacred fire burning all around him. After that he would eat seven grains of pepper and seven curry leaves in front of all of us. He spent nine days like this. I am a person who watched him at close quarters; even then if you don't believe—

MADHAVAN: Govindankutty and I would never say that you are lying, Father. There is no one in this whole world whose word we trust more than yours. However, we are merely saying that you happen to say such a thing because you have been given wrong information. In those nine days, how much time was that yogi alone and not seen by you or anyone else? He could have kept the things that he wanted to eat in a bundle or in some other form, and under the pretence of performing some yogic rites could have eaten behind closed doors. How can you be certain that that is not the case? You did not examine his body and the things he carried with him. Someone clever should stand on guard and check out whether he had eaten or not. You didn't do that, did you?

GOVINDAPANIKKAR: I did not think that he was a pretender. I will never believe that either. You believe only the things that you have seen. Madhavan, have you seen my father? I did have a father. Won't you believe it if I say that he is your grandfather?

MADHAVAN: (laughing) Why do you say this, Father? Is it not a natural phenomenon? I'd believe it even if you, my father, did not say so.

GOVINDAPANIKKAR: You said that you are not an atheist. Have you seen God? How can you believe in something you have not seen?

MADHAVAN: All right; this question of yours, Father, is a very good one. Let me try and answer it. Maybe Govindankutty will argue with me and defeat me in the argument—but I will tell you. I have not seen God. What and how God is I would be unable to say clearly. However, in this world, vaster than everything, I see a power that permeates all objects. It is that power I call God and think of as God. It is difficult to express and understand what this power is. I will say just one thing about that. In the absence of that power I think this world cannot be seen in the form that it has now. This power is seen in everything in the world. I see this power always when I think deeply of movable things, from man to a large black ant or tiny worms, or of immovable things, from mountains to grass, from the sun to all the other planets which move in the sky. I see it in things which can be seen, understood by touch, or heard at all times. It is this power that I consider to be God.

GOVINDAPANIKKAR: Govindankutty, didn't you say that God doesn't exist, that all inanimate and animate objects including man came into existence on their own? Let me listen to your reasons for it—after that I will listen to what Madhavan has to say.

GOVINDANKUTTYMENON: First of all, I didn't say that God doesn't exist. I just said that it cannot be believed or guessed from the things which can be seen in the world that God exists. I have read a few books written by great scientists and find myself in complete agreement with the opinions of some. One of the books written recently by a very intelligent sayiv Charles Bradlaugh is very convincing. Opinions and detailed arguments by many intelligent people have been astutely reported in this book. I have it here in my leather bag. I will read out parts of it, in Malayalam. Maybe then, you jeshtan, will be convinced that I'm right.

GOVINDAPANIKKAR: Whatever you might say, or whichever book you might read, in this birth I cannot even imagine there not being a God.

GOVINDANKUTTYMENON: Whatever I might say, whichever book I might read, Jeshtan, you need not accept atheism. However, will you believe me, if the matters I am going to speak about are positive?

GOVINDAPANIKKAR: Let me hear you.

GOVINDANKUTTYMENON: You should not hold on to your opinions in a stubborn way. You must consider the pros and cons of the matter. Only then will I talk about what I have to say.

GOVINDAPANIKKAR: Go on, let me hear you.

Govindankuttymenon took Bradlaugh's book from his leather case, lit a small candle, and looked through some papers. Then:

GOVINDANKUTTYMENON: Before I read each part of this book and talk to you, Jeshtan, I will tell you briefly what the beliefs of atheists are. They believe that the world came into being over a long period of time as a result of actions and reactions. The initial coming together of the elements—earth, air, fire, and water—resulted in the birth of various organisms. Valid reasons are shown for this. I don't think it will be possible for anyone to convince them that God exists. When we say that God exists, they will bring hundreds of proofs to prove that he does not. There is nothing in this world without its own properties. In actuality, intelligent people do not find any kind of consensus in the way Hindus, Buddhists, Muslims, Christians, or people from other religions talk about God. Bradlaugh sayiv has said many things about his own religion.

GOVINDAPANIKKAR: What is it—that his own religion is also falsehood?

GOVINDANKUTTYMENON: Bradlaugh's opinion is that nature and the order of all that's said about the creation of the world in the Bible is against reason, and if we consider it in the light of the knowledge that man has acquired now, that story of creation is unbelievable.

GOVINDAPANIKKAR: This sayiv is a great sinner.

GOVINDANKUTTYMENON: Maybe; but he is also very intelligent.

GOVINDAPANIKKAR: Because he says God doesn't exist?

GOVINDANKUTTYMENON: All intelligent people say that he is very clever especially if one reads his reasons for the non-existence of God.

GOVINDAPANIKKAR: It is almost a necessity for the world today to believe that there is no God. Therefore, this intelligent sayiv must have wanted to show how clever he was.

GOVINDANKUTTYMENON: Intelligent people feel obliged to correct the misconceptions harboured by people about certain matters of the world.

GOVINDAPANIKKAR: Have you made sure whether the knowledge of intelligent people now, or earlier, is correct?

GOVINDANKUTTYMENON: That is precisely why I say that we should reflect on the matters that intelligent people are discussing now.

GOVINDAPANIKKAR: Let me hear about those things.

GOVINDANKUTTYMENON: I will give you the gist in Malayalam of Bradlaugh's description of atheism. The atheist says:

I don't claim that God does not exist. I say that I do not understand the meaning of what you say is God. If I have to say that there is no God, I should know what it is that you call God. What can one say about something one knows nothing about? Then if you say that there is a special creator in the image of a man somewhere who has separately created all these living things that you see and that he protects them and destroys them, I will say that such a thing does not exist. That it is sheer stupidity. If you describe in words which are unintelligible to me I will be unable to conceive of God in my mind. I can never believe in the existence of something which I cannot understand.

This is the theory of atheists.

GOVINDAPANIKKAR: I have never heard of a more ridiculous theory. How can you not become silly if you read things like this? Look anywhere in the world, tell me where you do not see the glory of God's power. God has kept this world in such comfort and order! Without God how did this sun and moon come to be? Whose power is it that makes us live so comfortably in this world, in a state where we have enough food, sleep, and other things? Everything is done at the appropriate hour. Who is doing all this? Isn't it a merciful God? When there is need for rain, isn't it provided? Doesn't it quench the thirst of all living things? Doesn't the moon rise according to order and gladden the world? Don't grains and plants and other things grow exactly when we need them? How many comforts like these do we enjoy and each at the right time! How could all this occur without the might of God? Only crazy people will say that there is no God.

GOVINDANKUTTYMENON: All that you said is true—but you have only considered one aspect of this issue. I would admit that there is a merciful God in the world if all matters were to take place in a comforting, happy way and according to our needs. However, in reality that is not what we find.

Many accidents occur in this world. The power of God is not seen at that time. Living things die, or burn down for lack of water. Why is it that there is no timely rain? Animals burn in the ferocious intensity of the sun's rays. Trapped in forest fires and writhing in agony innocent animals roast to death. The daggers of the wicked wound the faithful Hindus, Christians, and Buddhists. A false witness can send an innocent person to the gallows. The sea erodes, places are submerged and people, both old and young, are drowned. Ships sink. People who do not have water drink the blood of their fellow-beings. Unable to bear their hunger, human beings kill each other and eat raw meat. Struck by lightning, innocent children die. A snake bites a hapless man while he is sleeping. A blind person painfully searching for a mouthful of food, falls into an unused well, breaks his neck and leg, suffers unbearable pain, and dies. People call out to God to save them from infectious diseases, wars, and droughts, and, not being saved, die. In these instances, why doesn't God's loving kindness and his power not save his creatures from grief? Brief respites due to some ordinary reason are looked upon as God's grace. However, Hindus and people of other religions offer worthless reasons for their sorrows and their continuance. In Hinduism, it is believed that sorrows are the punishment that God metes out to a person for all the sins committed in a previous birth. It is always better to let the person know that the punishment meted out to him is for the wrongs he has done. So how does it help if somebody is made to suffer without knowing why he is undergoing such pain? If punishment is for redemption from sin, shouldn't it be meted out with the knowledge of the sinner? Recently, a great scientist has written a book about this, I will give you a résumé of it. If I translate it directly, Jeshtan you will find it difficult to understand. This great scholar says:

Let us put aside the natural evil intention of a culprit who has brought about destruction or has attacked his fellow creatures. There is no other way to bring this offender back to society and its ways unless he is punished and helped to mend himself according to the rules made by man.

However, what is the evidence to show that it is God himself who is troubling his creatures in this manner? Let us set aside the debate regarding God's existence and for the moment believe that he exists. Ignore all the theses about the birth of sorrow. Then think of God as the ruler of the world. In such a situation, what reason can be shown to justify that this world ruler is troubling his creations? Is he punishing his creations in order to save himself or is he torturing people who have done wrong, for their good? Whatever be the case, can't the same God work out things without all this torture? We human beings feel pain if we inflict pain or sorrow on others, and we believe it to be a sinful deed. People who are learned teach those who are not, to love each other and also advise them on how to live well. But some people ignore this advice and continue to inflict pain on others. If such conduct is unacceptable in human beings, how much more unacceptable is it in God! If the kings who rule our country had the power to eradicate evil and instil goodness into the offenders, why don't they do so before an offence is committed? Never will such a thing be done. However, we human beings have no power to know the present and future. Surely, as you say, it is not possible for that God who is called the Merciful One not to have this power. God created man. It follows then that all our desires have their origins in him. Hence, God can, according to his will, either obliterate evil or aggravate it. Why doesn't he prevent man's inclination for evil? Why then should he scourge him after permitting him to indulge in evil deeds? Isn't this gross injustice? Will God do such a stupid and cruel thing? If we look at the punishments mentioned in the Bible, we see how intensely, mercilessly, and cruelly God has punished man. According to the Christian tenets, even if the culprit performs good deeds later, or repents, God does not show any mercy. Adam happened to commit a sin once. For that he and all his children had to burn in the fires of hell forever in a way in which they can't be redeemed. Because Adam sinned why should his descendants also suffer this great torture? If God can do things like this, where is his kindness and sense of justice?

This is how this great logician and scientist speaks.

GOVINDAPANIKKAR: In our Hindu Puranas nothing is said about the fact that there was a person called Adam. I won't believe this.

GOVINDANKUTTYMENON: You don't have to believe in Adam. The Puranas speak of many curses and sorrows which were the result of God's anger; in fact some of these were of greater intensity than what can be found in the Bible. The Puranas show that gods, human beings, and animals have at various times been at the receiving end of God's anger—not only of God's anger but that of sages, Brahmins, and chaste women too. As a result, they had to take many births and suffer a great deal in order to atone for their sins. Such lies and stupidity will not be found in the religious books of Christians.

GOVINDAPANIKKAR: You should not talk in this manner, Govindankutty. What do you know of our Puranas? Who will believe you if you call our great and ancient Puranas stupid and false merely because you have read an English book which was written just yesterday? Well, if there is no God, it means that you, Govindankutty, are saying that man came into being on his own.

GOVINDANKUTTYMENON: Not just mankind, but all these living things you see around came into being on their own and they fill this earth: this is what I am saying.

GOVINDAPANIKKAR: What when a man dies? Where does his life go?

GOVINDANKUTTYMENON: It doesn't go anywhere. It ceases to be. If you blow out a burning candle, where does the fire go? It doesn't go anywhere. It just ceases to be—it is the same with life also.

GOVINDAPANIKKAR: There is no alternative for man; if he dies, everything is over, isn't it? This religion of yours is good for devils—it is not good for anyone else. How did man get all these limbs and organs? With what logic was all this put together so neatly and in an orderly way?

MADHAVAN: All right, Father, your question is brilliant. With some changes it can sound like a question which a good English scientist would ask. I will rephrase it for you: Has this universe taken form on its own, without a creator? Is that your thesis, Govindankutty?

GOVINDANKUTTYMENON: Yes; I am saying that there is no evidence that it has been made by one creator.

MADHAVAN: State clearly and briefly why you hold that opinion.

GOVINDANKUTTYMENON: To say it clearly and in short is very difficult. Madhavan, like me, you too have read many books on this matter. Therefore, I will speak briefly in order to make jeshtan understand, though I doubt if my ideas can be amply demonstrated in a summary. I will read out certain parts of this book. Mr Bradlaugh's thesis is that what is said in the Bible about the creation of the world, its nature, and time is false and quite impossible. However, there is no need to talk about that here. If you think carefully and deeply about what scientists like Wallace, Darwin, and many others have said regarding the creation of the world, you can see that all these creations have come into being on their own through a birth process called 'evolution'. Darwin says:

Ordinary things naturally have contagion, growth, and destruction. One thing which stays in a particular manner with the passage of time acquires another shape and essence and it changes again. In this manner, in millions of years, one thing in its interaction and necessity of being with another thing casts off its first set of qualities and nature, and gradually acquires another. This is an innate power which is common to all things. The origin of man came about in this manner. In the beginning a creature with life, which was like an atom, improving gradually over a period of many years and according to the need and desire of life, and suitability of the bodily figure, evolved into the body and nature of mankind as we see it now.

As evidence for this Darwin has given many details. There are several parables to show that a distinct creator has not made all the things of this world in separate lots. When newly dampened mud is heated by fire and covered for four to five hours with a cold thing in order to prevent ordinary air reaching it, we will see on removing the cover lakhs of small forms like termites which are a type of white insect moving about. From where did these numerous insects come in such a short while? Did God make them then, were they given birth to, or did they come into being on their own when certain things interacted? An insect called the hornet picks out a termite or a worm and stores it in its nest. The worm becomes a hornet when it interacts with the latter for ten to fifteen days. If we look at minor things like this we get to see one thing acquiring the characteristics of another. Thus in this world, everything comes to be as a result of the ageless power of time and the interaction of one thing with another. It fills the earth thus and then it is destroyed. Huxley, an extremely intelligent person says,

If we look carefully and with scientific knowledge at all life forms and at all the bodies which have the unity of the five senses, we can see that each creature was born in the beginning as a result of definite reasons. The innumerable living things which we see all around us have come into existence from these reasons and we can see that they grow, spread and are destroyed. This is a power which is innate in many living things. There are no living beings without this power.

Bradlaugh responds:

On the basis of the knowledge we have acquired till today, it can be concluded that the nature and character of mankind today is not the same as earlier. They were like animals, fought with other animals, and lived in caves like creatures of the wild. Gradually, mankind became strong, intelligent, and capable of many things. In the same way, our knowledge can help us find out more about the condition of man several thousands of years ago.

GOVINDAPANIKKAR: Who will believe that man lived in a cave like an animal? Maybe in England it was like that. Likewise, even now there are people who are like animals. Aren't there, Madhavan?

MADHAVAN: Yes, in Africa there are men who live like animals.

GOVINDANKUTTYMENON: Long ago, in the times I spoke of, men were just as I described.

GOVINDAPANIKKAR: What is the proof for that?

GOVINDANKUTTYMENON: Scientific knowledge.

GOVINDAPANIKKAR: What science? Science made by the sayivs whose names you mentioned?

GOVINDANKUTTYMENON: They and people like them. What I am saying is based on many volumes of books which were written by people who have more scientific knowledge than even these men.

GOVINDAPANIKKAR: One of the things you said is also stated in the Hindu shastras. From being grass initially you have to go through several births to aspire to being human. But, all that comes about according to the decree of God, that is what our law says.

GOVINDANKUTTYMENON: All right, Jeshtan, do you agree with that much?

GOVINDAPANIKKAR: I have not agreed with anything you said. And never will, in this birth. Don't you say that there is no God? This is a very dangerous proposition; only a lunatic will say that there is no creator who is kind and all-knowing.

GOVINDANKUTTYMENON: I do not see such a person.

GOVINDAPANIKKAR: All right, let that be. These atheists have only recently started writing books. Long before that, now, and for more time to come, men have worshipped God in many ways and will continue to do so—of this I am sure. Govindankutty, will there be at least ten atheists in this world?

GOVINDANKUTTYMENON: There are several lakhs of atheists now in the world; however, not everyone knows them. In each religion, there are many atheists. But, when a count is taken, they are not separately accounted for. Among the people on this earth, four hundred five crore and six lakh are Buddhist, three hundred ninety crore and two lakh are Christians, two hundred four crore and two lakh are Muslims, one hundred seventy-four crore and two lakh are Hindus, and fifty lakh are Jews; and various others who worship idols are one hundred eighteen crore. This is what Bradlaugh writes. However, he shows that this account of religion is quite wrong. Among the learned and educated people living in Europe and America, a great many are atheists, but they are wrongly accounted as Protestants or Roman Catholics. There is no doubt that he is correct. Now in Keralam, in the census to be taken, I will be listed as a Hindu. However, in reality, I am not a Hindu at all. This kind of mistake is a common one. Therefore, it is nearly impossible to ascertain the exact number of people who do not believe that God exists.

GOVINDAPANIKKAR: What I hear is heresy! I will say it is the result of *Kaliyugadharma*.

GOVINDANKUTTYMENON: If that is so, then Jeshta why do you grieve over this? If in kaliyuga the God you refer to has decreed that men should become atheists, is it surprising that we have become atheists? Is there anything as unreasonable as the shastras of the Hindus? In one place it is said that the moment a man is born his destiny is engraved on his head or elsewhere by Brahma. If such a thing has been written and established, what power does man then have? You should live in this way; you should kill so many people, you should save so many people; you should do so many things,'—all these are already written and man is born with them. Then what self-power does that poor man have? He does what he has been ordered to do. Then why is he called a sinner or saint? In kaliyuga people will not remember God. They will commit sinful deeds. There won't be as much rain as is needed, the earth won't yield crops, there will not be purity and impurity, Brahmins will be tortured, cows will be slaughtered, evil people will prosper. Similarly, it is said that many such commandments have been made. Then why do you, Jeshtan, find fault when you see all these things happening according to the commandments? Aren't you also a person of kaliyuga? Don't these commandments apply to you also? It is a great pity that there is so much stupidity and unreasonable behaviour! Other than these books written by some Brahmins for their self-aggrandizement, there seems to be no other books to enlighten Hindus about such matters. Then what can we do? The poor people swallow all the stupidity in these books.

MADHAVAN: Govindankutty, what you have said just now is crass stupidity. If you knew something about a few of the valuable books written by Brahmins you would not have spoken like this. After reading books written by people like Bradlaugh, Darwin, Wallace, Huxley, and Herbert Spencer who have learnt only English, how can you say that valuable books have not been written by any Hindus?

GOVINDANKUTTYMENON: Madhavan, are you saying that the books which have been written by great scientists like Darwin and others are similar to the Puranas and the Mahabharatam, Bhagavatham, Ramayanam, and *Skantam* which are unreasonable and filled with unlikely happenings?

MADHAVAN: You should not speak in this hasty and irrational fashion. Think carefully before you speak. Herbert Spencer and others wrote recently. It is almost one or two thousand years since great writers and thinkers came to be among us Hindus. Similarly, English scholars too have acquired their knowledge about these one or two thousand years. They are surely more knowledgable than the earlier scholars for the simple reason that they came later. However, I am not finding fault with you, Govindankutty, for saying that Hindu religion is decaying; I do not doubt it. Nowadays Hindu religion propagates unreasonable and contradictory practices. It is the same with all the other world religions.

GOVINDANKUTTYMENON: Then, Madhavan, why did you find fault with me for saying that?

MADHAVAN: I shall tell you. You said that all the books of the Hindus in Sanskrit are likewise filled with matters which are contradictory in nature and that the poor people have no other books. I was also astonished at the way you listed the books in Sanskrit. Mahabharatam, Bhagavatham, *Skantapuranam* are important books of the Hindus. Isn't that what you said? That is very strange.

GOVINDANKUTTYMENON: Why, aren't these the main reference books?

MADHAVAN: Yes, these books are referred to in the same way as in English one refers to Milton's *Paradise Lost* and Shakespeare's plays. The things Milton, Shakespeare, and others have written are different from the writings of a Darwin or a Wallace. What is the connection between books which talk about the philosophy of Socrates and those by Milton and Shakespeare? In the same way, regarding the matters we have been discussing, the books for Hindus are not Ramayanam and Mahabharatam.

GOVINDANKUTTYMENON: Then what are they?

MADHAVAN: Shall I reveal to you that the thesis about atheism that you put forward now had been established by great Hindus about two thousand years ago?

GOVINDANKUTTYMENON: Is there something like that?

MADHAVAN: Of course. Don't jump to conclusions; listen to me patiently.

GOVINDAPANIKKAR: What are you saying, my dear boy? Have Hindus ever talked about atheism?

MADHAVAN: Without doubt they have. What was the thesis of Kapilamaharshi in what is called Sankhya? The Hindus expounded six schools of philosophy: Kapil's atheist sankhya philosophy; Pathanjali's yogas and Bhagavatgita; Jaimani's *Poorvamimamsa*; Vyasa's *Uttharamimamsa*—otherwise vedanta; Gautama's *nyayayika* thesis; Kanadan's *vaisheshika* thesis. It is Kapilan's sankhya that advises complete atheism.

GOVINDANKUTTYMENON: Is it so?

GOVINDAPANIKKAR: There is no atheism in our science. Certainly not.

MADHAVAN: Yes there is. However, that thesis is based on pure individualism—that knowing oneself is knowing God. Whatever it may be, all these are difficult to put across in a rational manner. I feel that nothing fruitful is going to emerge even if we argue about this matter for a long time. What Huxley—the scientist whom Govindankutty referred to—said about atheism, I remember verbatim. I will give you a translation of that. Father, you need to think about it and decide whether this great scholar is an atheist. Huxley says:

Unluckily I have had to read certain speeches written by some scholars who pretended to know about God's nature, form, and situation. These statements are illogical, false, even ridiculous. I have read only one other which matches this thing. There are statements by certain other atheists who oppose the thesis. I wonder whether these ill-aimed attacks are anything more than just that.

This is how Huxley's and the opinions of many other extremely intelligent Englishmen now stand. At the same time, none of these people are atheists. From Hindu philosophy itself we get to know that God is a power that cannot be understood and fathomed by ordinary people. There are many arguments for this. There is no need to talk about all this now.

Some intelligent people do not believe what many scholars in Europe (Darwin and others) have said about evolution and other things. In my opinion, atheism is a religion which is inimical to ordinary worldly pleasures. Not only is there no use propagating atheism in the world, I fear that it also complicates the lives of ordinary human beings. I shall state my reasons for saying so. Then I will talk about my own faith.

At all times, wise men should try to bring comfort to their fellow creatures. It is not possible for anyone to know definitively whether God exists or not. If learned scientists agree that God does not exist, they should resolve this doubt in a manner that can prove to be useful to mankind. If people truly come to believe that there is no God, the evils which will befall us consequently will be sufficient reason for intelligent people to discourage the spread of atheism. Ten reasons might be cited to show that God exists. The man who advocates atheism will use those very ten reasons to show that God does not exist, and do so in a way which will perplex the mind of the ordinary person and leave him to grieve. Isn't this really regrettable? If no harm is done by faith in God, why must that faith be riddled with doubts? If a person lies, steals, commits adultery, hurts his fellow creatures, or gives up dharma, other than the punishment such a deed will bring upon him, the fear of facing God, as a culprit, will at least act as a deterrent. I do not decry anyone who can prove and convince me that there is no power such as God. But if this cannot be demonstrated convincingly, why confuse and perplex ordinary mortals?

With the advent of scientific knowledge, many things, earlier mysteries, have been explained. We know about the origin, movement, strength, and philosophy behind these things. However, these 'sciences' do not help us understand the unknown power which is the reason for the existence of things. We can work out many tricks with the use of science because we know about the attraction between a magnet and iron dust. However, science does not reveal the initial reason for the existence of properties which are inherent in substances. There is no need for science to explain this. Science does not say that God does not exist. The aim of science is to comprehend the mutual workings between various things and to understand the intricate nature of those things in order to make them useful for human beings, thereby increasing the pleasure of living. But these sciences do not teach us anything about the condition of the human soul once it gives up worldly pleasures.

If you study the extremely reasonable philosophy of a set of believers called 'agnostics' in English, we find the claim of the atheists unreasonable and unbelievable. I am fully convinced that there is nothing like belief in God for mankind to be good and loving towards each other. Faith in God prevents people from indulging in cruel deeds and induces them to live by rules which lead to a judicious and comfortable existence for all. Particularly at the time of death, such people will undergo less suffering than those who have celebrated atheism in their lives. Faith is the only solace at the time of intense sorrow.

Isn't it wrong then that that faith in God which man has upheld for so long is denied in matters which are still so much in doubt and a move made to establish that there is no God?

Shouldn't we try to mitigate as much as possible the fear that human beings experience at the time of death? On realizing that he must give up his body, a person may become intensely sad and perplexed:

'Listen, you will die soon. Your health will not improve. Your life will be extinguished like this flame. You will be destroyed; you will leave behind your body, children, wife, mother, brothers, wealth, and all comforts.'

Just think of the predicament of a living being who has to listen to this and die in the midst of unrelenting sorrow.

On the other hand, think of the great comfort that your soul will derive if it has even a faint hope of salvation after death. It is better for mankind to have faith in God, especially if you think of your life moving into the intense darkness and unending sorrow.

Therefore, first of all, I will say that advocating atheism is something ignominious for human beings.

Now, I shall talk about what I believe in. Faith in God does not come about because of any reason. That faith can come even without reason. But you may ask how a man like you, Govindankutty, who is educated and who has given a lot of thought to such things, can acquire a faith like this. My answer is that though there are many things incomprehensible to man's sensibilities, he can certainly understand that there is an indescribable power that rules this world. I call this power God.

In my opinion, all the bounty and the perils seen in this world are necessary, and our creator's aim itself may be defined in this manner. All living things in this world are temporary. If it were not so I doubt whether this world would have survived for such a long time. If living things of the past fifty thousand years continued to live and mutiplied accordingly, this world would not be sufficient for everything and everyone to live in comfort.

Now we do not see a human being who existed a hundred and fifty years ago. They have all been destroyed. Think of how many hundred and fifty years have passed now. How many crores of people have been born in that period of time? How many have died? Countless. Indeed countless. If the decrease is not in proportion to the increase it is clear that this world would not have survived. It is by the order of our creator that destruction takes place in this world. Wise people are now aware that this is the condition of mankind. Even then, is there any man who is not frightened of death? Who is not shocked and perplexed when they hear that their life on earth is going to be terminated? Here we see an inexplicable power which sustains and destroys mankind. Sorrows and dangers convince us that wordly pleasures are nothing. We all admit that that is so, but we continue to ponder over these matters, forgetting that the world is momentary and insignificant. We do so because there is a great power of which we have no clear conception. I think of that power as God.

Let the world meet with many dangers, let regions burn without rain, let lightning strike and burn places, let the sea erode and drown nations, let there be earthquakes, let there be wars, let people die by the million; even so, at the very end we see that the transactions of the world increase with each passing year. Five hundred years ago there was more activity than there was a thousand years ago. One hundred years ago we see more activity than during the past two hundred years. More this year in comparison to last year, today more than yesterday. What is the reason for this? There is a power beyond everything which preserves the world from being destroyed, and because of that power this world continues on its path in spite of these destructions and sorrows. I call this supreme power God.

Then like the atheists say, if the world has come to be on its own and it does not depend on any special life-giving force, all the things and animals that are seen in this world need not stand forever in mutual parity and mutual dependence and they do not.

I say that the sun was created by God. No, the atheist says, it came into being as a globe with related reasons working together. For me, as well as for the atheist, it is amazing that despite so much light the sun can be so regenerative when it has the power to burn the earth to cinders, and that it stands all the time at the right distance from the earth. In general, if mankind thinks that the sun is a creation of God, is it right to invalidate the opinion? Won't this then cause sorrow to human beings? When he sees the bright glow of the sun, mankind imagines a much greater power as its originary source. Atheists do not say anything which can call to our minds other means that is more convincing. As matters stand like this, why should we accept the opinion of the atheist? With the knowledge called science it is possible to know a little bit about the round shape, heat, and the attractive power of the sun. It is not possible for science to know everything, like why and when such a globe came into being thus saving this earth and all the living things on it. If we go on talking about the matters related to the creation process called evolution, there is no doubt that we won't arrive at any conclusion on this phenomenon. Isn't it then more feasible to think that God exists? Heat, cold, rain, air, and other things which are great earthly forces benefit and comfort all the people in the world. Rather than make guesses as to how they came to be, isn't it better to think that there is a great power which is full of life, which organizes these lifeless things in this regular and correct way?

Think of the actions of a cow, an ordinarily stupid creature which thinks of nothing other than filling its stomach, a trait it shows immediately after giving birth to its calf. What it was carrying as a burden in its stomach until the time of birth, and what came out through its genitals, that animal does not know till that moment. It is amazing to see the love and affection this poor animal shows towards its young one and the hard work and enthusiasm with which the cow cares for the calf the moment it is born. The atheists talk about all this very accurately. However, I do not regard the issues that they bring up for discussion very seriously. Is there any reason to have an argument that there is a greater power above all this which sustains this world? We see even animals perpetuating their own kind, thus acting intelligently like human beings. From this we understand that there is a power called God. Govindankutty, you talked at length about all the sorrows in this world. Think about the comforts. If you calculate and make an account of how much land burns out with thirst as a result of no rain in one year, you will see that it is a tiny part of this earth. Take for instance a contagious disease like cholera. It could wipe out an entire population. It could leave a country depopulated. But ordinarily this does not happen. How many ships sink while they are on the sea? How many people who do not get water to drink, quench their thirst by drinking the blood of their friends? All these are probably meant to remind us that pleasures are never unalloyed. Even though we encounter difficulties, all things considered there is nothing as comfortable as life on this earth. I am not going to say anything further about this. The same intense eagerness to be in this world is witnessed in both the great king who resides in his grand palace, enjoying and revelling in all the pleasures and comforts, as well as in the poor man who toils for his livelihood and lives and spends his day in a shack. However old they may be, death induces in both of them the same kind of anguish and terror. Likewise, God has given the great king and the poor man similar pleasures. The great king opens his eyes to see and enjoy the beautiful red and yellow rays of the rising sun filtering through the golden satin curtains. The same rays give an equal amount of happiness to the poor man. The satisfaction which the king derives when he eats in beautiful golden trays filled with delicacies pleasing to the senses, is the same as the poor man's when he fills his stomach by eating plain rice and drinking water. The pleasure that the king experiences while he sleeps on his bed of flowers, is similar to the pleasure a poor man gets when he sleeps on his ordinary mat. Therefore, when you comprehend the rational cleverness with which the comforts of all living things are arranged there is no need to dispute the fact that there is a mighty power which governs this world.

If we take an accurate account of the happiness and sorrows in the world, we will see that there is more happiness, and the reason for that without any doubt is a great power. This I will emphatically and reverentially call God.

GOVINDAPANIKKAR: We have talked enough of this matter: none of us knows enough to conduct a philosophical discourse. First of all, I think I was wrong to ask you young people about this matter.

GOVINDANKUTTYMENON: Is this your opinion, Jeshta, in spite of all that we said?

GOVINDAPANIKKAR: What did you say? Both of you talked a lot of nonsense. What do you know about religion? It is my stupidity that I conversed with you on these matters. You have lost religious faith and the faith in your teachers, almost completely. Madhavan, though you believe that God exists, on examining the nature and characteristics of that belief I do not think that you have any special reverence, and fear of God than an atheist like Govindankutty. Come now, let's retire.

Govindapanikkar, Madhavan, and Govindankuttymenon lay down in the balcony upstairs to sleep. Madhavan had a lot to ask about Indulekha. Though he was reluctant to ask his father and Govindankutty, Govindapanikkar talked for some time to Madhavan about Indulekha's sorrow and about the condition of the Nambuthiripad. Some time was spent thus in conversation. Govindankutty then asked Madhavan:

GOVINDANKUTTYMENON: Are your friends, the babus, coming for the Congress session? I hear Babu Govinda Sen and Chitraprasad Sen and others are working enthusiastically for the Congress. Have they asked you to do anything special in this matter?

MADHAVAN: They have not asked me to do anything. Babu Govinda Sen is a great friend of the Congress. I once spoke at a meeting held at his residence.

GOVINDAPANIKKAR: I have heard that recently our countrymen had organized a meeting in which while everyone agreed that the English rule had proved advantageous to us in several ways, there were nevertheless some ills being perpetrated in the name of good governance. Are you referring to that meeting?

MADHAVAN: Yes.

GOVINDANKUTTYMENON: The Congress is proving ineffective; it doesn't have any substance—I think all this is a futile gesture.

MADHAVAN: This is indeed an exaggerated complaint, Govindankutty. Before you ridicule the efforts of the Congress, surely Govindankutty, you should have made Father understand clearly what the Congress is all about and what its aims are. Why don't you talk in particular about the nature and objectives of that group?

GOVINDANKUTTYMENON: Oh-ho! I shall talk about it, let Jeshtan hear. Some wealthy Hindus and Muslims, who can converse well in English, desire to form a government along the same lines as the English government. With this intention they have formed a group where they praise each other and pretend to be great and waste a lot of time. This is the Congress group. In no respect are we Indians the equal of the English. Aiming for equality may not be useful; there are many other things which we can attain easily and which are so much more productive. So why attempt that which is the trickiest feat of all?

The many liberties that English people enjoy have not been secured through the intervention of a group like the Congress. First of all, I am convinced that the voluble people who are desirous of this great independence are making this great clamour in English without thinking sensitively about it. If they are so passionately desirous of freedom and have so much pride in their race, why are they still under a foreign king? Let them fight and drive away the English. Let the babus rule the country. If England were to be subjugated by the Germans, do you think the English would form a Congress and plead with the Germans for pity? I don't think they will do such a thing. They will fight the Germans and try to drive them out. If you have any pride, that is what you should do. Is it laudable to pretend that you are proud and go on begging? When wealth, strength, greatness, and power are on their side, what is the use of barking and crying against them in this way? The Hindus and the Muslims have been overcome by the English in the same way. We have no wealth, no strength, no unity, no truth, no generosity, no education, no knowledge, no enthusiasm. Should people like this try to make a parliament for India? The English who have one religion and who are united are themselves finding it difficult to run a parliament properly. We Indians, who belong to diverse religious sects and who are terribly opposed to each other, are planning to form a parliament at the behest of these bearded English-speaking babus, Iyers, and Mudaliars. Nothing can be more stupid than this. People live in mutual peace because they fear the bullets of the English. If these Englishmen leave India tomorrow, we will see the boldness of these babus. They won't be able to protect the country even for a minute. If they really have a sense of pride, they would have acquired by now what they so passionately desire. Actually, these people have no courage, smartness, enthusiasm, and patience; they just want to make a lot of noise. They want to show how well they can speak English.

The English way of governance is acceptable to all. A few modifications in keeping with the changing times will suffice. Before we take on the burden of ruling this country, why don't we set right some of the ills that plague the country? Can't they do something to erase caste differences which necessarily stand in the way of prosperity? In order to prevent the country from declining into poverty, can't there be an attempt to teach Indians international commerce, agriculture, handicrafts, and industrial work? Why can't we try and rectify some of our domestic habits, our manners, and conduct? How many years has it been since the railway, telegraph, and other things which are such amazing techniques came to India? Why can't the Hindu and the Muslim learn to make and use these machines? Haven't the Europeans learnt the technique of manufacturing them? If we want a good iron wheel, don't we have to bring it from England? If we want an iron chain, don't we depend on England? If we want good materials from a needle to a battleship, don't we again turn to England? Aren't the people of this land ashamed of this state of affairs? First of all, shouldn't we try to make India the equal of England in such matters?

Only after resolving these numerous shameful matters should the people of India strive for freedom. Who will respect our demand if we do not effect these changes first? I have great contempt for this Congress. I feel ashamed when sayivs like Sir Lepel, Griffin and others talk about the natives of India. Many things that they say are true. Is it possible to ignore all this and desire that we equal Englishmen in the matter of our country's governance? If such a group forms itself, it will merely generate a lot of anger and noise, and waste a lot of money.

GOVINDAPANIKKAR: What Govindankutty says is right. Now the administration of our country is better than it was earlier and this will suffice. However, I do not agree with the absurd idea that caste differences should be eradicated.

GOVINDANKUTTYMENON: I shall not argue more about doing away with caste differences. However, Jeshtan, are you convinced about what I said with regard to the administration of the country?

GOVINDAPANIKKAR: Madhavan, don't you wish to respond to this?

MADHAVAN: I do not feel like saying anything, I am very sad. You have had a holistic education, Govindankutty, you have passed your BA and yet you talk so irrationally.

GOVINDANKUTTYMENON: I did not speak irrationally—show me the irrationality in what I said.

MADHAVAN: What you said is all nonsense. First of all, the aim of the Congress in India is not simply to make a parliament. No eminent person is of the opinion that Indians are equal to the English.

That there are many things to be rectified in India is correct. But merely because those matters have to be taken care of doesn't mean that we should not concern ourselves with the question of self-governance. If there is love and pride for the country, we should fight to recover it from the English. But it is also a fallacy to think that we are patriotic only if we fight to retrieve our country. Govindankutty, did you form such an opinion of the Congress after you read the histories of European countries? Just think of the story of England.

First, the Romans conquered the people who lived on the island of Britain. They ruled over it for some time. Then for some time they were under the Saxons and then the Danes. Finally, the Norman kings who were of French descent conquered Britain. Don't you remember what happened afterwards? Because these kings were powerful, didn't the British submit to them?

GOVINDANKUTTYMENON: They never submitted to them. These kings who came from outside united with the English people and became one with their ranks. The French simply left the kingdom. In the same way, should we allow the English people to rule over us till the great queen and others merge with our ranks?

MADHAVAN: I agree. Whether the English come here or we go there, it is the same. In our country, after the English rule began we have experienced prosperity and several comforts. That is why we Congressmen desire that gradually the English government and the Indian government should be united. We have directed all our efforts towards achieving this unity. As the Norman royalty became British royalty, we hope that English kings and English administration will become India's own. Initially the English and the Normans attempted to vanquish each other. When this could not go on any longer, they decided to forget their enmity and were united. Similarly, we and the English are fighting a battle of wits in the hope that the English will have faith in us and that the English government will not discriminate between us and the Englishmen. This cannot be achieved with guns and rifles, but by argument and discussion with intelligent Englishmen. If this strategy works, I can say that there has never been a party in India as capable as the Congress. However, I agree that this party should adapt itself to the changing milieu. Sometimes people unnecessarily, and without any adequate reason, find fault with the British government. I agree that this is a matter of concern. Even so, the English government has never been held in contempt by the eminent people of the Congress. We only request that each grievance be rectified as it comes up. After all this, how can you, Govindankutty, speak stupidly? The Congress has never denied that modifications need to be made. It is not possible for all the diseases of a patient to be cured at once with a single medicine. Each one has to be treated separately. But if that patient decides that he will take one medicine for all ills, he has no other choice than to suffer from all the diseases. It is not yet time for a group to form itself in order to work towards the eradication of castes. Even if something is done tomorrow to correct the functioning of the government, it will certainly be beneficial. I will tell you the reason for it. Caste, or what is said to be caste in India, depends on religion. Try as they might, the English people cannot remove the caste system from India, because it is deeply embedded in religion. If that practice has to be taken away from the Hindus and the Muslims of India, they have to be initiated into a religion which will prevail over their religious rituals. I cannot imagine such a special religion. Therefore, will it be possible if you try now to change a caste arrangement which is in accordance with the religions of India? It seems doubtful.

However, with the passage of time when knowledge increases, caste beliefs will gradually decline. They may finally be uprooted completely. In my opinion, trying to wipe out caste differences at this juncture might not be productive. However, think of the governance of the country. It is but a hundred years since the English began to administer the country. Even then, in such a short while, Govindankutty, think how much the people have learnt to appreciate the good governance of the English. Talk to a daily-wage earner or ask a fisherman and you will find the difference now. I am not claiming that he comprehends the workings of the civil and the criminal code but he knows that he can freely engage in anything which is not wrong and which he finds satisfying for his body and mind. Ordinarily this much knowledge is enough. Even in England and America, where ordinary people enjoy all the pleasures and every kind of independence, they have only as much knowledge of the subject of administration as the ordinary people of India. Isn't it rather silly then to say that all those who desire independence should understand the principles of governance as well as Gladstone does? It would be ludicrous to say that we should rule our country as in England only after women are given English education and we start manufacturing our own machines. Govindankutty, you also say that the people of India obey the English king because they are afraid of the bullets. This is not true at all. The power of the English has certainly struck terror in the hearts of evil people and good-for-nothings. But it has also earned the English the respect and appreciation of the good people. The whole country is under their control because the subjects love the government and because of the recognition of their ability to rule and look after their subjects. I have no doubt about this. If the English government had oppressed the people by being unjust like the kings we had before the English came, this government would not have continued for long in India! Also, Govindankutty, you say that we make speeches in English just to acquire fame as orators. It is not that we do not desire that kind of fame. But it is a mistake to say that it is just for that we are making speeches. These speeches are not only needed at this moment but have also proved beneficial to us. I will recount each of these benefits. First of all, the impartial people in England are convinced that there are many well-educated and intelligent Indians. This is the realization that these speeches have brought about. Secondly, due to this realization, many Englishmen believe that the Congress should be preserved. Thirdly, impressed by these speeches many eminent Indians who earlier disapproved of the Congress have now been won over. These merits which have been gained for India in so short a while are due to the extraordinary speeches of rational and eloquent people. If the Congress works in an orderly manner for some time, I have no doubt that Indians too will be able to get all the benefits which the English have been given by their government. Don't you realize, Govindankutty, how absurd it is to say that these speeches are mere bombast. However, I agree that sometimes some people from the Congress, some newspapers, some groups, and the books written by Congressmen or their friends have accused the English government untruthfully. This is a grievous fault. This can only be labelled great ill luck for India and the Congress. If this goes on it will be destructive for the Congress eventually. The distinguished Sir Oakland Colvin sayiv esq. once wrote a well-argued and beautifully phrased letter to A.O. Hume sayiv, about the mistaken accusations that the Congress had levelled against the Indian government. I was greatly disturbed to read the things mentioned in this letter. When the Indian government is careful that it should do all possible good for us, isn't it a grievous thing for some people to say that it springs from carelessness and evil intentions? If the English governors and the rulers of the country are not people blessed with great patience, how will they bear such accusatory statements? Had such accusations not been levelled against the Congress, it would have become more powerful long before this.

Initially, Lord Dufferin, the governor general, was supportive of the Congress. But he was unhappy to hear some people speak ill of the government. My constant thought and prayer are that the Congress should not, without cause, find fault with the English government. Instead, it should strive for India's prosperity and make India an independent country like England. There are many ways to achieve this without saying nasty things about the present government. The English government would never have thought that Indians should not benefit; or that Indians should continue as slaves of Englishmen. Had this been their intention, they would not have been so eager to educate us. They wanted us to be capable like them. Even little children can understand this. Those of us who are educated and knowledgeable should not decide that merits will occur automatically and be contented. We should try all lawful means to improve our situation. It is for this that the Congress Party has been formed. This kind of a party is indeed necessary. If at all someone in that party criticizes the government, I will brand him a mad man. Considering that we have been given the freedom to criticize, it is a great tragedy that we doubt the intentions of the government. If for these reasons the Congress suspects the trustworthiness of the government it will only lead to the destruction of society. All our deeds must be inspired by truth or a noble end is not possible.

Govindankutty says that Indians lack money, unity, truthfulness, enthusiasm, and other qualities. There's some truth in all this. But if there was no unity, the Congress would not have been able to work as it has worked. In such a big country, the kind of unity and togetherness we see has been possible because of the English language. If this language were to be more popular it would further strengthen our unity. Unity exists when people have similar opinions on certain key issues. This kind of unanimity of opinion can be achieved through the spread of education and knowledge. Furthermore, to Govindankutty's claim that there is no 'truth' I would just say that he has unnecessarily defamed the people of India. Govindankutty, how many truthful people living in India do you know? Haven't you read in the Puranas about people like Harishchandra, Aswatthama, Dasaratha, and others? From time immemorial India has been devoted to truth. I felt extremely sad when you suddenly said that we are an untruthful lot. You also said that Indians lack an enterprising spirit. This is also not strictly true. I have no doubt that in India the enthusiasm to learn and to gain knowledge is increasing and the courage and agility of the Indians can be determined only after we study the soldiers closely. It is possible, Govindankutty, that you may be a coward. It is common for a cowardly person to feel that all the others are cowards like him. I believe that many of the Congress babus, Iyers, and Mudaliars who were referred to in a derogatory manner by you as people who just make a lot of noise are people who are actually prepared to sacrifice their lives and their wealth for the prosperity and betterment of India. But who will listen if you say that victory should be won with intelligence! Who will agree if a fool says that courage can be determined only if ten babus or Iyers are seen fighting against the English government. Govindankutty, you said that you appreciate Sir Lepel, Griffin, and others criticizing India. I also enjoy that. It is true that we pay heed to our failures only when we encounter criticism from intelligent rivals. These people are clearly doing India a lot of good. When we continuously hear the insult that the eloquent babus, Iyers, and Mudaliars cannot find the strength to oppose Muslims, and that they are cowards, it actually makes us more energetic and determined. Therefore, let them say what they wish to say.

Govindankutty, I have given an answer to almost everything you said. Now I will briefly speak of the goal of the Congress in order to convince my father. I will move out of the Congress the moment I see it deviating from its professed goals.

Father's assumptions about the Congress are wrong. It was not set up to rectify the ills of English rule. From the time the English government started functioning, India has acquired multiple benefits.

The Congress was formed to try to augment these benefits. Can you ever find another people as intelligent as the English? I doubt it. This intelligence manifests in their sense of justice, impartiality, kindness, courage, initiative, and patience. It is with these six qualities that the English have managed to subdue so many countries in the world. It is India's great fortune that it came to be ruled by such an intelligent people. It is as a consequence of British rule that Indians have begun to experience the desire to augment their knowledge. If we ask the English to fulfil this desire, we fully believe that they will do so according to what is just. The Congress has been formed to work out these requests in a rational and appropriate way.

The English people are of the opinion that in all matters all people should enjoy independence. In several ways, this has worked towards the betterment of human society. In England, at this time no man can believe he is the slave of another. No man fears another for the performance of an action which is just. Though it is not possible for us to achieve all this immediately, the Congress is making a request that we should get something at the appropriate time. What is so wrong with this? It would be good I think, if the administration of the country is set up along the lines of the English not just in India but, if possible, also in Africa. But some people do not appreciate this demand for independent rule for they believe that they would be governed by incompetent people, not well versed in the art of governance. However illiterate a people, they certainly know about happiness and unhappiness. Isn't it stupid then to say that the people of India do not have the ability to distinguish one from the other? Let alone human beings, even animals can differentiate between the people who protect them with concern and others who are cruel towards them. What the Congress demands now mainly is to rule this country by enlisting the services of more of those people who can match the English in education and knowledge and who think like them. Is this wrong? Won't this be more beneficial to us? I agree that among our people there are many who are capable and know enough to administer and rule the country and it is the English who have made people like this. Shouldn't we request that these capable and educated people too be included in the government of this country? The Congress is mainly thinking of these matters.

It is true that in India we have more uneducated than educated people. But the mechanics of ruling the country are more or less similar among the people in different countries who live by ordinary business, agriculture, handicrafts, and daily wages. For example, look at the confusion that takes place in England when the members are elected to the parliament. Though everyone may not be knowledgeable, it is to be assumed that they will listen to the advice given by the more intelligent people amongst them and behave accordingly.

Caste, the lack of education among women, and other such things should not be cited as reasons for refusing the requests put forward by the Congress.

Impartial Englishmen are now of the opinion that more Indians should be involved in matters related to administration, dispensation of justice, and taxation, all of which will help in the spread of the nationalistic zeal. Such views are also being put into practice. All this is the result of the initiatives taken by the Congress over the past four years.

I believe that the primary protection that the English government has in India comes from the educated people. Only the educated will understand the merits and demerits of the English government. The kind of intense revolt which took place in India in 1857 cannot recur—not because the army has been strengthened and fortified but because of the spread of education and knowledge. A government's strength should derive from its subjects' knowledge, education, and love. How quickly the rumour spread all over the country in 1857; it was said that the grease on the ignition strips of the cartridges was actually animal fat and that biting it would make the soldiers lose caste, and people were quick to believe in that evil rumour, because at that time there were few knowledgeable people who could convince ordinary people that the English government would never behave so cruelly. Now there are many who understand the intricate details of English administration and they won't allow such lies to spread. Even then some wicked people find fault unnecessarily and because of this there is a feeling that educated people are against the English government. This makes me extremely sad. No eminent Englishman will demand that we should respect and fear them without reason. Father, I do not agree when you say that the English should continue to govern our country. After being educated like the Englishmen themselves and acquiring similar skills, who would not like to work in positions which match their abilities? Who other than mischievous people will say that this is wrong? Most people in England have great respect for this Congress.

Even when administrative reforms are demanded, or measures suggested by the people for the eradication of poverty are being implemented, foolish people like Govindankutty say: 'All of you do not belong to the same caste. First of all, unite all the castes. Secondly, educate your women. Discard the customary modes of eating, bathing. Learn how to make iron wheels and needles. Only then need you talk about matters like this.' Father, wouldn't you yourself feel that it is an irresponsible statement?

GOVINDANKUTTYMENON: I will admit that most of what I said is wrong if this is the nature of Congress. But I have read many speeches made by Congressmen which lack love and affection for the British government. When I read such statements I feel that people have only disgust for the English.

MADHAVAN: That is your interpretation of what you read, Govindankutty. If the English are hated, will this Congress enjoy so much respect in England?

GOVINDANKUTTYMENON: Only people who do not know about the situation of the Congress have respect for it. Great people like Lord Dufferin despise the Congress.

MADHAVAN: They do not despise the Congress. However, some meaningless speeches made by a few impatient people had displeased Lord Dufferin slightly. Despite this, he has a great regard for the Congess. Isn't it human to be displeased if a master is told that all the favours he has bestowed until now are worthless? All capable English people are of the opinion that capable Indians should be more involved in matters relating to the administration of the country. Lord Dufferin is also of the same opinion. Because the situation is like this it cannot be that they dislike the Congress. However, if the Congress moves away from its set goals and if it unnecessarily and untruthfully insults the British government, I will not be a friend of the Congress. Like Sir Oakland Colvin sayiv, I too believe that if the Congress abandons its professed goal its downfall is certain.

GOVINDAPANIKKAR: It is very late. I feel sleepy.

In this fashion, Madhavan and Govindankutty talked and went off to sleep. The next day they took the train for Keralam.

chapter nineteen

Things Which Actually Happened at Home during the Period of Madhavan's Journey

It is not possible to avoid saying something about the condition of Indulekha from the time Madhavan left Madras. Her grief was not of the kind that struck Madhavan's mother, or the others when they heard that Madhavan had left the country. Indulekha grieved mainly over two things: first, that Madhavan had believed the false story immediately and by doing so revealed how little he knew of her character and intellect; and secondly, even though she knew that Madhavan was a brilliant young man and that he loved her more than his own life, she feared that the intense sorrow of separation might drive him to end his life.

She did not mind that he had gone on a tour of the country. After completing one's education it was necessary to do so. There was nothing strange about that. She kept her intense grief to herself and I think it was the third day after Govindapanikkar and others went in search of Madhavan, that Indulekha appointed a man to stay close to the station and entrusted him to bring news of any telegraphic message. It is difficult to say exactly how Indulekha passed the time. She was usually beside Parvathiamma trying to comfort that mother in her sorrow. When she heard that Madhavan had gone away she somehow felt closer to Parvathiamma than to her own mother. Indulekha would not be separated from her at any time. Bathing, eating, and sleeping—everything was done together. However, Parvathiamma did not fully understand the situation between Madhavan and Indulekha. She knew that they loved each other. But that they were going to be husband and wife and that for Indulekha no one else was more important than Madhavan were not evident to Parvathiamma. It was almost one o'clock in the night when Parvathiamma sat up on her couch and asked Indulekha whether she was sleeping. Indulekha, who was unable to sleep as well, sat up.

PARVATHIAMMA: My dear girl, let me ask you something. Will you tell me the truth?
INDULEKHA: What is it you wish to know?
PARVATHIAMMA: Did you write to Madhavan expressing your dislike of him?
INDULEKHA: No.
PARVATHIAMMA: He gave you up for lost. That is why he went away.
INDULEKHA: Maybe.
PARVATHIAMMA: If you write to him in English saying that you will take him as your husband, in two days' time my son will be here. But ammaman has not permitted that. What can we do? It is my child's fate.

The poor woman began to weep.

INDULEKHA: You need not grieve about all this. He knows very well that I will have no other man as husband in this birth.
PARVATHIAMMA: Does Madhavan know about my daughter's feelings?
INDULEKHA: Very clearly.
PARVATHIAMMA: Then my son won't go anywhere. He will come back.
INDULEKHA: There is no reason for him not to return. But it is impossible to know what is happening there.

That night Parvathiamma understood something for sure—that Indulekha had decided to be Madhavan's wife.

A few days passed like this. That Madhavan had gone away became well known. The story also went about that it had happened because Shankarashastrikal had lied about Indulekha. A month later when Shankarashastrikal went to Chambazhiyot, he could hardly step out because of the way people scolded him. He sat in the temple, shamed and sorry. Indulekha was informed of Shastrikal's arrival. Immediately she sent somebody to summon him. When he found out that a man had been sent to call him, Shastrikal got the shock of his life. 'What a pity! I was the reason for bringing such great misfortune to two worthy people!' thinking which he began to weep. He was also afraid of Indulekha's wrath. All the same, he thought that it would be wrong not to see Indulekha. 'Whatever it is, let it be, I have not done anything knowingly. I wouldn't have done anything to harm Indulekha and Madhavan on purpose. For that, all-powerful God is witness.' This gave him courage. With his mind in a whirl, he went to Indulekha and stood before her.

However, Indulekha did not harbour any ill feelings towards Shastrikal. Indulekha had ferreted out all the details about what had happened. She even knew what Govindan had told Shastrikal at the inn.

She understood that Shastrikal's great affection for her must have blinded him to the truth and caused him to go off from there that very day itself. The reason for asking him over was to find out about his encounter with Madhavan just before he left.

The moment she saw Shastrikal, she pulled up a chair for him and asked him to be seated.

Shastrikal stood rooted to the spot and wept uncontrollably.

'Why do you ask to see this great sinner? Both of you are my life. God the creator! Unluckily, I was responsible for your calamity.'

INDULEKHA: Please sit down. I know all the details. This misfortune is the result of the strength of the love that Shastrikal has for me and Madhavan. You are not the only one who fell a victim to this misconception. Many have misunderstood the whole affair. I am not at all surprised by this. But I'm surprised and grieved that he too believed this so quickly.

As she said this, tears welled up in Indulekha's eyes.

SHASTRIKAL: (with words drowned in tears) A pity! A pity! If you, Indulekha, had heard the words I spoke—you yourself might have believed it for some time. I said it with such conviction. Also, Madhavan knows very well that I am a very good friend of yours. He heard me lamenting your deed. Is it surprising then that he believed everything! Everyone in that procession said that it was Indulekha in the palanquin. So please don't criticize Madhavan in any way.

When Indulekha heard this she felt greatly comforted to know that Madhavan had not done anything wrong. It did not matter to her much even if it was mistakenly thought that she had done something wrong.

INDULEKHA: When you spoke in this manner, what did Madhavan do?
SHASTRIKAL: By the time I spoke to him, many other people had told him about it. When he asked me whether what he had heard was right, and I nodded assent, Madhavan nearly fainted.

Unable to hear any more, Indulekha collapsed on the cot, crying.

SHASTRIKAL: Chi! Don't be sad, don't be sad. Everything will be all right. Every day in the evening I offer a puja to Bhagawati. The goddess will surely see that everything works out well.

Shastrikal stumbled out of Indulekha's rooms with tears in his eyes.

Indulekha spent the whole day looking out for a messenger from the station carrying letters. She ate and bathed to ascertain that no one ridiculed her. One day, around four o'clock, in the afternoon Indulekha fell asleep on the couch as a result of her general weariness and sleepless nights. Roughly around half past six she woke up with a start. 'Ayyoh! Ayyoh! did this Muslim stab and kill my husband? My husband is dead. I don't want to live anymore,' she cried out loudly. This cry was heard by people downstairs in Poovarangu. Immediately Panchumenon, Lakshmikuttyamma, and the others rushed up to her malika. They saw Indulekha lying on the couch, exhausted. Lakshmikuttyamma immediately supported her in her arms. Panchumenon drew her onto his lap. Her body was like a live coal. 'What is this, dear lord! Why is this girl burning with fever?' Panchumenon asked her, 'Dear child! Did you cry out loud?'

Indulekha tried to speak but couldn't. She asked for water. After she had sipped it, she noticed a number of people standing around her.

INDULEKHA: Everyone should leave. I want only my mother with me. I will tell my mother what happened and she will report to you, Grandfather. I cannot speak to you directly.

Perplexed, everyone except Lakshmikuttyamma went back downstairs.

INDULEKHA: Mother! I saw a nightmare. That is why I screamed. I dreamt that while Madhavan was travelling in a place near Bengal, a Muslim stabbed him in the chest and robbed him of all his wealth. Madhavan cried out 'God! How will my Indulekha live now?' This he said looking straight at me and died. I feel that Madhavan is in some danger.

When Lakshmikuttyamma heard this, she started weeping.

LAKSHMIKUTTYAMMA: My dear daughter, don't be sad. We see many irrelevant things in dreams. You should not take them all so seriously. Madhavan will come back hale and hearty. My daughter will join him and live a long and comfortable life.

INDULEKHA: My mother! I do not believe that dreams are harbingers of future events; however, sometimes it may happen that they are. Whatever it is, I was devastated.

LAKSHMIKUTTYAMMA: My daughter, you are running a very high temperature. You should cover yourself well and rest.

She made her lie down, pulled a sheet over her and sat beside her.

INDULEKHA: Mother, go and speak to Grandfather.

LAKSHMIKUTTYAMMA: Should I tell him now? Do you remember what you called Madhavan in your sleep?

INDULEKHA: No, what did I say?

LAKSHMIKUTTYAMMA: 'My husband.' Everyone heard you.

INDULEKHA: So what? Isn't he the person I wish to have as my husband? In this birth, no one else will be my husband. For me he abandoned everything and is now in great pain, all because of me. I do not know where he is and what he is suffering. If I regard such a person as my husband and if people get to know about it, I should be extremely happy. The moment I get to know of some disaster that has befallen him, I have no doubt it is going to be my death. See, this moment I have come down with an illness. If Madhavan comes back I will recover. Otherwise—

By the time so much was said, Lakshmikuttyamma burst out crying, 'My dear daughter, you shouldn't speak like this.' She fell on the cot, weeping bitterly.

INDULEKHA: Mother, do go and tell my grandfather. He awaits you downstairs. I am not afraid of anything. My mind is overcome with a certain madness. Grandfather may not be very pleased that I happened to call Madhavan my husband. So be it. But Kochukrishnanammaman brought me up very lovingly and he died before he could place me in a situation that would suit me. I did not want to live after his death. By the grace of God, in my teens, I met the person who could give my mind all the pleasures I felt I had lost. Mentally, I regard this desirable man as my husband. Now I am a little frightened whether it will work out for me at all. I am an unlucky person. That is why everything has turned out like this. However, I will not hide anything from my Kochukrishnanammaman's father. Mother, tell him everything and come back. I want you to lie down here beside me.

Lakshmikuttyamma rose sobbing and went down from the malika.

Here I have to tell my readers something special.

The dream that Indulekha dreamt in the evening at half past six and the robbery at the station by the 'sub-judge from Allahabad' occurred on the same day at the same time. Later Madhavan and Indulekha confirmed that it was so. But do not imagine that I believe that dreams are pointers to the past, present, or future. I do not know whether the human mind is capable or incapable of extrasensory perceptions. I do not yet believe anything that the theosophists say in this matter. However, all in all there is something I do believe: When you think of man's body and its natural functions, it can be said to be a machine with its several parts dependent on one another for it to work correctly and efficiently. But there are certain forces in the soul which we have not been able to understand clearly. Dreams are a whirl of the mind— a madness of the mind. Like the somnambulism and mesmerism that the English people refer to, it can be understood as an ordinary and natural emotion of the human mind during sleep. Sometimes, that emotion can be based on known causes. At other times it can occur for no reason at all. Sometimes we dream about situations which may never take place. One day a sayiv dreamt that a snake with its hood spread out was aiming to strike him. He started up, and opening his eyes saw a snake crawling away. Another sayiv dreamt that a very close friend of his whom he had not been able to meet for a long time came to his house and stayed with him comfortably for a couple of days. The dream actually came true. I have read about many such instances. Therefore, I am not unduly surprised by Indulekha's dream. Two or three years after this story of ours ended, Gopinath Banerjee wrote to Madhavan saying that two of the thieves belonging to the gang that had stolen Madhavan's things had been sentenced to death by hanging in connection with another robbery and murder. A good-looking young thief among them had admitted to committing many crimes, of having stabbed, shot, and poisoned about seventeen people. He had also confessed that he had stolen Madhavan's things; and had he not been able to rob Madhavan, this evil man would have killed him.

As Lakshmikuttyamma descended, Panchumenon and others were standing sorrowfully in the well of the staircase. He called her aside and asked her:

PANCHUMENON: Why did the child cry?
LAKSHMIKUTTYAMMA: (weeping) In her dream she saw that somebody had

stabbed Madhavan to death and in her intense grief, cried out. Now she is running a high temperature. Let me go upstairs quickly.

Panchumenon stood rooted to the spot in deep thought.

PANCHUMENON: This girl loves Madhavan so much! Shiva—Shiva! I did not know this the day I took an oath. Does the child know about it?
LAKSHMIKUTTYAMMA: Yes, she knows about it.
PANCHUMENON: She may be sad about that too.
LAKSHMIKUTTYAMMA: I think she is worried about that as well.
PANCHUMENON: If at least she is relieved of that sorrow, she will be comforted a bit. Call Kesavannambuthiri. Lakshmikutty, go upstairs quickly. Tell her that I am coming up immediately. Don't let the child grieve even for a moment.

Immediately Kesavannambuthiri came running.

PANCHUMENON: Indulekha saw a nightmare. Now she is running a very high temperature. I don't know what is happening. It is because of this child that I do not feel the loss of my Kochukrishnan.

Saying this the simple-minded old man burst out crying.

KESAVANNAMBUTHIRI: Chi! Chi! You shouldn't cry.

And that simple soul also wept.

PANCHUMENON: This illness and other problems are all because Indulekha is so fond of Madhavan. My oath that I won't give her to Madhavan must also contribute to her grief. Can't I do some penance for that oath? Will it cause any harm?
KESAVANNAMBUTHIRI: It is enough if you do penance. I will go and ask the family priest.

Annathiravaddhyar informed him that a penance would counter any adverse effects of retracting his oath.

PANCHUMENON: What is the penance?
ANNATHIRAVADDHYAR: Make gold or silver images of the letters that were used in the sentence of the oath and give them as an offering to Brahmin ascetics. On that day, do a small *vazhipadu* in the temple. It

would be ideal if the images of the letters are made in gold but they can also be made in silver.

PANCHUMENON: Let them be made in gold itself.

KESAVANNAMBUTHIRI: They should be made in gold then.

That very moment Panchumenon opened a chest and measured out the gold, weighing it before giving it to the goldsmith, counting the number of letters used for the oath—e–nte–shri–po–rka–li–bha–ga–wa–thi–ya–ne–nja–n–i–ndu–le–kha–ye–ma–dha–va–nu–ko–du–kku–ka–yi–lla—twenty-nine letters. When Shankaramenon doubted whether letters such as 'n' and 'nte' should be counted as letters, Annathiravaddhyar decided that they should be counted. Each letter was to be made in two gold *fanam*. After this had been ordered, Panchumenon went up to Indulekha's malika and sat near her to give her all the details.

PANCHUMENON: My dear child, I don't want you to grieve over anything. The moment Madhavan reaches here, I will hold your wedding ceremony.

INDULEKHA: Let your clear thinking guide all of us.

Indulekha ran a very high temperature that day and the next day. The third day the fever dropped a little. Then it was a cough, dizzy spells, and a persistent ache all over. Medications ceased to help her. A few days passed in this manner. By then the letters of the oath were prepared. Deciding that he should show these letters to Indulekha, Panchumenon put them in a measure and took them up to her malika. Indulekha who had been lying in bed, sad and tired, laughed out loud.

PANCHUMENON: I think my daughter is happy; now you will get better.

INDULEKHA: Yes, Grandfather, I am happy. Let things turn out well according to my grandfather's wish.

When they were chatting thus, Lakshmikuttyamma, Kesavannambuthiri, Shankaramenon, and others trooped in with the person who had been posted at the railway station for news.

The moment Indulekha saw him she sat up in bed but felt so giddy, she could not hold herself upright without support.

INDULEKHA: What, is there a telegram?

LAKSHMIKUTTYAMMA: There is a telegram, the stationmaster has said that it is happy news.

The telegraphic message was given to Indulekha. She read its contents aloud in Malayalam.

Bombay (9)

'Met Madhavan here today. He is absolutely fine. All of us are taking tomorrow's train home.'

When this was read there was not a person who was not happy. What should I say about Indulekha's happiness? Her giddiness, cough, body-ache— I do not know where they disappeared.

PANCHUMENON: (to Kesavannambuthiri) Look highness, the danger has passed and happiness restored to us the moment the images for the penance were made.
KESAVANNAMBUTHIRI: There is no doubt about that. This is God's grace and the blessings of the Brahmins.

Indulekha laughed. She didn't see any connection, much though she had thought about it, between the penance and the telegraphic message. But all those assembled there, except Lakshmikuttyamma, thought that Panchumenon was right. Everyone was very happy. That very day Panchumenon gave away the images. Annathiravaddhyar got around seven or eight letters. Our Shankarashastrikal got four or five. Some time later, after the feast for the Brahmins, Panchumenon noticed that Indulekha was looking much better. She had had a lot of *kanji* [rice porridge]. The cough and giddiness had almost disappeared. The ache in her limbs had subsided as had her exhaustion. The old man was happy. He believed that it was the fruit of his penance. He sat there talking to Indulekha.

chapter twenty

The End of the Story

Govindapanikkar, Madhavan, and Govindankuttymenon left Bombay and reached Madras. Madhavan went to meet Gilham sayiv and told him everything that had happened. Gilham sayiv laughed a great deal. Madhavan came away in great happiness after the sayiv said affectionately that he had been taken into the civil service. All of them set off for Malabar and reached home the next day. There is no need to talk about the happiness that Indulekha felt when she learnt of Madhavan's arrival.

Madhavan got all the news from his mother. He heard about the penance. While he was standing at the bottom of the stairs to Indulekha's malika, he saw Lakshmikuttyamma coming down the stairs.

Seeing Madhavan, she smiled and went back. After letting Indulekha know, she called him up. Madhavan went up the stairs and stood outside while Lakshmikuttyamma came down laughing.

INDULEKHA: (from within) You can come in. I cannot get up.

Madhavan walked in slowly. When he saw how exhausted Indulekha looked he could not control his tears. He sat on Indulekha's bed. Their tears spoke for them.

In this manner they spent the whole day. In the evening, when Panchumenon came upstairs and inquired about Indulekha's illness, he was very happy to know that she was much better. The seventh day after Madhavan reached home, a *swayamvaram* was held for Indulekha. It really was a swayamvaram—I do not hesitate to use that word. On the day of the swayamvaram, Panchumenon held an elaborate feast and did many other things for Brahmins. That very day he got a parcel Govinda Sen had sent from Bengal containing a great many expensive gifts more beautiful than the things received earlier. Indulekha and the others were very pleased. Barely a month after their wedding, Madhavan got an order saying that he had been taken into the civil service. They went to Madras with Madhavan's father and mother, and settled there comfortably. And thus ends our story on a happy note.

Afterword

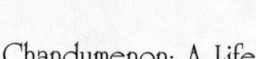

Chandumenon: A Life

Chandumenon was born on 22 Dhanu 1022, the corresponding date in the Christian era being 9 January 1847. He was born in a village near Thallassery in Malabar. He was the youngest of five children of Chittezhath Parvathyamma and Etapati Chandunair (1805–57). Had Chandumenon been brought up strictly in keeping with Nair practices of matriliny he would have been known as Chittezhath Chandumenon. However, when his father, who was in the judicial service and in the British government service, was transferred to Thallassery as the tahasildar there, Chandumenon's mother and the children moved with him. It is interesting that Chandumenon therefore grew up in something like a male-headed nuclear family. He takes as his family name, Oyyarath, the name of the house in Thallassery that they lived in and not his mother's or his father's family name.

Though schools were not common in his birthplace, Chandunair had been educated in Malayalam and had also gained some knowledge of the English language. His education led him to a job with the British government. He, therefore, insisted that his children be educated both in their mother tongue and in English. Chandumenon learned to read and write the Malayalam alphabets under the supervision of Korankurikkal, a well-known traditional teacher of the language. Whether it was the teacher who went to the student's home or vice versa depended entirely on the student's position in society. It is a measure of Chandunair's social standing that Chandumenon learned to read and write at his own home, moving to a formal school when he was much older. There, under Kunjambunambiar, the well-known Sanskrit scholar, he began studies in Sanskrit poetry, drama, and grammar. Since Chandunair desired that his son enter government service as well, he sent him to Thallassery Basel Mission Parsi High School for further education. In addition, he was tutored at home by K. Kunjanmenon, a translator in the Thallassery district court. However, his father passed away in 1857 when Chandumenon was nine years old. After this he was brought up under the care of his mother and his elder brother Shankaramenon for some time. His brother died six months later, and shortly after, his mother. Thereafter he was left in the care of his eldest sister Lakshmiamma who paid great attention to his education.

In 1863, at sixteen, while still at school, he cleared the uncovenanted service examination and continued with his education. At seventeen, while preparing for the matriculation examination, he received an appointment as the sixth clerk in the Thallassery Small Causes Court. There he caught the attention of Judge G.R. Sharp. The turning point in his life, however, came with an assignment as assistant to William Logan, the author of the famous *Malabar Manual*, also sub-collector at Thallassery. Logan, who learnt about Chandumenon's abilities had him transferred to the collectorate at Calicut. By all accounts, Chandumenon was of great help to Logan in the preparation of the *Malabar Manual*. Also, with Logan's encouragement Chandumenon became a dedicated reader especially of English novels, acquiring new arrivals as soon as they were published. He moved quickly up the ladder of government service, and by 1871 had become head munshi in the Calicut secretariat. In 1872, Chandumenon was promoted as head clerk in the Calicut Civil Court.

In his personal life also he was extremely lucky. In 1872, while he was working in the Calicut Civil Court, Chandumenon married Kanjoli Lakshmikuttyamma, the daughter of Kanjoli Lakshmiamma and Irinjalakuda Varambath Krishnanmenon. Going by Chandumenon's own account, in the Preface to the first edition, it is this beautiful and accomplished lady who inspired, nay troubled, him to write novels in Malayalam by insisting that he translate for her whatever he read. Chandumenon and Lakshmikuttyamma had five sons and two daughters.

On 11 June 1889, while at Parappanangadi, Chandumenon began to work on *Indulekha*. He completed the novel on 17 August in just over two months' time. The author claims that it would have been completed one month earlier in the first week of July had he not had to wait for the necessary books to write the controversial Chapter 18 of the novel. In 1891, he was nominated member of the Malabar Marriage Commission. The commission recommended major reforms. Chandumenon, however, wrote a long and justly famous dissenting note which had the support of a majority of the Nairs on the commission. He objected to changes that were being proposed in the time-honoured practices for two reasons: First, because the changes would upset the economy of the taravad system altogether, and second because the new legislation appeared to envisage the abolition of caste restrictions in marriage.

In 1892, while posted in Tinnevelly, he began his second novel *Sarada*, which he never completed because he suffered from a paralytic stroke in 1893 and had to go on leave. On his return to duty in 1896, he was posted to Calicut. In 1897, the British government honoured him by investing him with the title of Raobahadur. In 1898, the Madras University recognizing his merits, appointed him as examiner for the BL examination and honoured him further by nominating him a Fellow of the University. Chandumenon died on 7 September 1899.

A Note on the Communities

The communities to which most of the characters of *Indulekha* belong are the Nambuthiris and the Nairs. They belong to the two main castes in the former regions of Malabar, Cochin, and Travancore, which make up present-day Kerala. The Nambuthiris are Brahmins: they were primarily priests and landholders. A Nambuthiripad is of a higher rank than a Nambuthiri. The custom was that only the eldest male member of a Nambuthiri family could form a relationship with a woman from the same community. This marriage was called *veli* and was binding for life. Other Nambuthiris in the family formed contractual relationships with Nair women; these were termed sambandams. Polygamy was accepted. Nambuthiri inheritance was patrilineal.

The Nairs are a Sudra upper caste. They were a martial community and were landowners. The Nair taravad or joint family is governed by the Marumakkathayam law of inheritance. Marumakkathayam literally means descent through one's sister's children. A taravad consists of the descendants in the female line of a common ancestress. Members of the taravad collectively owned taravad property and lived together in one house. This house would be a *nalukettu* or *ettukettu*, a single quadrangular or double quadrangular structure with a courtyard in the centre and rooms opening out onto a veranda. There would be rooms upstairs expressly for the use of the womenfolk.

Taravad property was indivisible. Each branch of the taravad, meaning each sister in the taravad, would be of a different *tavazhi* or branch of the same joint family. The *Karanavan* who was normally the eldest male member, looked after the matters of the estate and family. The *anantharavans* were the younger male members of the family. Under the Marumakkathayam system, all the members of the taravad were entitled to their daily requirements of food, clothes, and toiletry, mainly oil, from a common pool of resources. Thus, the taravad defined and took care of its members' personal needs. Without the unanimous consent of the taravad women, family property could not be legally alienated.

One of the ritual practices which was prevalent during the nineteenth century and associated with a girl's life in the Nair taravad was the *talikettukalyanam*. This ceremony gave the right to the girl to take a sexual partner or enter into a contract or sambandam on maturity without much ceremony. The sambandam could be with a Nair man or a Nambuthiri. He could also be the Nair woman's 'bridegroom' from the talikettukalyanam. He gives her a *pudava* or cloth to mark their relationship. He visits her in her taravad but does not eat there. He remains a member of his mother's taravad, or in the case of a Nambuthiri of his own household. The couple could break the sambandam if they so desired, and either or both could enter another sambandam. A man had no rights over or duties towards his children. They bonded with the mother's family and often had little or no contact with their biological fathers. This system seems to have emerged as early as the twelfth century in Keralam.

The Marumakkathayam law of inheritance and the Nairs' 'matrimonial' relationships with the Nambuthiris ensured the indivisibility of the property of the Nairs as well as the Nambuthiris. This assured their place in the upper rungs of the communities in Keralam. However, the introduction of colonial rule into Malabar during the nineteenth century brought about changes into an agrarian economy which was prevalent earlier. Neither the Nairs nor the Nambuthiris actually cultivated land but they enjoyed a large share of the profits from the property. Educated Nair men during this time gained employment with the expanding British colonial bureaucracy and started accumulating property outside the taravad. They resented the appropriation of their privately earned income into the taravad property. With their interactions at their places of work, members of the Nair community were also exposed to Victorian notions of morality and with practices of Hinduism in the rest of India. The Marumakkathayam law of inheritance of the Nairs and sambandams made sexual proprieties and behaviour different from the Victorian norms of propriety. This produced great discomfort among the Nair men who began to question their marriage customs. These changes, both at the material and ideological levels, led to the reform of Nair matriliny.[1]

Legislation: A Rule of Propriety for Nairs

Right through the nineteenth century, Nair marriage, family life, and inheritance practices were subjected to criticism and ridicule. Colonial ethnographers were fascinated with this society for two reasons: their practice of matrilineal descent and inheritance, and the marriage contracts—sambandams—that were entered into at will and which could be dissolved in the same way by either party. The sambandams also attracted interest because a number of alliances were between Nair women, formally designated as Sudras, and men from the culturally and politically dominant caste of Nambuthiri Brahmins.

The 'inter-caste' or exogamous arrangements obviously created close bonds between the Nairs and the Nambuthiris. In terms of landholding, it worked in the interest of the consolidation of property units in both caste groups. However, socially the arrangement whereby a Nambuthiri man could 'claim' any Nair woman was a clear expression of Nambuthiri dominance. Only the eldest son in a Nambuthiri household married into the community. Other sons entered into sambandams with Nair women. Lalithambika Antherjanam movingly documents in her short stories and novels the problems that arose for Nambuthiri women—many of whom remained unmarried or were widowed young—as a result of these practices.[2]

Inheritance practices in the Nair community came under pressure principally from three groups: colonial authorities (and along with them a few very westernized Nairs), younger sons within the taravad—the anantharavans, and Nair men who were resentful of Nambuthiri rights over Nair women. Colonial authorities were disturbed by the 'unnatural' matrilineal form of inheritance and the relatively free arrangements that governed sexual relationships. However, they were also concerned that the joint ownership and indivisibility of taravad property would hinder the development of a money economy and discourage qualities of initiative and self-interest and habits of thrift and saving that were necessary for capitalist accumulation and growth of market economies. William Logan, whose work was a major resource for the rebellions against the landholding, rent-extracting *janmis* (mostly Nambuthiri Brahmins), clearly articulates this point.[3] He wanted that individual Nairs, be they male or female, should have the right to decide who should inherit their self-acquired property. 'Individual industry and thrift' would only thrive, he wrote, if the 'natural instincts' of the Nairs could be freely expressed.[4] The Raja of Parapanad stated in the Travancore Assembly that in the final analysis, it was not 'a desire to make marriage more binding or to make divorce more difficult' that drove Nairs to demand a change. According to him, the real reason was to 'keep self-acquired property out of the hands of one's taravad and rightful heirs' and to 'use it to make ample provision for the wife and children'.[5]

Anantharavans, who were beginning to see new possibilities in administrative jobs and in trade, resented the fact that they were not allowed to retain their earnings or share in the family property. These younger sons and less powerful lineages in the taravad began demanding an education in English. The karanavans were reluctant to pay for what was an expensive education for a large number of children, but were being increasingly pressured to do so.[6] For instance, *Indulekha* opens rather dramatically with an argument between the English-educated Madhavan and Panchumenon, the karanavan of the taravad, over the question of Shinnan's education, a man who belongs to a less important tavazhi of the taravad. Equally important, however, was the growth of the economy and the changes in land ownership and tenure that brought the taravad economy into crisis. K.N. Panikkar writes, 'Strife and litigation between *karanavans* and junior members of the family became the order of the day. "A house divided against itself cannot stand" reported the Marriage Commission, "and most *taravads* in Malabar are in this condition."'[7]

The resentment against the Nambuthiri man's right to take a Nair woman as his 'wife' (and the inclination of Nair women to 'accept' such suitors) was somewhat more widespread and accounted for much of the popular appeal of the call for restricting Brahmin privileges, and making Nair marriages more stable. Janaki Nair suggests that the changes in the ideologies of the family and sexuality that came with English education and the 'moral onslaught of the missionaries' fuelled the anger of people like Chandumenon.[8] Ideologically, the Nair system of marriage and sexual relations was criticized primarily for its 'looseness' and for the fact that Nair women seemed 'unnaturally' free and independent. It was relatively easy to enter into or terminate a contract. Ordinarily, a man obtained a woman's consent, negotiated with the karanavan and presented her with a set of clothes. Marumakkathayam

Law, writes Janaki Nair, 'condemned large numbers of Nambuthiri females to celibacy and forced Nair women to make themselves available for Nambuthiri (and Nair) men. The only written source for the Marumakkathayam Law was the *Kerala Mahatmyam*, an eighteenth century Sanskrit text which exhorted Nair women thus: "Let chastity be far from you: not the least sin attaches to its non-observance."'[9] A judgment made in the Madras High Court in 1869 decreed that 'the relation (sambandam) is in truth not marriage, but a state of concubinage into which the woman enters of her own choice, and is at liberty to change when and as often as she pleases'.[10] In brief then, the Nair system of sexual relations was a scandal, for colonial as well as for a 'Hindu' nationalism that was in the making.

However, there were several voices of dissent. One of those was that of Chandumenon who was a member of the Malabar Marriage Commission. He records in his Memorandum that the sexual relations among the Nairs should not be criticized on the basis of a few stray cases of 'professional prostitutes among Nair women, who do not know what the marriage tie means....'[11] There were also others: Sir James Stephen, speaking in the Viceroy's Legislative Council in 1872, said: 'Among the Nairs, there is, legally speaking, no such thing as marriage at all. In spite of this custom, marriage is practically as common and as binding among the Nairs as in many other races. The connections which they form usually last for life and are marked by a great degree of mutual fidelity.'[12] It is interesting that William Logan who was a staunch opponent of the system on other grounds and in fact lobbied for the new laws, dissociated himself from these 'moral' critiques. He wrote: 'A Nair usually only marries one wife, lives apart with her in their own home, and rears her children as his own also.'[13] I have already cited Chandumenon's comment.

From about the 1860s onwards, the Marumakkathayam system was increasingly challenged in public, both from within and without. Newspapers picked up the debate and carried articles that called for a change in the law. The principal demand was that the taravad property should be divisible. There were several demands that Nair sambandams be recognized by law so that they would be more like the permanent sacramental marriages that the British were familiar with, and which were practices of upper-caste Hindu communities in north India. The first formal initiative was taken in 1869 and a memorandum to this effect was submitted to the government. The movement was considerably strengthened by Logan's interest in it. Janaki

Nair writes, 'Logan produced one of the most exhaustive accounts of land tenures and caste systems in Malabar.' It was Logan who first pleaded that all adults, male or female, be given the 'power to regulate by will the successors of self-acquired property'. It was Logan who pointed to how 'individual industry and thrift' would flower if free rein was given to the Nair's 'natural instincts'. This 'natural instinct' favoured bequeathing his property to his wife and children rather than persons 'with whom he has little sympathy'.[14]

In 1890, the Madras Legislative Council admitted a bill seeking to legalize Nair marriages. The bill was not passed since there was considerable opposition. The government appointed a Malabar Marriage Commission in 1891, with T. Muthuswami Aiyar as president and Chandumenon as one of its members. They were required to say whether legislation was necessary and if so, 'what form it should take'. The report of the commission is a rich document of the many-faceted changes that were taking place at the time and the complex responses that were emerging. It is a fascinating document because there was much disagreement among the members. In the end, however, they recommended legislation. In a note of dissent, Chandumenon argued that legislation would precipitate the break-up of the taravad and destroy the very basis of Nair society and culture. Nairs were capable, he felt, of moving into modernity without giving up their own culture.

Chandumenon's novel, *Indulekha*, was written in the very midst of these discussions and controversies. It predates by a year or so his work with the Malabar Marriage Commission and his celebrated note of dissent. There is no doubt, given the cast of characters and the progress of the plot, that the novel is also an elaboration of what he considers the drama of this critical moment in the history of Kerala and of India. (To claim this, I hasten to add, is not to reduce the scope of this extraordinary work.) A large number of issues raised in this debate come up for elaboration and discussion in *Indulekha*. In one way or another, through character, dialogue, situation, or direct authorial intervention, questions of Nambuthiri dominance, the structure of authority in the taravad, western education, the demands of anantharavans, women's education, the study of English, the use of taravad property, matrilocality, and Nair marriage practices all come under scrutiny. Summarizing brutally, one might say that Chandumenon's response is that the Nair taravad can retain its structure and also be reformed. In other words, its 'evils' are not structural, but circumstantial. The novel shows what might be the nature and the process of this reformation. The controversial Chapter

18 of the novel, considered by many to be superfluous, is an extended discussion of a modernity and secularism that is appropriate, not only for Nairs but for India as a whole.

The Language of the Novel

In the preface to the first edition of *Indulekha*, Chandumenon claims, 'I have written this book in the everyday Malayalam that I ordinarily speak at home. I do have a little knowledge of Sanskrit, but on the whole, the Sanskrit words that I have employed are in the form in which they are commonly used by us Malayalis when we speak.'[15] The critical questions of course are what exactly is the significance of using a form of the language spoken in everyday contexts and who exactly is being referred to when Chandumenon says 'we Malayalis'. Historians of Malayalam language and literature have invariably taken Chandumenon's claim at its face value, rarely pausing to consider the more profound socio-political and literary implications of his claim. Yet, to a contemporary reader, one of the most striking aspects of Chandumenon's achievements in *Indulekha* is the artifice of the novel's prose and the enormity of his achievement. He is able to recreate in the formal writing of the novel's prose the effect of the everyday spoken language. In addition, he claims this form of the language as standard everyday Malayalam. In fact, what Chandumenon does is select from, stylize, and then consolidate the spoken Malayalam of the Nairs of his region. Principally, as a result of the phenomenal success of his novel, this dialect becomes the norm for what is today the standard educated form of the language. Benedict Anderson also points out such consolidation through print forms, 'the embryo of the nationally imagined community', and a national language. Anderson argues that it is such attempts that give 'a new fixity to the language'.[16]

Shortly before Chandumenon wrote *Indulekha,* Herman Gundert, missionary and lexicographer of German origin, had compiled a Malayalam–English dictionary (1872).[17] The revolutionary nature of Gundert's achievement lay in the fact that—and I cite from his preface—'the materials for this work have been collected during more than twenty-five years' study of the language. The words have been taken from all available sources, from the lips of speakers of all ranks, castes and occupations, from the letters and records of many different districts, and from the writers in prose and poetry of every age'.[18]

What is interesting is that while the dictionary opened up the possibility of a broad-based and more egalitarian form of the language becoming standardized, Chandumenon, through the much more persuasive form of novelistic narrative and dialogue deflected that earlier initiative. Instead, he effectively set up as standard the usage of a middle caste like the Nairs as standard. To this day there exists a certain productive tension between the more inclusive form of the language symbolized by Gundert's initiative and Chandumenon's more elite usage.

Though commentators such as Robin Jeffrey consider the end of the nineteenth century as a period of decline of Nair power, perhaps as a consequence of the considerable initiatives of Chandumenon, the Malayalam of the Nairs of this central Malabar region is, even today, the standard literary form of the language. This effort of recreation, within the artwork, of a language that had hitherto never been endowed with the dignity of art is an achievement of no mean order. Perhaps the fact that his wife Lakshmikuttyamma was his first audience made the task of writing 'as the language is spoken' easier and more 'realistic'.

ANITHA DEVASIA

Notes

1. For more details *see* Janaki Nair, *Women and Law in Colonial India: A Social History*, New Delhi: Kali for Women, 1996, 150–60; and K.N. Panikkar, *Culture, Ideology, Hegemony: Intellectuals and Social Consciousness in Colonial India*, New Delhi: Tulika, 1995, 176–99.
2. Lalithambika Antherjanam, tr. by Gita Krishnankutty, 'Life and Death', and 'Within the Folds of Seclusion', in *Cast Me Out If You Will: Stories and Memoir*, Calcutta: Stree, 1998.
3. These rebellions, loosely grouped under the heading Mapilla Rebellions took place, mainly in Malabar, right through the nineteenth century, culminating in the famous Mapilla Rebellion of 1921. For more details *see* Sumit Sarkar, *Modern India 1885–1947*, Delhi: Macmillan, 1983, 49–50, 216–17; *also* K.N. Panikkar, *Against Lord and State: Religion and Peasant Uprisings in Malabar 1836–1921*, Delhi: Oxford University Press, 1989.
4. Logan quoted in Janaki Nair, *Women and Law*, 154.
5. Robin Jeffrey, *The Decline of Nayar Dominance: Society and Politics in Travancore, 1847–1908*, Delhi: Vikas, 1976, 188.
6. K.N. Panikkar, *Culture, Ideology*, 191. The *Kerala Patrika*, Dec. 1885, published a letter commending an anantharavan for going to court against a karanavan, demanding expenses for English education.

7. Ibid.,192; *Report of the Malabar Marriage Commission*, 31.
8. Janaki Nair, *Women and Law*, 153; Panikkar, *Culture, Ideology*, 183.
9. Janaki Nair, *Women and Law*, 152.
10. Quoted in Panikkar, *Culture, Ideology*, 194.
11. Chandumenon's Memorandum in *Report of the Malabar Marriage Commission* 1891, 10.
12. Panikkar, *Culture, Ideology*, From NAI Legislative Department, Dec. 1890, nos 138–42, 194.
13. From William Logan, Report of the Malabar Special Commission, Madras, 1881, para. 483, quoted in Panikkar, *Culture, Ideology*, 194.
14. Janaki Nair, *Women and Law*, 154.
15. O. Chandumenon, Preface, *Indulekha* (1889), Kottayam: D.C. Books, 1993, 11.
16. Benedict Anderson, *Imagined Communities: Reflections on the Origin and Spread of Nationalism*, London: Verso, 1986, 47.
17. Scholars attribute the first Malayalam–English dictionary to Gundert. However, it is Benjamin Bailey from Kottayam who compiled the first printed dictionary—*A Dictionary of High and Colloquial Malayalam and English* in 1846.
18. Gundert, Preface, *Malayalam English Dictionary*, Kottayam: D.C. Books, 1992, n. paginated.

appendix I

Preface to the First Edition of Indulekha

Around the end of 1886, after I had left Kozhikode, I began reading a large number of English novels. Any time I had while not engaged in work related to my government job, I spent seated comfortably at home and reading novels. I noticed that this led to a growing dissatisfaction among my close friends, who would earlier have spent this time enjoyably in conversation with me. I did not as a consequence cut down on my reading in any way, but I did apply my mind as to how I might address that complaint. I tried reading a novel and then translating the gist of the story into Malayalam. I translated two or three novels in this manner, but I did not get the impression that my listeners particularly enjoyed it. Then at last, a translation of the late Lord Beaconsfield's *Henrietta Temple* appealed to one of them. From that point on, that person developed a consuming interest in hearing these novels being read, so much so that it soon became a passion. The pressure to translate became so strong that it was impossible for me to read a book on my own, because there would be insistence that I also read it out. Sometimes, even when I was reading a law book there would be an exclamation, 'That's a novel, translate it for me.' Things came to such a pass that I began to feel that I had made a bad mistake when I paid heed to her complaint in the first place. Finally, there was a request that I write out a translation of Lord Beaconsfield's novel. Initially I agreed to do this. However, when I tried translating some part of it, I realized that a translation of that kind would serve no purpose.

I do not think that it is particularly difficult to read a novel and then translate it orally in such a way that close friends of mine who do not know English can understand it reasonably well. On the other hand, I believe it is practically impossible to do a written translation in such a way that they will really grasp the import of the story. When one reads a written translation, one only understands what has actually been written. That is not enough. The actual force of an English work can be put across quite well in an extempore rendering because it is possible, even as each incident is being recounted, to supplement the translation with detail, example, and commentary, and to draw out the meaning implicit in the words with gesture and tone of voice. If you incorporate such description and commentary into a faithful written translation, there is no doubt that the work will get completely out of hand. Furthermore, if one were to simply translate the episodes where the *rasa* of *sringara* is dominant in an English novel into Malayalam, they would not be particularly enticing. Considering all this, I decided to write something like an English novel in Malayalam and promised the person who had been pestering me that I would do so. This contract was undertaken last January. With some excuse or the other, I managed to put off the matter until the month of June. Then the pressure on me grew unbearable and I began work on this book on 11 June; and finished on 17 August. This is the story behind the birth of this book.

I have no idea what my countrymen will think of a book like this. It is unlikely that those who do not know English will have ever read such a book. I doubt that those who are reading such stories for the first time will have the taste to appreciate them.

While I was writing this book, some of my friends who did not know English had asked me what I was writing about. When I explained to one or two of them what exactly I was writing, I did not get the impression that they were pleased. I know of one who said: 'What is the point? Why have you taken so much trouble over this? Of what use is it to write about something that never actually took place?' I have only one thing to say in response. Most of the books in the world are story books. Some of these stories are what is called history and these are based on actual events. As for all the others, these are stories that are simply believed to have taken place or ones that we suspect may or may not have happened.

In general, however, quite apart from whether the accounts are of events that actually took place or not, what people enjoy in a story is the skill with which it is told. Were that not so, we would not have had such a large number of books that are composed of stories. Informed people do not scrutinize a book to find out whether it is factual or not. It is the artistry of the

Appendix I 239

composition and the elegance of narration that they find elevating. When an intelligent and cultivated person reads a well-crafted story, he is all the time fully aware that the incidents related there have not taken place. All the same there is no doubt that he will experience the same force that he would have experienced, had he known the story to be true. Many serious-minded intellectuals are fully conscious that what they are reading has never taken place, yet they appreciate the distinctive skill with which an author unfolds a plot. Composed and well-bred people may find tears rising spontaneously to their eyes when they read passages that are full of pathos. Others catch themselves laughing out loud at a funny instance. Such things are everyday events among those who are knowledgeable. I feel that skilfully composed stories of this sort can also be used to entertain and educate the minds of ordinary people. That is why I believe that even if stories are not factual, it is wrong to say that they serve no purpose. The only real consideration is whether the story has been aesthetically told or not.

The other day, while I was checking the proofs of this book, another friend asked me what the book was about. In reply I just said that I would send him a copy after the book has been published and then he could find out for himself. I reproduce here his response: 'If you are writing about that body of knowledge called science in English, then it is worthwhile. There is no need for books of any other kind in Malayalam at the moment.' I was astonished at these words.

I have also been asked by some others whether people would enjoy a story that dealt only with the everyday life of our time and did not have anything that would excite wonder or amazement. This is my response to them: Before people here saw and began appreciating oil paintings of the kind that were done in Europe, they used to take pleasure in images of Narasimhamurthy that were impossible in reality, pictures of the lord of hunting and of monster-heads, representations of Srikrishnan standing with his legs twisted in a way that no ordinary biped can manage and playing the flute, images of the thousand-hooded cobra Ananthan and of huge demons—pictures that did not follow the rules of light and shadow, perspective or proportion and in crude colours. And they rewarded these artists with all kinds of gifts. Today many of those people have tired of such depictions and admire oil or water-colour paintings that depict people or animals or other things in their everyday form. The closer the artistic reproduction is to the natural model, the greater the honour and admiration for the artist. In the same way, a new taste will emerge with well-written stories about ordinary things and everyday events and replace the taste for the old stories of fantastic happenings.

However, I do not have even a grain of a feeling that the book I have written has achieved this beauty of style. If I have created such an impression in my readers, I regret it immensely. All I said was that if those who are capable of writing such stories well take the trouble to do so thoughtfully and with care, people will acquire the taste for them.

I have written this book in the everyday Malayalam that I speak at home. I do have a little knowledge of Sanskrit, but on the whole, the Sanskrit words that I have employed are in the form in which they are commonly used by us Malayalis when we speak. For example, though 'vyulpathi' [scholarship] is the correct form of the word in Sanskrit, it is ordinarily used by us as 'vilpathy'. I have written them in that popular form in this book. There are many other such examples: 'padu' [raw], 'druthagathy' [hasty], 'druthagathykaran' [rash person], 'yogyamaya sabha' [worthy council]. When such words and phrases are used along with other Malayalam words, neither the pronunciation nor the meaning remains what it was in Sanskrit. I want to alert my readers to the fact that I have used these words in this book in the way they are pronounced today in Malayalam. Let me also declare at this point that subject, verb, object, transitive and intransitive, are largely used in this book as they are in the spoken mode. I have not set aside the way Malayalis ordinarily speak Malayalam in favour of some pure Sanskrit form of the sentence.

While this book was under print I have been helped immensely by the superintendent of Spectator Printers, Mr Kochukunjan. The errors caused as a result of the intricacies of my writing were pointed out then and there by this capable youngster. I acknowledge this here with gratitude.

O. CHANDUMENON

Parappanangadi
9 December 1889

appendix II

Preface to the Second Edition of Indulekha

When I finished writing the Preface to the first edition of this book on 9 December 1889, I did not expect to write a second preface to this same book. Even if I had to write one, I did not even in my wildest dreams think that I would have to write one so soon. The first edition of this book which was put on sale in the beginning of January 1890 was sold out before 30 March. There was still a great demand for this book and this led to a second edition and therefore also to the writing of this preface.

Malayalis, who had not read in Malayalam any book in the manner of English novels, immediately read and enjoyed this book and praised it. Getting to know this has made me realize that I have been rewarded more than I expected for my hard work and I gratefully declare it here.

Many newspapers like *Madras Mail, Hindu, Standard, Keralapatrika* and *Keralasanchari* have praised my book. I have looked at many of the affectionate letters written by many great people praising my book. These people have shown that if Malayalam is written beautifully they can appreciate it wholeheartedly. I am touched especially by the people at *Deshabhimani* who do not know me at all but who appreciated my book. They also took pains to defend my book when certain people without any reason tried to malign it. At this point I must acknowledge with intense happiness but somewhat shyly that I had made a declaration in the preface to the first edition pointing to and doubting whether it would become difficult for my countrymen to happily appreciate my efforts.

I have also taken care to attend to the criticism made by some people about my book. I have accepted gratefully after giving as much of thought as is possible for me to the pros and cons of the suggestions made by them; subsequently I have made some improvements in the second edition.

However, it is commonplace for both qualified and unqualified people to talk about the merits and demerits of a book. The persons who hear about the merits and demerits pointed out by people do not think deeply about whether such people have actually got the ability to grasp the positive and negative aspects of a book. There is no doubt that this is a sad state of affairs for the authors. There have been such incongruous attacks on my book too.

Some people have criticized the second chapter where the hero and the heroine of the story express their love for each other. Their contention is that the love-struck Madhavan, his actions and words as a result of this do not have the majesty that is required of him; hearing him speak gives the impression that he is an immature fool.

Then another person has stated that since there are no proper links in what is said in the sentences, the book is difficult to understand. He has given an example—*Indulekha*, first (ed.), Chapter II, p. 9.

When I began writing this chapter, the fear that crept over me led to the sad conclusion that I might lack the ability to describe beautiful heroines.

This sentence has been cited as an example.

Then some critics have made this attack: Indulekha's lover Madhavan in his exhausted state because of the intensity of his love for her, utters some words that are inappropriate. In this lovers' quarrel, Indulekha calls Madhavan an 'idiot'. This they feel was discourteous.

Other than this, when Lakshimikuttyamma used the verb 'bandhavikkuka' [form a relationship] referring to the coming of the Nambuthiripad in a very insulting manner to Indulekha (*Indulekha*, first ed., p. 175) and when Cherusseri speaks to the Nambuthiri in an intensely contemptuous tone when the latter made a crude reference to Lakshmikuttyamma (*Indulekha*, first ed., p. 239) many people attacked me saying that my usage is indecorous. At that time I remembered a verse by the great English poet Alexander Pope. This I include below:

> In Poets true genius is but rare
> True taste seldom is the Critic's share,
> Both must alike from Heaven derive their light
> These born to judge as well as those to write.

The translation of this:

> It is very rare to see a true taste for poetry in poets. In the same manner, the critical ability can be seen seldom in critics.
>
> The ability to write for poets and the critical ability for the critics is a God-given gift which they should have at birth.

Before I bring this preface to a close, I have one more thing to declare: In the first preface to this book, I had written 'I began writing this book on the 11th of June and finished it on 17 August.' Many people commented that this could not possibly be true. Earlier I did not think that I would have to write a reply to this. However, I am going to talk a little about this because one of my friends, a barrister, Mr Alfred G. Gover sayiv had written happily about my book, and expressed surprise that this book had been finished so quickly. I had started thinking about the story far before the month of June. I had jotted down notes also by that time. On 11 June I really started writing it as a book. After some time the printing also started. If there had been no delay for some books to arrive in order for me to write Chapter 18, this book would have been completed long before 10 July. If you check the details of the dates entered in the office of the *Spectator*—the dates when I started writing it, and the dates when printing was started of each chapter and the details when it was sent to the office, there will not be cause for any doubt.

My readers might by now have come to know that an English translation of this second edition of the novel is being done by the acting collector, His Eminence W. Dumergue sayiv. More than half of the translation has been done. I have read the translation that is complete and come to understand that even the connotations of the sentences have been carefully understood and it is effortlessly conveyed in English. It is a special luck of the book and a cause for intense happiness and satisfaction for me that such a powerful person as this sayiv decided to translate the novel. I do not hesitate to declare this gratefully here.

My readers would have got to know that I have given permission and the authority to print the second edition of the novel to the Kozhikode Educational and General Book Depot. Therefore, the owners of the depot have printed this book at their expense. I handed over the printing because of the affection and warmth of feeling between the depot owners and me, and also because

I expected and believed that they would do a good job of it not thinking merely of the monetary benefits of the arrangement. My expectations have been fully realized when I see that the book has been so promptly and neatly printed and is ready for publishing. I have complete belief that eminent Malayalis will be extremely happy and that they will appreciate the efforts of this depot owner who is from elsewhere and who has done such laudable work for the promotion of the Malayalam language.

O. CHANDUMENON

Parappanangadi
31 May 1890

appendix III

Dumergue's Preface

If it is not true that no book should be written without justification, it is certainly true that no book was ever written with greater justification than the Malayalam novel of *Indulekha*. Valuable as the literature of the Dravidian languages may be considered for the purposes of archaeology or philology, nevertheless all those who have studied it with any other object in view must remember the sense of weariness and disappointment with which they rose from the task.

The popular literature, with all its unnatural and supernatural paraphernalia, belongs to an age when the human mind was still in a go-cart, its language is as obsolete as the language of Piers the Plowman, and as it is without exception founded on the venerable Sanskrit, there is a total absence of originality. But Mr Chandumenon has quit the well-worn track, paved with plagiarism; modern Malabar is depicted in his pages and the language of *Indulekha* is the living Malayalam of the present day. It is no part of my province or intention to discuss the merits of the work itself, but I may perhaps be permitted to observe that if this descent into a valley of bones which are very dry, is followed by their revival, the author deserves well of all who, from birth, inclination, or necessity are interested in a regeneration of oriental literature.

So far as Europeans are concerned, the value of a book like *Indulekha* can hardly be overestimated. Few amongst us have opportunities of learning the coloquial and idiomatic language of the country, which, so far as I am competent to express an opinion, is far more important for the ends of administration than all the monuments of archaic ingenuity which we read and mark and leave undigested under the present *Rules for the encouragement of the study of Oriental Languages*. In this respect, therefore, a novel supplies a distinct want, and I would respectfully commend this point to the consideration of the powers who regulate such matters.

Of all the recognized vernaculars in south India, Malayalam, being confined to one district in the Madras Presidency, and the native states of Cochin and Travancore, is least known to the world in general, and the influence of the new departure made by Mr Chandumenon would, therefore, in itself be limited to a narrow sphere. Hence, apart from the interest with which *Indulekha* inspired me, and the linguistic profit I derived from its perusal, I thought it desirable, with Mr Chandumenon's permission, to assist him in his declared object by translating the work into the lingua franca of the East. At the end of the volume will be found a few notes in which I have endeavoured to explain certain passages relating to the social and family system peculiar to Malabar. With regard to the translation itself, no one can be more painfully aware than I am myself of its many shortcomings, and I would beg those who honour me by reading it to remember, in criticizing the book itself, that the original must have suffered from the faults of the translation. In accepting, however, my due share of responsibility, I must express regret that, owing to a mistake by which an imperfectly corrected proof was used as the 'final revise', there have occurred, in the first half of the work, errors and misprints which would have disappeared on actual revision.

That the translation as a whole represents the meaning of the original, is guaranteed by the fact that the author himself did me the favour of perusing the manuscript copy and suggesting such alterations as were necessary; but at the same time I would ask those who sit in judgement on me to bear in mind that the translation is not intended as a 'crib', for the use of schools. Although I have generally adhered as closely as possible to the original, I have not hesitated to depart from the literal idiom on occasions when it would be unintelligible or discordant in English. For instance I may mention that, as pointed out to me by an eminent orientalist, the moon in Sanskrit is masculine, and therefore it was inaccurate to call that luminary 'the witching queen'. But I think that, very properly, a veil would have to be drawn over the fate of the Frenchman who rendered 'der mond' as 'le lune', and I confess that I have neither the courage nor the wish to tamper with the gender of the 'orbed maiden with white fire laden'.

Of Sanskrit I am ignorant, and obtained the meaning of some of the stanzas which occur in the original from the author and of others from a Telugu Pandit through transliteration, but for the verses in which that meaning has now been reproduced I am indebted to my wife.

Camp, Wynaad,
10 December 1890

W. DUMERGUE

appendix IV

Chandumenon's Memorandum to the Malabar Marriage Commission

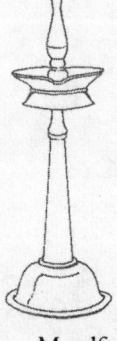

I wish to make a few observations separately about the proposed legislation in respect of marriages of the Marumakkathayam Malayali.

Myself a Malayali of this class and as such deeply interested in the question, I need hardly say that I have given my best consideration to the arguments advanced for or against the measure and that the opinion, I am about to express, is the result of a long, careful, and anxious consideration of the question in all its bearings and aspects. I have tried my best to ascertain the opinion of the people in general and have discussed the matter with many intelligent and enlightened men in Malabar. Here it is necessary for me to note that I do not attach much value to the evidence taken before the commission as a true reflection of the native public opinion in Malabar on the subject of the proposed changes in the marriage system. It appears to me that most of the witnesses that appeared before us, and many that answered interrogatories, had made up their mind beforehand, either to support or oppose the bill and did not care to represent public feelings on the subject.

As stated already I have spoken to many respectable Hindus of north and south Malabar on the subject and have no hesitation whatever in saying, from my personal knowledge, that the great body of the people or rather a very large majority, including, I may say, the whole of the aristocracy of Malabar, do not desire any change. I am fortified in this view by the unanimous opinion of the president and the other commissioners, who have passed a resolution to the effect that in their opinion, a large majority of the people did not desire any change. The large majority not only do not desire a change, but are, in my opinion, extremely averse to any change, or more correctly speaking, indignantly condemn the proposed measures. Here I must state my firm belief that the measure would not have met with such universal and so vehement an opposition from the public, had it not been for some of the provisions in the bill which, the people rightly think, have the effect of changing their nationality, their individuality as Marumakkathayam Hindus. There is hardly one Nair in one hundred, among the great body of the public of Malabar, who does not view with horror the provision in the bill as to the non-recognition or rather the abolition of caste for purposes of marriage and the provision that changes the fundamental principles of the law of succession of the Marumakkathayam Hindus. The provision regarding the registration of marriages and the removal of the hitherto observed rules of consanguinity and affinity are also equally disgusting to the public in general. In my humble opinion, nothing could have been more unfortunate for those few, who ask for marriage law, than to have published this obnoxious bill as the basis upon which legislation on the subject was to proceed.

Of course, I admit that there is a very small minority, a very infinitesimal fraction of the population, consisting of some of the English-educated men and a few others, who desire a change in our present system of marriage. They would have done better if they had consulted the public opinion thoroughly and carefully before bringing out such a bill. The violent changes in the the social and religious constitution of Nairs, introduced by the bill, naturally had the effect of making the orthodox Malayalis (and they are the large majority) hate the measure, as one designed for abolishing caste and Marumakkathayam system of succession, on the pretext of legalizing marriages. In this connection it becomes necessary to say a few words about the bill itself, in order to show the ideas of the people generally about the matters therein dealt with.

The bill opened with the following preamble:

Whereas it is expedient to provide a permanent form of marriage for *Hindus following the Marumakkathayam Law of succession* and to provide for the maintenance of the wives and children after the performance of such marriages; it is hereby enacted as follows.

Nothing could be more misleading than this preamble. A glance at the provision in the bill will show that, whatever may be the declared object of the bill, the matters dealt with therein are such as no one could have anticipated from a preamble worded as above.

The bill says that the law is intended for Hindus following Marumakkathayam Law of Succession. The people rightly ask, where we will find such Hindus 15 or 20 years after the bill becomes law. It is idle to say that the bill does not interfere with the taravads of Malabar. It destroys the taravad system altogether. The taravad property means the accumulations of wealth, acquired by the individual members of such taravad, and if the law holds, as the bill shows, that the individual acquisition should hereafter go to the wives and children of the person acquiring it and at the same time that the property, already accumulated, under taravad system, should be distributed and enjoyed according to the Marumakkathayam law, it is perfectly plain that the taravads cannot exist for any length of time. Therefore, in plain words, the bill aims at abolishing the taravad system altogether.

The public are struck with the provision which disposes of, in a summary manner, the caste system in Malabar. Whatever may be the prevailing opinion of a portion of the English-educated Malayali youths on the subject, there cannot be any doubt as to the fact, that all eminent English and native thinkers of the present generation, who are intimately acquainted with Indian Institutions and characters, have always thought that it would be highly impolitic, for the government, to interfere with the caste system in this country. On this point a distinguished law member of the Viceregal Council, an Englishman who had very carefully studied the question, in the course of his speech, on the Brahmo Marriage Bill, in 1872, said as follows:

> The institution, of caste in particular, whatever may be its evils, has provided safeguards against misconduct which it would be mischievous, in the highest degree, to sweep away like so much rubbish.

Under the bill, a young Nair, a junior member of a taravad, is at liberty to marry a Pariah woman and is of course entitled to live in his taravad with his Pariah wife. No social or religious rule can effectually interefere with his status on account of the marriage, for, he has the *express sanction of law* to marry the Pariah woman as a Marumakkathayam Nair. No Hindu can deny that such a rule violates the Hindu religious and social law in a most vital point. Still the bill is called 'a bill to provide a marriage law for Marumakkathayam Hindus'.

That the law of succession of the Marumakkathayam Hindus, as the law of all other Hindus, who follow Marumakkathayam or any other law of succession, is chiefly based upon religious rites, cannot be honestly denied by any one who knows the customs of Malayalis. The general principle of the Hindu law which guides succession is that '*he who is the spiritual benefactor of a deceased person shall succeed to the property of such person*'. That, according to the Malabar Law and customs, to a Marumakkathayam Nair, his *anandravers* are his *pindakartha* or the spiritual benefactors, no one can deny. That has been so ordained and it has been going on in accordance with such ordinance for thousands of years past. Even the most enthusiastic supporters of the bill, in their depositions before us, affirmed that a family of anandravers who omit to offer funeral cakes or observe pollution on the death of their Karanavan, forfeited their caste and status in society.* Such is the religious constitution of the relations between a Karanavan and Anandravan in Malabar, and it was in accordance with this relation that our law of succession was framed. If we ask the British government to alter the law of succession, could we also ask the government to alter our religious law, enacted according to the notions of Hindu sages and lawgivers for the spiritual benefit of the Marumakkathayam Hindus? Could we ask the government to legislate that the son shall be (pindakartha) the spiritual benefactor of a Marumakkathayam Nair in place of his Anandravan? I am sure the British government would indignantly refuse to legislate on the point even if we venture to ask them. As the British government would not interfere with our religious law, so they could not, according to their policy, interfere with our civil rights based upon such law, unless the people wish to change it or unless the exercise of such rights involve a crime or is opposed to public policy.

The Brahmos who wanted a marriage law had to declare beforehand that they had ceased to be 'Hindus'. They declared that they scorned to profess the Hindu religion and that they felt conscientious scruples in celebrating their marriages according to the rights of an idolatrous people. They declared that they had a religion of their own and that they wanted to regulate marriages according to that religion. Would any Nair in Malabar go to this length? It will be seen that the Government of India, even in the case of the Brahmos, wavered a good deal before giving them a law, because they were very anxious to know how it will affect the national Hindu Law. But the bill does not recognize this fact and legislates as if we did not form part of the Hindus or indeed of any nation recognized as such in India. Its provisions in this respect are most revolting to the tenets of our religion and a law which introduces

---

*The rites of passage in and out of life, namely birth and death, meant that the whole family was considered unfit to participate in any auspicious event. It was commonly referred to as a period of ritual impurity.

such sweeping changes in the constitution of Marumakkathayam Hindus does not deserve to be called a law for Marumakkathayam Hindus.

It is said that the bill is only permissive and does not compel Nairs to marry according to its provisions—and that if the Nairs do not like the law, they need not adopt it. This, I admit, is so; but it is necessary to consider the effect of making such a law available for the Marumakkathayam Hindus. Suppose an Anandravan of a taravad consisting of a hundred souls takes it into his head to marry according to this permissive law. He may marry a Pariah girl or a Nair girl of equal standing with him and bring her into the taravad house. What will be the consequence of this? If he brings a Nair girl she has a status quite different from that of the wives of the other members of the taravad and that is enough to produce great heart-burning among the other wives brought into the taravad and to destroy the peace of the taravad for ever. The children of the other wives may well be pointed to as bastards by the legal wife. If the Anandravan brings a Pariah wife, the consequences seem to me appalling. The whole of the members of the taravad, if they wish to keep up their caste and social status, will have to leave the taravad house and live elsewhere. Is this not very hard upon the poor Nair taravads of Malabar? And then as to maintenance suits and other suits resulting from such state of feelings between the members of a taravad, I am afraid that the already existing percentage of taravad suits will be multiplied hundredfold.

Such are some of the objections against the fundamental principles of the bill. I do not at all wonder that all true Hindus are indignant at such startling changes in their social and religious customs and ordinances, introduced on the pretence of legalizing our marriages.

Having stated as above my opinion that the people are quite averse to changes on the proposed lines in the bill, I have now to state my opinion whether the Marumakkathayam Hindus of Malabar have any system of marriage and if they have no system, whether they should have one, at least for the protection of the small minority who ask for it.

The Honourable Mr Sankarannair says in his speech that 'Though the Nairs are Hindus by religion their marriages are performed without any religious rites.' I must observe here that those who wish the change, including Mr Sankarannair, do not wish it on account of a desire to infuse more religious elements in our marriages. The bill has levelled down the sacred institution of marriage to a system of business relation or ordinary contract, enforceable at law. It seems to me that the reason of stating at the outset of this speech that our marriages are performed without any religious rites was perhaps to make it appear that our present marriage system is more vulnerable in its constitution than it would have been if any religious basis was accorded to it. I do not, of course, mean to say that our marriage system is altogether a religious institution. We, Nairs of Malabar, have very little of Hindu religious rites in any of our ceremonies. All our ceremonies are devoid of Mantrams or Sacraments as we are prohibited from studying or repeating Vedas. But whatever may be the basis of our present marriage system or whether it has any religious recognition or sanction, I must state here my opinion that a vast majority of the people of Malabar remain perfectly satisfied with the present system and should feel very unhappy if any new law to regulate marriage is thrust upon them.

It is always difficult to defend or justify the social and religious customs of oriental nations according to the European notions of morality and theology. Many customs sanctioned by our law and usage, and observed by us duly, appear to the Europeans extremely immoral and quite unjust according to their notions of morality. For instance, the Brahmins and Kshatriyas who are said to have highly religious marriages have polygamy as an institution sanctioned by Hindu law, and from the Himalayas to Cape Comorin you could find no orthodox Hindu, who would disapprove of polygamy as an immoral institution. Now polygamy is looked upon as a very immoral and shameful custom by Europeans. The Hindus know this very well. Perhaps some of the English-educated Hindus think of polygamy in the same way as the Europeans. Yet you will not find a single Hindu, whether English-educated or not, who would agree to the view that because polygamy is permitted and practised, the Brahmin marriage system is an immoral or defective system. Likewise, it will be difficult to find a Brahmin who would not feel horrified if he finds polyandry practised by a Brahmin woman. She and her paramor become outcastes the moment they are found guilty of polyandry. They are condemned and put out of society and looked down upon by every Hindu with the greatest contempt and horror. Now to an European the polygamous husband appears as immoral and wicked a person as the polyandrous wife appears to a Brahmin. But the custom permits polygamy and therefore the Hindu practises it and does not feel at all ashamed at his conduct. Such is the force the ancient customs and manners exercise over the minds of the oriental nations. I make these remarks simply to show that each nation values its own custom in respect of its marriage and other social and religious institutions independently of what other people think of them and to a certain extent each nation has got its own code of morality in respect of such institutions. In connection with the question of introducing new marriage systems, an eminent English lawyer, who was a law member of the Viceregal Legislative Council, once stated as follows:

Laws relating to such subjects as marriage have their root in the very deepest feelings and in the whole history of a nation; nor is it easy to imagine a more tyrannical or a more presumptuous abuse of superior force than that which would be involved, in any attempt to bring the views and practices of one nation upon such subjects into harmony with those of other nations whose institutions and characters had been cast in a totally different mould.

I would now describe briefly the ceremonies or formalities which constitute marriage among Nairs and leave it to others to say whether the ceremonies and formalities observed by Nairs, in order to constitute marital relations, have any religious element in them.

I think the Malayalam word 'sambandam' in its peculiar sense, as used throughout Malabar proper, Cochin, and parts of Travancore, conveys the same idea as the word marriage etymologically conveys in the English language, viz., 'the union of man and woman as husband and wife'. Sambandam is the principal Malayalam word for marriage as *vivaham* is in Sanskrit. Whatever may be the basis of the sambandams of the Marumakkathayam Nairs, there can be no doubt that the idea which the word conveys to a Malayali is the same as the word vivaham. This generic name sambandam, which in south Malabar between Calicut and Nedunganad and in Ponani, Cochin, and parts of Travancore, is the only word to denote marriage, includes,

1. *Guna dosham* as used in south and north Malabar.
2. The *podamuri* or its Sanskrit synonym *vastradanam* used in north Malabar.
3. *Uvamporuka* and *veedaram kyruka* of north Malabar.
4. The *kidakora kalyanam* of Palghat and parts of Nedanganad.

The podamuri, vastradanam, uvamporuka, veedaram kyruka, and kidakora kalyanan are local expressions hardly understood beyond the localities in which they are used, but there would be hardly a Malayali who would not readily understand what is meant by sambandam *todunguka*. The meaning of this phrase which means 'to marry' is understood throughout Keralam in the same way and there can be no ambiguity or mistake about it.

It is thus found that sambandam is the principal word denoting marriage among Marumakkathayam Nairs. It will also be found, on a close and careful examination of facts, that the principal features of this sambandam ceremony all over the Keralam are in the main the same. As there are different local names denoting marriage, so there may be found local variations in the performance of the ceremony. But the general features are more or less the same. For instance, the examination, prior to the betrothal, of the horoscopes of the bride and the bridegroom to ascertain whether their stars agree astrologically, the appointment of an auspicious day for the celebrations of the ceremony, the usual hours at which the ceremony takes place, the presentation of the *danom* to the Brahmins, the sumptuous banquet, the meeting of the bride and bridegroom in the central room of the house, the sprinkling of the rice on the head of the bride and the bridegroom, are features which are invariably found in all well-conducted sambandams in all parts of Keralam alike; but here I would beg to state that I should not be understood as saying that each and every one of the formalities above referred to, are gone through at every sambandam. I would only say that most of them are generally gone thorugh at all sambandams among respectable Nairs and I would further say that they ought to be gone through at every sambandam, if the parties wish to marry according to the customs of the country. I would now briefly refer to the local variations to be found in the ceremony of sambandam and also the particular incidents attached to certain forms of sambandam in Malabar. I shall describe the Podamuri or Vastradanam as celebrated in north Malabar and then show how the other forms of sambandam differ from it. Of all the forms of sambandam, I consider the podamuri form the most solemn and the most fashionable in north Malabar. Of course my description will be borne out by the evidence that is before us.

The preliminary ceremony, in every podamuri, is the examination of the horoscopes of the bride and the bridegroom by an astrologer. This takes place in the house of the bride, in the presence of the relations of the bride and the bridegroom. The astrologer, after examination, writes down the results of his calculations on a piece of palmyra leaf, with his opinion as to the fitness or otherwise of the match and hands it over to the bridegroom's relations. If the horoscopes agree, a day is then and there fixed for the celebration of the marriage. This date is also written down on two pieces of aalekam, one of which is handed over to the bride's Karanavan and the other to the bridegroom's relations. The astrologer and the bridegroom's party are then feasted in the bride's house and the former also receives presents in the shape of money or cloth and this preliminary ceremony which is invariably performed at all podamuri in north Malabar is called *podamurikurikal*, but is unknown in south Malabar.

Some three or four days prior to the date fixed for the celebration of the podamuri, the bridegroom visits his karanavars and elders in caste to obtain formal leave to marry. The bridegroom on such occasion presents his elders with betel and nut and obtains their formal sanction to the wedding. On the day appointed the bridegroom proceeds, after sunset, to the house of the bride accompanied by a number of his friends. He goes in procession and is received at the gate of the house, by the bride's party and is conducted with his friends, to seats provided in the *thekina* or southern hall of the house. There the bridegroom distributes presents, danom or money gifts to the Brahmins assembled. After this, the whole party is treated to a sumptuous banquet. It is now time for the astrologer to appear and announce the auspicious hour fixed. He does it accordingly and receives his dues. The bridegroom is then taken by one of his friends to *padinitta* or the principal room of the house. The bridegroom's party has, of course, brought with them a quantity of new clothes and betel leaf and nut. The clothes are placed in the western room of the house called padinitta in which all religious and other important household ceremonies are usually performed. This room will be decorated and turned into a bedroom for the occasion. There will be placed in the room a number of lighted lamps and *ashtamangaliam* which consists of eight articles symbolical of *mangaliam* or marriage. These are rice, paddy, the tender leaves of the coconut tree, an arrow, a looking glass, a well-washed cloth, burning fire, and a small round wooden box called *cheppu* made in a peculiar fashion. These will be found placed on the floor of the room aforesaid as the bridegroom enters it. The bridegroom with his groomsman enters the room through the eastern door. The bride dressed in rich clothes and bedecked with jewels enters the room through the western door accompanied by her aunt or some other elderly lady of her family. The bride stands facing east with the ashtamangaliam and lit up lamps in front of her. The groomsman then hands over to the bridegroom a few pieces of the new cloth and the bridegroom puts them into the hands of the bride. This being done, the elderly lady who accompanied the bride sprinkles rice over the lit-up lamps and the heads and shoulders of the bride and the bridegroom, and the bridegroom immediately leaves the room, as he has to perform another duty. At the thekina or southern hall, he now presents his elders and friends with cakes and betel leaf and nut. Betel and nut are also given to all the people assembled at the place. After the departure of the guests, the bridegroom retires to the bedroom with the bride.

This is an unvarnished account of a podamuri. Next morning the *vettilakettu* or *salkaram* ceremony follows and the bridegroom's female relations take the bride to the husband's house where there is feasting in honour of the occasion.

Uvamporuka or *veediramkyral* is a peculiar form of marriage in north Malabar. It will be seen from the description given above that the podamuri is necessarily a costly ceremony and many people find it difficult to celebrate it in due form for want of money. Such people generally resort to the less costly ceremony of uvamporuka or veediramkyral. The features of the ceremony are to a certain extent the same as podamuri; but it is celebrated on a smaller scale. There is no cloth-giving ceremony. The feasting is confined to the relations of the married couple. The particular incident attached to this form of marriage is that the husband should visit the wife in her house and is not permitted to take her to his house, unless and until he celebrates the regular podamuri ceremony. This rule is strictly adhered to in north Malabar and instances in which the husband and wife, joined by uvamporuka or veediramkyral ceremony and with grown-up children, being the issue of such marriage, undergoing the podamuri ceremony, some fifteen or twenty years after uvamporuka, in order to enable the husband to take the wife to his house, are known to me personally.

The sambandam of south Malabar and the kidakora kalyanam of Palghat have all or most of the incidents of podamuri, except the presenting of the clothes. Here money is substituted for clothes and the other ceremonies are more or less the same. There is also the salkaram ceremony wanting in south Malabar as the wives are not at once taken to the husband's house after marriage.

Immediately connected with the afore-mentioned marriage ceremony is another ceremony which is called *kettu-kalyanam* and which prevails among the whole Marumakkathayam people of all classes from Cape Comorin to Kavayi. Whatever may have been the origin of this kettu-kalyanam I have little or no doubt that the ceremony, as now observed, is essentially a religious ceremony which every girl in a Marumakkathayam family is bound to undergo, before attaining puberty, on pain of excommunication from caste. This view is supported even by the evidence now before us. As almost all the witnesses have described the details of this ceremony it will merely be a waste of time to recapitulate them here. This ceremony which is performed as a preliminary ceremony renders the girls eligible for marriage. The non-performance of this ceremony, before the girl attains her puberty, works a forfeiture of the caste of the whole taravad to which the girl belongs. It is said by some, who do not like our institutions, that when we look to the details of this ceremony, we find reason to think that the Nair girls, by undergoing this ceremony, become almost free to practise prostitution and lead an immoral life. It is said that by tying the *thali** on the first day and by cutting and removing it on the fourth day of the kalyanam ceremony, a marriage was first constituted and then dissolved and that after this dissolution, the girl is permitted to lead the life of a prostitute. Nothing could be a greater or more unfounded falsehood than this allegation. In my opinion, the kalyanam is a mere preliminary ceremony something like a *samskaram* among other Hindus which makes the person who undergoes it, eligible to marry. The fact that the ceremony is ordained to be performed before the girl attains her puberty is in my opinion a valid reason for supposing that except as a Samskaram, the ceremony has no connection with actual marriage. I do not think that where facts clearly disprove prostitution and immoral life in Nair women, we should have recourse to such arguments as these to show that the kalyanam ceremony is not intended or considered as a passport to prostitution.

The general notion among the people who do not personally know Malabar customs and institutions, is founded upon the Nambuthiri version of them and the *Keralolpathi* and the *Kerala Mahathmiam*. These two books that are supposed to give accounts of the Nair institutions, are works of the Nambuthiri Brahmin, who from interested motives, have always wished to make out that our women do not and need not practise chastity. The evidence given by some of the Nambuthiris themselves before us will, however, refute this doctrine and show that the practice has never been in accordance with it; but foreigners who wrote about Malabar in ancient times had the Brahmin version only to depend upon and the two works above quoted to consult. Hence, there is a general notion that we have no marriage system, but only concubinage accompanied with great laxity of morals. This notion must have, in the absence of evidence to the contrary, greatly influenced the high court of 1869, in saying as they did, about our marriage system, but I am hopeful that if matters are put in their proper light, the high court may change their view. Mr Logan who evidently has taken much pains to collect information on the subject, remarks on the marriage system in Malabar in the following words:

This part of the Malabar Law has in the hands of unenquiring commentators brought much undeserved obloquy on the morality of the people. The fact at any rate of recent years is that although the theory of the law sanctions freedom in these relations,

*further explained in the Glossary.

conjugal fidelity is very general. Nowhere is the marriage tie—albeit informal, more jealously guarded or its neglect more savagely avenged.

Mr Logan of course cannot easily divest himself of his early impressions on the subject received from the writings of Buchanan, Thackeray, Warden, Wilk, etc., and that is why he still says 'albeit informal'. Mr Logan's theory of law that sanctioned freedom in these relations was perhaps what he found in the *Keralolpathi* and *Kerala Mahathmiam*, the two recent Nambuthiri works composed with the evident object of degrading the social status of the Nairs.

As to whether our present marriage system deserves to be recognized by law as a valid and binding system, I think there cannot be two opinions. I ask that when the courts find that the allegations of the existence of promiscuous intercourse and laxity of morals and want of marriage system, etc., in Malabar are all absurdly unfounded, that when they find that the community of Nairs and Tiars, that is to say the respectable and a very large majority of it, observe the Marriage Law as strictly as any other nation in the world, when the court find these facts to be true, would not they hold, according to good conscience and equity, that we are entitled to the protection of the Penal and Civil Laws which protect other Hindu subjects of Her Majesty, the Queen Empress, in the enjoyment of their matrimonial rights.

From his speech, Mr Sankarannair himself does not seem to be quite sure as to what was the binding character of the customary law of marriage among Nairs, before the high court said in 1869 'the relation to be mere concubinage'. There can however be hardly any doubt on the point, notwithstanding what the foreigners wrote about it on imperfect and absurd information they received from the great enemies of the Nairs—the Nambuthiri Brahmins and Nambuthiri-ridden Rajahs and their people in the ancient days. To prove that the Nairs who were essentially a martial race, and were highly sensitive about any breach of their marital rights, had a valid and binding form of marriage, innumerable instances may be quoted from the ancient writings of well-informed men, our old country ballads and many other sources available. But I will quote here only one instance at present. The British commissioners of north Malabar once asked the Rajah of Chirakal to inform them what the law on adultery among Nairs was. In the reply, I understand from a credible source, will be found a statement from the rajah to the effect that he who committed adultery with a Nair's wife forfeited his life, that is that the husband had a right to kill the adulterer or the adulteress or both, on the spot, with impunity. To a martial race, summary laws of this nature suited better in those days than the elaborate hairsplitting Civil Law. Our race has, I admit, degenerated since these days. The martial spirit is dead under a powerful foreign government; but I think it was clearly the duty of British courts to have examined and ascertained, most carefully and thoroughly, the state of marital relations among Nairs, before deciding the question whether we had a marriage system or not and even if they found that there was no uniformity in the custom of marriage, the courts should have helped us by validating and upholding our present system, if they found it based on good moral principles and sanctioned by social usage. Sir Fitz James Stephen remarked in his speech on the Brahmo Bill of 1872 that

native laws should not be changed by direct legislation except in extreme cases though they may and ought to be moulded by the Courts of Justice so as to suit the changing circumstances of society. If this principle is fully grasped it will, I think, serve as the key to nearly every question which can be raised to the alteration of native laws.

Taking this principle as their guide, it will be enough if the courts will carefully enquire into the present state of things and ascertain whether we have a marriage system or not. As stated elsewhere, I admit that there may be Nair women who are professional prostitutes. But the existence of such men and women do not at all prove that we have no marriage system. The English, the French, and the other civilized nations, who have elaborate marriage law, have among them, many men and women addicted to immorality and whose practices, were it not for the laws against bigamy, would have been termed polygamy or polyandry, but that does not in any way weaken the marriage law in Europe. What the respectable portion of a community accepts and observes as their custom should be treated as the custom of that community, and is any one who desires a change in the marriage system prepared to say that respectable Nairs have no marriage? Even the great mass of evidence taken before us supports the view that Nairs have a system of marriage recognized by custom. I don't think that it is necessary to change our Marumakkathayam law of succession in order to have our marriages legally recognized.

It appears to me to be a simple denial of justice to Nairs, to say that because some Nambuthiri landlords successfully use their influence, that their wealth and position in Malabar give them, to seduce Nair women, that because there are professional prostitutes among Nair women, who do not know what marriage tie means, that because we follow Marumakkathayam descent of property, therefore we are not entitled to have our marriage, however solemnized, recognized by law. That our Brahmanical Hindu law recognizes as valid, marriages from which rights to property do not arise to either party to such marriage or their issue, is evident from the custom which some Nambuthiri Brahmins, who are recognized as Brahmins by the whole race in India, observe in north of Malabar, even to this day. A learned Brahmin of this clan was a witness before us and has described the custom. Their marriage is solemnized with all the religious ceremonies that are undergone at every Brahmin marriage in India. The *homam*, the mantrams, the *saptapadi*, etc., ceremonies are strictly and rigidly observed. Widowhood is recognized and observed as strictly as in other Brahmin class; yet the issues of such a solemn and religious marriage are Marumakkathayam Hindus and do not inherit their father's property, but follow Marumakkathayam law of descent. Now, would it not be great injustice to hold that adultery with a married lady of this Brahmin caste, enticing away the married woman of this caste, are not offences under the Indian Penal Code, because the Brahmins follow the Marumakkathayam system of succession, however solemn and binding their marriage may be? In my humble opinion, the system of succession to property has nothing to do with the solemnity or the binding character of a marriage founded upon our religious, moral, and social laws and customs, and if it can be shown that we have a perfectly good system of marriage founded upon our religious and social custom, why should not that system be recognized by our courts? That among Nairs there exist women who practise polyandry as a caste institution, recognized by our custom, is nothing but an unmitigated falsehood. It may exist in the nooks and corners of the district; but it is looked upon by the Nair community as a monstrous innovation due to the baneful Nambuthiri influence. If polyandry exists in a recognized form, let it be proved. Among the carpenter and blacksmith classes in Malabar, polyandry exits as an institution and we see every day the four or five chosen husbands among this class celebrating their polyandrous marriage openly according to their caste rules, and with much ceremony and pomp; but can even the worst and most uncompromising enemy of the Nair institutions point to a podamuri or uvamporuka or kidakora or any other recognized form of Nair sambandam, throughout the Keralam, at which a girl was wedded to more than one husband? If he can, I shall give up my contention and ask for legislation. I have not the slightest hesitation in saying that he would not be able to show a single instance of such a marriage whether in ancient or modern Malabar. Then, why cite the examples of the Nair harlots here and there, who are the slaves of the Nambuthiris and who form secret alliances with a number of men or who practise prostitution, as a profession! It is true that our women have no widowhood, but I suppose there are many Sudras in other parts of India, having an undisputed law of marriage, not observing perpetual widowhood among their women. Why then, I ask, should our present system be changed, our caste system and succession changed, our nationality destroyed?

I have nothing more to add to this separate memorandum of mine, except that if it is found that under our present system, adultery, enticing away a married woman, and other offences against matrimonial laws, recognized as penal under the Indian Penal Code, cannot be recognized as such, when committed in respect of parties married according to our present system, I should certainly solicit legislation in the way formulated by our President, the Honourable Mr Justice Muthuswamyiyer whose proposals are, in my humble opinion, the least likely to meet with opposition from the bulk of the Nair population of Malabar. My own opinions on each of the suggestions, made by the Honourable Mr Justice Muthuswamyiyer, are given in the resolutions recorded, and need not be recapitulated here.

The freedom to a Marumakkathayam Nair, to dispose of his self-acquisition by will, is what all the people of Malabar wish that they should possess. Wills or declarations of a deceased person, regarding the distribution of his self-acquired property have always been respected by Nairs and a legal recognition of it by courts will enable us to make sufficient provisions for our wives and children.

Calicut
1 July 1891

O. CHANDUMENON

appendix V

The President's Supplementary Memorandum to the Malabar Marriage Commission

The report of which a copy has been furnished by Mr Winterbotham was not before me when I drew up my memorandum on the resolutions recorded at the meetings of the commission at Calicut and with reference to the minutes of Messrs Chandumenon and Ramavarmatamburan. The report purports to be that of the majority of the commission and treats my memorandum as a minute of dissent. It, therefore, only remains for me to submit for the consideration of the government a few remarks on the alternative scheme of legislation proposed therein.

2. It will be observed that practically the report contains the views of three out of the six commissioners, viz., Messrs Winterbotham and Mundappabangira and The Honourable Mr Sankarannair, and I presume that the fourth, Mr Ramavarmatamburan, has signed it subject to the remarks contained in his minute. As, however, the opinions of all the six commissioners are before the government, the question whether the report in its entirety is that of three or four commissioners seems to be immaterial.

3. The grounds which led me to the conclusion that if legislation is expedient, it is expedient only on the lines indicated by me, are fully set forth in my memorandum. Turning to the alternative scheme, it embodies almost all the provisions of the Honourable Mr Sankarannair's bill which, it is clear from the evidence, are at variance with the marriage customs now obtaining in Malabar and are opposed not only to the feelings of the majority of the Marumakkathayam society, but also to those of the majority of that

section of the educated classes who are in favour of a marriage law. It ignores caste restrictions and the customary rules of consanguinity and affinity and retains the stringent provisions as to divorce and the rule of succession to self-acquired and separate property, as contained in the bill.

4. Before proceeding, however, to discuss the alternative scheme in detail, I think it is desirable to consider whether it is practicable or expedient to adopt it as a basis for legislation.

5. The first and most prominent objection is its revolutionary character. If it were put before the government that the Hindu law as administered on this side of the Ghats is a relic of archaic legislation; that the law of coparcenery is, in the opinion of some, unworkable and obstructive of the development of individual industry; that the succession of distant *sapinda*s to the exclusion of near blood relations is opposed to natural instinct; that the total displacement of daughters by sons in the line of succession is not in consonance with parental affection; that the theory of funeral oblations and spiritual benefit on which the Hindus rely is unreasonable; that if a law framed on rational basis were substituted, it would, in the course of a few generations, become the law of the people in general; that some of the English educated men who vehemently declaim against some of the provisions of the Hindu law may be treated as 'the leaven that will leaven the whole lump'; I entertain no doubt that the government will say, wait until the few induce the many to agree with them. In the meantime, sound policy forbids violent legislative action against the wishes of the bulk of the population, on the ground that they are 'uninstructed in the English sense of the term'. Yet, this, in short, is the basis on which the alternative scheme rests. The permissive character of the proposed marriage law is no justification where it alters the Marumakkathayam law of succession to self-acquired property and disturbs the domestic relation in a family corporation constituted as a Malabar taravad is.

6. The second objection is that the scheme departs from the lines laid down by the Government of India for the guidance of the commission. As I read their letter the expediency of legislation rests solely on the ground that the measure is either desired by the majority of the classes subject to the Marumakkathayam law, or is essential for the protection of the minority. In paragraph 59, the report says, '...we do not dispute the view that the proposed legislation is not at present desired by the majority; but we also believe that the uninstructed majority will rapidly follow the lead of the enlightened classes'. It proceeds to state that 'the great bulk of Nairs and Tiars are tenants of small holdings paying rack-rents and earning a scanty living by agriculture;

that they are totally uninstructed on the subject of the proposed legislation; and that 'the landlord and agricultural classes as a whole have little education in the English sense of the term and have that horror of innovation which characterizes most orientals'. The state of popular feeling on the subject, the several classes opposed to all legislation, and the section of the educated and official classes in favour of it on the basis of the existing custom are referred to in paragraph 18 of my memorandum. I would here ask whether it is reasonable to suppose that the tenants of small holdings would follow the lead of a few educated men and not the example of the *kovilagams* (families of ancient rulers), *naduvalia* (representatives of local chieftains), and of the aristocracy in general of the country and of their own landlords and agricultural classes?

7. In dealing with the question whether the measure is essential for the protection of the minority, the report adopts five of the grounds stated at the close of para 80 of my memorandum and omits the most important ground stated therein, viz., that legislation intended for a society as a body is expedient only on the basis indicated by imperative social customs and is likely to become popular and national in proportion to the extent to which such customs and other lasting social influences are taken into account. I must also add that in coming to the conclusion that legislation on such basis is expedient, I was influenced by the consideration that the opposition in north Malabar is due mainly to the obnoxious provisions of the bill indicated in my memorandum, and not to a belief that the customary marriage needed no protection or legal recognition. I also pointed out (paragraph 14 of my memorandum) that the educated classes were divided in opinion; that their number did not exceed a thousand at the most; that about 60 per cent of them desired legislation on the customary basis; and that the minority who were prepared to take the bill in its present form was too small to justify legislation on its lines. The report, overlooking the statements contained in this paragraph, expresses dissent from the view that the number of persons who would accept the bill is, as it stands, too small to render legislation on its lines expedient. I have referred to the recorded evidence and find that not more than a dozen out of 121 witnesses, orally examined, state that they would take the bill as it stands. Several of them object to some of the provision embodied in the scheme and state that their acceptance is only provisional on legislation on the customary basis being refused. I have also referred to the replies to our interrogatories from 822 persons and find that not more than forty agreed to the conditions of the bill, which the alternative scheme retains. I would pause here, and ask whose lead, it is expected that the uninstructed majority

will follow? Is it the lead of the 50 per cent willing to accept the scheme in its present form or of the 40 per cent of the English-educated men who are against all legislation or of the 60 per cent who would only accept legislation substantially on the customary basis. Again I find among the educated minority, who object to those provisions of the alternative scheme which are at variance with the custom of the country, a number of high court vakils, first-grade pleaders, district munsifs as also the Nair sub-judge of Tellicherry and the Nair high court judge of Travancore, and a number of intelligent men both in British Malabar and in Travancore and in Cochin. May I ask whether it is the lead of these gentlemen or of the educated men (about fifty according to evidence) that the uninstructed majority will follow? I fail to see how, on the evidence before us, the alternative scheme can be regarded either as acceptable to the majority or as essential for the protection of the minority.

8. The report states (paragraph 59) that the proposed law, if introduced, will not remain a dead letter and in support of this position refers to the fact that 'many of the strongest opponents' of the proposed legislation have expressed 'lively dread of its speedy acceptance by a large proportion of the people'. Extracts are given from the evidence of two witnesses (56 and 119). Here I would simply observe that I do not understand the intention of the government to be that an obnoxious law should be forced upon the people in anticipation of its being accepted by them in future. It is in my opinion clearly unsafe to disregard the popular feeling as evinced by the mass of the evidence recorded by the commission, upon the strength of statements made by some of the opponents of the proposed measure in which, in their anxiety to avoid it, they exaggerate what they conceived to be the ill effect likely to ensue from it.

9. Passing on to the form of legislation, I do not think that the government desire to improve the national morality by aggressive legislation. The first difficulty we had to face related to the form of marriage prescribed in the bill. It is discussed in paragraph 16–I of my memorandum and in paragraph 67 of the report. In the latter it is stated that the commissioners who have signed it do not in the least regard the acceptance of the procedure suggested by me as a sine qua non. I must here observe that no one that desires legislation needs a statutory form, or has scruples about going through the customary form, and that the introduction of the former is liable to be misconstrued as casting a slur on the conventional usage and as treating a solemn event as a business matter. A statutory form is of itself open to no objection, but the

question is whether it is either needed by or acceptable to the people for whom it is intended.

10. The next question we had to consider was how to meet the difficulty arising from caste restrictions on marriage. This question is discussed in paragraphs 16–II and III of my memorandum and in paragraphs 68–70 of the report. In the latter a solution is suggested in these terms:

> We would not, however, underestimate the difficulty. It is a fact that in numerous cases the parties to a marriage contracted in defiance of caste rules could not enter a taravad house without (in native opinion) polluting the whole family and rendering every member of it liable to boycotting and excommunication. It is just and necessary to protect the taravad from such consequences, and we would therefore provide that, if the difference in caste between the parties to a marriage be such that social usage condemns them to excommunication, the party so condemned shall lose his or her right of entry into, or residence in the taravad house, and that the man should lose his right of succession to the office of Karanavan.

This suggestion virtually annexes a penalty to violation of caste usage, and to this extent it amounts to a departure from the principle of neutrality invariably adhered to by the British government and a retrogression from the policy of Act XXI of 1850. It is moreover in direct conflict with paragraph 16 of the report where, assuming, contrary to the bulk of the evidence, that caste restrictions on marriage exist. As pointed out in my memorandum, caste is a quasi-religious institution, and any legislation validating marriages in contravention of caste rules will be regarded as an interference with their religious usage.

11. In this connection I may point out that the remark in paragraph 68 of the report is based on a misapprehension. The principles on which the caste difficulty should, in my opinion, be met in legalizing customary marriages are explained in paragraphs 16–II and III of my memorandum. In advertence to the doctrine of neutrality I stated that such restrictions should be tolerated in the same way as they are in the case of marriages contracted on this side of the Ghats so far only as they are referable to the rules of Hindu law. I stated also, that the society should be free to alter its customs with reference to the requirements of progress, and that this object might be effectually secured by inserting the words 'for the time being' and thereby imposing an obligation on the courts to recognize the custom actually existing at the time of marriage. That there was a decision at some former time recognizing a

different custom could not, as stated in the report, preclude the recognition by the courts of a subsequent modification of that custom. I may here quote Sir Fitz James Stephen's observations on the Brahmo Marriage Bill, to which Mr Chandumenon refers, viz., 'The native laws should not be changed by direct legislation except in extreme cases, though they may and ought to be moulded by the courts of justice so as to suit them to the changing circumstances of society. If this principle is fully grasped, it will, I think, serve as the key to nearly every question, which can be raised regarding the alteration of native laws.'

12. The next point on which the report dissents from my view is as to maintaining the customary restriction on marriage on the score of consanguinity or affinity. In paragraph 71, the report justifies the bill on the ground that the limitation therein contained has already been approved by the government. If it is intended to refer to the Brahmo Marriage Act of 1872, it must be borne in mind that that act requires a declaration from the parties to the marriage that they do not profess the Hindu religion, whereas the proposed legislation concerns those who profess that religion. Here I may ask whether any Marumakkathayam Hindu would declare that he does not profess the Hindu religion. Again, I would draw attention to the remarks contained in paragraphs 22–80 of my memorandum. Another reason assigned is that the Nairs and Tiars do not maintain ancestral trees and that it is difficult therefore to prove relationship beyond the fifth degree; but it must be observed that the family tradition kept alive by the observance of pollution on the occasion of every birth and death is relied on by the people as adequately supplying the want of family trees. According to the alternative scheme, if a taravad consists of members related to each other beyond the fifth degree, a marriage between them would be legal. It seems to me extremely undesirable to interfere with the custom in a matter like this; the marriage between parties descended from the same female ancestor being considered to be incestuous and to entail loss of caste.

13. I may here point out that, in regard to both caste restrictions and those founded on consanguinity and affinity, the alternative scheme differs from the bill submitted in 1884 by the committee consisting of Raja Sir T. Madava Row and Messers Logan, Wigram, Sankarannair and Karunakaramenon. Section 4, Clause 4 of that bill is in these terms: 'The relation of the parties must not be such in respect of consanguinity, affinity or otherwise that, according to any recognized custom, a marriage between them would be improper.' To illustrate the popular feeling on the subject I may, apart from

the bulk of the evidence before us, refer to the minutes of my colleagues, Messrs Chandumenon and Ramavarmatamburan, and the remarks of the sub-judge of Tellicherry and the high court judge of Travancore.

14. The provisions relating to divorce are discussed in paragraph 16–VII and paragraphs 17 and 18 of my memorandum, and in paragraphs 72–4 of the report. The ground on which my proposals rest is not, as stated in the report, that I consider the marriage to be a mere civil contract and as such dissoluble at will, but that a highly elaborated system of judicial divorce is ill-suited to the Marumakkathayam society just emerging from polyandry. The report states that whatever restrictions on divorce the government may deem indispensable in the interests of morality, the educated Malayalis will still beg for the legislation of marriage. Having regard to the evidence before us, I am unable to concur in this opinion. The alternative scheme appears to be open to the remark that a divorce law which, it is assumed, will generally be availed of two or three generation hence, is premature, and that the minority whose example is expected to influence the general Marumakkathayam population is, as already stated, infinitesimal. I have, moreover, only to refer to paragraphs 29 and 80 of my memorandum where I have considered the objections taken in the report. I still consider that where, as the report says, the standard of morality is low and the institution of marriage is in a state of infancy, my proposal to regulate divorce by judicial process and by the annexing of a penalty to abuse of the right of free divorce would be the first instalment of reform. The reform, whilst it is practicable, would be undoubted improvement on the existing state of things and would elevate the tone of sexual relation. It would also be susceptible of further development by paving the way for nationalizing marriage as a legal institution.

15. The next point of difference is that which relates to the right of succession to self-acquired property in cases of intestacy, which under the Marumakkathayam law as at present administered, vests in the taravad; the alternative scheme transfers it in whole to wife and children. This question is discussed in paragraph 24 of my memorandum and paragraphs 76–8 of the report. In the latter it is stated that a double system of inheritance prevails elsewhere, and that, though it may be incongruous, the incongruity does not occasion any insurmountable difficulty. The real question, however, is not whether there is any insurmountable difficulty, but whether it is expedient to introduce it by legislation. Again, it is suggested (paragraph 77) that the eager and unanimous demand for testamentary power betokens a general dissatisfaction with the existing law of intestate succession, implying thereby

that there is a general desire to give away the whole of the self-acquired property to wife and children. This inference is not warranted by the evidence. According to the evidence before the commission, many desire to give, and, when they make gifts inter vivos, do give a portion only, but a few give away the whole to their wives and children. It is true that the majority are not satisfied with the law of intestate succession to self-acquired property as now administered, but the general belief disclosed by the evidence is that this law is founded on an erroneous decision of the high court, reported in II. M.H.C.R. 162. That decision is, it is considered, based on a mistaken view of the custom of the country, according to which the acquirer's *taivali* relations, i.e. his brother, sisters, and sisters' children, are entitled to succeed in preference to the more distant members of the taravad. It is the desire to restore the previous custom which, together with the ground mentioned in paragraph 20 of my memorandum, accounts for the demand for testamentary power.

16. As regards the remark that the division into half and half is an unsatisfactory compromise, I have only to observe that where there are conflicting claims upon the bounty of the acquirer, viz., those of the wife and children on the one part, and of sisters and their children on the other, the best solution is a compromise based on the practice of those who make gifts inter vivos. If the self-acquired property is either too small, or in excess of what is required, for an adequate provision for wife and children, the inequality will be corrected by the acquirer himself by the exercise of his testamentary power. The real issue is whether it is the practice generally followed or the desire of a few that ought to be accepted as a guide in framing a law for the disposition of property in cases of intestacy. It must also be observed that in a society constituted as the Marumakkathayam society is, the affection for one's sisters and sisters' children is much stronger than it is elsewhere, and this makes the practice as regards the reservation of a portion of self-acquired property for them intelligible.

17. As for the religious objection considered in paragraph 79 of the report, it cannot be denied that the Marumakkathayam system is regarded by the masses as resting on divine ordinance and that any interference therewith against the wishes of the majority is liable to be regarded as an interference with their religious belief. It can, likewise, not be denied that the Marumakkathayam system imposes the obligation to offer funeral oblations on the sister's son and not on the son. The religious objection, therefore, urged by Mr Karunakaramenon is entitled to weight to this extent, viz., that

where there is no taravad property, the alternative scheme would give the whole of the self-acquired property to the son, while 'the key to salvation' is with the sister's son. From a strictly legal point of view, however, the religious obligation and the right of succession are correlatives as regards taravad property only, the self-acquired property being at the absolute disposal of the acquirer of the property, the obligation to perform funeral rites is peremptory, and neglect to perform them would entail forfeiture of caste. Therefore, although, in strict law, this obligation is independent of inheritance, yet policy requires that a legislative provision which would take away the means whereby the sister's son is enabled to discharge his religious duty should be guarded against. It is true, as stated by Mr Krishnamenon, a retired sub-judge, that, when Sriparasurama introduced the Marumakkathayam system, owing to the absence of the institution of marriage, it was not known who the father was, and this probably was the reason why the obligation was imposed on the nephew; but the ex-sub-judge's suggestion that, when the Marriage Act is passed and paternity rendered certain, the obligation would, under the ordinary Hindu law devolve on the son, is not tenable. It is not likely that his dictum, and the texts quoted by him, will be accepted by the people as sufficient to displace an ordinance of Parasurama in special reference to the Marumakkathayam system.

18. It only remains for me to notice the two side issues with which the question of legislation is complicated in the report. The first is whether the Marumakkathayam system is good or bad and whether a marriage law should or should not be so framed as to bring about its gradual decay and ultimate extinction. The report deals at length with this question, but the instructions of the government, as I understand them, do not require the commission to go into it. Assuming, however, that the commission is at liberty to go into it, and assuming also that it is desirable on economic grounds to break up the Marumakkathayam system, the fact that the great bulk of the people concerned are, as the evidence shows, anxious to maintain it, renders any legislation in that direction inexpedient. I would here refer to paragraph 24 of my memorandum. If the system is, as the report makes it, so unworkable, how is it that a very large majority of the Marumakkathayam classes base their objection to the Honourable Mr Sankarannair's bill on the ground that it tends to destroy it? I may point out that the opposition is the strongest in north Malabar where, as the report says, the natural feeling in favour of wife and children has become strongly developed. The effect of the evidence, as summarized in the concluding part of the above-quoted paragraph of the

report is that those who are in favour of legislation desire a marriage law to merely legalize what is already the prevailing custom; whereas the bill, as well as the alternative scheme, overrides the custom and aims a death blow at the Marumakkathayam system. The dewan of Cochin opposes all legislation on the ground that it would be ruinous to the taravad system. The dewan of Travancore, whilst approving of the proposal to introduce a marriage law, expresses the opinion that it should not be such as 'would sap the foundations of the Marumakkathayam system'. The Nair sub-judge of Tellicherry (Mr Gopalannair), adverting to the provision regarding succession to self-acquired property says:

I would certainly object to Section 84, clause (d) of the bill as it would be virtually interfering with the Marumakkathayam law of inheritance, which the majority of the people do not as yet want to set aside. As I learn from the Honourable Mr Sankarannair's speech in the Council when introducing the Bill, his object is to provide for such of the Marumakkathayam Hindus as wish it a form of marriage which the law will recognize, and so far I am with him, but I do not see why with a view of merely attaining this object we should startle the people of Malabar with innovation on their property law which the majority do not as yet want and which the exigencies of the case do not demand.

The Nair high court judge of Travancore (Mr Kunhiramannair) writes:

The proposed (d) as to succession deals, though indirectly, a death-blow to the Marumakkathayam system of inheritance. If the taravad is not to get a portion of the self-acquisition of its members, the Marumakkathayam taravad system cannot be properly worked or maintained according to the intention of its founders. The system has endured for ages, and the taravad is the best extant type of the primitive Hindu undivided family, whose cherished idea is to work for the good of the whole and not for the individual benefit alone; it has conferred domestic happiness in past ages on a large proportion of the inhabitants of the West coast, and it is not proposed to do away with the system altogether; if so, the soundness of the proposal (d) is open to question. In my opinion all that the State ought to do at present to satisfy the requirements of the progress of the Malabar society, is to declare marriages under the present system valid for the purpose of bringing the sinners against morality under the clutches of penal law, and to confer upon the wife and children a claim for maintenance out of the husband's self-acquisition, should he die without making due provision for them.

19. The second side issue raised is as to the theory of the Marumakkathayam system of sexual relation. This is discussed in paragraphs 80–90 of the report.

That the talikattu kaliyanam is only a preliminary caste rite and not a marriage is a fact as to which there is no difference of opinion. That prior to the introduction of podamuri and other species of sambandam (forms of individual marriage), the sexual relation was of a fugitive character and that there was no marriage in the proper sense of the term, is also not denied. But the question is not as to the primitive theory of sexual relation, but as to whether, as stated by the Honourable Mr Sankarannair, when asking for leave to introduce his bill, there is at present a marriage in practice, and if so, whether the customs relating thereto are such as would furnish a basis for legislation. As I read the report, this position does not seem to be disputed, for referring to the Marumakkathayam Hindus, the report states (paragraph 48) that 'they are all or nearly all of them better than their custom, and the majority (as we are told and believe) cleave to one woman for life'. Again, referring to the ancient notion, that chastity was not a virtue prescribed for Nair women, and that 'they were specially created for the Nambuthiri bachelors to play with', the report adds that 'Nairs will not submit to this teaching much longer'. The very same evidence, from which the above conclusions are drawn, associates the improvements in the relation of the sexes with podamuri and other species of sambandam. It is clear, then, that in the course of social progress the majority of the Marumakkathayam Hindus have engrafted forms of marriage on their ancient practice, that these forms are resorted to as overt acts whereby the intention to marry is manifested, and the sexual relation thus constituted in the majority of cases endures for life. This being so, the point for consideration seems to be, whether it is legislation on the customary basis or on the basis of the Brahmo Marriage Act (the so-called undenominational law) that will, by enlisting the sympathies of the people, more effectually help on social progress. The report, however, overlooking this consideration mixes up notions of the ancient polyandry with the present social marriage customs, and does not discriminate between a legal marriage and a social marriage. Further, by introducing other side issues, the report throws a cloud over the relations of the sexes as it now exists and states (paragraph 50) that 'Marumakkathayam was and still is destitute of the institution of marriage.' If the marriage customs are so bad as to render the sexual relation sanctioned by them nothing better than what it was in the primitive stages of the Marumakkathayam society, how are we to account for the admitted improvement in its moral tone, and how can legislation on the rigid lines of the alternative scheme be recommended? Our colleague, Mr Chandumenon, in his interesting memorandum, describes the marriage customs in detail, and they are accepted in the report as accurate. But the report states (paragraph 43) that, because a Nambuthiri Brahmin who goes through podamuri does not consider it a marriage binding upon him, it cannot be regarded as marriage in any other case. A Brahmin may not look upon any marriage other than Vedic as binding upon him; but it is no sufficient reason for concluding that as between Nairs, it is not regarded as binding either. On the other hand, that the Nambuthiri Brahmins themselves are compelled to go through the same formalities of wedding proves that, owing to social progress, the Nair women insist on giving the union the character of a marriage. However this may be, legislation with a provision for a declaration and its registration as suggested by me would make such marriages with even Nambuthiri Brahmins binding.

20. Our colleague, Mr Chandumenon, himself a highly educated and representative Malayali, whose opinion may be taken as reflecting the sentiments of a pretty large section of the educated classes, draws attention to the following observations of a member of the Viceregal Legislative Council:

Laws relating to such subjects as marriage have their root in the very deepest feelings and in the whole history of a nation; nor is it easy to imagine a more tyrannical and a more presumptuous abuse of superior force than that which would be involved in an attempt to bring the views and practices of one nation upon such subjects into harmony with those of other nations whose institutions and character have been cast in a different mould?

21. I must here add that when I expressed an opinion generally in favour of the bill framed by the committee appointed in 1884, I had not before me the evidence which I now have as to the provisions relating to divorce and the right of succession of the wife and children to self-acquired property.

22. In conclusion, I have only to state that after giving my best consideration to the subject, I cannot persuade myself to believe that the alternative scheme is expedient.

Bibliography

Achuthan, M., *Nirdharanam*, Thrissur: Current Books, 1991.
Aiyappan, A., 'Fraternal Polyandry in Malabar', *Man in India* 15, 1935, 109–18.
Anderson, Benedict, *Imagined Communities: Reflections on the Origins and Spread of Nationalism*, London: New Left Books, 1983.
Antherjanam, Lalithambika (tr. by Gita Krishnankutty), *Cast Me Out if You Will*, Calcutta: Stree, 1998.
Armstrong, Nancy and Leonard Tennenhouse (eds), *The Ideology of Conduct: Essays in Literature and the History of Sexuality*, New York: Methuen, 1987.
—— (eds), *The Violence of Representation: Literature and the History of Violence*, London: Routledge, 1989.
Armstrong, Nancy, *Desire and Domestic Fiction: A Political History of the Novel*, Oxford: Oxford University Press, 1987.
Arunima, G., 'Colonialism and the Transformation of Matriliny in Malabar, 1850–1940', Unpublished PhD dissertation, Cambridge University, 1992.
Asad, Talal and John Dixon, 'Translating Europe's Others', in Francis Barker et al. (eds), *Europe and its Others*, 2 vols., Colchester: University of Essex, 1985, 170–77.
Asad, Talal, 'The Concept of Cultural Translation in British Social Anthropology', in James Clifford and George E. Marcus (eds), *Writing Culture: The Poetics and Politics of Ethnography*, London: University of California Press, 1986, 141–64.
Asad, Talal (ed.), *Anthropology and the Colonial Encounter*, New Jersey: Humanities Press, 1973.
Bakhtin, M. M., *The Dialogic Imagination: Four Essays*, Michael Holquist (ed.), tr. by Caryl Emerson and Michael Holquist, Austin: University of Texas Press, 1981.
Balakrishnan, P. K., *Chandu Menon: Oru Padanam*, Kottayam: Sahitya Pravarthaka Cooperative Society, 1964.

Balakrishnan, V. and R. Leela Devi, *Mannathu Padmanabhan and the Revival of Nairs in Kerala*, New Delhi: Vikas Publishing House, 1982.
Barthes, Roland (tr. by Annette Lavers), *Mythologies*, New York: Hill & Wang, 1974.
———, *S/Z*, New York: Hill & Wang, 1974.
——— (tr. by Stephen Heath), *Image Music Text*, London: Flamingo, 1977.
———, *The Rustle of Language*, New York: Hill & Wang, 1986.
Basnett, Susan and Andre Lefevere (eds), *Translation, History and Culture*, London: Pinter, 1990.
Bassnett-McGuire, Susan, *Translation Studies*, London: Methuen, 1980.
Basu, Aparna, 'A Century's Journey: Women's Education in Western India 1820–1920', in Karuna Chanana (ed.), *Socialisation, Education and Women: Explorations in Gender Identity*, New Delhi: Orient Longman, 1988, 65–95.
Bayly, Susan, 'Hindu Kingship and the Origin of Community: Religion, State and Society in Kerala, 1750–1850', in *Modern Asian Studies* 18.12, 1984, 177–213.
Belsey, Catherine, *Critical Practice*, London and New York: Methuen, 1980.
———, *The Subject of Tragedy: Identity and Difference in Renaissance Drama*, London: Methuen, 1985.
Benjamin, Andrew, *Translation and the Nature of Philosophy*, London: Routledge, 1989.
Benjamin, Walter (tr. by Harry Zohn), 'The Task of the Translator', in Hannah Arendt (ed.), *Illuminations*, London: Collins, 1973, 69–82.
Bhaskaranunni, P., *Pathonpatham Nuttandile Keralam*, Thrissur: Kerala Sahitya Akademi, 1988.
Borthwick, Meredith, *The Changing Role of Women in Bengal, 1849–1905*, New Jersey, Princeton: Princeton University Press, 1984.
British Government of India, *Report of the Malabar Marriage Commission, with Enclosures and Appendices*, Madras: Malabar Marriage Commission, 1891.
Caplan, Pat (ed.), *The Cultural Construction of Sexuality*, London: Tavistock Publications, 1987.
Chaitanya, Krishna, *A History of Malayalam Literature*, New Delhi: Orient Longman, 1971.
Chakravarty, Uma, *Rewriting History: The Life and Times of Pandita Ramabai*, New Delhi: Kali for Women, 1998.
Chanana, Karuna, 'Social Change or Social Reform: The Education of Women in Pre-Independence India', *Socialisation, Education and Women: Exploration in Gender Identity*, New Delhi: Orient Longman, 1988, 96–128.
Chandumenon, O. (tr. by Appadurai), *Indulekha*, Madras: Malar Nilayam, 1956.
——— (tr. by W. Dumergue), *Indulekha*, 1890, *Indulekha: A Novel from Malabar*, Calicut: The Mathrubhumi Publishers and Printers, 1965.
——— (tr. by R. Leela Devi), *Indulekha, Crescent Moon*, New Delhi: Pankaj Publications, 1979.
———, *Indulekha*, Kottayam: Sahitya Pravarthaka Cooperative Society, 1981.

Chandumenon, O., *Sharada*, Calicut: Poorna Publications, 1990.
———, *Indulekha*, Kottayam: D.C. Books, 1993.
——— (tr. by Sudhamshu Chaturvedi), *Indulekha*, New Delhi: National Book Trust, 1994.
Chatterjee, Partha, 'The Nationalist Resolution of the Women's Question', in Kumkum Sangari and Sudesh Vaid (eds), *Recasting Women: Essays in Colonial History*, New Delhi: Kali for Women, 1993, 233–53.
———, *The Nation and its Fragments: Colonial and Post-colonial Histories*, Delhi: Oxford University Press, 1995.
———, *A Possible India: Essays in Political Criticism*, Delhi: Oxford University Press, 1998.
———, *The Present History of West Bengal: Essays in Political Criticism*, Delhi: Oxford University Press, 1998.
Chinnamma, K., 'Nair Strikalude Thalkalika Vyavasthakalum Unnamana Margangalum', in *Lakshmibai* 9.2, 3 & 4, 1913, 53–60, 117–24, 156–65.
Choondal, Chummar and Sukumaran Pottekkattu (eds), *Malayala Pathra Charithram*, Ernakulam: Fr. George Veliparambil, 1977.
Chummar, T. M., *Bhasha Gadhyasahitya Charitram*, Kottayam: Sahitya Pravarthaka Cooperative Society, 1955.
Collins, Mrs Richard, *Khathakavadham*, 1877, Kottayam: D.C. Books, 1990.
Darwin, Charles, *The Origin of Species. By Means of Natural Selection: Or the Preservation of Favoured Races in the Struggle for Life*, New York: New American Library, 1958.
Das, Sisir Kumar, *1800–1910: Western Impact, Indian Response*, Vol. VIII of *A History of Indian Literature*, 10 vols, New Delhi: Sahitya Akademi, 1991.
———, *A History of Indian Literature 1911–1956: Struggle for Freedom: Triumph and Tragedy*, New Delhi: Sahitya Akademi, 1995.
Dasi, Binodini, ed. and tr. by Rimli Bhattacharya, *My Story and My Life as an Actress*, New Delhi: Kali for Women, 1998.
Derrida, Jacques (tr. by Barbara Johnson), *Dissemination*, Chicago: The University of Chicago Press, 1981.
——— (tr. by Peggy Kamuf), *The Ear of the Other: Otobiography, Transference, Translation*, New York: Schocken, 1985.
———, 'Des Tours de Babel', in Joseph F. Graham (ed. and tr.), *Difference in Translation*, Ithaca: Cornell University Press, 1985, 165–208.
Devasia, Anitha, 'Dreamers and their Dreams: Women's Utopias of the Early Twentieth Century: Begum Rokeya Sakhawat Hossein's *Sultana's Dream* and Charlotte Perkins Gilman's *Herland*', Unpublished M. Litt. Dissertation, Central Institute of English and Foreign Languages, Hyderabad, 1990.
Devasia, Anitha and Susie Tharu, 'Englishing Indulekha: Translation, the Novel and History', in Prafulla C. Kar (ed.), *Critical Theory: Western and Indian*, Delhi: Pencraft International, 1997, 56–78.

Devi, Mahasweta (tr. by Gayatri Chakravorty Spivak), *Imaginary Maps*, Calcutta: Thema, 1993.

Disraeli, Benjamin, *Henrietta Temple: A Love Story*, 1836, London: Longman's Green and Co., 1870.

Dumont, Louis, 'Marriage and Status, Nair and Newar', *Contributions to Indian Sociology*, 7, 1964, 80–98.

Eapen, K. V., *Church Missionary Society and Education in Kerala*, Kottayam: Kollet Publication, 1985.

Fanon, Frantz, *The Wretched of the Earth*, Harmondsworth: Penguin Books, 1967.

Fawcett, F., *Nairs of Malabar*, 1901, New Delhi: Asian Educational Services, 1990.

Forbes, Geraldine H., 'In Search of the "Pure Heathen": Missionary Women in Nineteenth Century India', *EPW*, 21,17, 26 April 1986, 2–8 (WS).

Foucault, Michel (tr. by A. M. Sheridan), *The Birth of the Clinic: An Archeology of Medical Perception*, London: Tavistock Publications, 1973.

——— (tr. by Robert Hurley), *The History of Sexuality: Vol. I: An Introduction*, Harmondsworth: Penguin Books, 1978.

——— (tr. by Alan Sheridan), *Discipline and Punish: The Birth of the Prison*, New York: Vintage Books, 1979.

———, *Power/Knowledge: Selected Interviews and Other Writings 1972–1977*, Colin Gordon (ed.), Brighton, Sussex: The Harvester Press, 1980.

Fuller, C. J., *The Nairs Today*, Cambridge: Cambridge University Press, 1976.

Fuller, Marcus B., *The Wrongs of Indian Womanhood*, Edinburgh: Oliphant Anderson, 1900.

Gentzler, Edwin, *Contemporary Translation Theories*, London: Routledge, 1993.

Gopalakrishnan, P. K., *Navakerala Shilpikal: O. Chandu Menon*, Ernakulam: Kerala History Association, 1982.

Gough, E. K., 'Changing Kinship Usages in the Setting of Political and Economic Change among the Nairs of Malabar', *Journal of the Royal Anthropological Institute*, 82, 1952, 71–88.

Government of Kerala, *Kerala Through the Ages*, Trivandrum: Department of Public Relations, 1976.

Guha, Ranajit (ed.), 'Chandra's Death', in *Subaltern Studies V*, Delhi: Oxford University Press, 1987, 135–65.

Huxley, Thomas H., *On the Origin of Species or the Causes of the Phenomena of Organic Nature*, Ann Arbor: The University of Michigan Press, 1968.

Innes, C. A., *Madras District Gazetteers: Malabar and Anjengo*, Madras: Government Press, 1908.

James, Siby, 'Hegemony and Culture: The Case of *Indulekha*', *Haritham*, 5, 1995, 69–77.

Jeffrey, Robin, *The Decline of Nayar Dominance: Society and Politics in Travancore, 1847–1908*, Delhi: Vikas, 1976.

Jeffrey, Robin, *Politics, Women and Well-Being: How Kerala Became 'A Model'*, Delhi: Oxford University Press, 1993.

John, Mary E., *Discrepant Dislocations: Feminism, Theory, and Post-colonial Histories*, Delhi: Oxford University Press, 1996.

Karlekar, Malavika, 'Kadambini and the "Bhadralok": Early Debates over Women's Education in Bengal', *EPW*, 21,17, 26 April 1986, 25–31 (WS).

———, 'Women's Nature and the Access to Education', in Karuna Chanana (ed.), *Socialisation, Education and Women: Explorations in Gender Identity*, New Delhi: Orient Longman, 1988, 129–65.

———, *Voices from Within: Early Personal Narratives of Bengali Women*, Delhi: Oxford University Press, 1991.

Karve, Irawati, *Kinship Organisation in India*, New Delhi: Asia Publishing House, 1968.

Kaviraj, Sudipta, *The Unhappy Consciousness: Bankimchandra Chattopadhyay and the Formation of Nationalist Discourse in India*, Delhi: Oxford University Press, 1995.

Kishwar, Madhu, 'Arya Samaj and Women's Education: Kanya Mahavidyalaya, Jalandhar', *EPW*, 21,17, 26 April 1986, 9–24 (WS).

Kochuthomman Apothecary, Kunnukuzhiyil, *Parishkarappathi*, 1892, Kottayam: Vidhyarthimitram, 1977.

Kooiman, Dick, *Conversion and Social Equality in India: The London Missionary Society in South Travancore in the Nineteenth Century*, New Delhi: Manohar, 1989.

Kopf, David, *British Orientalism and the Bengal Renaissance: The Dynamics of Indian Modernization 1773–1835*, Berkeley: University of California Press, 1969.

Kosambi, Meera, 'Women, Emancipation and Equality: Pandita Ramabai's Contribution to Women's Cause', *EPW*, 23, 44, 29 October 1988, 38–49 (WS).

Krishnapillai, N., *Kairaliyude Katha*, Kottayam: Sahitya Pravarthaka Cooperative Society, 1975.

Kumar, Ravinder, *Essays in the Social History of Modern India*, Delhi: Oxford University Press, 1983.

Kumaran, Moorkothu, 'Indulekha', *Bhashaposhini*, 11, 7–8, Meenam 1907, 194–201.

———, *Oyyarath Chandu Menon*, Thrissur: Kerala Sahitya Akademi, 1932.

Kunjanpillai, Elamkulam, *Kerala Charithrathile Iruladanja Eedukal*, Trivandrum: Educational Supplies, 1953.

———, *Studies in Kerala History*, Kottayam: Pub. by the Author, 1970.

Lakshmi, C. S., *Women in Society, the Face Behind the Mask: Women in Tamil Literature*, New Delhi: Shakti, 1984.

Lawrence, James H., *The Empire of the Nairs*, 1811, New York: Scholars Fascimilies and Reprints, 1976.

Liddle, Joanna and Rama Joshi, *Daughters of Independence: Gender, Caste and Class in India*, New Delhi: Kali for Women, 1986.

Logan, William, *Malabar*, 1887, 2 vols., Madras: Government Press. (Reprinted, with additional papers, in 3 vols., Madras 1951.)

Lyotard, Jean-François (tr. by Geoff Bennington and Brian Masumi), *The Postmodern Condition: A Report on Knowledge*, Minneapolis: University of Minnesota Press, 1984.

'Malayali Vivaha Bill', *Malayala Manorama*, 17 May 1890, 3.

Menon, A. Sreedhara, *Trivandrum, Kerala District Gazetteers*, Trivandrum: Government Press, 1962.

———, *Cultural Heritage of Kerala: An Introduction*, Cochin: East-West Publications, 1978.

———, *A Social and Cultural History of India: Kerala*, New Delhi: Sterling Publishers, 1979.

———, *Keralasamskaram*, Kottayam: Sahitya Pravarthaka Cooperative Society, 1987.

———, *A Survey of Kerala History*, Madras: S. Viswanathan Printers and Publishers, 1991.

Menon, Dilip M., *Caste, Nationalism and Communism in South India: Malabar 1900–1948*, New Delhi: Cambridge University Press, 1994.

Menon, T. C. Sankara, *Makers of Indian Literature: Chandu Menon*, New Delhi: Sahitya Akademi, 1974.

Moore, Lewis, *Malabar Law and Custom*, Madras: Government Press, 1905.

Mukherjee, Meenakshi, *Realism and Reality: The Novel and Society in India*, Delhi: Oxford University Press, 1985.

———, 'The Unperceived Self: A Study of Five Nineteenth Century Autobiographies', in Karuna Chanana (ed.), *Socialisation, Education and Women: Explorations in Gender Identity*, New Delhi: Orient Longman, 1988, 249–72.

Mukherjee, Sujith, *Translation as Discovery and Other Essays on Indian Literature in English Translation*, Hyderabad: Orient Longman, 1994.

Mullens, Catherine Hannah (tr. by Rev. Joseph Peet), *Phulmoni Ennum Koruna Ennum Peraya Randu Strikalude Katha*, Kottayam: D. C. Books, 1989.

Murshid, Ghulam, *The Reluctant Debutante: Response of the Bengali Women to Modernisation, 1849–1905*, Rajashahi: Rajashahi University Sahitya Samsad, 1985.

Nair, Balakrishnan, 'The Nair as Warrior', *Calcutta Review*, 100, 1895, 375–82.

———, 'The Sterner Aspects of Nair Life', *Calcutta Review*, 104, 1897, 272–6.

———, 'The Origin of the Malabar Nairs', *Calcutta Review*, 107, 1898, 111–20.

———, 'The First Great Malayalam Novel', *Calcutta Review*, 109, 1899, 243–61.

———, 'The Nairs: A Race of Hereditary Fighters', *Malabar Quarterly Review*, 1.2, 1902, 83–97.

Nair, Janaki, *Women and Law in Colonial India*, New Delhi: Kali for Women, 1996.

Nair, Manakad Sukumaran (script by), *Indulekha*, Changanacherry: Assissi Printing and Publishing House, n.d.

Nambuthiripad, Moothiringote Bhavatharatan, *Apphante Makal*, Trissur, Kerala Sahitya Akademi, 1989.

Nandy, Ashis, *The Intimate Enemy: Loss and Recovery of Self under Colonialism*, Delhi: Oxford University Press, 1983.

Narendran, K. M., 'Mrigabalikal, Vijayothsavangal', *Mathrubhumi Aazhichapathippu*, 25 Oct. 1988, 6–9 and 31–35.

Niranjana, Tejaswini, 'Translation, Colonialism and Rise of English', *EPW*, 25, 15, 14 April 1990, 773–9.

———, *Siting Translation: History, Post-Structuralism and the Colonial Context*, Berkeley: University of California Press, 1992.

Niranjana, Tejaswini, P. Sudhir, Vivek Dhareshwar (eds), *Interrogating Modernity: Culture and Colonialism in India*, Calcutta: Seagull, 1993.

'One Malayali's Response to the Bill', *Malayala Manorama*, 25 May 1890, 2.

'One Malayali's Response to the Bill', *Malayala Manorama*, 31 May 1890, 2.

Padmavathiamma, K., 'Parishkrithareethiyilulla Malayali Vivaham', in *Lakshmibai* 8, 1913: 238–48.

Paniker, Ayyappa K., *A Short History of Malayalam Literature*, Thiruvananthapuram: Department of Public Relations, Government of Kerala, 1998.

Panikkar, K. N., 'Land Control, Ideology and Reform: A Study of the Changes in Family Organisation and Marriage System in Kerala', *The Indian Historical Review*, 4, 1, 1977, 30–46.

———, *Against Lord and State: Religion and Peasant Uprisings in Malabar 1836–1921*, Delhi: Oxford University Press, 1989.

———, *Culture, Ideology, Hegemony: Intellectuals and Social Consciousness in Colonial India*, New Delhi: Tulika, 1995.

Panikkar, T. K. Gopal, *Malabar and Its Folk*, 1900, New Delhi: Asian Educational Services, 1983.

Parameswarannair, P. K., *Aadhunika Malayala Sahityam*, Kottayam: Sahitya Pravarthaka Cooperative Society, 1954.

——— (tr. by E. M. J. Venniyoor), *History of Malayalam Literature*, New Delhi: Sahitya Akademi, 1967.

———, *Malayala Sahitya Charitram*, New Delhi: Sahitya Akademi, 1985.

Parashar, Archana, *Women and Family Law Reform in India*, New Delhi: Sage Publications, 1992.

Parry, Benita, *Delusions and Discoveries: Studies on India in the British Imagination 1880–1930*, New Delhi: Orient Longman, 1972.

Poovey, Mary, *The Proper Lady and The Woman Writer: Ideology as Style in the Works of Mary Wollstonecraft, Mary Shelley and Jane Austen*, Chicago: University of Chicago Press, 1984.

Puthenkalam, J., *Marriage and the Family in Kerala with Special Reference to Matrilineal Castes*, New Delhi: Print and Community Centre, 1977.

Rabinow, Paul (ed.), *The Foucault Reader*, Harmondsworth: Penguin Books, 1984.

Raghavan, Puthupalli, *Kerala Patrapravarthana Charitram: Oru Padanam*, Trichur: Kerala Sahitya Akademi, 1985.

Rajarajavarma, Vadakkumkur, *Kerala Sahitya Charitram: Charchayum Puranavum*, Kottayam: Sahitya Pravarthaka Cooperative Society, 1968.

Ramakrishna, V., *Social Reform in Andhra, 1848–1919*, New Delhi: Vikas Publishing House, 1983.

Ramanpillai, C. V., *Marthandavarma*, Kottayam: D.C. Books, 1992.

Rao, Jayasrinivasa, 'Concept of Women's Education in the Early Kannada Social Novel', Unpublished paper, 1996.

Rao, M. S. A., *Social Change in Malabar*, Bombay: The Popular Book Depot, 1957.

Report on the Administration of Travancore for the Year, M. E. 1057, AD 1881–2, Trivandrum: The Travancore Government Press, 1883.

Report on the Administration of Travancore for the Year, M. E. 1060, AD 1884–5, Trivandrum: The Travancore Government Press, 1886.

Said, Edward W., *Orientalism*, New York: Pantheon Books, 1978.

'Sambandam', *Malayala Manorama*, 25 May 1890, 2.

Saradamoni, K., *Emergence of a Slave Caste: Pulayas of Kerala*, New Delhi: People's Publishing House, 1980.

Sarkar, Sumit, *Modern India, 1885–1947*, Delhi: Macmillan, 1983.

Satthianadhan, Krupabai, Lokugé, Chandani (ed.), *Saguna: The First Autobiographical Novel in English by an Indian Woman*, Delhi: Oxford University Press, 1998.

Sattianadan, Krupa, *Kamala: A Story of Hindu Life*, Madras Christian College Magazine, 1888.

Schneider, David M. and Kathleen Gough, *Matrilineal Kinship*, Berkeley: University of California Press, 1961.

Seshagiri Prabhu, M., 'A Note on the Word Nair', *Malabar Quarterly Review*, 1, 4, Dec. 1902, 347–9.

Sunder Rajan, Rajeswari (ed.), *The Lie of the Land: English Literary Studies in India*, Delhi: Oxford University Press, 1991.

Tagore, Rabindranath (tr. by Surendranath Tagore), 1919, *The Home and the World*, Madras: Macmillan, 1989.

Teltscher, Kate, *India Inscribed: European and British Writing on India 1600–1800*, Delhi: Oxford University Press, 1997.

Tharakan, Michael P. K., 'Socio-Economic Factors in Educational Development: The Case of Nineteenth Century Travancore', *EPW*, 19, 45, 10 Nov. 1984, 1913–28.

———, 'Socio-Economic Factors in Educational Development: The Case of Nineteenth Century Travancore', *EPW*, 19, 46, 17 Nov. 1984, 1959–67.

Tharu, Susie and K. Lalita (eds), *Women Writing in India, Vols I & II: 600 BC to the Present*, Delhi: Oxford University Press, 1993.

Thomas, M. V., *Mahacharithamala 20: Biographies of O. Chandu Menon, C. V. Ramanpillai, Uroob*, Kottayam: Kairali Children's Book Trust, 1981.

Vanamala, Vijaya, 'Conservative or Radical? Jane Austen and the Feminist Consciousness in the Late Eighteenth Century', Unpublished M. Litt. Dissertation, Central Institute of English and Foreign Languages, Hyderabad, 1992.

Velayudhanpilla, P. V., *Indulekha Padanam*, Thiruvanthapuram: Prabhatham Printing and Publishing Company, 1990.

Venuti, Lawrence (ed.), *Rethinking Translation: Discourse, Subjectivity, Ideology*, London: Routledge, 1992.

———, *The Translator's Invisibility: A History of Translation*, London: Routledge, 1995.

Warrier, Raghava and Rajan Gurukkal, *Kerala Charitram*, Calicut: Vallathol Vidyapeetham, 1992.

Watt, Ian, *The Rise of the Novel: Studies in Defoe, Richardson and Fielding*, London: Chatto and Windus, 1967.

White, Hayden, *Tropics of Discourse: Essays in Cultural Criticism*, London: The John Hopkins University Press, 1978.

Glossary

aalekham: palm leaf manuscripts.
Amaravati: the city or capital of Lord Indra.
anandravers: inheritors, in the Nair system, the nephews.
chakravaka: a mythical bird which stays with its mate by day and parts from it when evening falls.
chenda: a percussion instrument struck with a stick.
faded leaves: a customary way of referring to lovers separated.
fanam: coin current during the pre-British period; four gold or five silver fanams were equal to a rupee.
gopurams: a spire-like structure rising from the roof, like the dome of a temple.
Indulekha: Now a common name for women, it means the crescent moon. It also means an initial scripting.
jeshtan: it is a form of address for an elder brother.
kadukan: single-stone earrings, worn by men.
kalapura: place where sheaves of paddy are threshed.
kalam: storeplace.
kali: the expression can also mean rage.
kalyanam: auspicious.
Kamadevan: the god of love.
kannil: in the eye.
Karanavan: the eldest male member of the Nair joint family, who is also the administrator.
karanavars: plural; also includes other senior male members of the family.
kasu: 1/448 part of a Travancore rupee.

komatti: an abuse, since komattis are traders, especially when spoken by a Brahmin.

Kubera: Ravana's wealthy brother and owner of *pushpakavimana*—the name of the aircraft Lord Brahma gave to Kubera. The converse would be Kuchelan who had twenty-seven children and did not have enough money for even a single meal.

kuduma: In the nineteenth century, Nair men generally grew their hair and tied it up on one side of the head. This knot of hair is the kuduma. Men took pride in their hair, oiling it and washing it everyday. The kuduma was a mark of caste distinction.

kuri: the marking on the forehead, with holy ash or sandalwood paste.

kutta: a term of endearment in north Malabar.

maddalam: a percussion instrument played by hand.

mana: household of a Nambuthiri.

Manmadhan: the God of Love.

maraan: the sweeper and drum beater of a temple.

Meghdantan: He is making up names. This name means a person with teeth like a cloud.

melmundu: a cloth thrown over the shoulders and covering the breasts/chest.

mukillatha: lacking a nose.

mundu: an ankle-length piece of cloth secured around the waist worn in a slightly different style by both Nair men and women in Keralam.

Mudaliar: caste title of a prominent Hindu community from Tamil Nadu.

nalukettu: a single quadrangular structure (house) with a courtyard in the centre and rooms opening out on to a veranda.

Nambuthiri: the highest caste of Brahmins in Keralam.

Nambuthiripad: hierarchically higher than Nambuthiri.

ootupura: place were Brahmins are fed—every important taravad would have an ootupura, where as a routine, the household serve meals to Brahmins.

paatom: tax paid by a tenant to the owner.

paladapradhaman: a dessert made from milk, sugar and flattened stripes of steamed rice.

palkanji: rice porridge with milk, a light meal.

para: a solid measure, normally used for grains, most commonly paddy; roughly equivalent to eight kilograms.

pattar: a Tamil Brahmin considered lower in the caste hierarchy to Malayali Brahmins.

pinda: regular offering to ancestors.

podamuri: one of the symbols of a Nair wedding ceremony. The Nair groom gives his bride a length of fine cloth or a set of fine clothes.

prarambham: The Malayalam word *prarambham*, is in the singular but we have chosen to translate it as beginnings rather than a beginning or the beginning, both of which are possibilities because there are several embryonic moves embedded in this opening chapter, including the beginnings of the story, the novel in Malayalam, a new Malayalam prose and realism!

purathalam: a veranda-like semi-private room from which a staircase leads to the private rooms.

rashi: a pun here. The word means fortune/gate.

rudrakshamala: a necklace made from the seeds of the rudraksha tree worn by devotees of Shiva and used to keep count while saying prayers.

sambandam: literally, 'relationship'. The Nair marriage unmarked by sacred rituals.

sathrasala: a place where free food and accommodation is arranged.

sayiv: in Keralam, an Englishman is called a sayip (sahib)—sayiv is a variation.

Shishupalan: King of the kingdom of Chethi. He was killed by Srikrishnan.

strivesham: A female character—literally translated, this would be donning the costume of a woman. Kathakali performers were all men.

taravad: Nair homestead. See afterword (p. 228).

ruby teeth: teeth stained delicately by chewing betel leaves: a sign of beauty.

thali: the leaf-like gold ornament which Nair women wear after their talikettukalyanam.

talikettukalyanam: In the context of this work, in the Nair system the fastening of a thali around a young girl's neck was done before she matured. It did not signify marriage.

thekkini: southern side of the main building (nalukettu).

Thiruvathirakuli: Thiruvathira nakshatra in the month of Dharvi in the Kollam era is the birthday of Shiva. As part of the ritual connected with the vows and fasting, women take a group bath very early in the morning in a pond. Maidens do this as a discipline to get a good husband and married women for a long married life.

thoda: ear ornament, worn by women.

ulappenna: an oil used by royalty.

uri: a measure of rice; about one-fourth of a kilogram.

uuku: evening rituals among the Nambuthiris.

vara: a linear measure of 36 inches.

vasuri: smallpox; here marked by the disease.
vastradanam: see 'podamuri'.
vazhipadu: an offering promised to a deity.
veli: a marriage in the Nambuthiri community to a woman of the same community.
vettilapetti: a box to store betel leaves, areca nuts and flavourings.
vivaham: wedding.
Warrier: caste name of a people who attend to the menial chores in a temple and whose main occupation is tying the garland for the deity.
yugam: According to Hindu cosmology there are four yugas—Krutha Yuga, Thretha Yuga, Dwapara Yuga and Kali Yuga. It is believed that evil things happen during Kali Yuga. It is believed that Kali Yuga began in 5105 BC and will continue for a period of four lakh thirty thousand years.

CIS 4em 362
11/7/9